Wendy Perriam

was born in 1940 and educated at a
St Anne's College, Oxford. After
succession of more offbeat jobs, ranging from the bizarre to the
banal, she now writes full time.

Her novels, which include *Born of Woman*, *The Stillness The Dancing*,
Sin City, *Devils, for a Change*, *Fifty-Minute Hour* and *Bird Inside*, have
been acclaimed for their exuberant style, their provocative mix of
the sacred and the profane, and their extraordinary power to
disturb, amuse and shock.

She is currently working on her eleventh novel and some new
short stories.

WENDY PERRIAM

Cuckoo

Flamingo
An Imprint of HarperCollinsPublishers

Flamingo
An Imprint of HarperCollins*Publishers*
77–85 Fulham Palace Road,
Hammersmith, London W6 8JB

Published by Flamingo 1993
9 8 7 6 5 4 3 2 1

Previously published by Paladin 1992
Reprinted once

First published in Great Britain by
Michael Joseph Ltd 1991

Copyright © Wendy Perriam 1991

The Author asserts the moral right to
be identified as the author of this work

Photograph of Wendy Perriam by Jane Bown

ISBN 0 586 09130 0

Set in Baskerville

Printed in Great Britain by
HarperCollinsManufacturing Glasgow

Then wonder not to see this soul extend
The bounds, and seek some other self, a friend: . . .
For 'tis the bliss of Friendship's holy state
To mix their Minds and to communicate.

John Dryden Eleonora

For Vicky Wilmot

Thanks for fifteen years of Mind-mixing!

1

Typical of Charles to decant his sperm sample into a Fortnum and Mason's jar. Empty of course, but it had once contained gentleman's relish, and Charles was, if nothing else, a gentleman; one who had better things to do than mess about taking freshly-decanted semen up to Harley Street. He had a more pressing appointment – negotiating the revision of a multi-million oil contract in Bahrain. No wonder they hadn't had a baby. Charles was never in England at the right time of the month. He'd be streaking over the Med by now, sipping cocktails on Concorde, while she strap-hung on the tube.

The train jolted, suddenly, and Frances lurched forward. It seemed strange to be travelling on the tube again, struggling in the rush hour, but without her job, carrying a scant two milligrams of her husband's seed instead of a bulging briefcase. She almost hankered after those old, punctilious, nine-to-five days (more often nine-to-seven), with her thick-pile office and her chromium-plated secretary, when she'd solved problems by her own application and initiative, instead of waiting on the whim of Mother Nature. Conceiving a baby was proving the biggest hurdle in an otherwise effortless career. She had even ditched the career, to make it easier. But the in-tray in her womb stayed strictly empty.

A man got off at Charing Cross and she slid into his seat. She felt she had a right to it, not pregnant (yet), but carrying the stuff of life. She cupped her hands more firmly round the jar, shrouded in its paper bag. It would be blasphemous to drop it, after what Charles had been through to produce those vital drops.

He'd sidled into the bathroom that morning, with the empty jar concealed beneath the *Investor's Chronicle* and *The Financial Times*, and remained there, in nerve-racking silence, for close on an hour. She had tried to concentrate on his breakfast, crisping the bacon the way he liked it and squeezing Spanish oranges into cut-glass tumblers, over ice. She had made the tea, heated the croissants, sorted his letters into Urgent, Personal and Dross. Still no husband.

She had opened her own mail, to try to pass the time – an invitation to speak on 'Women In Publicity' at the Graphics Society September meeting; the pick-of-the-month from *Classics Choice* (Riccardo Muti's recording of the Cherubini Requiem); a begging letter from 'Save The Seal'; a plea from the Residents' Association to use her house and services for their Christmas jamboree. She tossed them to one side. Even without her career, her life was still nine to seven. She was busy, committed, conscientious. Yet, somehow, it all meant nothing. If she had written a begging letter on her own behalf, all it would have asked for was a baby.

Slowly, she walked upstairs to the bathroom and listened a moment outside the locked door. Silence. No heavy breathing, no rhythmic creaking. Not even a tap running, or the cistern flushing, to indicate completion and success.

'Can I – er – lend a hand?' she called.

'No thanks.' He sounded as if he were refusing the garrotte, or a term's hard labour in Siberia. He couldn't be anywhere near it, with a tombstone voice like that. And why be so damned independent? The doctor had suggested that she more or less do it for him, yet he wouldn't even let her in the bathroom.

She mooched downstairs again. The croissants had shrivelled, the tea was over-stewed. She sat at the table, staring at the tasteful hessian wall, torturing the empty orange skins into a shredded, soggy mess of peel. It was absurd to be so tense, but that sample was desperately important. She had endured all the tests herself and had been pronounced in perfect working order. But Charles had resisted. He wasn't the type to take his trousers down before even the most eminent of Harley Street physicians, let alone entrust his semen to tin-pot laboratory technicians who had taken sandwich courses at provincial poly-technics. Charles was a snob, even when it came to a sperm count. He should have had one years ago. She was already in her thirties – there wasn't time to go on relying merely on chance, or luck, or the inexorable vigour of the Life Force. He'd only agreed at all after watching a documentary on artificial insemination, where one of the donors was a drop-out on the dole.

Perhaps she'd been too insistent. She was all too aware of the demands and pressures of his job. Sometimes, there wasn't even time for routine sex, let alone infertility investigations. Charles' life was perpetual overtime. But if he didn't produce that sample, they might as well give up. He was so damned proud, he'd never try again. It was bad enough not conceiving in the first place. Fathering a child was something elementary. Any school leaver could do it, in a ten-minute tea-break, so why not Charles Parry Jones Esquire, MA (Cantab.), FCA?

Frances bit into a burnt corpse of a croissant and put it down again. It seemed sacrilegious to eat, when Charles was struggling with his half of the reproductive process. Or was he? Knowing her husband, he was more likely to be poised on the lavatory, writing a report on Prophylactic Cash Flow Analysis. He hated wasting time. Even at breakfast, he dictated his letters into a tape recorder between mouthfuls of poached egg, and he'd spent a fortune on sleep tapes. Charles rarely had a dream – he was too busy with 'Beginner's Sanskrit', or plugged into 'Budgetary Control for Micro-computers'. Sometimes, she wondered if he even wanted children. A keen prospective father wouldn't take an hour to produce a teaspoonful of sperm.

She picked up his Urgent pile of letters, the largest of the three, and weighed it in her hands. 'Urgent' meant business. Charles' work was like a barrier between them. Of course she admired his zeal and energy, his never-failing enterprise, but why couldn't he devote a little time to his future son and heir, rather than lavish it exclusively on the tax and investment problems of the Western hemisphere? If he couldn't even masturbate without using the other hand to write a memorandum, then she and their relationship came a very poor second to Messrs Caxton, Clarke and Parry Jones. And the poor unborn infant would be lucky if it even came third. She'd been prodded and poked a score of times in the cause of procreation, poured out libations of blood and urine without complaining, and here was Charles baulking at a trifling sperm sample.

Perhaps the atmosphere was wrong. Shiny white tiles and an impending flight to Bahrain weren't the most suitable setting for sexual success. She was always nervous herself about him flying, even now, when he boarded Concorde as casually as if it were a country bus. There were so many risks to a man in his position – a crash, a coronary, a kidnapping, a hijack. He was such a solid character, if anything happened to him, the world would crumble in sympathy. She felt strangely light and insubstantial when he was away, as if part of her had been amputated. Sometimes, she wondered if she even existed, except as his reflection. Was that why she wanted a child? A Charles in miniature? He was a big man, in every sense, and had never been a baby himself – you could tell. He'd sprung into the world fully grown, with a schedule in one hand and a computer in the other.

Frances switched on the radio and tuned from *Thought For The Day* to *Morning Concert*. Neville Marriner was conducting Elgar. She turned him up louder. Perhaps the *Enigma Variations* would reach Charles in the bathroom and return him to the task in hand.

'Christ, Frances! Did you notice how Marriner dawdled through that first variation? Elgar took it twice as fast, when *he* conducted.'

Charles had emerged, looking enigmatic and impeccable. Six foot of navy pin-stripe, topped by a lean, pale face, with surprisingly full lips. The mouth seemed out of character with the rest of him. It was too sensuous, too curving. Everything else about him was thin and stern. Charles was a straight line. He never slouched nor sprawled. No paunch, no bulges, no moral kinks. Frances glanced at his face – it was utterly composed. No flushed cheeks, no air of achievement. Not even the jar.

'Nice bacon,' he grunted. 'It's the Cullen's isn't it?'

She found the sample, later, on the bathroom sill, concealed behind the Harpic: a few oozy gobbets of greyish phlegm, already congealing in its jar. Could that be life material, half-way to a baby? What a messy, complicated business reproduction was! No wonder Charles was hostile. He liked things to be orderly, and if they weren't, he made them so, forged or forced them into shape. He'd have preferred to have a baby computer-fashion, feeding in the relevant information and masterminding a safe, no-nonsense, fully automated, remote-control delivery, without all the mess and fuss of haphazard sperm and elusive ova.

*   *   *

Frances gazed around the crowded carriage of the underground. All those seething people were almost proof of nature's random method. Their parents hadn't had test-tubes or computers. World population stood at some four and a half thousand million at the present. That meant four and a half thousand million spermatozoa had successfully found an egg and fused with it. Not to mention all the countless million others, in preceding centuries. Why should Charles' sperm be so recalcitrant? She opened the Fortnum's bag a crack and stared at the curdled junket at the bottom of the jar. Was something wrong with it? Did it have its own, conservative ideas about procreation or world population control? Or was it simply proud and stubborn, like its owner, too fastidious to scramble up slimy cervix walls into the hurly burly of the womb?

She steadied the jar on her lap, fanned herself with her still unopened copy of *The Times*. The train was stiflingly hot and had unaccountably stopped between Oxford Circus and Regent's Park. If there were a breakdown on the line, the sperm would die and the infertility investigations come to a screeching halt. None of the passengers spoke, few even bothered to look up from their newspapers. She fumed at their impassivity. *They* might have time to wrestle with the crossword half the morning, or goggle at Page Three, but she most certainly did not. Mr Rathbone had stressed how important it was that she didn't hang about. Sperms were like goldfish – they perished when out of their natural element. She closed her eyes and willed the train to move. It didn't. She wondered if she could sue London Transport for the murder of four hundred million spermatozoa. Veritable genocide. Rathbone had told her that was the number in just one ejaculate. No wonder women always felt inferior. They simply didn't operate on that overwhelming scale. The carriage shuddered, sighed, jolted forward twenty yards, then stopped.

'Murderer!' she muttered.

The train let out a screech of protest and revved into motion, rattling and pounding into Regent's Park Station. Frances leapt out with her jar.

'Splendid, splendid, Mrs Parry!' chuntered Mr Rathbone, as she almost collided with him in the Harley Street laboratory.

11

He always called her plain Mrs Parry, without the Jones. She wasn't sure if he were merely absent-minded, or whether he did it in the interests of brevity, or vaguely democratic bonhomie. He looked far too respectable and avuncular to be a gynaecologist, trespassing among women's private parts and messing about with Fallopian tubes and foetuses. He had short, no-nonsense grey hair, combed strictly to one side, and half-moon spectacles. He shook her hand, whisked the jar away, and closeted himself with two technicians and a microscope.

Frances sat and waited, leafing despondently through *Country Life*. Whatever Rathbone's pronouncement, there was going to be a problem. If Charles' sperm were deficient, he would never forgive himself, nor her for proving it. She wasn't sure if she'd forgive him, either. But even if it were entirely satisfactory, they were still no nearer having a baby.

Rathbone returned, looking flushed and jubilant, as if he had just given birth himself.

'Well?' said Frances.

'Very much alive and kicking! No problems there. Want to look?'

Frances moved into the inner room. It seemed impertinent to be prying into Charles' emissions, when he was captive on an aeroplane. She looked. Hundreds of tiny punctuation marks were writhing under the microscope, leaping and lunging in an ecstatic John Travolta dance.

'Are you *sure* that's Charles' sample? I mean, you haven't muddled it up with someone else's, have you?' Charles was such a controlled and sober person, it seemed most unlikely that he should harbour such giddy, madcap sperm.

Mr Rathbone smiled his eighteen-carat smile. 'No doubt at all, my dear. Your husband's semen is eminently satisfactory. There's clearly nothing wrong on *his* side.'

Frances sat down suddenly. She was glad, yes of course she was. It was unthinkable that Charles should be defective, even in a sperm count. Charles never failed. He'd won the form prize every year at Radley and then gone on to get a highly satisfactory 2/1 at Cambridge. He'd come third out of twelve hundred candidates in his accountancy examinations and he could play Liszt's *Harmonies Poétiques* without even looking at the music. A man of that calibre simply wouldn't produce sub-standard spermatozoa. So why did she feel disappointed, resentful even? Did she *want* him to fail? She hated failures just as much as he did. She had married him precisely because he outshone her in everything, and that wasn't always easy. She had a degree herself, a good one, but it wasn't Oxbridge. They'd met at a golf competition – the Pearson Mixed Foursomes – but her handicap was double his. They both spoke French, but Charles' accent was almost imperceptible. They both liked art, but Charles could tell a Canaletto from a Guardi at a glance, even from the back of the gallery. And he wasn't even smug. He was too serious for that.

'Well, I suppose it's my fault.' Frances swung her handbag angrily against the chair.

'We don't talk about faults, my dear. And, as you know, all your own tests were completely satisfactory.'

'Well, what *is* it then? We've been trying long enough. I've been following your instructions like the Bible.'

Rathbone clasped his hands together, as if he were praying. 'Call it Factor X, if you like. Something mysterious we can't put our finger on. In ten per cent of all cases we investigate, we find absolutely nothing wrong. It might be the colour of your eyes, the weather, the type of book you read . . .'

'Mr Rathbone, I'd appreciate it if you could take this subject seriously.' They paid him enough, for heaven's sake, and all he could do was produce idiotic jokes.

'But I *am* serious, my dear. I'm often amazed myself at the oddities of medical science.' Rathbone shifted his gaze to the leather-bound blotter on his desk. 'Some women are actually allergic to their own husband's semen. They make immune bodies to it, as if it were an invading germ. We don't know a lot about it, but it's one of the subjects being kicked about by the boffins at the moment.'

'You mean a woman who's perfectly fertile might simply not conceive because she and her husband were – well – sort of biologically incompatible?'

'That's it exactly. And if the same woman had intercourse with a different man, one whose semen she accepted, she might very well get pregnant.'

Frances shrugged. 'That's all very well if you believe in polygamy, but I haven't got a different man.'

Rathbone grinned conspiratorially at the tradescantia trailing across his desk. 'You could always try the milkman, my dear. I'm joking of course.' Frances stared. He sounded deadly serious. 'But – well – it has been known, Mrs Parry. And if you both want a baby so badly . . .'

I'm not sure Charles *does* want one. She didn't say it. It sounded ungrateful after all Mr Rathbone's efforts, but to have a baby with a tradesman – Charles would expire. He believed in people sticking to their proper stations. Mr Rathbone really was eccentric. He looked like an elderly bishop with his black coat and his pinched, ascetic face, yet here he was more or less encouraging her to couple with the milkman.

'But, Mr Rathbone – think of all the problems. And, anyway, couldn't people tell? What about paternity tests and blood groups and all that sort of thing?'

'Why should any husband bother? He'd just accept the babe as his own. They do, you know. And even if he were one of the rare suspicious ones, paternity tests are still notoriously unreliable – one of those grey areas of great complexity, which can always be obligingly confused.'

Frances frowned. 'But surely you're not seriously suggesting . . .'

'Of course not, my dear. Just a tip other women have found fruitful – ha ha – forgive my little joke. No, the best thing for you, Mrs Parry, is to forget all about this baby business and find yourself a little job.'

Frances stood up. She found it infuriating when men referred to women's jobs as 'little'. No red-blooded man ever did a 'little job'. But however responsible and arduous the job, if a woman took it on, it automatically shrunk in status.

She'd worked for years, for God's sake. And in a big job, a man's job; had only given it up to have their non-existent baby. Maybe that was the trouble. She'd worked too long through all her fertile years, never doubting for a moment that she and Charles would produce their perfect 2.5 progeny the minute she stopped the Pill. Everything else had always gone right for them. Charles and Frances Parry Jones, the perfect couple. She wondered if their friends hated them, those well-bred, well-fed friends, who only said what was allowed in the rules. Who had written all those rules? Was it Charles, or his mother, or God,

14

or the Royal Mid-Surrey Golf Club, or the Richmond Residents' Association?

Oh yes, they had it all. The elegant house on Richmond Green where they'd moved after their impeccable country wedding. The charming Norman church and the chic Vogue dress. Yet, she'd cried all night before the wedding, and hadn't even known why. Gone through the ceremony like a puppet, smiling and mouthing until her face ached. It had seemed strange taking on his name. Frances Parry Jones was such a mouthful after plain Franny Brent. (Charles refused to call her Franny.) The name had always weighed her down. Like the house. The expensive, tasteful, dark, funereal house – Charles' house, not theirs, too big, too perfect, for a pair of newly-weds. All the furniture came from his mother (who looked like a bow-fronted chiffonier herself) – Georgian desks and Chippendale chairs, priceless and uncomfortable antiques you couldn't loll or sprawl in, and so much labour. Brass to polish and parquet to shine. Not that she had to do it. Charles' mother found them Mrs Eady, another glum, sombre, unaccommodating thing. They never seemed alone. Mrs Eady in the mornings, grumbling about the rain ruining her washing, or the sun spoiling the furniture; Charles' gilt-edged friends in the evenings, and the golf crowd at weekends. There wasn't much of Franny left. Even her career was always overshadowed by Charles'. A Public Relations executive with a flair for fashion couldn't hold a candle to an international finance consultant. Sometimes she wondered if she wanted a baby only to complete her, to give her a role and status denied to her by Charles. Something which wasn't dark and overshadowed and antique.

'Mr Rathbone, *please*. There must be something else you can do. I'm not a person who gives up easily, you know that. I don't mind what I go through . . .'

'My dear Mrs Parry, conceiving a baby is not meant to be an endurance test. If you could only relax, it would probably happen anyway. There's nothing wrong with you, you know. Your temperature charts are perfect, you're ovulating nicely, you've had a D and C, your tubes are open . . .'

'Yes, I know all that, but nothing ever happens . . .' She shrugged towards the door. It was stupid wasting time with this second-rate charlatan. She should have chosen a doctor with verve and dynamism, a man more like Charles. That was the trouble with having a husband like Charles – all other men seemed feeble in comparison.

'Sit down, Mrs Parry, I can see you're very overwrought. Look, there is one last thing I could suggest, although I hesitate . . .'

What was he up to this time? A test-tube baby in a milk bottle, care of United Dairies?

'Well?' She strummed her fingers along the padded leather chair-arm. Rathbone was such an old muddler. Even now, he wasn't looking at her, but punching his pen nib through the larger leaves of the tradescantia.

'I could perhaps put you on one of the fertility drugs – just for a short trial period.'

God Almighty! Sextuplets crawling over the front page of the *Sun*, television cameras peering down her womb, their house overrun with nappies . . .

'I . . . er . . . don't think Charles would be too keen on a multiple pregnancy.'

Rathbone laughed. 'No cause for alarm, my dear. I was merely thinking of Clomid. One of the less dramatic drugs. You may get twins on Clomid – 6.9 per cent I think the incidence is, but nothing worse than that.'

Twins? Charlie and Franny? Two in one? Rather convenient, really. Save time, save money. Charles would approve of that. She opened her bag and took out her leather-covered memo-pad. (A present from her husband. Where other wives received boxes of Milk Tray, she was given memo-pads.) 'Right, what is it? Where do I get it? When do I start? What are its side effects?'

Rathbone needed pushing. He was far too ready to sit back and talk about relaxing. He could have put her on the Clomid months ago and the twins would be almost toddling round the golf course by now.

'It's very rarely given where women are ovulating as regularly as you are. That's why I hesitate. . . . On the other hand, it may just work. It does seem to make a better ovulation. Now what you do is . . .'

Frances uncapped her pen and recorded Rathbone's instructions to the letter. She mustn't get it wrong. Somehow, she felt this was going to be the answer – a wonder drug and twins.

'Expect nothing, Mrs Parry – it's much the best way. Then you won't be disappointed. And, don't forget, it's most important to relax. Try to forget all about conceiving. There are other things in life, you know. Enjoy yourself. Take up a little hobby.'

Little, little. Why was everything so infuriatingly little? She already had a hundred little hobbies – golf, tennis, music, art – the versatile woman who could turn out a soufflé or a fashion report with the same easy flair. But what was all that, when you couldn't do the one thing that *made* you a woman? She was just an outward shell – smart clothes, fine accomplishments, but nothing inside. No baby, no womb working for its living, a hollow, a void, a failure.

The sun was shining as she stepped outside. The sky was too blue for London, flecked with little puffy clouds which would have looked better on a chocolate box. Façades again. A smug heaven smiling down on all the world's misery. It probably smiled like that on Vietnam. Or Auschwitz. Ridiculous to be so bitter. Hundreds of women couldn't conceive. Ten per cent of all marriages were infertile, hadn't Rathbone said? Discounting those who had their babies by the milkman. Did such things really happen? She and Charles were so ludicrously sheltered. Charles' mother pursed up her lips if anyone so much as mentioned the word intercourse (let alone anything shorter), and her own mother thought a lesbian was a type of French table fowl. All around them were murder, infidelity and rape, and the worst any of them had managed in their two combined families was to get a parking ticket.

She crossed the road into Cavendish Square. A blackbird was singing in a tall plane tree and the grass was as bright as the enamelled surface of a Holman Hunt. She longed to lie down for a moment and sun herself among the daisies and the sparrows. But Charles had taught her that time was a precious commodity, not to be squandered. Every minute must be squeezed to yield maximum productivity. She bent down and let her fingers brush against the daisies. She'd squeezed all those minutes and what had she got to show for it – an elegant house, run as rigidly as NASA, a filing cabinet crammed with past PR campaigns, a full diary, and an empty womb.

She left the square and crossed the road into the back entrance of D. H. Evans. She had promised Charles she'd buy him a new umbrella. Charles hated rain. He always cited it as one of the proofs of the non-existence of God. Any sensible craftsman would have made a world in which water seeped upwards into the fields, not downwards on to people's city clothes.

'Men's umbrellas, please?'

She should have gone to Brigg's of Piccadilly – Charles preferred his brollies hand-made – but she felt too tired to jostle with the crowds in Regent Street. She tried to decide between a Peerless with a boarskin handle and a Fox with a real gold band, both black, both expensive. Another woman was buying a Union Jack umbrella in red, white and blue. She'd love to see Charles holding that above his pin-stripes. Or a Snoopy umbrella which said 'Just singin' in the rain'. Charles never sang, except at his Old Boys' Reunion Dinner, once a year. She took the Peerless.

She stood by the escalator, reluctant to go home. Charles would phone from Bahrain – a brief, formal phone call – yes, the flight had been fine; yes, he was tired; no, he hadn't had time for sight-seeing.

'Goodbye, darling.'

''Bye.'

'Love you.'

'Love you too.'

The formula, then silence. The house to herself. Piano practice or an educational cassette. Cooking for the freezer or brushing up her bridge. Preparing that speech on Women in Publicity, ploughing through the latest Günter Grass. Mustn't waste a moment. Charles had it all worked out. Günter Grass wasn't waste, but Herman Hesse was. (Charles hated wishy-washy, unsubstantiated mysticism.) A Stravinsky concert counted, but Malcolm Arnold didn't. She felt he marked her like a teacher. Three gold stars for practising her Bach. Two black crosses for yawning through Proust. It wasn't all bad. It gave life a point and purpose. Charles swept her and the house into his own inimitable system, so that everything was certain, predictable and tidy. Charles ran his existence by a system of colour-coded notebooks – black for petty cash and bills outstanding, brown for household maintenance, green for his yearly gardening plan. There was even a crimson-coloured notebook for Christmas, with a countdown to the 25th, and a birthdays and anniversaries book, so they'd never forget a date or lose a friend; a check-list for holidays and hospitals; a household inventory; and a filing system which took up three-quarters of his study. Frances wondered sometimes if he had a notebook labelled 'Frances' (blue to match her eyes) which reminded him to buy her flowers on Fridays, and check her share returns, and spend three and a half minutes pleasuring each breast before he entered her. He did do all those things, and if sometimes she wanted to scream when he handed her another bunch of poker-faced carnations, that only proved what an ungrateful bitch she was.

She jumped on the escalator. She didn't feel like going home. First floor, fashions; second floor, coats; third floor, baby wear. She went right on up to the third. The word 'baby' was like a magic lure. While she'd been working, she'd hardly considered the whole teeming business of reproduction. It was something tedious and distant, which no doubt she'd get round to, all in good time, when she and Charles had fulfilled their other, more crucial ambitions. But, now, motherhood was almost an obsession. The whole of Oxford Street seemed to be seething with prams and pregnant women. London had turned into an ante-natal clinic. Every magazine was fixated on fertility. She'd cancelled the *New Yorker* and taken out a subscription to *Mother and Baby*. She pored over advertisements for front-fastening nursing bras and disposable nappies. She hid it all from Charles. Publicly, she went on reading Stendhal or Sartre, or discussed the anomalies of police pay, or whether the Arts Council was under-represented in the provinces. But underneath, there was a second, hidden life, where she peered into prams and studied her monthly cycle like a secret vice. She was almost ashamed of it. Women weren't meant to want babies any more – only equality, and freedom and leisure. She had all those. Sometimes she suspected it wasn't even the baby she wanted, but the pregnancy itself, that essential, biological badge of womanhood, whatever the libbers said. A unique, almost mystical experience that served as your membership card. It was like sex – if you hadn't had it, you were shut out from the closed circle of other women, a stranger to their conversation and their coven.

And, yet, pregnancy was almost obscene. Frances glanced at the hugely pregnant woman in front of her, choosing a fluffy pink jacket from the display rack. It annoyed her sometimes, watching these casually pregnant women lumbering all over London, displaying themselves in public. This one probably hadn't even planned it. Perhaps the Durex had broken or her husband came home drunk. Maybe she had seven kids already, didn't need another one? She looked ordinary enough, pale, with lank brown hair scraped back into a rubber band. But young – you had to give her that. *She* hadn't wasted the best years of her marriage, being important and expensive and sterile.

She stared at the woman's stomach – vast, disgusting almost. Unthinkable to look like that. She herself was small and slim, with tiny hands and feet, and not a trace of flab. She had her weak points, of course, but at least there was nothing gross about her. A belly like that would be out of the question. She picked up a vest, a tiny scrap of cotton which wouldn't fit a doll.

'May I help you, madam?'

Frances let it fall. She was trespassing, had no right to be there. She hadn't joined that magic sisterhood. She squeezed past the stomach and on into the toy department. Another world apart. She and Charles were both only children, so there weren't even nieces and nephews to buy for. She stopped in front of the teddies – expensive ones, with real suede paws, cheap ones with yellow mangy hair, enormous ones with eyes as big as paper-weights, and tiny ones for hanging in a pram. Perhaps she'd buy a toy for their baby – to make him more real. If she believed in the baby, maybe she would have him. There was always so much doubt, like with God, and Peace, and Love, and Perfect Sex, and all those other desirable things which never quite happened.

She moved past the bears to seals and otters. Perhaps Charles would prefer a more serious beast – he believed in educational toys. He'd probably have the baby on sleep tapes, as soon as it was born. If it slept eighteen hours a day, as the baby books claimed, it would be a genius before it was even weaned.

'I'd like to choose a toy for a baby.'

'Certainly, madam. What age is the child?'

'Well . . . still very young.'

'You can't go wrong with a bear, then. A nice cuddly teddy.'

It was then she saw the lions. Proud, dignified creatures with magnificent manes and greeny-yellow eyes. A Leo would be perfect – Charles' own birth-sign and the king of beasts. Infinitely more suitable for Charles' child than a nice cuddly anything. All the lions were ridiculously expensive, but Charles wouldn't mind. He insisted on quality, even in a toy.

She didn't want it wrapped. It seemed cruel, somehow, to reduce a lion to a brown paper parcel. She tucked him under one arm and smiled. She felt a little better.

Frances sat in her Ince and Mayhew chair, with a Haydn string quartet on the stereo, and *The Bostonians* ready at her side, to read when it finished. Five gold stars. The lion sat opposite, ensconced in Charles' chair. He looked faintly sardonic, as if life in Richmond Green left a lot to be desired. It was dark, quiet, lonely. She'd go to bed early; always did when Charles was away. She switched off the lights, locked the front door, wrote a note to the milkman. 'No milk.' She stopped suddenly, in the middle of the 'm'. Milkman – secret stud for all Mr Rathbone's patients, father of a million happy babies. She didn't even know what their milkman looked like. He came very early, before they were up, and she didn't pay him in person. He left the bill in a milk bottle and Charles sent the cheque care of United Dairies.

Had Mr Rathbone been serious? He sounded it. When he was joking, he pushed his spectacles half-way down his nose and put his funny face on. She hadn't seen a trace of it. Would other women really take chances like that, risking random fathers for their children? How could you ever find out? People never said anything except what was allowed in the rules. In their set, it was always Sunday supplement conversation – David Hockney's latest swimming pools, the new Buñuel at the Curzon, the test score, the Third World. But not their own world. Nothing lower than their heads. All the rest was unknown territory. Even with people one was closest to, her parents, for example. In thirty odd years, they'd never talked about anything personal. Her mother could be frigid and her father suicidal, for all she knew. They stuck carefully to safe, uncensored subjects – the pros and cons of organic fertilizer, why the National Trust should increase its admission fees. Charles was even worse. He kept his feelings in a safe, double-locked behind a steel wall, and only let them out occasionally, in meagre dribs and drabs; then banged the door tight shut again. She had never seen him cry. He rarely even shouted.

And, yet, she couldn't imagine a baby that wasn't nine-tenths Charles. It was always a boy, with Charles' straight, fair hair and full lips, with his tidiness, his order, his punctuality. No Parry Jones baby would dribble or doze, or mess up its nappies, or arrive off schedule.

Perhaps it would be better to have a baby by the milkman. A normal, messy, uninhibited infant, with no ambition. Sometimes she longed to be like that herself. But she had always been ordered and ambitious. She couldn't blame Charles. He'd simply made her worse.

She rummaged in her bag and found the small white tablets Rathbone had prescribed for her. 'CLOMID' said the label. They looked more like humble aspirin than a wonder fertility drug. By some strange coincidence, it was exactly the right day to begin the course, the fifth day of her cycle. Perhaps it was a sign. She swallowed a tablet with a glass of milk. Milk – with any luck, she'd be ordering more in future. She screwed up her note to the milkman and started another.

'Please ring.'

2

There were lions everywhere. Real, fierce ones with ravaging jaws and roars like the doorbell. The largest beast pealed mercilessly into her left ear. The sound of a maddened, hungry doorbell. It *was* the doorbell. . . .

Frances groped out her hand and grabbed a tail. The lion was sleeping upside down beside her.

'Hell!' she muttered. 'The milkman.'

She pulled on her Harrods house-coat and loped downstairs.

'Coming!' she called through the locked door, struggling with stiff bolts. She hardly dared look up. She felt like the Princess in the fairy tale, face to face with her frog prince.

First, she saw his shoes. Scuffed black lace-ups from Freeman, Hardy and Willis. Her eyes moved slowly up towards his trousers – grey turn-ups with a hole in the knee, brown plastic belt, navy nylon anorak. A small man, a thin man, but what about his face? Adonises could be pint-sized. She took a deep breath and jumped from grubby grey collar to flabby white face. Three warts, two faded eyes and a gingery moustache. It was the only hair he had. His peaked United Dairies cap covered only half of his shining bald head. Yul Brynner? No, Yul Brynner was a he-man. This was a shrimp. And not even pink. A dead shrimp, pale and bloated. He looked as if he'd been drinking too much of his own pallid milk.

'Yes, madam?'

They still said 'madam' on Richmond Green – one of the reasons Charles chose to live there.

I'd like you to sire my baby. No, she couldn't say that. 'I wondered if you had any . . . yoghurt?'

'Strawberry, blackcurrant, or mandarin?' His voice sounded like gravel plopping through porridge. Perhaps he had a younger assistant, one of those cherubic boys with soft skins and golden hair. Colette had extolled the virtues of the youthful male. But was it safe to father children under age?

23

'Strawberry, blackcurrant, or . . .' He began his litany again.

'Lovely weather, isn't it?' Frances smiled her best blue-chip smile. Anything to keep him there. She glanced in the direction of the milk float – there didn't seem to be a boy. Only a mangy dog sniffing at the bottles. 'I mean, it's surprising to see the sun after all that rain.'

He grunted. 'Or we do have the plain. That's a penny cheaper.'

Perhaps he had a day off, and another, younger fellow took over, a Kevin Keegan, or a Bjorn Borg. 'Of course it *is* July. I suppose we should expect a little sun.'

He took a step backwards. 'So you won't be wanting yoghurt, ma'am?'

'Er . . . no thanks, not today.' She closed the door. No yoghurt, no strawberry-flavoured baby. The whole thing was utterly ridiculous. Even if he had been Adonis, what on earth could she have done? Asked him in and demanded a free sample of his double jersey cream? Told him she was doing a market research survey on South Thames milkmen and would he please strip off? Mr Rathbone should have sent her a handbook on how to seduce milkmen, like the instructions he enclosed with her temperature chart. She knew those off by heart: take the temperature every morning, by mouth, before rising. Do not eat, drink, smoke, talk, move, *breathe*, before recording it. Start a new line on the first day of every period and plot the graph for that month. A dot for every day. She'd grown accustomed to her little dots – her start to the day, like Charles' exercises or the Morning Service.

Every time they made love, a small neat circle went around the dot. She was often tempted to add a few more circles. They never seemed quite enough. Either Charles was away, or exhausted. He refused to rush it, was a perfectionist even in the bedroom. No snatched five-minute snacks, but a four-course meal with all the trimmings.

Apart from the paucity of circles, the charts were perfect. Some women had erratic charts, so Rathbone said, with temperatures rising and falling completely at random, but hers were as neat and orderly as her life. Twenty-eight-day cycles to the minute, the little dip just before ovulation, the one-degree rise exactly on day fourteen. Up and down it went, exactly as it should, and in and out went Charles' thing (work permitting), following its curve. And absolutely nothing happened: no continued rise denoting pregnancy, but down again, start again, new line, new chart.

The trouble with the charts was that they killed all spontaneity, more or less ordered you when to make love, when to abstain. And if Charles was away on those few vital, fertile days, she felt almost bereaved. In the last year alone, she had followed him to outlandish and unlikely places, just so they could put a circle round the dot. Once, they were grounded in Alaska with engine trouble, followed by a blizzard, and Charles was so upset about missing his International Tax Conference in Hawaii that he couldn't even get it up. Another time, she'd spent seven rain-sodden days trailing round the Isle of Man, trying to prise Charles away from three hundred identical accountants, and eventually collapsing with 'flu and pharyngitis (and still no circles round her dots).

She couldn't really blame Charles. For almost eighteen months now, they'd done it on the right days, and she had stayed on her back for thirty minutes afterwards, with her legs stuck up in the air (Mr Rathbone's Holy Writ again). And still no results – except backache and lost sleep.

Frances scanned *The Times* and nibbled on her starch-reduced roll. Two gold stars. Charles liked her slim and well-informed. She'd planned a round of golf today. Laura had taken time off and was collecting her at ten. She felt a dart of envy. When every day was more or less a day off, freedom lost its flavour. She didn't even feel like golf. Once, it had been crucial to drive a ball cleanly down a fairway and two-putt every green, but now it seemed absurd to lavish all that ardour and attention on a tiny white ball. When Laura knocked, she was still dawdling through the paper in her house-coat.

'Good God, darling, have you gone down with the dreaded influenza?'

'No, I'm just a bit ungolfish.'

'Impossible! Look, have a cup of coffee and you'll feel better.'

'I've had three and I feel worse.'

'Well, make me one, then. To tell the truth, I've only just crawled out of bed myself. Do you know, Frances, this is the first time I've ever caught you in your nightie! If that indefatigable spouse of yours ever had a free minute to communicate with lesser mortals, I'd tell him what wicked things you get up to when he's three thousand miles away.'

'Yes, it's my chatting-up-the-milkman gear!' With Laura, you had to be flip.

'Frances, if you're going to have a fling, for goodness sake aim high. A diplomat, or something. Far better perks, and a decent pad to do it in. Personally, I just wouldn't fancy a milk float. All those empty bottles banging against my breasts.'

Frances tried to smile. It was all talk with Laura. She spattered her conversation with wild allusions to her tempestuous life, yet most evenings she was closeted with Clive and half a dozen poodles, in front of *Nationwide*.

'Laura, do people really have all these affairs?'

'Which affairs?'

'Oh, come on, you know what I mean. You can't pick up a women's mag these days without some article on "Why You Need a Latin Lover" or "How To Stop Your Husband Finding Out". It's credible, until you bring it down to actual individuals. I can't imagine Mrs Eady with a lover, even an Anglo-Saxon one. And what about Viv? Does she have affairs?'

'Can't you use the word in the singular, darling? You talk about affairs like eggs, as if they came in dozens. I should have thought one affair was more than enough for anyone.'

'Well, one, then. Does Viv have even one?'

'How should I know? You're closer to her than I am. I doubt it, frankly, with all that surplus avoirdupois. Unless, of course, she's found a fellow with a fat fetish.'

Laura was a bitch. She wasn't slim herself, but it was the sort of flesh you called voluptuous, rather than obese. She pushed away the sugar bowl and prised open the tiny silver snuff-box which held her saccharin. 'Frankly, I think it's all a ploy, darling. A hidden plug for male superiority. You know the sort of line – now women are liberated, all they want is men.'

Frances frowned. 'But most of those articles are written by women. The liberated kind.'

'Oh, half of them are probably men in drag. Haven't you noticed how androgynous most women's libbers are? Facial hair and baby slings. The poor male ego has taken such a bruising recently, they'll stoop to anything just to shore it up again. Frankly, it tends to put me off them. There's nothing sadder than a drooping ego.'

Frances glanced across at her. Laura's elegant long legs had been dipped in sheer black silk, and were crossed provocatively at the thigh. Her three-inch heels lengthened them still further. Even when she changed into her golf clothes, the men still goggled. Laura loved it. She lapped up men like cream, then spat them out again.

'Quite honestly, Frances, I haven't bothered with affairs since I drew up a balance sheet on them. You know, pros and cons. The pros took two lines, and the cons four pages. I simply can't be fagged risking syphilis, BO, boredom, trichomonas, guilt, or cancer of the cervix – to name but a random few.'

Or pregnancy, thought Frances. Laura had been sterilized ten years ago, as casually as if she'd had her hair cut. She herself had been shocked when she heard. Sterilization seemed a violent act, a desecration, almost. She knew all the arguments, of course – over-population, strain on natural resources, wrong to bring a child into a wicked world. But that was only talk. Women didn't get their tubes tied because harvests had failed in Bangladesh, or Peking was stock-piling the Bomb. Laura wanted to keep her leisure and her looks, her independence, her freedom to travel, her glossy, streamlined job. Frances almost envied her – just to be that certain. Laura never agonized. She knew what she wanted and she got it.

Frances removed a wilting carnation from the stiff flower arrangement on the table. 'Do you think Viv . . .?'

'What about her?' shouted a voice from the hallway. Viv had let herself in, the back way, and was standing panting at the door. 'Sorry I'm late. Midge refused to go to school. She crawled underneath the hall seat and clung on to the legs. It took three of us to prise her out.'

'Little monster,' muttered Laura, who regarded children as a lower form of life. Strange, thought Frances, how children wormed their way into everything. Women who didn't have any were set apart, put in a special category, frigid, selfish, spoilt. It was true they were less restricted – their lives weren't swallowed up in rose-hip syrup or school bazaars, or parcelled out among a dozen grabbing hands. All the same, it seemed a strange basis for alignment. Viv was friendly with the most unlikely people, simply because they had a school or a Brownie pack in common, whereas she was lumped with Laura, on the arbitrary basis that neither had a child.

In fact, she felt pulled between the two. Laura's elegant, untrammelled life was not unlike her own. The difference was that Laura enjoyed it. Her glass and concrete office and her *Homes and Gardens* house (complete with rich, phlegmatic husband) apparently fulfilled and satisfied her, so that she didn't yearn for children, or that elusive Something Else. And, yet, she didn't want to be a Laura, with a padlocked womb and a solid silver locket in place of a heart.

Neither did she want to be a Viv – an overweight earth mother who had run to seed. Yet Viv lived far more fully and unselfishly than she or Laura ever could. Viv had five kids and a heart big enough to fit them all. Viv was warm, real, safe, easy, comfortable. And – Laura would have added – stolid, slovenly and boring. Chewing-gum on chair seats and marbles dropped in cornflakes packets. When Frances thought about her own child, it never looked like Viv's, with their runny noses or filthy fingernails. It never had rashes or earache or diarrhoea, or answered back, or was stupid at arithmetic. She relied on Charles to produce a model infant, something she could stand on the mantelpiece and admire like a flower arrangement.

And yet Charles had produced nothing, whereas Viv's David had fathered five, and he was away even more than Charles – a sales engineer with three-month stints abroad. Viv snatched her babies from him between electronic equipment exhibitions in Frankfurt, or customer conferences in Singapore, and then set about having them as casually as other women had summer colds or dandruff. Eight months gone with Rupert, she'd dug up their wilderness garden, single-handed, and transformed it into a sand-pit for the older children. Now, it had reneged into a wilderness, but that wasn't the point. What was astonishing was Viv's slapdash attitude to pregnancy itself. It seemed too sublime a condition to treat so cavalierly. If she herself were pregnant, she knew she would view her body as the Temple of the Holy Ghost, yet there was Viv wedging that sacred bulge into the bowels of the motor mower or squeezing it underneath her oily, stalling Volkswagen.

Even now, she looked *enceinte*. (Although she wasn't. The bulges had stopped with Rupert. David had insisted that number five be their finale, and had doubled his stint in Singapore to underline the point. He was still there now, leaving Viv a widow until October.) She sat slumped in a chair, in one of her old maternity smocks, bunched around the middle with what looked like a piece of hair ribbon. The fragile Sheraton strained stoically beneath her eleven stone.

'Playing golf in your nightie?' she grinned, plugging her mouth with a chocolate biscuit, as if it were a deprived and hungry child.

'She's betraying us with the milkman, Viv!' Laura wrinkled up her twice-remodelled London Clinic nose. 'Rating United Dairies above the Royal Mid-Surrey Golf Club is almost certainly a treasonable offence.'

'Oh, Laura, do stop. If you want to know, I've actually decided to go and get a job.'

'A job, darling. But you've only just stopped working.'

'No, I've been idle for over a year. It doesn't suit me.'

'Idle!' There was a faint groaning sound as Viv bounced forward on the chair. 'You must be joking. You and Charles don't know the meaning of the word. I've never known such a pair of eager beavers in my life – so many committees and commitments, I have to book a year ahead just to have coffee with you.'

'So it's back to the world of the plunging bosom and the plummeting hem. Well, old Peters will be glad. He always fancied you.'

'Don't be silly, Laura. Anyway, I'm not going back. Not there. It's too much of a strain, with all my other activities. I just want a little job.'

'What, like reorganizing British Rail?' Laura spooned cream into her second cup of coffee.

'You're crazy,' said Viv. 'You don't have to work at all. You don't even have the excuse of escaping from the kids. If I were you, I'd loll around drinking schnapps and reading Mills and Boon.'

'With the occasional breathless little foray into United Dairies,' added Laura.

Frances escaped into the kitchen to make more coffee. Everything was joke and chatter with her friends. She burned to examine motives and morality, or probe into philosophy and purpose, but it was one of the rules, not to be too serious. There were whole layers of life, waiting and wasting underneath, while they all frothed and frittered on the surface.

'What sort of job do you want?' Viv shouted through the open door.

'Oh, I thought I'd work in a florist, or something.'

'You're nuts, Frances! You'd be bored stiff in a day. All those dreadful damp daffodils and people weeping over wreaths.'

'Well, what *can* I do? I don't fancy teaching. I don't want anything too arduous . . .'

'How about a traffic warden? You'd look fantastic in the uniform. And you could give me special permission to park outside Sainsbury's.'

'Get a fun job,' urged Laura. 'You've been so bloody serious all your life. It's time you broke out. How about a croupier? Or a bunny girl?'

'What, with my figure? They don't take 34As.' Back to the silly chat again. She felt like screaming at them, laughed instead. 'Anyway, Charles would go berserk.'

'Charles needn't know. I read about a girl the other day, a diplomat's daughter. She took a job as a high class courtesan, and her father thought she was having music lessons. He even dropped her there each evening, with her Chopin.'

Viv gulped down her fourth chocolate biscuit. 'Shouldn't we set off? Or I won't get my eighteen holes in before it's time to meet the kids.'

'Sure you're not coming?' asked Laura.

'Positive.'

When they'd driven off, she wished she'd joined them. Golf was probably no more absurd than anything else in life. At least it had rules which couldn't be broken. The other rules seemed remarkably fragile. Middle-aged wives are faithful to their husbands. Middle-class graduates take serious jobs. But were they? Should they?

She spread out the local paper and last night's *Evening Standard*. Scores and scores of jobs she couldn't do: computer operator, laboratory technician, tool maker, *chef patissier*. What was one paltry arts degree and ten years' experience in public relations, compared to this ocean of skills she knew nothing of? She didn't want to go back to the fashion world. Oh yes, it was well paid and well regarded, but such a trivial world, where bitchy people took fatuous frivolities desperately seriously. She wanted something in which steel-souled philanthropists got to grips with life-and-death emergencies. A missionary, a bomb-disposal expert, a lion tamer. She grinned at the lion which was squatting on a kitchen stool. It already seemed a friend.

That sort of mission was impossible. She couldn't bring the Gospel to savages in Botswana, when Charles needed her in Richmond Green. In any case, she had to conserve her energies. One of the reasons she hadn't conceived when she first came off the Pill was the stress of her career – she was sure of it. This time it would be a gentle, unambitious little venture; yes, a little job, *pace* Mr Rathbone.

But what should it be? Whatever Viv said about damp daffs, a florist's would be ideal. A most suitable background to conceive a baby in, all those buds and blooms. But no florist's post was advertised. How about a waitress? There were scores of openings there, except Charles would disapprove. And supposing one of the members of the Royal Mid-Surrey Golf Club should come in as a customer and catch their ex-Lady Captain slopping about with trays of shepherd's pie. She turned back to the 'situations vacant'.

Temporary Owner-Drivers Urgently Required
Medfield Mini-Cabs

A driver. Now that was something she could do. She had her own car, an elegant Citroën which spent a lot of its life yawning in the garage. Driving was simple and soothing and wouldn't overtax her. She'd still have vital energy to spare for circles round the dots. And it could be called a fun job. Not as daring as a bunny girl, but then you didn't need a forty-inch chest to be a driver – it would only encumber the steering wheel. But at least a little

31

daring. Wasn't there some risqué film called *Confessions of a Taxi Driver?* Charles wouldn't allow his wife to be a taxi driver. But as Laura had said, Charles needn't know. Well, need he? He was away for a week in any case, so she could just try it out. She almost ought to break a rule, on principle. She'd been so obedient all her life, so careful and professional, never taking risks, never acting foolishly. She suddenly wanted to turn round and stick her tongue out, shrug off all those cautions and prohibitions, and, if not plunge in the deep end, at least put a toe in the water.

She picked up the phone. 'Medfield Mini-Cabs? Hallo, I'm phoning about your advertisement for drivers. Yes, of course I'm a woman, what did you think? Oh, I see. Good Lord, what prejudice! I've got a remarkably good sense of direction. It's nothing to do with sex – I could read a map when I was eight. Yes, a '79 Citroën Pallas. Of course it's got four doors. Clean licence? Yes. What, you want me to come now? Right, give me half an hour.'

She took the stairs two at a time. She'd got an interview and she wasn't even dressed; wasn't sure she wanted a job at all, let alone a crazy one like this. She hunted through her wardrobe for something suitably severe; didn't want anyone to get ideas. She pulled on a sludge grey suit and a pair of walking shoes, and peered in the mirror. She still looked too demure. Her Minton china look, Charles called it. Charles loved fine china. Her dark hair was cut like an elf (an elf with a healthy bank balance and an extremely good hairdresser). Her eyes were blue, a very deep intense blue. Inestimable eyes, Charles had called them, when he'd first fixed his own lighter ones upon them and promptly decided they were assets he should invest in. He approved of the fact she had dark hair and blue eyes, which seemed to make her special, or at least superior to those who automatically associated blue eyes with fair hair, and dark with dark. She didn't like her nose. It was too small and insignificant, but she'd learned the trick of not seeing it when she looked in the mirror. She focused on her eyes instead, or on her even teeth.

She wished she were an inch or two taller. It might help as a driver. Small women were always treated as even more fragile and feeble than the big ones, and it rankled. She kicked off her brogues, put on her highest heels.

'Lord! You're a littl'un,' muttered the small, greasy man in shirt-sleeves, stirring his coffee with a custard cream. The Medfield office was a dingy room sulking above a coin and stamp shop – girlie posters on the walls, nothing on the dirty concrete floor. The man fished half a soggy biscuit out of his cup and dried it on the blotter. 'I'm Reg,' he said, 'the boss. You must be Mrs Jones.'

'Yes.' She had dispensed with the Parry. 'And if you're worried that I can't reach the pedals . . .'

'All right, keep your hair on, Mrs Jones. You're the women's lib one, aren't you?'

'Certainly not! I don't believe in women's liberation, not as it stands, in any case. It needs total re-thinking and reform . . .'

'Well, we don't get many women on this job, lib or otherwise. But with the summer hols coming up, I can't be choosy. Sit down.'

The interview took exactly twelve minutes, half of which Reg spent answering outside calls. Did she have a police record? Did she know the area? Could she add up?

'Now, listen . . .'

'OK, OK, I'll take you on. Though I wouldn't, if I weren't desperate. I've nothing against you personally, mind, but women are invariably born with no sense of direction.'

Frances opened her mouth to object, but Reg was rattling on about insurance, commission, and methods of payment.

'Phone in tomorrow for your first booking. Nine o'clock sharp. No excuses. We'll take it from there.'

'*Tomorrow?* Good gracious! I don't think that's . . .'

'And don't forget to see that bloke I mentioned. He'll fix up your insurance right away, if you say I sent you. OK? Close the door behind you. There's a draught.'

She reeled to the nearest café and ordered a black coffee, to recover from the shock. She never acted impulsively like this. She should have gone to a professional employment agency and taken a job more suited to her station in life. She grinned into her Danish pastry. No one except Charles used expressions like that.

The trouble was, her station in life was so exceptionally narrow. She'd never had a job which wasn't sheltered and respectable;

never even had a lover. Oh yes, a few tepid paddlings when she was at university, but they didn't really count. Then Charles had taken over and insisted on an early marriage, before she'd even sat her degree and long before she'd had a chance to taste the wide and wicked world. And here she was, aged thirty-four, and fifteen years married, Charles' creation more or less, accomplished, efficient, successful, and barren. Charles was ten years older, or maybe a hundred years. She loved him, she admired him, she depended on him almost frighteningly, and yet sometimes she felt he'd taken away all her spontaneity, kidnapped her youth, and locked it in a bank vault.

She selected a second Danish pastry, even larger and stickier than the first. (Three black crosses. Charles hated obese women and bad teeth.) Was the job an act of rebellion? Mrs Parry Jones, mini-cab driver, stuffing herself with pastries, and wasting Charles' precious time. Perhaps she'd do worse – waste the whole day window-shopping and sprawling in the sun. She'd be a working girl tomorrow, so she'd treat herself to a little indulgence today. It wasn't easy. She was so accustomed to being useful and committed, it seemed sinful to miss the Save Wildlife fund-raising tea-party, and to turn down a freelance fashion job when her old boss phoned in a panic and begged her to do it for him. Worst of all, Charles' eye seemed to peer down at her from the sky in mingled disbelief and horror when she switched the Bach recital over to Radio 2 and lay down to doze in her bikini on the lawn.

She was due for drinks with Clive and Laura in the evening. She cancelled that as well. Laura was still more maddening on her own home ground – all fizz and façades – and Clive made a life's work out of being unobjectionable, and hid behind half a dozen clichés and the whisky bottle. Besides, she felt it was important not to see anyone before she started the Medfield job. They'd all make witty remarks and say how amusing she was (meaning downright stupid) and then she'd weaken, and instead of ringing Reg in the morning, she'd be chairing the meeting for the Richmond Residents' Association or practising her Mozart. She'd written a new rule for herself: do something impulsive, ridiculous, and jolly well enjoy it. She had and she would.

She was watching a thriller on ITV when Charles phoned,

just before ten. She switched it off hastily – his all-seeing eye was frowning from Bahrain.

'Miss you, darling.'

'Miss you too.'

'Good flight?'

'Not bad.'

The shorthand of her marriage. She could have done it in her sleep. 'How did your paper go?'

'So so.' (That meant brilliant.)

'Hotel all right?'

'Not bad.' (Five star, with all the trimmings.)

'Are they working you hard?'

'No, not really.' (Fourteen-hour day and homework on top of it.)

'Poor darling.'

'No, I'm fine.' (Man is born to labour.)

It was comforting, predictable. Charles never let her down. Cards for all their anniversaries, phone calls for his trips away. And yet, somehow there was a barrier between them. She longed for her bare soul to rub against his, for their two minds to crash into each other and send up showers of sparks. But all that happened was this kid-glove conversation, this whirring of words. They never seemed to meet head-on, only obliquely, and, even then, there was a moat and a drawbridge up on Charles' side.

'Charles,' she said suddenly. 'I . . .'

'What, darling?'

'I . . . love you.'

'Yes, of course, love you too.'

The formula again. That wasn't what she'd meant to say. But how could you start on all those forbidden, complicated things, via a crackling line half a world away? She could picture Charles in his Turnbull and Asser maroon silk dressing-gown, with all his possessions arranged in straight lines in the drawers; the items on the dressing-table drawn up in military formation, the alarm clock set for earlier than he needed it, the memoranda on the bedside table.

Suddenly, she missed him. The second bed looked cold and empty, his brown spare slippers gaped on the bedside rug. She reached out and picked up the lion from where it had fallen on

35

the floor, tried to turn it into Charles. It wasn't easy; Charles was hairless and didn't have a tail. She turned the other way and imagined Charles beside her, stroking her breasts the way he always did, seriously and with total concentration, as if he were trying to increase their output or improve their dividend. Charles approached sex like a business meeting, a challenge he must meet with unqualified success. It *was* always successful – when they had the time for it. They did all the right things in the right order. She sometimes even came, and pretended quite convincingly the other times. They tried new positions and never skimped on foreplay. They'd ploughed through Masters and Johnson and the Hite report. Yet, somehow, they both remained detached and apart. However hard their bodies thrust and thrashed, the heads above were looking the other way, averting their eyes. She found she was making a shopping list, or working out a problem, at the very moment Charles was spurting into her.

She worried, sometimes, that there was something wrong with her. She never felt abandoned or overcome with passion, like all the books described. Did Laura scream and squirm in ecstasy? Did Viv cry out 'I'm *dying* with it, Fabrizio,' like a Bertolucci heroine? She'd never know. It was bad enough never having had another man. Being faithful was almost a perversion these days, more pitiable than being scrofulous. You were more or less obliged to pretend to affairs – hint at torrid entanglements and abandoned couplings, to give yourself a modicum of self-respect.

She picked up the lion and held him close against her breasts. His tail dangled down conveniently against her pubic hair. She tried to move herself against him. 'I'm dying with it, Fabrizio,' she whispered. And yawned. It really was more tempting simply to go to sleep.

3

Frances hated going into pubs alone. It was almost three o'clock, closing time, and the Bricklayer's Arms was noisy and crowded. How, in heaven's name, was she supposed to find a Mr Smythe? She whispered to the barman and then wished she hadn't. 'Any bloke here for a Medfield Mini-Cab?' he shouted, fortissimo. 'Lovely lady driver! Don't all rush at once.'

She tried to ignore the catcalls. Mr Smythe was struggling through the crowd, a small, spindly man, with an apologetic moustache in one shade of ginger and a toupee in another.

'Medfield?' he grunted. His voice was surprisingly deep, as if God had made a mistake and given him the voice of a Titan.

'Yes. Where to?' She'd learnt already to cut through the formalities. Even the female passengers seemed to want her life history, and she didn't intend giving it to anyone.

'Broke down, didn't I? Right on the way to a fancy customer. God knows when I'll see my car again. You need wheels in this job. I'm a salesman – suppose they told you, didn't they? Hygi Hankies, South West London area.'

He paused, as if for congratulation. Frances said nothing. She was fighting her way through two dozen beer-laden stomachs.

'Must admit I've never heard of Medfield. All women drivers, are they?'

Frances side-stepped a lighted cigarette. 'No.' Monosyllables were safer – she'd discovered that the first few days. There were only two female drivers to twenty-three males, but she wasn't going to tell him that.

The air outside smelt blessedly fresh. 'Where to?' she asked again, opening the car door and holding it for him.

'Thanks, Miss, but I'll sit in front if it's all the same with you.'

Frances left him to open the front door himself, and edged over as far to the right as possible. 'Where are you going, Mr Smith?'

'Smythe, with a "y", dear. Lesley Smythe. Pleased to meet you. Nice little car you've got here. Not that I'd ever touch a foreign car myself.'

'Mr Smi – er – Smythe. I'm due to finish at five o'clock sharp, so if . . .'

'Sorry, dear – thought they gave you all the details before you picked me up. Sunbury Trading Estate, please, and fast. I should have been there half an hour ago.'

Frances did a neat U-turn and accelerated sharply, feeling irritable and out of sorts. The job had proved a disappointment. She'd gone into it as a sort of holy rebellion, expecting excitement and regeneration, and all she'd found was traffic jams and crude boring passengers who wouldn't stop nattering, or tried to chat her up. A drawing-office assistant had spent the whole journey to Gerrards Cross and back again telling her what an intrepid drinker he was, how many times he'd lost his licence, and how he rigged the breathalyser. And an electronics engineer from Staines had boasted about fathering three babies on three different women and not paying a penny for any of them.

She glanced at Mr Smythe, who was waving what looked like a strip of blue and white awning above his ginger head.

'The Hygi Hankie, dear. Quite a different little product. I wondered if you'd ever come across it?'

'No,' she said.

'It's half-way between your fancy handkerchief and your all-purpose Kleenex. Man-made. Man-size. No washing, no ironing, no wispy bits of paper sticking to your nose. One a day, throw away. Lasts all day even when wet.' He blew his nose loudly.

The product demonstration, Frances assumed, making a mental note to gargle that evening. She hadn't realized what a germy job cab-driving would prove to be. She'd already risked two colds, three coughs, one roaring influenza, and a bad case of eczema.

Mr Smythe finished blowing and started doing unspeakable things with the handkerchief. 'You see, it still holds together even with the heaviest cold. I can guarantee you'll never go back to ordinary hankies, once you've tried ours. What about your husband? Men are mad for Hygi, you know. You're married, I presume?'

'Yes,' said Frances firmly. She usually got that one in, somewhere near the beginning of the ride.

'The only way to be, isn't it? I'm widowed myself. Twenty-five
years we had together. You should have seen the stuff we got on
our silver wedding! Bloody great teapots, silver cocktail shakers.
The wife did all the catering herself. She wasn't well then, but
she never said a word. Six months later, she was gone. Want
a Polo?'

Frances shook her head. She'd earned a hundred black crosses,
on the strength of the job alone, without ruining her teeth on
top of it.

'Two years, it took me, to get over it. You never do, though,
do you? Of course, we had the boys, but they were always closer
to their mother. The older boy married, though I must admit, I
didn't like his wife. She dyed her hair. Turn left at the garage
and then it's first left. You needn't wait. I'll make my own
way back.'

He tipped her generously and left her two boxes of Hygis and
half a tube of Polos. She watched his small figure breezing up to
the ugly red-brick factory, preparing his patter; wondered how
many doors were slammed in his face in the course of a normal
working week. She hadn't been exactly friendly herself. Quite the
stuck-up, frosty little bitch, in fact. But, somehow, the way he
mixed up death with silver cocktail shakers . . . Maybe Charles
was right – it wasn't what you said, it was the way you said
it. Charles meant it cynically, but it seemed to operate in life.
When his partner's wife died, for instance, the poor bereaved
fellow carried on like the matinée idol of a cosmic tragedy –
until someone caught him fondling his secretary in the back of
his new Mercedes, just three days after the funeral.

No, she mustn't think of what went on in the backs of cars – or
not until she'd handed in her notice. That was the reason she had
to be so sparing with her sympathy. You offered them a friendly
ear, and soon they were grabbing something further down. No
wonder women didn't work as cab-drivers. Yet, Laura would
have handled it superbly, slapping them down with just the right
mixture of flattery and fury, so they'd be eating out of her hand
by the first green light. And Viv would be maternal and relaxed,
chatting and sympathizing, and even managing to enjoy herself,

for heaven's sake. She slumped at the steering wheel. Perhaps she was a misfit, only functioning when she was in her own neat, safe world, with Charles by her side, pointing her in the right direction and engraving her soul with his maxims for life.

She cruised through the side streets, searching for a phone box. 'Reg, it's Mrs Jones. I'm signing off now. I'll ring you in the morning, and bring my cash in then.'

'Do me a favour, love. I'm desperate for drivers and there's a Mr Bradley called from Acton. 57, Wyndham Road. Doing his nut, he is. He's been waiting half an hour already, and he's got to get to Southmead Polytechnic, urgent. He's got a load of stuff. Sheep, I think he said.'

'Sheep?'

'That's what it sounded like.'

'Reg, I'm not only exhausted, but I draw the line at animals. Even that wretched Mrs Barker's lap-dog ruined my upholstery.'

'Well, forget about the sheep and rescue Mr Bradley. I doubt if they're real ones, anyway. You don't get sheep in Acton.'

The pips were going and she didn't have another coin. 'OK love?' Reg shouted. 'You'll do it for me then?'

'OK.' Frances swore silently. Blast Mr Bradley and his flock of sheep. On the other hand, there was nothing to go home for. Charles was away till the following evening, and the house always felt lost and limp without him, as if it had shed its stuffing and its spine.

The traffic was appalling. She tried to take a short cut and landed in a cul-de-sac. She hoped Mr Bradley wouldn't storm and shout. Some of the passengers almost attacked you, the minute they opened the door, lambasted you for being late, or ruining their plans. It was rarely her fault, anyway. Reg ran the firm on a shoestring and had no idea of management. He took the scanty profits, and she and the other drivers took the ample abuse.

Mr Bradley didn't appear to be in. She knocked twice and then rang. Silence. That was another disadvantage of the job. You trailed all the way to some outlandish place and then found the passenger had disappeared. On Tuesday, she'd waited two whole hours at the airport for a Mr Wong (Peking), and when at last

40

the flight arrived, he wasn't even on it. You didn't get paid for all that wasted time. OK, she didn't really need the money, but the principle was wrong. She knocked once more, and began to walk away down the crumbling stone steps. Acton looked dingy and faceless, as if it had been overlooked or abandoned by the Great Builder in the Sky.

'Hi there!' said a deep voice from the direction of the dustbins. Frances looked up and saw a pale blue corduroy bottom and two matching legs. The head was out of sight, the arms elbow-deep in tins and tea leaves.

'Would you be looking for James, by any chance?' The voice was muffled – there was still no head.

Frances stopped in her tracks. 'Who?'

'Jim. He gets all the good-lookers – lucky bloke. Flat 3, top floor. Just walk up. The bell's out of order.'

Suddenly, the bottom turned round and a top came into view – quite an appealing one. The red and white checked shirt was open to the navel, revealing an exotic purple vest and a mass of hair curling on the chest. The hair on the head was lighter, streaked by the sun into stripes and shadows. The eyes were yellowish green, the mouth grinned. There were tea leaves in his hair.

'I was searching for a fish-hook,' he explained. 'The one that got away. You wouldn't have a fish-hook concealed about your person, would you?'

'No,' said Frances. She genuinely wished she had. It suddenly seemed important to be the sort of female who walked around with fish-hooks in her handbag.

She took a step towards the dustbins. 'Would Jim be Mr Bradley?'

'What?' He was sitting on the largest dustbin now, pulling the petals off a dandelion.

'Mr Jim Bradley?'

'Mr Ned Bradley.'

'Ah, you know him then. Where is he? I understand he ordered a mini-cab.'

'He did, he did. About a hundred years ago. Sadly, it never came.' The dandelion was only a stalk and a centre now. He twisted it through his lowest buttonhole, disturbing the hair.

41

'Oh, it did. It has, I mean. I'm it.'

'You're Medfield Mini-Cabs?' He laughed delightedly and the stalk fell down inside his shirt. 'My stars were right, for once. "An apparent disaster will be turned to your advantage." Star-Scope in the *Mail*. Terrible rag, but I read it. What are you born under?'

'I think it's Virgo.'

'Think? You should know, my love. Astrology rules our lives. That's bad, though.'

'What is?'

'Well, Sagittarius and Virgo. They're horribly incompatible. I think I'd better walk to Southmead! On the other hand, there may be some mitigating factors. Perhaps our moons are in the same sign, or we've both got Libra ascendant. Shall we risk it?' He slithered off the dustbin and brushed his blue bottom. His trousers were deplorably tight. Frances tried to concentrate on higher things.

'Look, let me get this straight. Are you Mr Bradley?'

He nodded. 'Call me Ned.'

She tried to ignore his cheerful grin. 'The Mr Bradley who ordered a mini-cab?'

'You're quite a girl, aren't you? Is this interrogation part of the service? Yes, of course I ordered the bloody cab. I was just about to phone and tell them what I thought of them. But perhaps I can tell *you*. I'd like that. You're pretty and bossy and you've got the most smashing blue eyes I've ever seen. And you're lovely when you're angry. That's what they say in bad B-movies.'

She drew herself up to her full five foot. 'I understand, Mr Bradley, there were also some sheep to be transported.'

'Christ! I'd clean forgotten about the little blighters. You're a clever girl, you know. You deserve a reward.' He handed her a second dandelion, allowing his hand to brush against hers for longer than it should. There were strange foreign colours mixed and marbled in his eyes. She tried to look away. He wasn't even handsome – too small, too messy – so why on earth should he light up everything around him? Even the dingy house and the bedraggled front garden leapt into shining focus when he looked at them. He took the steps three at a time and then ran back to fetch her. 'I'll need your help with those godforsaken creatures.

Do you mind? How about a coffee before we start? To give us strength. Come in, come in. Welcome to my shambles!'

Reg had said emphatically that Mr Bradley was in a rush, and if he wasn't, then she most certainly was. She had letters to write, and a list for Mrs Eady, and her notes to prepare for the Historical Association. Just because she'd been dazzled by too much charm and a couple of dandelions . . . 'Look, Mr Bradley . . .'

'Ned.'

If only he wouldn't sparkle like that. It was easy being cold and offhand to the Mr Smythes and Mrs Barkers, but this one seemed so sunny, he was frost-proof.

'Have *you* got a name?' He had suddenly, maddeningly, lured her through the front door. The house smelt of cats. The hall was high and bare, with flaking yellow paint.

'Mrs Parry J . . .'

'Oh, just my luck, a Mrs. Shouldn't I have guessed. Jim gets all the single ones. Let's pretend you're single, shall we? What's your first name?'

'I only took this booking as a favour, Mr Bradley. I was on my way home, and . . .'

'Home to hubby?'

'No, my husband's away, if you must know.'

Why in God's name had she told him that? He was rude and nosey enough already, without her breaking all the rules she'd made. Charles always advised her to create a new set of rules for every situation, so she'd drawn up her Medfield Mini-Cab Code the very first day – coldness, caution, and monosyllables; no names, no revelations, no chats, no chatting up. And yet here she was almost moving in with Ned.

He walked through a dirty corridor into a jungle of a kitchen. 'Coffee or tea? Except there isn't any tea.'

'Look, Mr Bradley, I make it a rule never to mix business with pleasure.'

The near-naked chest collapsed with laughter. 'Do you know, I never knew people actually said things like that. Let alone laser-sharp girls with eyes like damn great sapphires. And I bet you don't take sugar.'

'No.' Well at least it was a monosyllable. He was so relaxed and easy, he made her feel ridiculous. She was safe enough, really. There were people upstairs and it was still broad daylight.

He was searching for the coffee, which he found at last in an empty Campbell's soup can. 'I had to pinch the jar for bait. Do you find you're always needing empty jars?'

'No.' Another monosyllable. She was still keeping to the rules.

'I suppose you're not a fisherman?'

Frances picked her way through an assortment of empty cardboard boxes. 'Fisher*woman*. Or would it be fisherperson?'

Ned turned round and grabbed her arm. 'Are you one? How absolutely incredible. Do you know, I only ever met one woman who fished, and I think she was pretending. To be a woman, I mean. Coarse or sea?'

'I beg your pardon?'

'Well, do you fish in rivers or in the wide open brine?'

'I'm sorry to disappoint you, Mr Bradley, but I don't fish at all.'

'Oh, just my luck. Why did you say you did, then? Never mind, I expect you're a scuba diver or a Black Belt, or something just as worthwhile. Black or white? Don't say white, until I've sussed out the milk situation.'

The kitchen clearly contravened the requirements of the Health and Safety Act. An overweight black cat was sitting in the larder gobbling the remnants of a greasy chicken carcass. The cooker was tangled with dangerous-looking wires, which trailed, unsheathed, across the dirty floor. Every surface was covered with what appeared to be the contents of a jumble sale – a broken bird cage, a tea-stained set of Shakespeare's tragedies, a left slipper, a right gumboot, a stack of broken 78s, and three-quarters of a bust of Cardinal Newman.

'Sit down.' Ned cleared a space on a home-made pine bench. Frances sat, gingerly. A second cat sprang on to her lap, turned round three times and settled down with a sigh.

'Rilke,' he announced. 'I can't introduce you, as you've only got a surname and cats prefer people to have Christian names.'

She stroked the silky fur. At least he must be educated if he called a cat Rilke. One gold star – she couldn't grudge him that, and perhaps her Christian name as well.

'Happy to meet you, Rilke,' she said. 'I'm Frances.' The cat closed its eyes and purred.

'Amazing what they do for a cat. It's like Jim. People go on their knees for Jim, reveal their whole life histories, lend him a fiver. Alas, I'm only human.'

If she grinned like that at everything he said, it would give him ideas. She pretended she was smiling at the cat, though she didn't much like cats. They were unhygienic and left hairs on your clothes. Still, she had to admit Rilke was rather a charmer, with his long swishy tail and appreciative purr.

'My kingdom for a cup!' carolled Ned, searching the breadbin, but finding only a packet of mortar mix. 'There's never a cup in this kitchen. Do you mind drinking out of a vase? You do mind. I can see it on your face. Right, a cup it shall be. Hold on a minute, I might have a mug in here.' He opened the fridge and Frances peered in, under his arm. It was almost empty, save for two or three glass jars. The coffee jars. Except they weren't coffee. Frances clutched her stomach.

'There's something – er – *moving* in your fridge.'

'Yes. King rag and Dungeness lug, that's all. Bait for the thirty-pound cod I plan to catch each week. I keep it cool in there.'

Frances stared into the cruel hooked mouth of a twelve-inch worm with a myriad little legs. A second worm was writhing in the sand at the bottom of its jar.

'Look, Ned . . . (if she used his name, at least it would sound less rude). Please don't bother with the coffee. I never drink coffee after five, anyway.' She didn't want to offend him, but it was crazy risking some lethal disease – fish poisoning or dysentery – for the dubious benefit of a vaseful of Maxwell House.

He didn't look the least offended. 'Tell you what, we'll have tea at the Poly. They flavour it with cyanide and have the cheek to charge 12p – and that's subsidized – but at least you get a mug. In fact you get a real cup and saucer, and I can see you're a cup-and-saucer girl. A matching cup-and-saucer girl, in fact.'

'A Minton china matching cup-and-saucer girl.' It was quite a fun game to play and he laughed so nicely when she joined in.

'Right, coffee cancelled, sheep reprieved. Cats fall out, Frances follow.'

He marched out of the kitchen into another, far less tangled room. She did follow, amazed at her own submission. The room was almost elegant, with its high moulded ceiling and dove-grey walls. In front of the sofa stood a flock of paper sheep, fleeces white and woolly, noses black and shiny. A large green cardboard tree soared above them, heavy with white lace blossom, and a Dresden shepherdess smirked through her frills, brandishing a gold-foil crook.

'Oh, isn't it gorgeous!' Frances fell on her knees in front of it, caressing the curliest of the sheep.

''Course it is. I made it. Now wait a tick. It all folds into itself, for easy transportation, as they say in the blurb. Here, give me a hand with that tree, will you. It's losing half its leaves. Gently does it. I hope you've got a big car.'

Frances hardly heard him. She was still bewitched by his handiwork. 'So you're an artist?' That would explain the shambles. Artists were always bohemians – it was one of Charles' rules.

'Oh no, I'm not, my love. I'm a part-time lecturer in Media Studies, whatever those may be.'

'Then how . . .?'

'Oh, just a sideline. I've always loved making things. It's the Poly dance tonight – end of term rave-up. This is just part of the decorations. We're having a pastoral theme – green fields and dreaming spires, you know the sort of thing. The Poly's such a bloody ugly building, the poor deprived students have to invent their cardboard fantasies. Another bloke's bringing Morris dancers – plastic ones, of course.'

'But it's perfect. And so beautifully made. You've really got talent.'

'Thank you, I'll be blushing in a moment. Now perhaps you'll allow me to address you by your name?'

'Well, I . . .'

'Thanks, Frances. Nice name, it suits you. But what on earth are you doing, driving a mini-cab?'

She wished she knew herself. 'Look, aren't you going to be late for this dance affair?'

Ned dismantled the shepherdess's crook and tucked it under

one arm. 'Horribly. I promised to be there hours ago, to fix this lot up. Not that they'll miss a few sheep. There are plenty of other lazy sods to help lay out the drinks. Hold on a tick, I suppose I'd better grab a jacket.'

She was glad to see the jacket matched the trousers. Rather unusual, a suit in pale blue corduroy. It would have looked better cleaned and pressed, but a man who was so clever with his hands could perhaps be forgiven for neglecting his clothes. Though the purple vest was definitely a disaster.

Ned wolf-whistled the car and settled himself in front. She couldn't object – the sheep needed every inch of grazing space at the back.

'Know the way to the Poly?'

''Course.' It was back to monosyllables. She should definitely control herself if she'd started taking an interest in his vests. He talked enough for both of them and, somehow, he kept turning her monosyllables into jokes, and then she had either to laugh, or to defend herself, and either way she was using far more words than one. She was amazed when they reached Southmead. There was still a lot of traffic and it should have taken the best part of an hour, but they seemed to have arrived in seconds.

The building was long, low and so ugly, it was almost endearing; the foyer crowded with students who overflowed into the concrete garden outside.

'Cash or account?' said Frances. It was high time she got back to a business-like approach, and back home, too, while she was about it.

'Account? You must be joking! A penniless teacher like myself? I cadged a lift with a friend today, but he let me down, the swine. Medfield was only a very last resort. A lucky one, though, I must admit.' The greenish eyes had a deplorable knack of knifing right into her when she was off her guard. 'And I shan't give you a tip, unless you help me with my sheep. You can park the car just here in front.'

'Well, I can't be long. I . . .'

'Ned! Thank Christ you've arrived. We're knee-deep in nymphs and shepherds, and not a bloody sheep to be seen.' A large, bearded man who looked like Christ's bigger brother almost capsized Ned with a friendly slap on the shoulder. Ned dropped the tree and showered himself with white lace apple-blossom.

'Get off, you brute! And say hello to Frances.'

'Who?'

'Frances Parry something. She's a deep-sea angler, and incidentally the best woman driver I've ever met.'

'Hi. I'm John.'

Nobody appeared to have a surname. Charles was most punctilious about introductions. Both names repeated twice, distinctly, plus a brief description of the person's job, interests and station in life. Well, Ned had done almost that, even if he'd got it all wrong. Another gold star. Somehow, she liked awarding him gold stars. She held on happily to two furry legs, while Ned and John manipulated the rest of the sheep through the door and up the staircase. They were assaulted by the wailing vibration of a group and vocalist, performing at the back of a large, dark hall, which was crowded with students and dizzy with revolving lights. Although it was early and still light outside, the party was full-blown. Paper flowers were festooned across the ceiling, and five and a half lopsidedly curvaceous dryads sprawled along one wall. A huge cardboard sun blazed in one corner, with golden paper streamers lurching from its centre, some already torn and trailing. John dodged a herd of dancers and a clump of polystyrene marigolds, and began to nail the sheep in place, just above the bar. Frances clung on to a woolly tail, while Ned made minor adjustments to the shepherdess's undergarments.

'Great!' said John, standing back and surveying the pastoral idyll. 'Absolutely great! I'm only sorry I couldn't come and fetch them. Car blew a gasket.'

'I'm remarkably glad it did.' Ned's strange marbled eyes looked almost black in the darting light. 'How a blown gasket led me to True Love. Read next week's enthralling instalment as the Ice Maiden of Richmond prepares to walk out in high dudgeon . . .'

He made it sound so ludicrous, she had to walk right back again, even smiled to show she hadn't meant it.

'Have a drink before you go.'

'Thanks. A gin and Italian.'

'Sorry, love, it's warm beer or Algerian plonk in this hell-hole.

But you do get a plastic glass. And they don't go in for lugworm.'
This time, they grinned together.

'Do you teach?' asked John. She could see he was trying to
be civil, distracting her from the worst of Ned. She wasn't sure
whether she wanted to be distracted.

'No, I . . .' She broke off. It was all so confusing. What *did* she
do, and who was she? She'd no business to be there at all, at this
most peculiar party, where everyone was dressed alike in tattered
blue jeans. In her and Charles' set, there were rules for party
dressing, and if you were brave enough to resist the regulation
dark suit or long skirt, the least you could do was to sport a
velvet jacket or a kaftan and be classified as 'arty'. Of course
you owned blue jeans – they were regulation too, but expensive
ones, kept clean and pressed, and worn only for a strictly defined
period on Saturday mornings, after shopping and before golf.

This mob looked as if they'd slept in theirs, and their accents
were so slovenly. In her day, students wore neat grey flannel
trousers and respectable tweed jackets, and didn't sound like
garage mechanics every time they opened their mouths.

'Ned, I simply must get back . . .' Charles was phoning
early with details of his return flight. She never missed his
phone calls.

'What? You'll have to shout.'

It was impossible to speak against the din, even more impossible
to sneak away. She was interred in a cage of shrieking sound.
Every time she tried to squeeze between the bars, the music
closed her in tighter and tighter, so that she was trapped between
flickering ceiling and vibrating floor.

'Want to dance?'

'No, I . . .'

Her voice was dashed to pieces by the drums. She was a
tiny pebble pounded by thundering waves of music, waves
coloured scarlet by the third glass of plonk which had somehow
disappeared down her throat.

'Come on, then.'

Ned dragged her into the centre of the room and she was
suddenly part of the stamping, thumping harmony of blue
jeans, hearing the music now from the inside out. Her arms
and legs didn't know what to do with themselves – she was

more accustomed to dancing the slow foxtrot at one of Charles' black-tie affairs. She was stiff like a piece of driftwood, stranded like flotsam thrown up by the tide. She envied the students now. However shabby, they were so much freer than she was. They weren't worried about ruining their Russell and Bromley patent leather shoes in the spilled beer on the floor, or agonizing because the assistant English lecturer split his infinitives. They just let go and poured themselves into their bodies. She glanced at the girl beside her – eyes closed, head thrown back, torso moving to some wild inner rhythm. Her partner was hurling himself from side to side, hands clapping, feet stamping, no spoilsport mind to tame or censor him. All around her were jostling bodies, setting up vibrations between them, like electric currents. Somehow she had to switch herself into them – turn off the harsh, glaring light in her head, and lose herself in the darkness.

She moved a little closer to Ned. He wasn't even touching her, but she could feel him like a hot, wiry animal, a body coloured by the ever-changing lights – a scarlet Ned, a green Ned, blue, silver, spotted, gilded, striped. The music lapped at her skirt and swept her into its insistent rhythm. Slowly, she submitted, shutting out everything except the hall, the sound, the moment. She felt the throb of the guitars surging into her like a blood transfusion, their noise no longer frightening, but reassuring, like the roar of life. She was plugged into some great power machine, with Ned as generator. Her feet didn't belong to her any more. They were Ned's feet, doing only what Ned dictated. She was losing all her boundaries. All shapes and colours had run into each other, and she and the room and the rhythm were merging into one warm, wine-red cell, with Ned as the nucleus of it all. Rules were broken, clocks smashed. There was no time, except the beat of the music and the flash and stamp of a thousand dazzling feet.

Half a lifetime might have passed, for all she knew, or half an hour. It was impossible to know. She couldn't think, could only submit to the music and let it master her.

Suddenly, there was a shattering blast of silence. She faltered a moment, almost fell. Her life-support system had been switched off and the harsh fluorescent lights switched on. The band had stopped for a break and a beer. She felt jolted out of a dream. People were pressing all around her, laughing and shouting, surging towards the bar. Ned was joking with a clutch of colleagues.

'Drink, Frances?' he yelled.

'Yes. No. I . . .'

He couldn't hear her, anyway. He was only one of a hundred sweaty bodies, pinioning her arms, trampling on her feet. Someone handed her a pint of bitter, frothing down the sides. It wasn't Ned. He was trapped further down the bar, exchanging jokes with the under-age barman, who was wearing a paper hat and looked as if he had slipped away from playschool.

'I don't drink beer.' No one heard. Her Young's Bitter benefactor had already turned his back. She had to drink it, anyway, to stop it slopping down her dress. It tasted sharp, strange – almost good. She gulped a little more.

'Oh, one of the boys now, are we?' Ned was elbowing his way towards her, a plastic tumbler balanced in either hand. 'I've just broken the bank buying you a glass of Château Southmead 1981, and there you are, knocking back the bitter like a front-row forward! Don't worry – I'll drink it myself. This is Les, by the way.'

'Hi!' said another pair of faded blue jeans, distinguished, this time, by a studded leather jacket and dark glasses. Staff, student, or Hell's Angel on a heroin charge? There was no way of telling. She smiled nervously at her own distorted reflection in his lenses. She felt foolish, out of place. So long as the band had kept pounding out that deep-ocean rhythm, she had been engulfed in it, safe in it, but now it had stopped, she was a dead fish beached on a dry strand.

'Ned, I really ought to go.'

'Go? Go where? This is the only place it's at.' Les's voice was the scrape of an iron chain on a stone jetty. The accent started North of Manchester and finished East of Liverpool. He was working through a packet of onion-flavoured crisps, spraying Golden Wonder crumbs in her direction. 'Are you the Principal's Secretary or sent direct from Rent-a-Bird? We never get tailored skirts and high heels in this dump. Unless perhaps you're acting President of the Real Female Campaign – the next thing after Real Ale. Pleased to meet you, anyway. I'm Les Davies, Head of Workshop Technology.'

'Oh, I . . . see.' She didn't. She wished Ned would rescue her, but he was too busy with his one-man-band of fruit pie, sausage roll, and double dose of wine. Her own beer had already reached mid-tumbler. Suddenly, she didn't care. Her stomach was gently swelling and distending like a plump hot water bottle; hops were skipping through her bloodstream, all her limbs turning into froth. If she missed Charles' phone call, well, he'd simply have to try again. Why should she always rush back home, ready to do obeisance to that prim grey receiver at its very first whimper? Charles was dwindling, anyway, crumbling into a broken crisp. There was only her glass, looming large and insistent in front of her, eighteen-carat gold spun into booze.

Les was joined by Gareth, Gareth by Dylan, as Manchester and Liverpool gave place to South Wales. She was somehow in the middle of a magic circle, and Ned was transforming her into a deep sea diver, a racing driver, a cat-charmer, a fisherwoman. Everyone was laughing and admiring. Why should she contradict him and turn herself back into a dreary tax consultant's wife, or a telephone answering machine? It was really rather delightful to hear how she'd caught her second ten-pound turbot, or won Le Mans by a nail-biting front axle. Anyway, the music had started up again, roaring through her head, shattering the glasses, emptying the bar. She had to follow it. It was like the tide, dragging her in, dashing her down.

Now, it was easier to dance. She didn't even have to look at Ned, but could feel him through her feet and through her heartbeat, plunging her under, swirling her round, as rules and Richmond soared out of the window in a white avalanche of sound. The music was no longer pain. The screaming guitars were only fronds of seaweed, the feverish drumbeats only froth and spume. Even the beseeching, shrieking singer had been turned into a stream of silver bubbles. She was drunk, dazed, crazy, and she ought to go straight home. But she didn't really own herself; the music was in charge. She was only a pounding, syncopated part of it; couldn't stop the ocean single-handed. If she left, or wavered, the whole reverberating harmony might stumble into discord.

She *was* stumbling. Ned's small, hot hand had snapped across her back and ripped the rhythm into shreds. He was shouting something at her, underneath the drumfire, guiding her through the tangle of dancers, across the beer-swilled floor towards the exit.

'Hot!' he panted. 'Need some air.'

The swing doors clashed behind them, muffling the music to a muted roar. She blinked against the harsher light outside, crash-landed on blundering feet, almost deafened by the quiet. They were in a small, fuggy corridor, with windows all along one side. Ned pushed one open and gulped down air like beer. It was dark now outside, and his pale torso cut into the dead black square of sky and quickened it. His shirt was open almost to the waist. His body shouted at her. With Charles, it was always the clothes you saw first: Savile Row pin-stripes or Christian Dior tie, all style and surface, with nothing real or risky underneath. But Ned was naked flesh and blood – hot hands, live hair, real sweat mixed and shaken in some dangerous, heady cocktail. His clothes were hardly there.

Frances shivered suddenly. Reality was surging back like a spoilsport wave of nausea. She could feel Young's Bitter heaving against her stomach, nagging in her head. What in God's name was she doing, gate-crashing a party, losing track of time, making unfair comparisons with her husband, when she should have been sitting safe at home, waiting for his call. She pulled her dress to order, smoothed her tousled hair.

'What's the time?'

'Time to kiss you.'

His mouth was hovering dangerously close. She tried to dodge away. He had a large wet patch under each armpit, and she could smell the raw, brutish odour of his sweat.

'My watch has stopped.' She glanced at its gold face. The hands pointed stupidly at seven.

'Southmead Poly must have overpowered it. It does have that effect on people.'

'Ned, do stop fooling and tell me the time.'

'Only if you call me Ned again. I like the way you say it. Like a very special sergeant major.'

'Ned, I . . .'

'No, not like that. Nicely, the way you did before. OK, OK, I'll tell you. Hold on a minute . . . at the third stroke, it will be 22.02.'

'You're joking!'

'Well, that's only British Summer Time. It's after midnight in Ethiopia, and more or less siesta time in Las Vegas. Let's pretend we're in Las Vegas.'

'Ned, it can't be after ten!' How on earth could a whole evening have drained away like that? She had only stopped for one small drink, one short dance. Charles would have phoned her several times by now. She had assured him she'd be home by early evening. She'd missed the sacred formula: Love you. Love you, too. He might even have rung round all her friends to find out where she was.

'Look, Ned, I simply must go home. Now.'

'You said that three hours ago. You can't leave yet, in any case. There's the pagan fertility rites at midnight. We all do disgusting things with nymphs and sheep, and the odd science student gets sacrificed. It's a riot!'

Why did that wretched word 'fertility' worm its way into everything? Every time she heard it, it was like a twinge of pain. It was as if she wore a label round her neck: 'damaged goods', 'substandard', 'infertile'. That was another reason to get home – her charts were waiting for her, her own private fertility rite. And Charles' final phone call.

'No, I'm not arguing, Ned. I'm going.'

'Christ, you've got eyes like blue steel knives! How many men have you cut into little pieces? Please, oh please, may I be your next willing victim?'

He didn't try to kiss her again. She felt irrationally disappointed. He didn't even ask for her phone number. If that pushy passenger she'd driven to Uxbridge had the cheek to demand it, after only two miles up the A4, then why shouldn't Ned? No, that was absurd. She'd told him herself she didn't mix business with pleasure. She'd already lost her head, lost her boundaries, and it was time to regain control.

She almost ran downstairs and out into the car park. Ned panted after her and stood by the door of the Citroën, one hot hand clasped over hers on the steering wheel. She didn't remove it. It would be cold and dark at home.

'How will you get back to Acton?' she asked.

'Are you offering me a lift?'

'Certainly not.'

'Well, I'll have to walk then, won't I? Dynamic Southmead lecturer dies of exposure on Hogarth flyover.'

'People don't die of exposure in July.'

'No, but they die of disappointment.'

'I'll send you flowers.'

'Will you?' He looked pleased like a child, stuck his head through the open window. His breath smelt faintly of low-grade Beaujolais. 'Dandelions. Lots and lots of them.' His lips were only inches from her right eye. 'I like you, Frances.'

'Yes ... well ...' She turned on the engine, so she needn't answer.

'Say "Ned" again.'

'Don't be silly.'

'Please.'

'Ned.'

'Again.'

'*No!*' She almost ran him over as she drove off. It was asking for trouble, playing romantic moonlight scenes with some casual stranger she'd literally picked up. There'd be no more passengers, in any case. Charles was due home in a mere twenty-four hours, and she couldn't carry on the job with him around. The evening had been just a mad midsummer fling, a muddle-headed mutiny which mustn't be repeated.

The phone was ringing when she walked in. Charles' voice sounded faint and indistinct, as if he were speaking from the wrong end of a telescope. It was almost one A.M. in Bahrain. He should have been asleep.

'Where on earth have you been, darling? I was getting really worried. I've phoned three separate times.'

'I went to a party.' She never lied to Charles.

'A party? Where? On your own?'

'No, some friends of Viv's.'

It wasn't quite a lie. Viv was bound to have friends at Southmead Polytechnic. They looked her type, bearded and provincial.

'I see.' He didn't.

'I'm missing you.' She wasn't.

'Well, back tomorrow.'

'I'll meet you, shall I?' She'd been to the airport five times in the last seven days, knew the journey backwards.

'No, no, please don't.' He never wanted her to meet him from his trips, always took a mini-cab. Perhaps it would be Medfield. She could just imagine Reg saying: 'Put your foot on it, love. There's a Mr Parry Jones doing his nut at Terminal Three. Raring to get back to his faithful little wife.' Well, she was faithful, wasn't she? One perfunctory party and a spurned kiss didn't count.

'Listen, darling, we've had some damned good news on that rubber plantation.'

'Oh, yes?'

'We're going to repossess it, almost certainly, plus ten years' profits and full compensation. The shares are bound to rocket. Oppenheimer's delighted.'

'Really, Charles?' She tried to sound equally delighted. Charles' work was the most fascinating thing in his life, so she always aimed to give it due respect. But, sometimes, she wished he did something humble and simple and more comprehensible, like running a sweet shop. Or teaching Media Studies, with a sideline in sheep.

'They're just perfecting a new cross-bred rubber tree, which combines the best of the Malaysian and Indonesian strains. It's particularly suitable to the soil out there, so the total yield . . .'

'The line's awfully bad, darling. I can hardly hear you.' Odd, when she could still hear the music. It had poured into the tele-phone exchange and was pounding down the wires – drumbeats and guitars and the deep-sea snort of a tenor saxophone.

'Rubber Futures are low at the moment, I know that. But with so many people turning to commodities as a currency hedge . . .'

Unforgivable to be listening to a second-rate rock group when Charles was expounding the mysteries of the commodity market. She tried to concentrate, return to the safe ritual; waited for a pause. 'Miss you, darling.'

'Miss you, too.'

If she wasn't really missing him, it was only because she was tired. She'd be relieved when he was home again – always was. She replaced the receiver and walked slowly up to bed. This time, it would be a most important homecoming, since she'd already reached day eleven. She opened the bedside drawer and spread out her temperature chart. She'd written a small C in black biro for every day she'd taken a Clomid. Five black Cs. Any day now, there would be that little dip in her temperature, followed by a rise. It was essential Charles was in there, when it happened. She mustn't miss it this time, not with Clomid and the chance of twins. She wouldn't press it the first day he got home. He was always tired then, anyway, and jet-lag might affect his sperm. But the day after, there must be no excuses. She'd cook him his favourite *entrecôte chasseur* and drape herself in her Janet Reger nightie. From then on, every other day. 'Miss no chances, but don't wear him out' – that was Mr Rathbone's little maxim. Sperm needed forty-eight hours, apparently, to recover its strength. She put ticks in her diary for the Tuesday, the Thursday, the Saturday, and the following Monday. Hell! The Monday would be difficult. Charles was doubly pressured on a Monday and often stayed late at work. Whatever happened, she must give up her own job. She'd need all her vitality to lure Charles into bed on the right nights, couldn't risk his anger over Medfield. Anger might endanger an erection, and erections were far more important in her life than driving Mr Smythes to John O'Groats.

She placed the thermometer neatly on the bedside table, together with the chart and a blue biro. The dots were done in blue, the Cs in black, the dates in green, and red crosses for the five days of her period. (She'd learnt a lot from Charles.)

She shut her eyes and returned to the Poly dance. Ned's corduroy suit had been cleaned and valeted, his hair cut and styled at Michaeljohn. They were foxtrotting together in the ballroom of a stately country mansion. The sprawling plastic marigolds had rearranged themselves into formal phalanxes of expensive hot-house flowers. Dylan, Gareth, Les, were impeccable in cashmere dinner jackets and velvet cummerbunds. Ned's dandelion had turned into an orchid.

'I like you, Frances,' he whispered, as he entwined it in her hair.

The music had surged back, bludgeoning the silence of the bedroom, though she could still hear his voice throbbing and strumming above it.

Strange how loud and clear the line was, now.

4

'Charles, *please.*'

'For God's sake, Frances, I can't.'

'Can't? You mean won't.'

'Look, I'm sorry, but I'm totally non-operational at the moment. I've got a hell of a problem on.'

'You've always got problems. I'm getting sick of it. Your work comes between us like a great Berlin Wall. We can never relax because the bank rate's up, or the exchange rate's down, or the balance of payments is precarious.'

'Well, this time, it's nothing to do with work.'

'I don't believe you.'

'In fact, I really ought to talk to you about it.'

There, he'd got it out at last. He'd have to tell her sometime, so it might as well be now. Except he didn't have the words. All his life he'd got to grips with things, papered over problems, talked his way through crises. But, now, he was dumb. He couldn't even concentrate on the latest tax concessions from Zug. He was struggling through the German text, but all he could see were his wife's accusing eyes tripping him up on every printed page. He had come home from the airport, laden with his Glenfiddich and her Chanel, flushed with achievement, happy to be back. *Coq au vin* for dinner, an Ashkenazy concert on the radio, and eight blessed hours' sleep without a mosquito net, or prayer calls wailing through the dawn.

The next morning, a phone call. One brief call and his world in smithereens. Frances' world hadn't even flickered. She didn't know, she couldn't know. And here she was, bleating on about a child, when the very word suddenly made him sick.

If only it hadn't been fucking day thirteen. Just his luck – her temperature had fallen on the morning he came home, that vital little dip she waited for so avidly each month. Day twelve, day thirteen, day fourteen – that's all he ever heard. The whole universe was centred on his wife's Fallopian tubes. She had her own private clock and calendar, set differently from everybody else's. If they were toasting Christmas, she was weeping because her period had come. If Russia dropped an atom bomb on Richmond, she'd still be lying there, taking her temperature for a full three minutes by her watch. Christ, how tired he was of that passion-killing thermometer, the way it ruled their lives.

He rubbed his eyes, tried to make sense of his economic forecasts. God Almighty! Frances' little blue dots were straying even here. He couldn't see his own charts, only the one-degree fall on hers. Frances had marked it with as much elation as if it were a dramatic fall in the minimum lending rate. The little blue dot swelled into an accusing finger. He was meant to chase it up, turn it from a paper cypher into something bigger and more permanent. He couldn't. There was nothing there between his legs – only jet-lag.

He put his work away. You couldn't plot financial trends from the data of a woman's menstrual cycle. Frances was sitting in the bedroom, trickling Chanel between her breasts. He watched her in the mirror, draped in her best satin nightie, and wearing anguish like a decoration. He had never liked the nightie and he couldn't cope with anguish. He was damned if he'd allow her to lure him into bed, and then be forced to lie beside her like some limp laughing stock. And yet he cared for her – loved her even, if he dared use such a word. That's what made the whole thing so disastrous. He walked across and kissed her on the throat.

'I'm sorry, darling.' He'd apologized fifty times already, and each time diminished him. He wanted to overpower her with his strength, to shower on her anything she asked for. Yet, the only thing she did ask was a kid. And that he couldn't give her. Not at the moment, not while . . .

'You just don't want a baby, do you, Charles?' She was twisting her wedding ring round and round on her finger. 'Why don't you be honest? It's so frustrating being messed about by gynaecologists and swallowing dangerous drugs, when you won't even come near me.'

'Look, Frances, I've had bad news. It's nothing to do with you and your blasted babies. Don't you understand?' There he was, barking at her again, when he wanted to be rational. His head felt like a battleground, with Frances' voice the endless whine of gun-fire in his ears.

'How can I understand, when you keep the whole thing secret? I'd like to help, honestly I would. Couldn't we just lie together? Just for comfort. We don't have to do anything. It might even help you to relax.'

'No.'

She was scrubbing at her lips, almost rubbing off the skin. He longed to take her in his arms and kiss her better, confess the whole damned muddle and have her understand. But if he kissed her, she'd only ask for more. He hated having to produce it on demand. She was already nuzzling at his back. 'Let's just touch each other, Charles.'

He moved away. Let's just bloody fuck, that's what she meant. The egg's ready, I'm ready, and there's nothing else that matters in the world. He could almost see her cosseting that egg, wrapping it in tissue like the emeralds he brought her back from Bogota. More infinitesimal than a pin-prick, one hundred times smaller than a frog's egg. That's what she had told him – Frances always had her facts. And yet the tiny egg had grown into a carbuncle, filling the room, blotting out everything else in her life.

Two days later, it was dead. It lived only a day like a mayfly, and it had died unfertilized. Frances mourned it as if it were a child already. He could hear her tears sniping through the bedroom. He hated tears. They made him feel guilty and angry and helpless, all at once. If only she realized what a mess he was in himself. There were worse things in the world than not conceiving. He wanted to shake his fist at the whole cock-up of a universe and shout at it, for making everything so difficult for both of them. Instead, he calmed his voice, took a step or two towards her.

'Look, just relax, darling, give it time.'

'But I haven't got that much time, Charles. I'm already old to be a mother, and I've only got two more months of Clomid left. Rathbone won't let me take it any longer, in case of side effects. We've wasted this first month completely. I might as well have chucked the tablets down the drain.'

'Well, let's concentrate on next month. Things will be different then. I'll have sorted out my problems and . . .'

*   *   *

60

Charles had still said nothing. He and Frances sat like stiff cardboard cut-outs on each side of the dead marble fireplace, dinner uneaten in the dining-room, coffee cold on the table. Only the clocks made conversation. Charles had the usual papers on his knee, but his eyes were closed. He never sat in silence, wasting time. Frances felt marooned, shut out behind the barrier of his eyelids. She leant across and took his hand.

'Shall I put the concert on?' Boulez was conducting Boulez.

'No thanks.'

Charles never missed a Boulez concert. He set his life to music, more or less. She was so used to his evenings of quadraphonic Karajan or veteran Toscanini, she felt almost threatened by the hush. He preferred pre-Romantic, or post-Mahler composers, the stern ordered cadences of Buxtehude, Rameau, and the Bachs, the lucid intellectuality of Schoenberg and Webern. The nineteenth century left him wary. He hated raw emotion running riot in his music; insisted on structure and control. Their whole married life had been wreathed in Telemann and Pergolesi, Berg and Hindemith. Sometimes she'd resented it. How could you switch on *Armchair Thriller*, with Monteverdi's *Vespers* praying through the house, or get a word in edgeways when Stockhausen's querulous ring-modulators were monopolizing the conversation?

She suspected Charles used music like his work, as a barrier between them, protecting him against too much conversation or the danger of deep communication. Music filled all the cracks and spaces in their life, like cultural polyfilla – blocking precious crevices which might have been used for something spontaneous and intimate.

But now that Charles had switched to silence, it was worse. The whole house seemed to hold its breath, as he sat dumb and inaccessible behind the drawbridge of his face. Menace oozed out of the heavy mahogany furniture and hung like a cloud in the air. It was only a few days since he'd returned from Bahrain, but it felt like a whole lumbering century, crawling at snail's pace through her mind and turning her and the house grey before its time.

Wednesday dinner, they ploughed through grilled haddock.

61

His face was still shuttered, all the blinds down. But at least he was eating.

'Nice?' she asked. He needed encouragement.

'Mmm.' He didn't even look up.

'Not too salty?'

'No, fine.'

They were back to monosyllables, almost like Medfield. She was sorry now she'd given up the driving job. It would have provided a distraction from Charles' misery, and in his present condition he wouldn't have even noticed she was working. She longed to help him, comfort him, but Charles' pride dictated that he should never need help. She had learnt not to fuss, not to ask questions, though this time she was worried, since the whole Parry Jones efficiency machine was clearly shambling to a halt. It was only tiny things, insignificant to other people, but for her they were warning signs. He'd started ripping open his mail in the mornings, instead of slitting it neatly with his silver paper-knife. He scribbled notes on scrappy bits of paper, rather than in the correct colour-coded notebook. Some plants arrived from Fernstream Nurseries, and he left them dying and unopened in the hall.

She wished to God he'd switch to a different profession – anything, so long as it was less high-powered and stressful. A teacher, for example, with shorter hours and longer holidays. They hardly knew any teachers – Charles regarded them as non-productive leftists. She stabbed a potato and suddenly saw Ned's grin skulking at the bottom of her plate. Ned was a teacher. Or at least he was when he wasn't a shepherd or a fisherman. She grinned back.

Charles pushed away his haddock. 'What's the joke?'

'Nothing.' Funny how you could meet a hundred people and forget them instantly; then a special one popped up and imprinted himself indelibly, for no real reason. Well, no more reason than purple vests and lugworm. She prodded her courgettes. 'Oh, Charles . . .'

'What?'

'It's hell here, at the moment. If work's such a strain, you ought to take a rest. It's bad for both of us.'

'We're going out on Tuesday.'

'That's only dinner. You need more than Amanda Crawford's fricassee of veal to buck you up. You're in quite a state, you realize.'

'Yes, I know.'

She was amazed that he admitted it. 'Why don't we go away then, just for a day or two? You need a break from the office.'

'It's not the office, Frances, not this time. Look, I think I'd better talk to you about it . . .'

She suddenly felt frightened, stared down at her plate. Ned's grin had disappeared into the gravy. There were only Charles' pale full lips facing her across the table. He leant across and kissed her. The kiss continued, though she tried to pull away. Charles never mixed up sex with mealtimes. Another sign of strain.

'Let's make love,' he urged.

'But we haven't had our pudding.'

'Bugger the pudding!'

'Charles!'

'I want you, Frances.'

But I don't want you, she almost said. She somehow lost all interest once she'd passed day sixteen and there was no hope of a baby. The whole act seemed meaningless. But Charles was now unbuttoning her blouse. She'd never known him like this, spontaneous, on heat. Normally, he waited till after the late night news; did things at the proper time, prepared the room and atmosphere – dimmers on the bedside lights, the curtains drawn, a record on the stereo. They didn't actually make love in their own bedroom, but in a spare room with a double bed. It was beautifully furnished, but used only for sex, as if they might contaminate themselves if they did anything else in it. Their own bedroom had single beds. Charles claimed he got too hot if he slept with her beside him, and he didn't like the covers rumpled up.

She had no reason to complain. It was always a superb performance in the spare room, though she sometimes wished it wasn't quite so formal. It reminded her of church, the way Charles went on – his hushed voice throbbing through the sacred gloom. She felt she ought to burn incense, or wear a cassock. It would be fun to giggle with him sometimes, or munch Mars bars under the blankets.

Even now, he didn't skip the preparations. She could hear him running his pre-intercourse bath. She went into her own, smaller bathroom and took a shower. It was part of the schedule. Showers, deodorant, aftershave, foreplay. She unscrewed the scent he'd brought her from the airport, watched a drop dribble down between her breasts, breasts still small and firm. She wondered what would happen if she ever had a baby. Would they sag and droop like Viv's? She'd seen Viv naked once and it had shocked her – the earth mother parcelled in her own flesh. She was glad she had a waist, and a small neat bottom which didn't ooze all over the chairs. Even five children and all that teeming fecundity couldn't make up for looking like Viv. Was that why Charles didn't want a baby, because he didn't fancy her fat and slack and marked? But why couldn't they talk about it, as other people did? Charles was like an iceberg – she knew only the tip which showed above the surface, not the depths submerged beneath. He was acting strangely even at the moment, demanding sex in the middle of a meal, when he'd refused it on those vital fertile days. It wasn't even lust – he was too miserable for that – more like desperation. There was an iron coating even on the kiss.

She arranged her body neatly on the bed. Rathbone had advised her never to refuse him. If she cold-shouldered him at any time, he might be less eager in that all-important middle of the month. Charles walked in, naked except for his underpants. It was one of his quirks, always to leave his pants on till the very last moment, as if he were ashamed of what they hid. He had a tall, slim body, muscular and well-made. Not that she ever saw much of it. As soon as they were undressed, it was under the covers for both of them. She sometimes felt he'd have preferred to do it in his pinstripes.

She slipped off the bed to find a suitable cassette. Charles kept his cassette deck in the spare room, so that even their love-making was duly harmonized.

'No, don't bother with the music, darling. I've got to talk to you.'

Frances clutched the Brandenburg Concertos like a shield in front of her. Charles never talked when he made love, always claimed it spoilt his concentration. It seemed strange to talk stark naked, anyway, ranged on opposite sides of the room as if they were about to fight a duel, the silence between them solid, like a piece of furniture.

'Well?' she said, defensively.

Suddenly, he switched on the radio and Bartok roared into the room. He hated Bartok – all that bilge about the brotherhood of nations and the treasurehouse of peasant warblings. Even now, she could hear the gutsy folk rhythms bringing Hungary to Richmond; wild sweeps from gypsy violins stampeding through suburbia.

'It's too loud, Charles, turn it down.'

He took hold of her instead and pulled her to the floor. He was breaking all his own rules – no Sleepeezee mattress or elaborate coaxing foreplay. Just the rough scratch of the carpet underneath her bare buttocks and his angry thing tearing in and out of her, and Bartok bawling on the dressing-table.

'Frances, you've got to listen to me . . .'

'How can I listen with this noise?'

He was thrusting harder, out of time with the music, wrenching her body into a discordant key.

'I can't hear, Charles. And you're hurting.'

It was impossible to talk. His mouth was crushing hers. Behind her head, she could hear another voice, the suave bellow of the Radio 3 announcer, turned up to a hundred decibels. Bartok was over, and the roaring, booming Eton-and-Oxford larynx introducing a talk on modern physics.

'Heisenberg declared that in their new designations as conjugate observables . . .'

'Look, Frances, I didn't tell you before, but . . .' He was hammering into her, as if all the pent-up misery of the last few days had broken through a dam and come pouring out. This wasn't making love; it wasn't even sex, but some strange pagan rite, some terrible release. Fifteen years of bedroom courtesy and drawing-room control had snapped. He was rutting like an animal.

'I didn't want to deceive you. I agonized for years . . .'

How could he talk and do it at the same time? She tried to exchange his voice for Heisenberg's.

'Indeterminacy ruled that no quantum mechanical system could simultaneously possess . . .'

The whole of Surrey could hear this physics lesson. It was so loud, the room resounded with it, Heisenberg battering into her, along with Charles.

'In fact I wouldn't have told you even now, if only . . .'

'I can't hear a word you're saying, Charles.' She didn't want to hear, didn't like the words. They were making terrible black stains on her mind, like blots of ink, spattering a clean white page. Her head had fallen back against the skirting board. He was ramming it against the wood, pinioning her arms too tight beneath his own.

She tried to concentrate on the rational order of a measured world.

'. . . this Platonic central order, with its universal symmetries, constitutes the rationale for a mathematical equation applicable to all systems of particulate matter . . .'

It didn't sound convincing in that barbaric roar.

Charles was almost coming. She could feel him revving up, slamming her spine against the floorboards. She tried to pull away, but he resisted. He was talking, explaining, yet coming at the same time. She closed everything against him, even her ears, refused to accept the irrational things he was telling her.

He was still thrusting, still coming, whispering now, almost incoherent. Across their coupled bodies crashed the last blaring words of the broadcast. 'Thus, on the sub-atomic level, the traditional idea of scientific causality had been split apart.'

Everything was split apart. Not just sub-atomic particles, but their whole sheltered, blue-chip, pre-Einstein universe. Charles was slumped on top of her, wet and silent now, inert.

'This talk can be heard again, next Friday morning, at eleven.'

'No, Charles,' she shouted. 'No! It can't be true. I simply don't believe you.'

5

'Viv, I'm sorry to barge in like this, but . . .'

'What on earth's the matter? You look completely washed out.'

'I . . . haven't slept for two nights.'

'Are you ill or something, Frances? There *is* a virus going round . . .'

'It's Charles. He's . . . Look, it's rather confidential. Can we talk in private?'

'Well, there's no one here except Midge and Rupert, and half a dozen cats. The only word Rupert understands is "more", and Midge is ill in bed. Come in.'

Rupert was sitting on his potty, red in the face with effort. The remains of seven breakfasts were littered on the kitchen table, the sink an avalanche of nappies. Viv cleared a space among the bacon rinds and cleaned up Rupert on the table. His podgy fingers made patterns in the butter.

'I was in the middle of feeding him when he started poohing. They time these things so badly! Mind if I continue?'

'Not at all.' Frances averted her eyes as Viv unlatched one huge breast and hoisted it off her stomach. Rupert lost himself among the folds. He was over a year old, but Viv loved breast-feeding. She'd be offering the nipple to her fourteen-year-old, if inconvenient things like school hadn't come between them.

'Go on, love, sit down. Now what's the trouble?'

Frances removed a half-chewed rusk from her chair-seat. 'Charles has got a daughter.'

'*What?*'

'By another woman.'

'You're joking.'

'No. She's fifteen.'

'Fifteen! But that's almost grown up.'

'Precisely.'

'But didn't you know? I mean where's she been, all this time?'

'With her mother.' Her dark, passionate, tempestuous slut of a mother, who helped herself to babies without the little matter of a husband.

'Frances, I can't believe it. Not Charles.'

'Oh no, not Charles – that's what we all thought, didn't we? Charles is so faithful and upright and considerate and *busy* and . . . But he isn't, Viv. It's all a lie. He's a bigamist, more or less. I've worked it out. He must have conceived that baby less than a year before we were married, and she was born only weeks before the wedding. How on earth could he have gone ahead and married me, mixed up with all that? And then kept it a secret all these years.'

'Frances, I'm stunned. I simply don't know what to say. Look, let me get you some coffee. You must be absolutely shattered.'

Frances turned away. Viv smelt of milk and unwashed babies. 'No, Viv – thanks – I can't keep anything down. Do you know, I was sick when he told me. I couldn't stop vomiting. I knelt on the floor in the lavatory and shivered all over. And Charles just lay on the bed reading. He was actually reading, Viv. I saw him. A book on business management. I mean, how *could* he?'

Viv stowed her breast away and came over to squeeze her hand. 'It was only because he couldn't face you, sweetie. He can't really have been reading. He was just trying to hide. He must feel desperate himself.' Rupert was screaming in deprivation. Viv turned back to him and stirred puréed prunes into cold porridge.

'It was even worse the next day – yesterday, that was. Christ! It seems a hundred years ago. Charles took the morning off from work. He never does that – it's unthinkable – he's far too busy. I thought it was a sort of present to me, to make me feel better, give us time to talk about it all. But do you know what he did? He went straight out into the garden and started planting out spring cabbages. Forty or fifty of them, in dead straight rows. He just went on and on, in the pouring rain. You know how wet it was? Well, he didn't even notice. He had this measuring gadget and he spaced every seedling exactly eighteen inches apart. I watched him. He was soaked through and absolutely fixated on those cabbages. He grew them from seed in the greenhouse and he's been fussing over them ever since. He didn't even look up when I went out to him. He might as well have gone to work and been done with it.'

Viv scooped dung-coloured porridge from her housecoat and spooned it back into Rupert. 'I'm so sorry, love. I only wish I could . . . Look, how on earth did you find out about it? I mean, if he managed to keep it secret all these years . . .'

'He told me. Oh, he had to. The mother's dumped the child on him. She's going back to Budapest.'

'*Budapest?*'

'Yes, she's Hungarian. Came over at the revolution and has lived here ever since.'

'So why's she going back?'

'Oh, some story about her grandmother dying. Cancer or something. But there's more to it than that. The grandma's got a flat in Budapest and I think she wants to get her hands on it. She's sick of England, so she's making sure she's in at the kill. Decent flats are like gold-dust in Hungary.'

'But why can't she take her daughter with her?'

'That's what I said. But they don't want to disrupt her education. Magda's quite bright, apparently, and preparing for her O-levels. They think she'll get at least eight or nine. The system's totally different in Hungary, so she'd have to start a new syllabus, in a different language. If she stays where she is, Charles thinks she might get into university. The mother's all for it – she never had much schooling herself.'

That was only half the story. The better half. There was some rotten Romeo mixed up in it as well. Charles had been cautious, telling her only what he chose. But she could guess the rest. His Hungarian whore didn't want a teenager messing up her new little love-nest. Or maybe the man himself had refused to take her on. Miklos he was called – a fellow Hungarian. He wouldn't welcome a half-English love-child cramping his style, another man's brat, any more than she wanted a half-Hungarian one ruining her own life, even if it was her husband's child. What a sordid mess the whole thing was. That's why it hurt so much. She had always prized her marriage as impeccable and ordered, and now Charles had dragged it down in all this mire and confusion. Even the way he'd told her had made it so brutal. Blurting it out like that, when he was actually making love to her, lying on the floor.

Magda's mother must have taught him things like that. Every time he'd been to bed with her, he'd brought the taint of that other woman with him. Perhaps he'd sometimes slept with both of them on the very same day, had her juices dripping from his body. How could she say all this to Viv; kind, shambling Viv who never had bitter, jealous thoughts, or felt like murdering a child she'd never seen?

'Oh, Viv, if only . . .'

'Coo-eee!' The front door creaked and slammed. Viv got up, Rupert still clinging to her dressing-gown.

'Oh hell, that's Rachel. She's bringing some guppies.'

'Bringing what?'

'Guppies. Fish. Philip's hamster died, so we've got to make it up to him. Look, don't worry. I'll tell her you're not well.'

Rachel breezed in, with two jam jars and a grizzling three-year-old. 'Hi, girls! Any coffee going? In exchange for half a dozen tiddlers and a water snail.'

'Well, just a quick one, love. Frances isn't feeling too good.'

'Oh, bad luck. Got your period? No, don't touch, Bella.' The child had opened Frances' bag and was fiddling with a lipstick. Rachel scooped her up and bounced her on her knee. If only she could cuddle a child, Frances thought, instead of hating it. Charles' child had been tiny once, like Bella – whining, maybe, but harmless, blameless. Even now, she was still a child, still innocent. Any other woman would accept her, love her even. Was she a monster to feel so hostile, a selfish bitch without the normal, decent, female sentiments? It wasn't easy. Bella was Rachel's own kid, not a faceless fifteen-year-old, living proof of her husband's infidelity.

It still seemed almost unbelievable. Everything had changed in just one evening – an endless evening of talking, shouting, arguing. She had done the shouting. Charles had clammed up almost as soon as he'd told her. And when, at last, she emerged from the lavatory, he was lying in bed in his pyjamas, with his hair combed, and his face composed, as if nothing had happened, as if the sex and the outburst and the shock of telling her had sobered him up, and the other, wilder Charles had disappeared into its cage. He was now all reason and self-control. She hated him for it. Breaking her life apart and not even raising his voice.

And the way he said 'my daughter' – it made her almost sick again. How could he have a daughter who wasn't hers as well? Another secret woman in his life, all these years, deceiving her and double-crossing her, and negating all the love and trust she'd thought they'd shared. How could he do it, a man so methodical and orderly, and who loathed deceptions, if only because they couldn't be tidied up and indexed? Did he have a notebook for the Other Woman – scarlet for lust – in which he noted down their couplings, the heart-breaking conception of their child?

'Have a biscuit.' Rachel passed the tin across. 'I adore these chocolate gingers.' Rachel broke a piece off and stuffed it into Bella's mouth. The child spat it out, examined it, and put it back again.

'How's Charles, Frances? Busy as ever?'

'Er . . . yes.'

'I envy you. My spouse sits at home half the time, fiddling about with model aeroplanes. Hey, Viv, you don't want a guinea pig, do you?'

'I don't mind. We've got three already.'

Viv had room for all creation, and she couldn't accept one abandoned child. 'Look Rachel, I don't want to sound rude, but Viv and I . . .'

'You want me to go. OK, I'm going! I've left the oven on, in any case . . . Say goodbye nicely, Bella.'

The door slammed and Viv sat down again. 'Now, Frances, tell me more about this child. Magda, you say. It's a pretty name, isn't it? Poor kid, though, it must be awful for her.'

'I hate her, Viv. Oh, I know it sounds brutal, but I feel I simply hate her. Just for existing. For ruining everything between Charles and me.'

'But you haven't met her yet. Give her a chance. She may be quite a sweetie.'

'I'll hate her even more, if she is.' She hated herself, as well, for saying it, knew it sounded cruel. She'd always regarded herself as a decent sort of person, up till now – not as tolerant as Viv, perhaps, but basically humane. She'd never realized one could feel so bitter, violent almost. It had shaken her faith, not only in Charles, but also in herself. Why, in God's name, did he ever have to tell her? If only he'd sent Magda to a friend's house, or bought her her own flat, or insisted she went back to Budapest. He'd tried, she knew he had. He'd offered boarding school in Scotland, or private tuition back in Hungary – anything. But that wretched woman had refused it all, blackmailed him, more or less, threatened to tell her if Charles didn't, or just turn up with Magda on the doorstep. She shuddered. At least she'd been spared the sight of Charles' mistress in the flesh, his fingerprints all over her, her womb engraved with his initials.

Viv was stacking dishes. She popped a discarded crust into her mouth, almost absent-mindedly, as if she were a waste disposal unit. 'Perhaps Magda's mother will have her in the holidays. That's half the year, at least.'

'No, I don't think so.' Miklos was the stumbling block. She probably saw him as her last chance of marriage, or romance, or even affluence. Charles had hinted that he wasn't badly off.

'There's a man involved, Viv. The perfect match. They're both Catholics, and both from Budapest. What I imagine's happened is that he insists on going back there, with his bride in tow, and refuses to be saddled with anything as unromantic as a teenager. So she dumps the child on us.'

'Look, be fair, Frances, love. She has looked after her for fifteen years. That's quite a stint on her own – without a husband to support her.'

'She should have thought of that before she had the kid.' She could hear herself sounding bitchy and unreasonable. Just because Viv had five children herself, and lived her life around them, she imagined everyone else was overflowing with the breast-milk of human kindness. Nice to be a Viv . . .

'Look, Frances, just love her enough and she'll accept you. They always do. Can't you see her as a sort of big baby, or an adopted step-daughter? You always said you wanted a baby.'

Frances burst into tears. Rupert joined in, louder. Midge trailed through the door, flushed and spotty in a torn nightie.

'Why is Auntie Frances crying?'

'She's not, darling, she's got a bad cold.'

'*I*'ve got a cold, haven't I, Mummy?'

'No, you've got measles, love. Now you pop back to bed and I'll bring you some nice warm milk.'

'I hate nice warm milk. Auntie Frances *is* crying, Mummy.'

72

'Yes. Well, we'll make *her* some milk, shall we?'

'That's the worst thing, Viv, the very worst thing about it.'

'What is? You ought to have something, you know, just a drink, or . . .'

'The baby thing. I've never said much to you about it, Viv. I'm proud, like Charles. But we've been trying for years to have a child. Charles was always rather odd about it, never wanting to discuss it, just said vague, evasive things like "no rush" or "wait and see". I thought it was male pride. He wouldn't even have the proper tests. Well, he didn't need to, did he? He'd already proved his rotten fertility. But he let me go on thinking it was him. I'd had all the investigations and they'd found nothing. So, naturally, I assumed it was in his department. Well, up to last month I did. And now . . .'

'But, Frances, maybe that was kind of him. Not to let you blame yourself. You'd have felt much worse if you'd known.'

'I *do* feel worse. I feel absolutely betrayed. He's deceived me over everything. Every single minute of our marriage has been a lie. Every time I've talked to him, he's not been the person I thought he was. Even our wedding was a lie. He was married to her already, more or less.'

'He wasn't, Frances, that's just the point. He couldn't have wanted her, not really. Not to marry. He married *you*. It was probably just an affair which went sort of sour on him, but because she had his child, well . . .'

'Careless bitch! As if there weren't coils and pills and things. I bet she did it on purpose, just to trap him.'

'That's probably it, love. But it didn't work. He still loved you and wanted to marry you.'

'But how will I ever know? I can't find out whether he loves this woman, whether he ever loved her, how much he's been seeing her. How well does he know his own child, for example?'

'Well, how well? Surely he told you that.'

'Hardly at all, as far as I can gather. He's been sending them money, but he didn't seem to see Magda much after she was five or six. I think she got in the way of the affair, so to speak. The child embarrassed him.'

'Poor kid. She must be feeling desperate, with no proper father and her mother waltzing off without her.'

'Oh Viv, don't say that. I do feel sorry for her. In theory, anyway. But I'm so shocked and . . .'

The doorbell rang. "Doctor!' carolled Midge. She was naked now, except for her father's fishing cap.

'Midge, where's your nightie?'

'I piddled on it.'

Viv groaned, and turned to Frances. 'Will you be all right, love? I won't be a minute. Make yourself some toast.'

Food solved everything for Viv. She had even plugged Rupert with a biscuit to keep him quiet. Frances could hear her slow, easy voice rising above the doctor's baritone. She glanced at Rupert, who had regurgitated breakfast dribbling down his chin. She could never be a mother. All those gynaecological tests were just a sham. She lacked that vital ingredient which allowed you to love a child, even through prunes and piddled nighties. Rupert knew she was a brute, the way he stared at her, coldly almost, with his huge, undissembling blue eyes. She didn't like Rupert and she couldn't love Magda. True, a teenager wouldn't be sicking up its breakfast, but it would still be a body. There was something so physical about a child – its smells, its noise, its orifices. She always noticed it at Viv's, especially when all the family were there. Five mouths munching, five noses running, ten hands grabbing . . .

'Keep her on liquids for the moment. Plenty of fluids. And try not to let her scratch the spots . . .'

The doctor was booming his way out again. Viv returned to the kitchen, started washing up. Frances slumped back in her chair, as if to dissociate herself from the messy cluttered table. There were crumbs in the marmalade and tea stains in the sugar.

'Frances . . .'

'Mmm?'

'I'll have her.'

'What?'

'Magda. I'll have her – here. I'll look after her. Another kid around the place won't make much difference. She'll be company for Bunty.'

'Viv, you're an angel!'

'No, I'm not. I'd quite enjoy it, actually. And if you say she's Roman Catholic, well, she'd be better off here in a nice safe Papist family than in your godless set-up.'

Frances grinned for the first time since Saturday. 'Oh, Viv, it would be wonderful. If I just didn't have to have her all the time, sleeping with us, and eating with us, and reminding me every minute of . . . I mean I'll come and visit her – every day if you like – and buy her clothes and take her to museums and . . .'

'Well, that's settled, then. Perhaps she'll like babies and give me a hand with Rupert.'

Frances leaned across and picked up Rupert from his high chair. He felt heavy and uncomfortable against her shoulder. 'Rupert, you're gorgeous. Please try and like Magda.' Rupert screwed his face up in a wail. She returned him hastily to Viv, and the wail changed key into a gurgle. So she couldn't even hold a baby properly. She groaned, aloud, despairingly.

'What now?'

'It's no good, it won't work. I must be out of my mind. Magda's not a parcel to be delivered to any new address. She's Charles' own flesh and blood. Charles may even want her, Viv. That's why he agreed. He's bound to feel an obligation. He probably loves her. He'd never let her live with you, in any case. I don't want to be ungrateful, Viv darling, but you know what he feels about cats in the bed and . . . Look, please don't be hurt. It's just my stupid husband. He's obsessed with hygiene and order and . . . Oh, I'm as bad, I know I am. How any godforsaken child will stick the course in our double-wrapped, sterilized ice-house, I can't imagine.'

Viv was disentangling nappies from the washing-up. 'I must admit your place does look a bit like a museum. Everything in glass cases – even you. Please Don't Touch the Exhibits.'

'Oh, Viv, are we really so awful?'

'No worse than cats in beds, I suppose. I turfed all six out of Tessa's bed this morning. We're just two extremes. Perhaps that's why we're friends.'

Frances wondered if they really were friends. Somehow it was difficult to be friendly with someone as messy and disorganized as Viv. It got in the way of everything. Perhaps she only used Viv – wept on her shoulder whenever there was a crisis, or popped in for coffee when all her more sophisticated friends were out. She was beginning to dislike herself, using people, hating people, barring access to her home and heart. Viv was a saint, compared

75

with her, splitting her life into seven pieces and keeping only the smallest for herself. And willing, now, to offer that to Magda.

'Viv . . .'

'What?'

'Thank you.'

'What for?'

'Oh, for listening and . . . everything. I do feel better, honestly.'

'When's Magda arriving?'

'Wednesday. I've only got five days to get her room ready.'

'Just a sleeping bag and a few posters on the wall. That's all they want, at that age. Bunty moved all the furniture out of her room in the name of Freedom for Botswana, or some such.'

Frances closed her eyes. Problems, problems, problems. She picked up her handbag and the long, elegant umbrella. 'Goodbye, Viv.'

She heard Rupert crow with laughter as she closed the door.

6

Viv really was absurd. A sleeping bag for Charles' only child! A posture-sprung four-poster was more the thing he'd have in mind. And a Regency desk or two, and the collected works of Henry James. Viv made everything so easy. Another loaf, another pint of milk, another child. Her life was built for children, like her house. Everything was shabby, grubby, friendly, worn, comfortable. Dinky toys down the lavatory and soggy biscuits embedded in the chairs. Viv would do anything for anyone, but you always had to share her – with noise, and smells, and pets and brats.

Frances brushed cat hairs off her dress, glanced around her own house, which looked chilling, almost sterile, more a show-house than a home. The photographs and ornaments were sited with exact precision. She bought flowers to match the curtains, arranged magazines in rows, as if it were a dentist's waiting-room. She could hardly remember now if she'd been so finicky before she'd ever met Charles, or whether she'd changed to humour him. Her own home had been strict, not so much tidy as double-locked and barred. Everything was dangerous or forbidden. Her mother regarded childhood as a period of continuous peril. Ponies only existed to be fallen off; fairgrounds broke your neck or picked your pocket; holidays abroad were a foreign plot to give you sunstroke or diarrhoea. Children themselves were risk and ruination, who would wreck your figure before they frayed your nerves. It had been almost a relief to escape to Charles' regime. At least he had a plan to beat the perils. She sometimes wondered what she might have done, if she hadn't had a Charles. Could she have discovered that life wasn't as hazardous as everybody claimed?

She stretched out on the Victorian chaise-longue and tried to see the room through Viv's eyes. It didn't look like a museum – she was too good a home-maker for that. It was elegant, yes, but comfortable. The Victorian copper log basket was filled with hand-picked logs, attractively arranged – real logs, but not for

77

burning. The log fire was a sham, an artificial hearth, courtesy of the Gas Board. It was cleaner than the real thing. She and Charles hated grime. They also hated shams. But the real logs somehow redeemed it. She got up to switch it on. It wasn't cold, but she felt stiff and shivery. She hadn't slept at all, the last two nights. After hours of agonizing, they had lain in their single beds, turned away from each other, facing their own bare strip of wall. Strange how life continued. Time still ticked on, sixty minutes to an hour, exactly as before. The sun came up and set again. The milkman delivered Charles' skimmed milk and free-range eggs.

She had stared out of the window, this dreadful, drunken morning, and everything appeared so ordinary. Dogs peeing on the grass, commuters plodding to the station, a plane doodling through the baby-blue sky. The trees were lush, unruffled; the pavements still divided into squares. She couldn't understand it. The way she felt, the world should be uprooted and capsized, trees turned bare and blasted overnight. Her own world was in ruins, and the real one hadn't blanched.

Other mornings, she'd looked out and felt a sort of wonder that everything was happening as it should, as if Charles had been put in charge of the whole universe – trains and planes running on schedule, delivery vans unloading bread and newspapers, postmen linking Surrey with Snowdonia, road sweepers keeping the entire planet clean. Her own shining house was somehow part of it, and Charles' work, his lists, his notebooks, all had their place in this cosmic harmony: clocks ticking, computers whirring, machines thumping and pumping, the whole earth, ordered, punctual.

But not the last two days. The busy world whirred on, but she was a piece chipped out of it. She had been rubbed out like an error, deleted from the timetable. Her day stretched in all directions, with no point to it, no boundaries. How could she ever have thought it worthwhile to toil across the golf course, or bother with committee meetings? And what was the point of eating and sleeping, when your husband had a mistress and a daughter? She didn't want to cook. Impossible to sit opposite Charles at the table, guzzling mouthfuls of cardboard *entrecôte*, when he'd betrayed her with that very same mouth.

But what would they do? Sit and drink their normal Tio

Pepes? Talk about the weather? The usual platitudes seemed precious now.

'Had a good day?'

'Busy.' (Always busy.) 'And you?'

'Quiet.' (Often quiet.) 'Nice lunch?'

'Tolerable. Went to Simpson's with a couple of accountants.'

'Hope you didn't choose steak. That's for dinner.'

Well, it wouldn't be, not now. He could get himself a sandwich, or go and ask Piroska to cook Hungarian goulash for him. Was that the woman's name? Something outlandish and fancy. And Magda Rozsi wasn't much better. People in their circle didn't have daughters called Magda Rozsi Kornyai. And what about their circle? How in heaven's name were they going to explain away a teenager? They could call her a niece, but Charles was an only child. And supposing Magda blabbed? Could they invent a deceased first wife for Charles? But why would he have hushed it up? You didn't hide legitimate daughters for fifteen years. All their friends would jeer and tittle-tattle. They'd lose their settled, precious way of life, their reputation as decent people who could be invited anywhere.

Every time she thought about the problem, some new dimension punched her in the face. Charles' mother, for example, his staid, sheltered mother who wouldn't even read the newspapers because they were full of 'shocks and horrors'. Perhaps she'd take back all her furniture, or refuse to lend them her country cottage any more.

Frances sagged down in the chaise-longue, her body like a crumpled paper bag. She turned off the fire, and obediently the flames subsided. Was *she* an artificial fire? So that Charles was forced to find a red-hot Piroska, a blaze of Hungarian passion burning up his schedules and consuming all his rules? She didn't want to know. She walked slowly upstairs to the bedroom, with its whipped cream walls and rosewood furniture. The single beds looked cold and smug, as if they had never been ruffled in their lives.

She lay face downwards on the pillow and cried. She never cried. Tears ruined the complexion. She listened to the noise of her own sobbing, almost from outside it. A strange, animal noise. If only she could be more like an animal, abandoned and

79

spontaneous, instead of imprisoned in her head. Animals cared for other creatures' offspring. Dogs suckled fox cubs and hens mothered ducklings. But what about the cuckoo? It laid its eggs in the pipit's nest, and soon all the other nestlings were pushed out and starved. That's what Magda would be – a greedy little cuckoo, commandeering the nest.

But she still had five days. Anything could happen in five days. Piroska might relent, or Magda refuse to live with them at Richmond, and run away and join a commune. . . . She eased up from the bed and rummaged in her wardrobe, looking for the lion, the toy she had bought for her non-existent baby. The only baby now was Charles' – a stranger and almost grown-up. Even if they did conceive their own child, it wouldn't be a new experience for Charles. She couldn't cherish it as his first-born. That had been Piroska's privilege.

She took the lion back to bed with her. It had a friendly sort of grin, almost a Ned grin. It looked like Ned, in fact, the same streaked golden mane and greenish eyes. Charles had raised an eyebrow when he saw it. He never encouraged anything frivolous. In the early days, when she'd wanted a kitten, or a ball-game on the beach, or a nightdress-case in the shape of a giraffe, he'd made her feel childish and stupid even for asking; bought her a real leather briefcase instead, with a combination lock.

She sat on the counterpane with the lion cradled in her arms. Her head was like a child's tin drum, pounded by a hundred throbbing drumsticks. She couldn't bear to think. Wherever she looked, there was only chaos and deception. She swallowed four aspirin and an Equinil on top of them, and put herself to bed.

She dreamt she was climbing up the decks of a tall ship with no solid sides or rails, but only high, trembling scaffolding. She climbed higher, higher, higher; the wind screaming in her ears, the waves like foaming troughs. Everyone else was dying – pale and hopeless bodies cocooned in tight white blankets like larvae, stacked in rows. She stepped over and over them, and suddenly she was on the topmost mast, and a harsh light was stabbing her eyes and some terrible sickly smell shoved right up her nostrils, the smell of forced carnations. A double bunch, double-wrapped in cellophane, with Charles on the other end of it. And behind him again, that harsh ship's light, the bedroom light, assaulting her eyes.

His mouth was saying something. She tried to concentrate. Body and mind seemed to have drifted miles apart from each other, and she couldn't join them up. She shut her eyes and the smell of carnations swooped right inside her skull. She opened them again. Charles was bending over her, the cellophane rustling against the counterpane. Carefully, she watched the movements of his mouth.

'Are you all right, darling?' it appeared to say. She nodded. The mouth moved again – she wished it wouldn't. She was so incredibly tired, she'd rather sleep than lip-read.

'Look,' it was saying, hesitantly, almost desperately. 'Piroska's had to leave immediately. The grandmother's had a stroke. I'm sorry to spring this on you, darling, but Magda's ... er ... downstairs.'

7

She wasn't a child. She had a full mouth and large breasts, and was five foot four, at least. She wasn't a woman, either. Her face was a blank on which nothing had ever happened, a child's face, smooth and blameless. Her eyes were large and dark, but the light had gone out of them. They looked inward and backward, as if they had followed her mother to Hungary. Apart from the mouth, she was nothing like Charles at all. Her hair was almost black, and hung wavy and tangled to her waist; his was fair and straight. Charles was tall, lean, upright, spruce, almost pollarded; she was broader and wilder, slumped round-shouldered at the table, her legs sprawled out in front of her. She wouldn't even look at him.

Breakfast had lasted for a hundred years and she'd still eaten only three dry scratchy cornflakes.

'How do you like your egg?' Frances asked, at last.

'I don't eat eggs.'

'Bacon?'

'Nope.'

'No thank you.' That was Charles. Magda didn't show she'd heard him, just stared down at her plate – willow pattern, blue and white. She seemed to have run away from them and strayed into that willow-pattern world, hiding behind the windmills, slouching through the cold blue fields.

'Do you like school?' Frances knew it sounded stiff, but couldn't think what else to say; felt dumb and paralysed.

'No,' said Magda dully.

'Would you like some toast?'

'No,' the girl repeated.

Charles didn't say 'no thank you'. Magda looked too miserable for that. How, in God's name, Frances wondered, was she going to get through the day? Well, they'd have to buy some clothes, for a start. Magda couldn't go out in those tatty frayed jeans and that torn man's shirt with half its buttons missing. She'd

82

brought one pathetic bag with her, and that was mostly full of records.

'Do you like clothes, Magda?'

'Yeah.'

Well, that was something. She wondered if Charles would agree to elocution lessons. And certainly a change of school. His daughter needed polishing.

'Would you like to go shopping today? We've got Dickins and Jones in Richmond. Or Top Shop – that's where all the teenagers go.'

'I'm not a teenager.'

'Of course you are, Magda.' Charles got up almost angrily, pushing back his chair. 'I'm sorry, but I've got to leave. I'm meeting Oppenheimer at ten o'clock sharp and I can't be late.'

It was Saturday, but Charles still made appointments. This one had been fixed long before he knew of Magda's arrival. And yet Frances felt resentful. It was so easy for him to escape. How could she argue with an all-day conference at the airport? Charles was meeting his millionaire client and an international banker on a stop-over flight between Hamburg and Buenos Aires. Even daughters didn't disrupt that sort of sacred mission. She clutched at his sleeve.

'Well, have a good day.' The formula again. Anything to keep him there.

'And you.' A peck on the cheek. Would he kiss Magda? He seemed uncertain, made a movement towards her across the breakfast table, and caught his elbow on the marmalade. When Magda picked it up, her hand was trembling.

'Clumsy old me!' Charles was trying to be jokey, sounded merely bogus. 'No, don't see me off. You stay here and finish breakfast. I'll try to get back early.'

'Early' for Charles meant seven or eight o'clock – a whole ten hours away. How would she survive that grey, aching stretch of time with a strange pale creature in the house, who said only no and no. They'd never even finish breakfast. Magda had spooned in two more cornflakes and held them in her mouth without swallowing. Frances got up and tried to speak to Charles with her hands, her eyes, anything – speak to him in code, in signs: don't leave us, cancel your appointments, we need you. He slipped a wad of bank notes into her hand. 'Have a little lunch out. Buy some clothes. Get her hair done.'

She turned away, furious. Money healed everything for Charles. Carnations to cancel out adultery, lunch in Harrods to pay for a broken night. God! What a night, worse than the previous ones. She hadn't really known where Magda ought to sleep. The house was big enough, for Christ's sake, yet slowly they'd taken over all the rooms. Charles' study, Charles' workshop, her sewing-room, her dressing-room, the lumber room, the love-making room, the television room. There didn't seem to be a place for Magda. Finally she'd put her in the sewing-room, on the top floor. She rarely sewed these days.

'It's nice and quiet up here.' (Out of the way, as far from us as possible.) And then she'd lain awake, regretting it. The sewing-room was small and faced north. Viv would have snuggled Magda into her own bed with half a dozen cats. Or at least given her the studio, a warm, spacious room which got all the sun. But there were precious things in the studio, the Mackmurdo chair, the two John Piper watercolours. And supposing Magda split Pepsi on the mid-Victorian patchwork?

Frances had tossed and turned in her own warm, expensive bed, listening to the silence. Charles hadn't even come upstairs. He was working on a complex tax return. Or so he said. She wished she'd kissed Magda goodnight. It had seemed impossible. If Magda had been three, she might have kissed her, wooed her with a teddy bear and read her 'Goldilocks'. But Magda wasn't three. She had full high breasts, bigger than her own.

She had stood at the sewing-room door, trying to look calm and normal and welcoming. 'Goodnight then, Magda.'

''Night.'

'Got everything you want?' My house, my husband, my sewing-room.

'Yeah.' Why couldn't Piroska have taught her child how to speak?

'Well, goodnight,' she'd said again.

''Night.'

She'd still lingered, holding the door handle. It didn't seem enough to say goodnight. She'd offered Ovaltine, but Magda wouldn't touch it.

'Hungry?'

'No.' If only she wouldn't flatten her vowels like that. A foreign accent would have been preferable – charming even, and certainly classless.

The child must be hungry, however she denied it. None of them had eaten, only played at it. Magda had jabbed the food around her plate for an hour and a half, and all she'd swallowed was two peas and half a glass of water.

'I'll be off, then. Sleep well.'

'Yeah.'

Yeah. Oh yeah. Of course they'd sleep well, all of them. Charles escaping into his midnight calculations, she herself wondering why hugs were so impossible, Magda sobbing under the bedclothes.

Was the child sobbing? She sat up and tried to hear. The sharp cry of a night bird ripped through the silence, but nothing else.

She crept upstairs and listened outside Magda's door. She heard the laburnum tree shift and sigh a little outside the window, and a tom cat courting. She opened the door a crack.

'What d'you want?' The voice was fierce, almost rude. It came from by the window, where Magda was standing, still dressed and wide awake. She wasn't crying. She looked as if she had never cried in all her fifteen years. Her face was stiff and wary.

'You're spying on me.'

'Of course not, Magda, I just wondered . . .'

'Go away.'

'I thought perhaps . . .'

'I said "go away".'

How dare a mere child tell her to go away in her own house. Rude, ungrateful little bitch! 'Look, Magda, if you want to be difficult, please yourself. But we've got to try to live together. So you might as well . . .'

Ridiculous, taking that tone with a child, a miserable, frightened creature who belonged nowhere and owned nothing. I'd like to be nice to you, Magda, really I would. Give you a hug, put my arms around you. But I've no idea how to even get near you. I'm not as heartless as I seem. Or maybe I am. Perhaps I'm a monster, a snobbish, steel-trap of a woman, completely lacking in maternal feelings. Is that why I've never conceived? I'm too

85

bloody mean to be a mother? I can't blame Charles any more. He's proved his fertility, hasn't he? You're the living, breathing proof of it. That's partly why I hate you, Magda. Oh, I know it's unfair. It's not your fault, and I'm sorry for you, but . . .

You're beautiful. I wish you weren't. Your hair's magnificent. I could never grow mine as long as that. Perhaps Charles will make you cut it. You've got your faults, though. You're too tall for a child, and your hands are large and bony. Why don't you wash your feet?

She took a step inside the room. 'Listen, Magda, I'm sorry I was sharp. Why don't you have a nice warm bath? It might help you to sleep. I could give you some bathsalts, lovely pine ones, which turn the water green.' She did really long to give her something. A hug was impossible, but bathsalts, biscuits, time to talk. So long as Magda went on saying no, they'd never break the barrier between them.

'No.'

'All right, then, I'll go away.'

'No.'

'You don't want me to go away?'

'No.'

She sat down on the bed. It wasn't good for the mattress, but it might be a start. 'Why don't you come and sit beside me?'

'No.'

Christ! what a little minx she was, slouched beside the wardrobe, jabbing her feet against the wood, expecting them all to wait on her and worry about her, and spend the whole night trailing up and down stairs. She felt stupid sitting on the bed – trapped and vulnerable. Where in God's name was Charles? Hiding behind his tax returns, frightened of his own daughter. How could you be frightened of a schoolgirl? Yet, she was herself; she was.

Magda looked even paler now, sort of shrunk and faded, as if Mrs Eady had put her in the washing machine on the wrong programme. She probably hadn't slept at all, and she couldn't cope with breakfast. Frances cleared the toast away – no point forcing her. She brightened up a little after Charles had left. Frances wondered if she was angry with him, too. Both of them furious with Charles. By having a daughter, he'd betrayed his wife, and by having a wife, he'd disowned his daughter. Perhaps she could use it as a bond between them.

'Magda?'

'Yeah?'

'Look, first of all, let's get one thing straight. It's "yes", not "yeah".'

'Yeah, I know.'

'Well, why don't you say it, then?'

'Why should I?'

'Because it's correct.'

Magda shrugged. 'Don't care.'

No, thought Frances, you don't. Your fingernails need cutting, and your breasts are far too heavy to go around without a bra like that. And you haven't brought a flannel with you. She tore a piece of paper from the memo-pad hanging by the dresser and made a shopping list: flannel, slippers, bras, blouses, skirt, shampoo . . .

By twelve o'clock, they'd only got the slippers and shampoo. Magda refused to wear skirts or bras. She didn't make a fuss, she just said no, but in such a pale fierce way, Frances didn't argue. She wouldn't even have a proper pair of shoes.

'But you can't go out in those.' They were combat boots, with heavy studded soles and knotted laces.

'I won't go out, then.'

'Don't be silly, Magda. I want to take you out. I've already planned a visit to the V. and A., with lunch in town beforehand. You can't go dressed like that.'

'Well, I'll have to stay at home.'

'Magda, *please*.'

'What's the V. and A., anyway?'

A voice behind her chipped in. 'A boring old museum which kids get dragged to in the name of culture, and then inflict on their own children as a just revenge.'

Frances whirled round and came face to face with blue corduroy and a grin.

'Mr Bradley!'

'Ned. What's all this, then? Another Medfield job? Guided tours of Richmond, I suppose. Is this your passenger?' He stopped in front of both of them, barring their way, and grinned full-frontally at Magda. 'Pleased to meet you. Ned Bradley's the name. Friend of Frances, and enemy of all museums.'

She'd never seen Magda smile before. It was a slow, unwilling smile, but at least it displaced the scowl she'd worn all morning. She felt a surge of gratitude. Ned was like a human de-icer.

'This is Magda.' She and Charles had decided to dispense with Magda's surname for the moment. She had, of course, taken her mother's name, which was all but unpronounceable. And until they'd decided who Magda was supposed to be, a surname posed problems. 'She's our – er – guest at present. We're just buying her some clothes.'

'No, we're not,' said Magda.

'Do I detect a clash of interests? I suppose Lady Frances insists on twinset and pearls, and you refuse anything but a boiler suit.'

'Yup,' said Magda. 'Though I wouldn't mind some cords. Like yours.'

'Well, you won't find them in this dreary old emporium, my love. They only sell grey suits for grey people. I'm just off to buy some gear myself. Going to a jumble sale. You'd better come along.'

'A jumble sale!' Charles' daughter in second-hand clothes which might have come from slums or syphilitics . . .

'Well, let's be fair to it, it's really a summer fête. Big do, in fact, with all the sideshows. Guess the weight of an anorexic goldfish – you know the sort of thing. But they do have an old clothes stall. One of the best round here. I come every year and sniff out all the bargains.'

Magda took a cautious step forward. 'Do they have cords?'

'Oh, stacks of 'em. Boiler suits, dungarees, ex-army stuff – all the "in" gear. It's held at a school where I used to teach. I still know half the staff and they put things by for me.'

Frances ignored him. 'Magda, the last thing you want is junk clothes. You've got enough of those already. You need some respectable outfits – skirts and blouses, a decent little dress or two.'

'Why?' said Magda.

'Yeah, why?' said Ned.

The two were near conspirators, slumped together against the window of a record shop, their messy, casual clothes almost matching. Ned slid his bottom down the window and balanced on his haunches. 'There's a nearly-new stall, as well – you'd get a decent dress there. They even sell period clothes, Queen Victoria's knickers, Second Empire ermine tippets.'

Magda giggled. 'Come on then, let's have a dekko.' They plunged arm-in-arm down the High Street, Magda almost skipping. She couldn't be missing her mother much, if a few germy cast-offs were enough to distract her. No, that was totally unfair. But somehow the sight of Magda treating Ned like a brother – or worse – made Frances bristle. Ned was *her* property, and she didn't want him mixed up with sordid reality. If anyone were going to hold his arm, it shouldn't be a pushy, problem kid.

'Magda, will you please come back . . .'

Ned came back instead. 'Be a sport, Fran. You'll love the fête! There's a donkey derby and a very classy dance display. We could make a day of it. I'll treat us all to tea.'

'We haven't had our lunch yet and I've already booked a table at Valchera's.' Charles' restaurant, where the waiters all paid homage to him. Where else could she take his child?

'I don't want lunch, I want tea.' Magda had trailed back and dumped her shopping bag on the pavement. She was staring into the record shop. 'Please, Frances.'

Frances could see the pale, pleading face reflected in the window. The kid was asking for something. Why not give it to her? 'All right then, but only for an hour. We'll have to do the proper shopping afterwards.'

They walked through Richmond, three abreast, across the roundabout and down the Lower Mortlake Road.

'Brent Edge Comprehensive!' Ned announced, as they stopped in front of a Dickensian blacking factory. Plastic pennants were fluttering in the wind; rock music blaring out across the road and on through half of Surrey. Two scruffy boys in school uniform were standing just inside the gates, playing mouth organ and accordion.

'Please give generously,' said the placard propped between them. 'Headmaster, staff and 2000 boys to support.'

Ned tossed them a coin and made straight for the jumble. Half a hundred female welter-weights had had the same idea. Ned fought with Crimplene bosoms and knuckle-duster handbags. An irate matron started a tug-of-war with him. They landed up with one sleeve each of a velvet smoking-jacket.

'We need help against these Amazonian hordes,' he muttered. 'Hold on a sec, there's Mac.' He nodded to an out-of-work gangster with a patchwork waistcoat and the dirty debris of a beard, who was serving behind the stall.

'Hi, Mac, meet my harem. Magda, Franny – this is Neil Macauley. Teaches Comparative Religion to the drop-outs. Got any decent cords, Mac?'

'Who for, you or the ladies?'

'All three of us. Three for the price of one! And none of your Shylock tactics.'

Mac dug about under a pile of assorted outerwear. 'You don't want a wet-suit, do you? Genuine hundred-per-cent British rubber. Donated by a diver who never re-surfaced. No, wait, here's something better.' He slung a pair of black corduroys into Magda's arms. 'Special price for you, love – 20p. Try 'em on. You're not really allowed to, but if you crawl behind the counter . . .'

'Magda, you can't possibly wear those.' Frances dodged thirteen stone of polyester polka-dots, advancing on her from behind.

'Why can't she? They're cheap at the price.'

'Yeah, why can't I?'

'They're filthy, to start with, and . . .'

'It's only good clean dirt. Gives them a bit of body.' The polka-dots had overtaken and were blocking the view.

'Don't be silly, Ned. They're men's jeans, in any case.'

'I don't care, I *want* men's. I want them exactly the same as Ned's.'

Ned was wrestling with a pair of purple Levis and some smaller jeans in a dirty shade of grey. He shook an ersatz Boadicea off the other end of them. 'I don't really think you can tell the sex of jeans. They're unisex, like goldfish.'

Magda crawled up from underneath the stall, the cords so tight they looked as if they had been painted on her.

'They're far too tight, Magda, you can't sit down in them.'

'I'll stand up, then . . .'

Mac laughed. 'That's the spirit, dear! Look, I'll make it 15p. But only for you, mind.'

Ned squeezed between a dropped bosom and a brass-bound handbag, and took Frances' arm. 'Go easy on the kid, love. One pair of cords can't hurt.'

She wished he wouldn't interfere. Magda was already far too free and easy, calling Ned by his Christian name, and leaning against him like that, when she'd only just been introduced. With a mother like hers, she needed watching. Easy for Ned to spoil her, when he didn't know the facts. It wasn't his problem; he didn't have to live with her. He was right, though. It wasn't really Magda's problem, either. She hadn't asked to be conceived. And anyway, she'd probably worn this sort of gear all her life. Magda in cords hadn't brought the world to a halt yet.

'All right,' she said gruffly. 'She can have them.'

'Great!' said Ned. 'I'll take these two pairs as well.' He rescued his booty from a materfamilias with a terrier grip. 'What's your best price, Mac?'

'50p the three. And I'm more or less giving them away.'

'Daylight robbery. Make it forty.'

'Forty-five.'

'Done!' Ned handed across a pocketful of loose change and looped the jeans around his neck.

'Who are those ones for, Ned?' Magda was clinging on to his arm, stroking the Levis.

'Purple for me, grey for Franny.'

'I never wear jeans, and would you please not call me Franny.' She was being shoved from behind, against the hard wooden stall. There'd be splinters in her skin, and God knows what else if she wore other people's cast-offs.

'They'd look smashing with your eyes, that sort of feline grey. It's more or less the colour of my cat.'

'I distinctly remember your cat as being black. With a small white patch on his back left paw.'

'Yes, Rilke. You never saw Hallam – he's the grey one. But fancy you remembering. Cor! I wish I was a cat – they've obviously got a way with women. I bet nobody'd ever remember the colour of *my* back left paw.' Ned ducked beneath a pair of seersucker biceps and stormed the counter again. 'If you don't like jeans, I'd like to buy you something else, Fran. Hey, Mac, what you got for a natty dresser?'

Mac flung a silver lurex top across, with a *décolleté* neckline and sequins round the sleeves. Ned caught it in mid-air.

'This is absolutely you, Fran. Just the thing for Conservative Party coffee mornings. You get a very decent class of jumble here, you know. Even Mrs Thatcher buys from Mac. OK, you're not impressed, I can tell. Let's try the Bargain Box, then.'

He dipped into a cardboard carton labelled 'Rockbottom Prices – we must be daft' and came up with a large straw hat. Plastic cherries dangled across the broken yellow brim and purple ribbons cascaded down the back. He set it rakishly on her head, ruffling her Evansky hair-do. 'Miss Brent Edge 1981, chosen unanimously from a thousand breathless finalists!'

Frances almost shook him off. His humour was E-stream and the hat worse. She could hear herself sounding harsh and irritable, like the worst sort of spoil-sport. Why couldn't she just relax and enjoy a summer afternoon, as Magda was now doing? She looked a different child without her scowl, looping diamanté earrings over Ned's earlobes and trying on a stripey blazer back to front. Ned seemed to know how to tame and thaw her . . . which only made it more difficult. He was like a grinning reprimand, his easy banter showing up her shrewishness. She didn't want to be a shrew, but there was some strict headmistress of a voice, sitting in her head, nagging and prohibiting, casting a blight on everything. It reminded her of her own mother's voice, anxious, life-destroying. 'Don't get your feet wet, Frances; dogs bite, Frances.' Her mother would run a mile from jumble sales. 'You'll only pick up germs, Frances, after they've rooked you . . .' But why repeat her mother's maxims? The umbilical cord had been cut long since, and she was free to go her own way. Grudgingly, she picked up the hat.

'What about that tea you promised?'

'Oh, it's not time for tea. Let's have ices first. They've got a Dayville's tent here. I'll treat us all to triple scoops.'

They sat in the stuffy tent on collapsible stools. Ned wore the hat back to front, a frayed purple ribbon trailing in his cornet. He leant across and licked the nuts off Magda's ice. 'Here, do a swap. A lick of my Rocky Road for a bite of your Strawberry Fizz.'

Frances seethed inwardly. Ned had no right to make Magda's manners worse than they were already. He'd bought them all giant-sized cornets with hot fudge sauce and nuts. No gold stars. Ice cream was fattening, and chocolate ruination for the skin. Delicious ruination, none the less. She'd never had a Dayville's, could almost have enjoyed it, if it weren't for Charles' prohibitions. It was so difficult, being torn all ways, her mother's voice in one ear, Charles' in the other, and another, new-hatched voice urging, 'Go on, spoil yourself.' She might have heeded that one, if she and Ned were on their own. It had been a bonus to bump into him at all, but she was annoyed that it had happened when she was playing dreary mother, so he'd see her as a nagger and a killjoy. And Magda herself had come between them, slipping triumphantly into the role of Ned's playmate, and making her the odd one out. It could have been far worse, though. She might be marooned now in Valchera's, toying with her vichyssoise, a sullen rebel facing her across the table, and the afternoon stretching to infinity. Ned had worked wonders with Magda, no doubt about it, but she almost resented the fact that he had succeeded where she and Charles had not. Everything was so confusing. Perhaps she was simply tired. Three sleepless nights hadn't helped, nor a daughter delivered like unsolicited goods. The fête was mercilessly noisy, crowds jostling and jabbering, loudspeakers blaring, one announcer out-shouting another.

'A little girl has been lost. She's sobbing her eyes out in the Red Cross tent. Her name's Lucy, and she's wearing a blue dress and red wellies. If anyone . . .'

'Poor sod, she'll get trampled in the rush.' Ned had demolished his cornet in half a dozen bites. 'Hey, girls, let's splurge all our cash on the donkey derby.'

'Oh, yeah, Ned! Can I ride a donkey, Ned? Ned, d'you think they'd let me?'

All those Neds! Supposing Magda repeated them at home, made Charles a carbon copy of the whole mad afternoon. It was time to make a break.

'Magda, we haven't bought your shoes yet. Or your bras.'

'Donkeys don't wear bras.'

Ned and Magda giggled, clearly in alliance.

'Magda, love, if you go and find the donkey man, he'll turn you into Lester Piggott. He's a pal of mine . . . just say Ned the Red. Here's a pound to back you, and don't you dare fall off. I

93

can't afford to lose my stake. It's all I've got for Sunday lunch. Otherwise I'll have to eat roast Rilke and mint sauce.'

Magda galloped off, with the pound in one hand and her cornet in the other.

'See you at the tote!' Ned yelled, turning back to Frances. They were suddenly alone, with a hundred other bodies pressing round them in the tent. It was almost frightening to have his full attention, to stop being a stepmother, and become something dangerous else. His sticky fingers were already stroking down her arm. She shook them off.

'Relax, Fran. You're all uptight and tense. It's a lovely day, sun's shining fit to bust, birds singing their crazy little hearts out. Why are you all screwed up?'

'I'm not screwed up, I . . .' Christ! She couldn't cry. Not in an ice cream tent, not in front of everybody, not – oh, please God – not in front of Ned. Her face was crumpling up, losing control of itself. There were tears on the plastic table, tears on Ned's red-checked arm. Somehow, she was holding on to it, and he was leading her to the back of the tent and seating her gently on an upturned packing case. She tried to pull her face back into shape, to make her voice behave.

'Look, I'm sorry. Stupid of me. I'll be all right in a . . . Oh Ned, it's . . . it's *not* a lovely day.'

'Of course it's bloody not, if you're unhappy. It's a swine of a day. What's the matter, Fran?'

'Oh, nothing.'

'Everything?'

She nodded.

'Husband?'

'No.' How in God's name had he guessed?

'Really no?'

'Well sort, of. It's . . .' She shook her head. 'I'm sorry, Ned, I just can't tell you. Magda might come back. Can you see her?'

Ned got up from his knees and peered through a gap in the canvas. 'The donkey man's flirting with her. Joe's a shocker – teaches woodwork when he's not chatting up the chicks. He likes them dark like that, and barely out of gymslips.'

'She's beautiful, Ned, isn't she?'

'Not bad. I prefer the older woman, actually.' He had a store of grins in different colours – wild crimson ones for poly rave-ups, and soft blue ones for weepy afternoons. She smiled back.

'That's better. Now come on, girl, tell Uncle Ned what's up.'

'But, Ned, I hardly know you and . . .'

'Good God! Haven't we been introduced? I must have overlooked it. How terribly remiss of me. I do apologize. Edward Charles Bradley, DFC, OBE, Commanding Officer, Southmead Polytechnic.'

Frances dabbed her eyes. 'Is your second name really Charles?'

''Fraid so.'

'That's my husband's name.'

'Poor sod. He could always change it.'

'He likes it, actually.'

'And what about Magda? That's an unusual name.'

'Yes.'

'Italian?'

'No, Hungarian.'

'She sounds English enough.'

'Yes.'

'She's the problem, isn't she?'

Frances chewed her thumb.

'Aren't you going to tell me about it?'

The loudspeaker was booming out again, fighting with the rock music and the raucous laughter of the ice cream lady. 'Lucy is still lost. She says she doesn't know her other name, but she came with her granny. If there's any grandma who's lost a Lucy . . .'

'Well?' said Ned. He was almost whispering, but his soft voice swamped loudspeakers.

'It's Charles – that's my husband. He, I mean, she – she's his daughter. She's my husband's daughter.'

'By another woman, you mean?'

Frances nodded. How could he sound so calm about it? Why didn't he leap to his feet, or gasp in shock? She should never have told him, anyway – a stranger, an inexperienced bachelor. He could never understand.

'Who wasn't his wife?'

'No-o.'

He couldn't have heard her properly, just sprawling there,

plying her with questions, as if they were filling in an application form.

'I see. How long has she lived with you?'

'About eighteen hours.' A month, a century.

'Christ! I'm beginning to get it. Where's her mother?'

'Gone back to Hungary.' Bitch, deserter.

'Permanently?'

'More or less, as far as I can gather.' How could she know, when Charles wouldn't tell her anything?

'But you knew about her?'

'No.' Nothing. Fifteen years of falsehood.

'You mean, it was a complete bolt out of the blue?'

'Mm.'

'Fran, that's really bloody tough. I'm sorry. She's living with you, is she?'

'Mm,' she said again. Breaking up my life.

'Well, it won't be for long, I suppose. How old is she, seventeen?'

'Fifteen.' Still only a child. A child with a woman's body. It might be years and years. Maybe she'd stay for ever, forcing herself between her and Charles, growing bigger and bigger, like a cuckoo . . .

'It's a funny age. I used to teach them once – here, in fact – between these hallowed walls. Give me the Poly any day! At least they've reached the age of reason. At fifteen, they're emotionally in nappies, more or less. Maybe I could help you with her, Fran. I'm good with kids.'

If only someone could help – take the child away, make everything all right again. 'I'm afraid not, Ned. It wouldn't work. I hardly even know you, should never have really told you in the first place.'

''Course you should. You've got to talk to someone. You're crazy, Fran, all tied up with rules, as if you're following some formal book of etiquette. People aren't strangers, even if they've never met. They've got the human condition in common, which is more important than the same Alma Mater and all that sort of crap. We don't have to be formally introduced by our frock-coated fathers at the Hunt Ball before I'm allowed to care about you, Franny.'

96

A nice word, 'care' – and he did care. She could hear it in his voice. 'Look, Ned, I'm sorry, but I'm not in a position to be friendly with you. I'm married, for one thing.'

Ned was still on his knees beside her, at the back of the tent. 'So is Charles.'

'What's that supposed to mean?'

'Well, he hasn't treated you exactly handsomely, has he?'

Frances flushed. 'Look, Ned, the Magda thing . . . He was still single when it happened, more or less.'

'More or less?'

'I'm sorry I ever said anything.'

'I'm only trying to help. Why shouldn't you be friendly with a guy, when your husband's busy clocking up affairs?'

'He doesn't have affairs. Not any more.'

'How do you know?'

'Well . . . he's too busy – he wouldn't have the time. And he's not the type, in any case.'

'It's not a question of types, my love. Anyway, how about this other woman? Or did she conceive Magda via the Holy Ghost?'

'Ned, please. That was ages ago and I don't wish to discuss it. Now will you please move over and let me get up. We've left Magda quite long enough.'

'OK, but promise me something first.'

'What?'

'You'll wear your hat.'

He placed it on her head, almost tenderly, arranging the streamers on each side of her neck and kissing the space between. 'Franny?'

'What?'

'You look quite beautiful.'

After the donkeys, they tried the rifle range. Frances won a pink plaster ashtray in the shape of a pig. Magda swapped it for an ancient parasol she'd bought for 20p at a stall marked 'Odds and Ends'. The sun kept fighting with the clouds, and when it rained, they all three sheltered beneath its ragged flounces, pressing close together. The rain plopped through the rents and fell on Frances' hat. She could feel Ned's thigh warm against her own.

'Happy?' he asked.

She nodded, astonished to be happy, wandering around a run-down comprehensive in a field of mud and litter, with a tomboy on one side and a shambles of a teacher on the other. She'd sent her mother packing to her split-level house in Cheltenham, and at last she felt relaxed. She must never see Ned again, though, especially now she'd told him about Charles. It could only be dangerous, disloyal, but there was nothing to stop her spinning out this one sweet afternoon. Ned had a knack for making things good fun.

'Are you good at running, Magda?'

'Yeah. Why?'

'Let's go in for the three-legged race together.'

Frances sat and watched them pull each other over, panting and laughing. They came in last and won a booby prize, a little plastic brooch.

'Shame! Give it to your daughter,' yelled a man in the crowd, as Ned pinned it on his shirt front. Magda couldn't be his daughter – he wasn't old enough. And yet a casual onlooker had turned them into an instant family, a messy, happy family, munching toffee apples and sprawling on the grass. Strange to be a threesome like that, an ordinary family with no Charles to cosset and control her. Would she be happier, freer, or poorer and duller? Ned was everything she disapproved of – scruffy, casual, pushy, puerile. Yet already he'd changed the day from Rocky Road to Strawberry Fizz.

The sun came out and stayed out. Ned and Magda won the egg-and-spoon race. Ned was munching his box-of-chocolates prize. 'You'll get fat,' said Magda.

'I am fat. Open up, Franny, for a Brazilian almond whirl.'

His fingers tasted of candyfloss and hot pennies. He traced them along her lips, kidnapping the last piece of almond for himself. The loudspeaker was blaring out again.

'The next race will be the Barefoot Contessa's Mid-Fête Marathon. Any lady over eighteen who takes her shoes and stockings off is eligible to enter . . .'

'This is it, Fran! Your big chance. Quick, take your shoes off!'

'But I can't run in this tight skirt.'

'Put your jeans on then – quick – the catty ones. Come on, hurry! They're all lining up.'

She hardly knew what she was doing. Magda unzipped her skirt for her, while she removed her tights and eased the jeans on underneath. She could see Ned looking at her, her bottom sticking out provocatively, the fabric straining against her thighs. She must be out of her mind – changing her clothes in public, running in madcap races. Supposing she were seen. There might even be people from the Golf Club there – Charles would never live it down.

Bugger Charles! She sprinted towards the starting-line and squeezed in between a pair of bunions and a bad case of pigeon toes. Everyone was giggling and joking – including the announcer.

'Aren't they a lovely lot, then? All those bare feet ... Wow, what a turn-on! Right then, girls. Ready, steady ...'

Frances was running like a lynx. The bare feet made it easier. So did Ned, shouting on the sidelines, 'Come on, Fran, come *on*!' as if he'd bet everything he owned on her. She willed her feet to go faster, could feel the grass skimming underneath them, cold and slippery. She was way in front, streaking ahead of all the rest. It paid to be small sometimes, small and swift and streamlined. She almost fell across the piece of string held taut by two PT teachers. The crowd was clapping wildly, as someone pinned a red rosette in the middle of her chest. 'First' it said. A camera snapped. She was a Brent Edge celebrity, a barefoot contessa with muddy feet and grass between her toes. Ned and Magda were slapping her on the back, as she collapsed in a heap between them.

'Cor,' said Magda, admiringly. 'You can't half run!' Ned twisted a buttercup through her hair. 'Beautiful *and* clever,' he said.

They lay on the grass, still tangled together. Frances closed her eyes. The noise and glare slipped away and she was alone with Ned in an enchanted garden, running like Atalanta up Mount Parthenus. No, that was wrong. Atalanta lost her race; all the goddess gained was a suitor and three golden apples. Well, she had Ned and a plastic peg-bag as a prize. And a pair of cat-grey jeans.

'Lucy has been claimed and is now happily reunited with her

Granny in the tea tent. And if anyone else wants teas, I'm told there's a very good line in half-price sausage rolls . . .'

It was still warm, but the sun was nudging its way down the sky, looping long shadows across the grass. Frances opened her eyes, reluctantly. She didn't want anything to move or change, just to stay ideal and immobile like a picture in a Greek frieze.

'Ned, I simply must go.' Her voice was a spoil-sport, detached from the rest of her.

'What about the Dance Display? A hundred little Markovas pounding through *Swan Lake*. We can't miss it.'

'But I daren't stay any longer. I've wasted the whole afternoon as it is.'

'Wasted?'

'I'm sorry, I didn't . . .' A Charles word, wasted. Charles would be back by now, wondering where they were, creaking into his father role, laboured and precarious.

'My husband's coming home early, especially to see Magda.'

Magda bit into her half-price sausage roll. 'I'd rather see the dancing.'

'Magda!'

'Tell you what, let's grab a beer and a hot dog, have a quick peek at the Nureyevs and then push off, OK?'

An obese and red-faced matron was pounding an old Bechstein. One swan had lost its feathers and another picked its nose throughout the *Danse Hongroise*.

'You've got mustard on your chin,' Ned whispered, as he leant across and licked it off. 'And the most incredible blue eyes I've ever seen.' He was murmuring in her ear. She could smell his warmth, his sweat.

'Ned . . .'

'What?'

'Nothing.' How could she tell him she felt different and peculiar? He seemed to have hatched some new and hidden part of her which had lain dormant for so long, she'd almost forgotten it was there. It seemed stupid to swap this shabby, scuffed school-hall for her elegant house in Richmond. But again her voice rebelled.

'Ned, I *must* go. Now. Don't argue.'

'OK, love, relax. There's no hassle.'

They sauntered back to Richmond Station. Ned was taking

the Broad Street line to Acton. Frances felt sick and strange. They'd stuffed themselves with junk food the whole afternoon, rolled about like gypsies on the grass. Tomorrow, it was back to normal, with regular mealtimes and perhaps a museum, so that Magda could be shown life in its true, grey, sober colours. She was leaping ahead of them, jumping over cracks in the pavement. Ned dropped back behind.

'Don't forget, Fran, I'm around if you want me.' He stuffed a piece of paper in the pocket of her jeans. 'That's my number. Phone any time. I'd like to help.'

'Look, Ned, I don't really think . . .'

'OK, please yourself.' He loped off towards the platform, the straw hat perched absurdly on his head.

'Ned, that's Frances' hat!' Magda almost threw herself upon him, snatching the straw hat and confiscating it. They wrestled for a moment, then he hugged her – a casual but affectionate embrace. Frances watched with envy. So, a hug was as easy as that.

Magda dawdled slowly back to her, passed the hat across. There was a short, embarrassed silence.

'Magda.'

'Mmm?'

'I think I'd better change.'

'Change? But you're only a couple of minutes from the house.'

'Yes, but Charles will probably be home by now, and he likes me, well you know . . .'

Magda shook her head. 'No, I don't know.'

Frances disappeared into the station Ladies' room and re-emerged with her skirt on. It felt heavier and scratchier than she'd remembered it. It was also disgracefully creased from its sojourn in a plastic bag. She stuffed the hat at the bottom of the shopping basket, with the pink-pig plaster ashtray and the peg-bag.

They walked in silence back across the Green. The sun had disappeared behind a cloud, the colour seeping slowly out of everything – grass, sky, their own Cambridge-blue front door. Charles met them in the hall, his new paternal smile highly polished, wary. He was still in his pin-stripes and he too looked colourless. She could hear Stravinsky's *Orpheus* weeping from the drawing-room, the plaintive clarinets accusing her. How could she have endured Brent Edge punk all afternoon, when there were harmonies like this?

'I was worried about you, Frances. I came home especially early, planned to take you and Magda out to dinner. I've booked a table at Valchera's.'

'I'm sorry, darling, but I don't think we could manage it. We've been eating all afternoon.' A second Valchera's table swept away. Vichyssoise and crêpes suzettes dethroned by candy-floss and Dayville's. Her three-scoop Strawberry Fizz nudged her in the guts.

Magda was hiding behind her scowl again, had re-erected the barriers. Charles did his best to bring her out, his voice trampling on the *Orpheus*, frail, limpid music which couldn't fight with conversation. Frances listened anxiously as an ostinato screwed the room tighter and tighter in its relentless circling.

Charles turned to her instead, since he could get no word from Magda. 'Pleasant afternoon?'

'Very pleasant.'

'Bought the clothes?'

'Some.'

'Why the black?'

'I beg your pardon?'

'Well, it's a little funereal for a child, isn't it?'

'She likes black.'

Silence. Black silence. 'How was Oppenheimer?'

'Fine.'

'Would you like a chop for supper?' God I'm going to scream.

'Thank you. Nice.'

Not nice. Not nice at all. Ridiculous. Unbearable. 'I'll just have a salad. I'm not hungry. Magda?'

'Yeah?'

'A chop for you?'

'Nope.'

'Salad?'

'Nope.'

'No, thank you,' Charles said tersely. Frances winced. Christ, not again, she prayed, not the whole stiff, funereal, screaming farce again: Magda slouched at the table, fiddling with a fork,

Charles chewing a pork chop, no talk except the odd strained monosyllables. She suddenly remembered Ned's scrappy piece of paper, stuffed in her jeans pocket. She'd forgotten all about it, hadn't even looked at it. It might have fallen out . . . 'Excuse me a moment, would you?'

'Of course.'

Always so damned civil, she and Charles. She rushed out to the hall, rummaged in the shopping bag, found the piece of paper still crumpled in the pocket. 'Rilke is flattered you remembered him. His business phone number is 749 2348, extension Ned. P.S. Swap my ice cream cornet for your eyes.'

Crazy, puerile Ned, she thought, suppressing a broad grin. It wasn't even funny.

8

Charles washed his hands with the yellow scented soap in the marbled hotel basin. Five matching yellow towels in assorted sizes hung neatly on a heated rail. He pulled crossly at the smallest one, dried between his fingers. He hated hotels – too many bloody mirrors. The bathroom itself was like a mirrored coffin, reflecting him full length, in parallel. Six separate Charleses dried their hands; twelve hands replaced the towel, dead centre, on the rail; six double faces grimaced at themselves.

If he moved a fraction to the right, Laura edged into the mirror, reclining on the bed in the adjoining room, naked except for the fine silver necklet he had bought her.

'Charlie.'

He wished she wouldn't talk – she was getting as tedious as Frances. And he'd told her a hundred times about the Charlies.

'Charles . . .'

'That's better . . .'

'Come here, sweetest.'

'Just a moment.' Christ! She couldn't want it again. He had a heavy afternoon ahead of him. One of Laura's attractions was that she was a short-and-sharp girl. None of that nonsense about multiple orgasms and the earth moving. Laura was more like a man – one big bang and all over. Though her face and figure were anything but masculine – thank God. He inched to the right again, eyed her in the mirror. She was a female you were proud to be seen with: voluptuous, fleshy, elegant; neither her auburn hair nor her scarlet talons quite what God had given her, but striking none the less. And a sharp and witty woman who understood his work, respected him for being who he was.

He needed that respect, sometimes wondered whether Frances really fathomed the cruel pressures of his job. He could hardly afford to be a person any more. His profession had set him up as a deified decision-machine, cold, efficient, steely. His day existed only to solve other people's problems and survive other countries' crises; his evenings and weekends merely to keep up with the crippling burden of research. If a client quizzed him on custodial charges in Nauru, or Copper Futures on the Tokyo Exchange, he had to know – and instantly. And there were thirty-eight important clients, all pushing him for data. Multi-million banks and multi-national corporations picking his brains and probing his judgements; off-shore banana republics demanding instant fiscal programmes; oil princes expecting razzmatazz and homage with their ten-year economic plans. His own life was squeezed between them. Even a mistress had to be slotted into a lunch hour, and then paid for with half a night of homework. The same with music. If he listened to a concert on the radio, he had to make up lost time by swotting through the early hours. Sometimes he only snatched the last movement of the final piece, or taped the programme while he studied in another room, hoping to play it back in his car, or during meals.

Even in his sleep, strange jumbled images of dollar signs and silicon chips howled in the cold factory of his head; accusing columns of figures hurled themselves out of their tidy phalanxes and multiplied each other over and over, until their seething numbers spun into infinity. Some nights, he dared not sleep at all. One miscalculation could cost him half a million pounds and all his self-respect. Even in his so-called rest hours, he must remain constantly, relentlessly alert.

It wasn't easy. If he were irritable or tense, it was only because he had been forced to divide his mind into thirty-eight pieces and give each one simultaneous attention. That's why he needed a Laura in his life – a retreat, a haven, somewhere he could move out of the jangling computer of his mind, back to the solid base of his body, and remind himself it still existed.

It would be hellish, giving her up. True, she was already more demanding, and the 'Charlies' were intolerable, but she was still a prized possession, something luxurious, unique, like his Bristol 411, and his eighteenth-century office with its Adam ceilings and its Goya aquatints.

He replaced his underpants, to rule out second helpings, returned slowly to the bedroom.

'Lover . . .' Laura whispered.

105

'Mmm?'

'You don't really mean it, do you?'

'Laura, I've got to mean it. I can't inflict any more on Frances at the moment.'

'Frances doesn't know.'

'She might get to know, darling, and I just can't take that risk. Not now. Not with Magda.'

'So, I'm to be sacrificed for Magda?'

Charles kissed her heavy breasts. 'It would have ended, anyway. These things always do.'

Laura pushed him off. 'Don't be a bloody hypocrite! You had no intention of ending anything, until that godforsaken brat turned up. Look, I'm sorry, Charles, but . . .'

'It's not for ever, sweetheart. It's just a break, that's all, until things are better organized. I've got plans for Magda. Boarding school, for instance.'

'Frances won't agree to that. She's against boarding schools on principle, for girls. I've often argued with her over it. She thinks . . .'

'She may think rather differently, when it's in her own interests.'

'Charles, you're such a cynic. Just because your own principles are sandwiched between your interests, it doesn't mean that Frances' are as well.'

He removed Laura's groping fingers from his thigh. 'I'm sorry, darling, but I've already written to the Sacred Heart at Westborough.'

'A convent school? What a load of humbug, when you don't even believe in God.'

'I'm not the one who's going.'

'Well, is Magda religious?'

'I can't say I've noticed. But her mother's Roman Catholic.'

'Ah yes, I know the type – it's quite OK to screw, so long as you don't prevent the babies. I suppose that's how Magda arrived on the scene.'

'No.'

Laura laughed, slid her hand down Charles' leg again. 'Don't sulk, it doesn't suit you. Poor Frances – you knocked all the God out of her when she was a pious young thing carolling away in the church choir, and now you reinstate religion just to wrap your daughter in. She won't like it, Charles, you know. Frances agonizes over that sort of thing – indoctrination, freedom of choice. She's got quite a hefty conscience.'

Charles sat up on the bed. 'You seem inordinately fond of Frances at the moment. I can't say I've noticed it before.'

'Well, screwing your best friend's husband never does the friendship any good. Nor the screwing, really.'

'So you're complaining about my performance, are you, now?' Charles eased up to his feet, drifted to the window and stared out at the garden spread below. Two spaniels were copulating underneath a willow tree. Bitches didn't criticize their dogs.

'Oh Charlie, don't be so paranoid. You don't think I'd put up with you if you weren't a fantastic lover, do you? I've no complaints as far as bed's concerned. I just don't want to be turfed out of it.' Laura snaked her long legs farther down the covers, as if to stake her claim. 'You always suit yourself, Charles. When *I* had scruples about Frances, you kissed them all away with a load of balls about self-fulfilment and post-Freudian morality. But now you're wrestling with your own guilts, they . . .'

'No one said anything about guilt, Laura.'

'You hate the word, don't you? Guilt demeans a man, so you call it something else. Principle, convenience . . .'

Charles walked slowly to the wardrobe, where he had hung his clothes on hangers, whereas Laura's strewed the floor. He dragged on his white lawn shirt, immaculately laundered by Apex Valet Service. Perhaps he wouldn't miss her, after all. When they'd started their affair, she'd saved her astringency for the Labour Government, or her husband, instead of turning it on him. She had never nagged or grumbled in the early days, just thrown off her clothes and opened her legs, always ready for him, purring. He didn't have to waste an hour or more, coaxing her, preparing her, as he always did with Frances. There was no need to say he worshipped her, or that life was dust and ashes in her absence, or all the other crap his wife expected. Laura would have laughed, said, 'Shut up and get on with it,' and then come quickly and efficiently. Other women's orgasms were something of a nightmare. Half the time you suspected they were pretending, and the other half they didn't even have one, though they still made those wild noises, so that you feared you'd ruptured them, until you discovered they were only crawling along to ecstasy in bottom gear and were never going to make it. Even with Frances, there were doubts. She seemed to come – sometimes – and so she bloody ought to, after all the time he lavished on her, but there was no full stop, end of paragraph. It took him an age to get her there, and then twice as long returning her to base. Laura didn't need all that after-sales service; soothing and reassuring and saying, 'Yes, wasn't it wonderful,' but just rolled over and went to sleep, or got up and poured them both a Scotch.

But things were changing. Already Laura had started interfering and complaining. If she refused to lie low for the moment, well, there were always other Lauras. His home life was far too precious to be sacrificed. He tensed, felt her prowling hands again. She'd come up right behind him, and was trying to ease his Y-fronts down.

'No,' he said abruptly.

She knelt in front of him, rubbed her head against his thighs. She was teasing him now, kissing everything except his cock. It annoyed him, really, the way it always responded to her, even now, when they were meant to have finished, and he had an investors' meeting to attend in half an hour. He was stiff again and she was sucking him, at last, with as much relish as she sucked an ice cream cornet. Frances didn't like ice cream, and frankly, he understood the way she felt. With Laura he got the best of both worlds; she tongued him (to perfection), but didn't demand it back. Laura wasn't mercenary, except out of bed. Maybe some other guy sucked her off – certainly not her husband, who preferred horse-racing to sex – but he didn't want to know. So long as he didn't have to push his own face into some steamy, strange-smelling thicket, he wasn't complaining. Laura thrived on thickets, and he could always pay her in silver.

The silver chain he had bought her dangled against his thighs and distracted him from the wilder sensations between them. He let his head fall back against the wardrobe, gripped the wooden doors.

It was hard work, a second climax. Once, the sight of Laura's naked breasts had been enough to make him come, but even mistresses palled. He shut his eyes and summoned the new office secretary from her typewriter. Obediently, she slid out of her dress and took him in her mouth, her lips taking over from Laura's. It was a slow, arduous climax, demanding every ounce of concentration. But the more effort he put into it, the more gratifying it was – he found that with most things in life. His entire body was joining in. His head felt light and spinning, his hands and feet had disappeared. He was only a pillar, thrusting and thrusting, reduced to one wild stab of pleasure. He was no longer being gentle, or sparing the new secretary's small, shy virgin mouth, no longer cared if he choked her. She was only a slot, a socket, something he controlled. He slid almost out and felt the air cold for a second against his cock, then in again – warm and burning-wet. Out, then in; cold, then hot. His body was a force, a rhythm, reduced to six inches of sensation, yet those six inches bigger than the six-storey hotel.

He hadn't believed he could come another time – there was nothing left inside him – but Avril-from-the-office had turned nothing into a tidal wave. Her prim lips were dragging out of him the entire Atlantic Ocean. Everything he owned was in her mouth – his sperm, his guts, his money, power, spurting down her throat. He had grabbed her head, and his fingers were digging into her scalp, as he thrashed out the last dregs. Then, suddenly, there was only an empty bag between his legs and Laura's auburn hair twisted between his fingers, and his own breathing, dangerously loud.

Avril had tripped back to her IBM Executive. It was Laura who was licking her lips, as she knelt back on her heels. She was a swallower, thank God. After a climax a man felt foolish enough, without the woman spitting him out or washing him off. Laura made the whole thing acceptable, bridged the aching gap between ecstasy and self-disgust. She gulped down sperm in the no-nonsense way she ate oysters at Wheeler's; wiped her mouth, re-applied her lipstick, and ten minutes later, she'd be discussing the retail price index like an intelligent colleague.

It certainly made it easier. He could zip up his pants and return to more important things, cross sex off the list and put it away till next time. Frances expected full-scale action replays with commentary and flashbacks. You couldn't fit her in between a hectic morning with a bankrupt shipping company and a three o'clock investors' meeting. And she wasn't one for mouths.

'It's such a waste of sperm,' she objected, on one of the rare occasions they'd lifted their veto on oral sex. 'You can't have a baby that way.'

Christ! Those bloody babies, they got in the way of everything. That was the reason he'd first escaped to Laura. Sex for Laura was an end in itself, not a baby-manufacturing process. She didn't keep bleating on about embryos or oocytes, or litter the bed with charts and turn the whole performance into dreary paperwork. For Frances, he'd become a stud, a prize stallion to fill her belly, rather than her cunt. Thank God, it didn't fill. He didn't want another Magda.

He slumped down suddenly on the edge of the bath, had returned to the bathroom for the third shower of the lunch-break. Magda – beautiful and terrifying. A stranger made out of his body, with his own chromosomes staring out at him through her dark, angry eyes. What he felt for Magda must be somewhere near love, whatever love was. Yet the child had brought only misery – not only to himself, but now to his mistress and his wife. He had hurt all three women, and yet he loved them all, to some degree. Better not use the word 'love' – he couldn't define it, and he suspected words that resisted definition. Besides, how could you love someone and destroy her in your own mind, as he did with Frances? Ripped her to shreds and served them up to Laura as a peace-offering; criticized her maternal urges and then expected her to mother the child he'd had by another woman. He closed the bathroom door. He wanted the mirrors to himself, not half a dozen Lauras sneaking into them, fishing out stockings from under the bed, or stubbing out fag-ends in dirty coffee cups.

Frances folded her clothes and didn't smoke. Frances was neat, reliable and punctual, and he had made her so. One of the reasons he loved Frances (that forbidden word again) was that he had helped create her, built her up from small, promising beginnings, like his practice or his garden. All three of them were blooming, and it was credit to him. But now he had blighted Frances – with Magda. The whole tidy garden had been trampled on and bulldozed.

For years, Magda had been only a faded photo in his double-locked office drawer; a monthly cash transfer from his bank to Piroska's; expensive presents for birthday and Christmas, ordered by phone from Harrods and sent direct. Plus some small, sticky residue of guilt, pride and fear, locked away even more securely than the photograph. Piroska had hardly bothered him for months – the odd letter, the occasional gift, school reports duly forwarded and returned. He kept her now only as a standing order on his bank account.

Then everything had changed. Piroska sprouted teeth and claws, and a Hungarian lover with a good line in invective. He couldn't refute their joint accusations. Yes, he had neglected Magda, left Piroska to tarnish in a Streatham backstreet, while he shone centre-stage in Surrey. For a nightmare week, he wrestled with past and present, trying to square duty with expedience.

And then he saw his daughter. Eleven years had turned her from a faded photo into a woman with all her outlines sharp. He felt something dangerously like desire, struggled to change it into pride. This dazzling creature was his own flesh, his own achievement. He had fashioned her out of his body, and was experiencing the thrill of ownership. He wanted the world to bow down and acknowledge her as his. She was a priceless possession which must be restored and overhauled, moved into a more favourable environment. She would only lose value, rusting where she was.

The stumbling block was Frances. He couldn't force this new acquisition on his wife and expect her to groom and polish it, along with all the rest. For seven anguished days, he fought against Miklos, Piroska and his new paternal pride – and lost. He couldn't fail to lose, because fundamentally, he wanted Magda with him. It wasn't simply duty, though there was some of that as well. Piroska had done her stint for fifteen years, without much help from him. But there was a deep desire to be completed by a daughter, vindicated even. He wanted almost to flaunt his fertility in front of Frances. He hated her constant innuendos that it was his deficiencies which prevented her from conceiving, that he was somehow less than a man because he couldn't sire a child. Well, here was his child and his manhood, all in one. He tried to turn it to Frances' own advantage, to offer her the child she craved, without the mess and disruption of a baby. No broken nights, nor nursery tantrums, but a ready-made family, to meet her desperate need. After the first shock, she might even come to welcome it. She could graft her maternal urges on to Magda, and turn *fait accompli* into deep fulfilment.

It hadn't happened. There were still broken nights and nursery tantrums. One simple child had turned their whole existence into a battleground, with Frances as the casualty. Magda hadn't graced their life as he'd imagined, reclining elegantly beside him on the sofa, alluring and intelligent, listening to Beethoven sonatas when he could spare the time, or joining him for a few quick holes of golf. All she'd reclined on was his Queen Anne gate-leg table – cracked it right across – and used four-letter words when he switched off the wild din she claimed was music. It hurt to see his own flesh refusing to wash her hair or cut her nails, refusing even to turn into his daughter. And Frances making things still worse by constant recrimination and complaint.

He slapped the soap against his thighs, working it into a lather. He wished to God he could wash all women away – their shrill, insistent voices, their continual contrariness, their infuriating habit of serving up guilt with dinner, or grudges with sex. The soap slid away from him and skidded along the bottom of the bath. He grabbed it angrily, digging his nails into the bar, as if to pay it back. Even if he escaped from all his females, there'd be more within a week. He didn't want women – they were an expense and a distraction – yet still they wormed their way into his life, and some part of him clung on to them. Even when Magda was born, he'd been glad she was female – as glad as he could be in the circumstances.

He remembered his first glimpse of her in that sterile Streatham hospital. A dark head and a white blanket. And Piroska radiant and transformed, her breasts like soft white cheeses. Frances was right to want a baby – there was something miraculous about it. That was why she angered him by always dragging the subject under a spotlight, probing it, examining it, reminding him of his own inadequacies both as a father to Magda, and in failing to become one in their own relationship.

He stepped out of the shower and rubbed himself briskly with the largest yellow towel. No point agonizing. Too much

112

speculation was a danger and a waste of time. The relationships he'd planned as a refreshment from the pressures of his work were turning into further stresses, his personal life becoming as fraught as his professional one. He had to take a stand. Basically, it was a question of priorities. Each problem, each woman, must be assigned to its pigeon-hole, and dealt with in order of importance. Worry itself was profitless, and guilt a sign of moral bankruptcy. It was only females who confused him and sex which weakened him. In his study, or his office, he didn't give way to spineless introspection. He must return to the office and his own consummate control. If he left in five minutes, he'd have time to draft a report before the meeting. And the wasted lunch-hour could be repaid in midnight oil.

Laura trailed in, wearing one stocking and a bra, and slipped her hands underneath the yellow towel. He caught her wrists and held them.

'I've got exactly three minutes,' he said and kissed her throat. The kiss took just two seconds – he could spare those. They'd be the last she'd be getting for a while.

9

'Can't you spare me even a minute, Charles?'

'Well?' Charles was peering over his amplifier, adjusting the balance of the speakers, fiddling with the bass control.

'No, sitting down properly. I need to talk to you, want your full attention, for a change.'

'Why say a minute, then, when you mean half an hour?' Charles removed the Schoenberg and returned it to his alphabetical record storage cabinet, after Scarlatti and before Schütz.

'I'm sorry. I suppose I should have booked a formal appointment. But considering it's your daughter I want to talk about . . .'

'Must you keep referring to Magda as "my daughter"? Can't you use her name?'

'She *is* your daughter, isn't she? Or are you ashamed of the relationship?'

'No, I'm not ashamed. But you use it as a battle-cry, and a way of getting at me. I've told you I'm sorry, Frances, several times in fact. Do you expect me to go on prostrating myself for the rest of my life for springing Magda on you? Where is she, anyway?'

'At Viv's.'

'She's always at Viv's.'

'She likes it there.' And no wonder, Frances thought. Viv and David weren't always drawn up for battle, circling each other, torturing. Viv's house wasn't wrapped in cellophane and tissue paper, with 'keep off the grass' printed all over the garden. 'That's what I want to talk to you about. Magda's made friends with Bunty, so Viv suggested we try to get her into Highfield.'

'What's Highfield?' Charles hunted down a Satie which had strayed behind the Schoenbergs and filed it back in order.

'Charles, you know it's Bunty's school. You've even been there.'

'Christ, that bear garden!'

'It's not a bear garden, it's a perfectly respectable place.

114

Magda's not used to private schools, in any case. You told me yourself she'd been stuck in her local comprehensive . . .'

'Yes, and look what it's done to her.'

'I'm not suggesting she stays there. She couldn't, anyway. It's a dreadful journey, now she's moved from Streatham. But she'd have a ready-made friend if she went to school with Bunty. They could travel together. Viv could even pick them up.' Frances had it all worked out. If Magda couldn't live at Viv's, she could do the next best thing, stay there as much as possible, make bosom friends with Bunty, and keep out of the way.

'It's not a Catholic school.'

'Well surely you don't want Magda to be brought up a Catholic, do you?'

'She is a Catholic, Frances.'

'But you hate Catholicism. You spent the first few years of our marriage forcing your atheism down my throat. I suppose that was just a reaction to being caught out by a religious fanatic who wouldn't use the Pill.'

Frances had never spoken to Charles like that before. She could hear her own voice, harsh and hectoring. It was usually a soft silk voice, but Magda seemed to have turned her into some bristling, prickly thing; released some cruelty in her, which she never knew existed. Even in the matter of the school, she was being selfish and hypocritical, considering her own peace and privacy, rather than Magda's happiness. Yet the child could be happy at Highfield. It was a decent school, not too demanding, and she would start with the advantage of a friend in her own year. If Charles were really worried about religion (and it seemed preposterous), then Magda could attend catechism class with Bunty. That would leave Sunday mornings Magda-free as well, maybe all day, if Viv suggested lunch. Sunday lunch at Viv's house had been known to last until five.

She knew what Charles wanted – to send Magda to St Helier's, a small private school on the Green. They had no canteen facilities, so Magda would be home for lunch; the school holidays were longer there, and they had every Wednesday off. Magda would be far too close to home. She could almost see the convent from the window of her bedroom, whereas Highfield was two miles away. If Magda went to St Helier's, she'd soon look down on the Highfield girls, and the friendship with Bunty would swiftly peter out. Somehow, she couldn't handle Magda on her own, must have Viv as ally.

Charles sat down, at last, but now he was reorganizing his briefcase, setting out the papers in neat piles on the table, pausing a moment over a letter or memorandum, and then relegating it to the appropriate section. She never had his full attention, always had to share him with books, or music, or paperwork. Yet wasn't she the same herself – with Magda – grudging the child her undivided attention? Both she and Charles tried to squeeze caring and conversation in among the chores.

Charles stowed a stray sheet of paper into a loose-leaf file, and placed it at the far end of the table. 'I've more or less decided on boarding school for Magda.'

'Boarding school! But you don't believe in them for girls.'

'It's you that don't believe in them, my darling. You have an amazing habit of kidnapping my rubber stamp for all your own views. But never mind. I'm sending her for your sake. It's the obvious solution. She'll get a first-rate education and you'll only have to see her in the holidays.'

'It's not that I don't want her, Charles . . .'

Charles snapped his briefcase shut. 'Frances, for God's sake, be honest.'

How could she be honest? Tell her husband that she wished his daughter dead. No, no, not dead, that was truly wicked. Just negated; someone who had never been; a bad dream she could wake up from, and find that Charles was still her exclusive property, no Magda, no Piroska. And yet wasn't it just as wicked to wish a child away? A sort of late abortion? She had never believed in abortion, nor in boarding schools. So how could she shatter her life principles on the stony rock of one oppressive child? Charles didn't seem to find it difficult.

'She'll be away more than half the year as a boarder. And even in the holidays, they take them on school trips – skiing in the Alps, or pilgrimages to Rome.'

Frances fiddled with a paperclip. It was tempting, certainly. They could choose a school deep in the country, too remote for frequent visiting, wipe Magda out from September to Christmas. Or could they? Did you forget the foetus you flushed down the

116

lavatory? However many miles they put between them, Magda would still be there, still alive, still suffering.

'Yes, but Charles, she's just had one big upheaval in her life, losing her mother and coming to live here. If we pack her off again before she's even . . .'

'No one's packing her off anywhere, Frances. Don't distort everything. I've spent a lot of time and trouble on the problem, and I've found a very decent convent school. The nuns are kind, but strict. Magda needs that. She's had no discipline at all.'

And whose fault was that? Frances bit back the remark. Her husband looked irritable enough. He had picked up a bronze sculpture, a small figure of a girl, and appeared to be trying to wrench its head off. How, in all conscience, could he suggest a convent school? He had drilled into her long ago the dangers of indoctrination. An indoctrinated Magda might be easier, of course. The nuns could make her docile and obedient, force her out of jeans into stern blue gymslips. Break her spirit, break her heart.

Charles traced a finger along the bowed bronze legs. 'She'll pick up some accomplishments at a convent – embroidery, piano lessons, skills they don't bother with at Highfield.'

'Charles, you can't be serious. Magda wouldn't do embroidery!' He must be blind to the reality of his own daughter. Did he see her as he wanted her to be, instead of the angry, slouching rebel who had actually arrived? No, that wasn't fair. Magda had another, sunnier side, the one she showed at Viv's. She found her voice at Viv's, even laughed, occasionally; helped with the children. But back with them, she froze again, returned to the sullen waxwork who had been moulded in mid-scowl.

Frances jabbed the paperclip, hard, into her palm. She'd tried, for heaven's sake; had the whole studio redecorated, so that Magda would have a nicer room. She'd replaced the Victorian patchwork with an easy-care quilt, and teamed it with frilled curtains in a stylish pattern of blue and purple cornflowers. She'd adapted the scheme from a picture in *Homes and Gardens* and persuaded Reggie, their elderly tame painter, to complete it in just a week. She had tried to keep it a secret from Magda, which wasn't easy with the smell of paint and Reggie underfoot, but Magda was often round at Viv's, or deafening herself with Radio Caterwaul at the very top of the house.

On Saturday, the room was completed. She had added the last touches: a row of children's classics on the new bookshelves, a bunch of real cornflowers from the garden, a quilted nightdress-case she had made herself. The surprise was planned for after dinner. Magda had spent the whole of roast lamb and apple pie defying them. She had eaten the pie with her fingers and then wiped them on the tablecloth. She refused to remove the badge on her shirt which said 'FUCK OFF, I'M A JUNKIE'. She informed Charles he was a Nazi, and damned Richmond as a dump. She herself had tried to keep the peace; she didn't want the evening spoilt. They had trooped upstairs together, stopped outside the studio. The room looked delicate and charming, its hazy blues and mauves contrasting with the dazzling white of the fluffy goatskin rug.

'It's yours,' she'd said to Magda. 'Your very own room. You can have your friends here, play your records. We've even got a really special desk for your homework.'

The windows were wide open to dilute the smell of paint. An oleander bush pushed against the panes, scattering fragrant blossoms on the sill. The walls matched the curtains in a tapestry of rambling flowers. The quilt was plain blue terylene, frilled round the edges, and there were cushions of the same material on the graceful bedroom chair. Charles had chosen the pictures carefully – the John Pipers were too precious for a child – but he had replaced them with some Edward Bawden watercolours, tranquil landscapes in muted, low-key colours. The desk was his own, a Regency jewel, which she'd harmonized with the modern furnishings.

'Well?' she'd said, smiling. They were still outside, all three of them, as if the room were too immaculate to enter. She and Charles were looking at Magda, waiting for her reaction. They knew she wouldn't rave, but . . .

'It *stinks!*' the girl had shouted, and rushed up to her old room, muttering obscenities about stupid fucking frills and poncy flowers.

On the Sunday, Charles had summoned Magda to his study and dealt sternly with the 'fuckings'. He then forced her to move in among the cornflowers and the terylene; explained how much

118

the room had cost, in terms of time and trouble. Magda had said nothing, just jabbed her foot against his desk.

She obeyed that evening, sullenly, dumping all her possessions on the floor, a tangled mess of shoes, jeans, records, junk. She tacked punk posters over the gilt-framed Bawden prints, stuffed the cushions under the bed, flung the nightdress-case in the dirty linen basket. Then she put her wildest, rowdiest rock group on the stereo and played it at full blast, over and over, long past midnight. When Frances knocked, she didn't even answer, just turned it up louder still. At three A.M., the house was vibrating with drums and screaming with electric guitars. Frances lay alone in bed, staring up at the quaking ceiling and the wincing chandelier, torn between fear, fury and exhaustion. Charles had escaped, caught the late-night plane to Paris for an emergency board meeting of a French property developer.

When he returned, the stereo was broken, and Magda and the rock group had fled to Viv's.

'I've written to the nuns already,' he was saying. 'They've sent a prospectus. The fees are very reasonable. They've got lovely grounds, even a trout stream and a lake. I really think it's the best thing in the circumstances.'

Frances took an apple from the fruit dish and laid her cheek against its cold green skin. Boarding school would mean quiet uninterrupted nights, tidy rooms, well-mannered meals . . . She bit into the apple with sharp teeth. 'We can't send her, Charles. I know we can't. She'd hate it.' Her friend Theresa had run away from a convent boarding school when she was only seven. And then been expelled at seventeen The only men she'd ever seen in the hundred years between were an octogenarian gardener and a Polish priest with a private line to Hell. They'd taught her that dancing was dangerous and Protestants were damned, and she'd spent much of her childhood praying fervently for her favourite Auntie Annie, who was a C. of E. ballroom-dancing teacher.

Oh, yes, it would be idyllic to have the house to themselves again, to springclean Magda off the premises and return to their civilized, sound-proofed way of life. But to sacrifice a child for your own peace and privacy . . . Theresa had told her how she'd cried every night with earache, and the nuns had instructed her to welcome the pain, and offer up her little agonies for the Holy Souls in Purgatory. They'd even had to keep a Penance notebook, a record of all their penances and privations, so they could tot up how many souls they'd saved. It sounded like something out of Charles' system, except Charles didn't believe in gratuitous suffering. He suffered only in the cause of efficiency and order, or of Britain's financial solvency.

'Look, Charles, I'm sorry if I've been too hard on Magda. But don't send her away. She's suffered enough.'

She was surprised by her own words. Here was a chance to put half of England between herself and Magda, and she was turning it down, refusing the very thing she'd wanted since the child first set foot inside the house. It wasn't just a prissy desire to live up to her principles, though that was there as well. She did oppose boarding schools and religious education, and everybody knew it. Even if she'd borrowed her beliefs from Charles to start with, they were firmly grafted in her own mind now. But there were deeper feelings, too – irrational but important ones. She yearned for a child and Magda had arrived. Only a mockery of the child she wanted, a bane, not a blessing, but perhaps also an initiation, or a trial. The way she treated Magda might determine the fate of her own baby, its very existence, even. Charles would scoff at such superstitious *non sequiturs*. She almost scoffed herself. But some strange inner voice kept repeating, 'Would you send your own child away?' The answer was an unequivocal no. So, how could she send Magda?

Her friends would know she'd only done it to get rid of her. Laura would mock, and Viv would agonize. Ned would fight a duel with Reverend Mother. But why bring him into it? He wasn't even a friend, and there were enough complications without invoking the bolshie views of a half-baked anarchist. Yet Ned was the only one who'd really understand those inner promptings, those voices which urged, 'Love, don't destroy.'

But she couldn't love. There was only a gaping hole where that emotion should have been. Perhaps it would be kinder to send Magda away, than keep her in a house without affection. Maybe she was wrong about the nuns, and they knew more about love than she did. She felt pulled in all directions. Not only inner voices, but Charles, Laura, Viv, Ned, all nagging to be heard.

'Look, Charles, I think we ought to discuss it further. It's a very big decision.'

'It's a very simple decision, if only you'd keep emotions out of it.' Charles was replacing the contents of his briefcase now, working from the right-hand pile in towards the left. She had no idea what he was really thinking. He knew Piroska didn't want their child at boarding school and that Magda herself had no desire to go. Was it easy for him to override all three of them? Perhaps he realized that it would be to their advantage, in the long run. Charles was often maddeningly correct in his decisions.

He winced suddenly, as the front door slammed and footsteps hammered down the hall.

'Mrs Parry Jones!' It was Bunty, in muddy jeans and her brother's climbing boots, with something cradled in her arms.

'Take those ... clodhoppers off in here, please.' Charles frowned at the marks on his silk Kashan carpet. Bunty pulled off the boots without undoing them, and placed her bundle gently on the floor. It got up and shook itself, standing on four uncertain legs.

'Isn't he *lovely*?' Bunty crowed. 'Magda found him in the pond. Someone tried to drown him, the stinker! I'd drown *him*, if I could catch him.'

Chocolate-brown eyes stared into ice-blue laser ones, six feet higher up. The puppy dropped his first. His tail had also dropped.

'Kindly remove that creature from my drawing-room.' Charles' voice had turned a ball of fur into a ravening lion.

'W ... where's Magda?' stumbled Frances, praying that the puppy wouldn't relieve itself on Charles' precious Persian rug.

'Waiting in the garden. She didn't dare ask you. Well, you wouldn't mind, would you? I mean, he's Magda's dog already. She rescued him, you see. He's only small. I don't think he'll grow much more. You can tell by the legs.'

Frances shut her eyes. Perhaps the small, bedraggled, trembling wretch would have disappeared when she opened them again. It hadn't.

Charles was reinforced concrete towering over a small, pink Bunty made of plasticine. She tried to slip between them.

'Charles dear, it's not Bunty's fault. Let's take the puppy into the kitchen, shall we? And make some tea.'

121

'We've just had tea.'

'Bunty and Magda haven't, darling.'

The puppy was exploring Charles' trouser-leg. Charles almost kicked it off and put half a dozen Persian-carpet dragons between the two of them. 'I've got some reports to finish for Oppenheimer. I'll be in the study if you need me.' He was already halfway through the door. 'And I want that animal removed.'

Charles had a talent for escaping. Frances had never really noticed it before Magda arrived. His daughter had obviously inherited the same characteristic.

'Magda should have asked me herself, Bunty. It's no good running away from things.' She shuddered at her hypocrisy. Given the chance, she'd run away from things herself – other people's children, for example.

Bunty's pink-rubber face was screwed up in supplication, pale eyes fixed on Frances, like another dog. 'She was afraid you'd say no. You won't, though, will you? She's never had a pet, you see, never in her life. Her mother went out to work, and anyway, she had asthma, so Magda wasn't even allowed to keep a cat.'

So, Bunty knew the whole story, did she? A latch-key mother with asthma didn't sound too cheerful, but none the less she was forced to harden her own heart. 'I'm sorry, Bunty, but I shall have to say no.' Or rather Charles would. Charles always avoided animals, and disturbances, and . . .

'But *why*? He won't be any trouble. Magda will look after him.'

No trouble. A boisterous smelly dog shedding its white hairs on Charles' dark sombre life, chewing up his carefully constructed barriers, peeing on his principles, barking at his platitudes, scratching up his whole perfect system.

'Look, Bunty dear, my husband simply prefers not to have animals in the house, that's all.'

'But what about Magda? She lives here as well, doesn't she? Why can't *she* have a pet? Mum said she could adopt one of ours. But it's not the same, is it, not like having one of your own?'

'No, it's not the same.'

The puppy was shivering on the cold kitchen tiles. Bunty took off her jumper and wrapped him in it. Frances walked over to the stove. 'I'll warm some milk for him.'

'Oh, thank you, Mrs Parry Jones.' Bunty and the puppy were crushed against her chest in a hug. 'You'll let Magda keep him, then? I *knew* you would. I told Magda you would. Shall we call her in?'

Frances longed to say yes. What was the point of a home, if nothing was allowed to live in it? And yet, there was something safe about rules and prohibitions. Elegance and order wrapped you in a sound-proof, chaos-proof cocoon. Magda had already ripped it open and let in a dangerous cacophony of sounds. If she went any further, they'd soon be overrun. First a drowned rat of a puppy, then kittens, snakes, ponies, boyfriends, gangs. Their house wasn't built to stand it; she and Charles weren't programmed to withstand an invasion on that scale.

Even when Magda brought her Streatham friends back, she felt threatened, a prisoner in her own home, confined to her study, while Magda's rude rebellious cohorts terrorized the house. One of them had struck a match against the Bechstein and another ate lunch in her vest.

There was some small serpent-trail of envy mixed in among the fear. She had never been allowed Magda's freedom, to come and go as she pleased, to have cash on demand for anything that caught her eye, to shrug her shoulders at every social nicety. It had always been 'Money doesn't grow on trees, Frances', 'Take the cake nearest to you, Frances', 'When I was your age, I didn't . . .' Yet mothers only did things for your own good. Rubbish! Mothers could hate and break and envy and destroy. Mothers turned puppies into principles, and simple requests into catastrophes.

She moistened a sponge with warm water and cleaned the puppy's coat. He whimpered, shut his eyes. He was only a baby, really. Just one, small, harmless animal – would it really be so unendurable? She fondled his ears with her free hand and went on dabbing his fur, until it showed up white, with two brown patches.

'He's not exactly a beauty, is he?' She stared at the spindly legs, the dumpy little body, the ears like small pink flaps.

'No, but he's sweet, isn't he, Mrs Parry Jones? You must admit he's sweet.'

'All right, he's sweet. If you insist.' She poured milk into a saucepan and heated it gently. She'd never had a pet herself.

Her mother regarded all animals as dirty or dangerous, and her father was the sort of man who instantly reported any dog he saw fouling the pavement. At the age of eight, she'd adopted the butcher's dog, a white bull terrier which dribbled. She'd sneaked into the butcher's shop every day, after school, and sat in the sawdust feeding him her ration of jelly babies. Her father had discovered her one Thursday afternoon and locked her in her room until the morning. Since then, she'd avoided dogs.

Perhaps she could start again. Why repeat the old restrictions, or say no to Magda because she'd been refused herself? Her father was only a plot now, a square of turf and a headstone. The puppy was alive.

'Do you know if he's house-trained, Bunty?'

'Oh, yes, I'm sure he is. And even if he's not, he won't take long to learn. He's very intelligent, you know. Does that mean you're going to let Magda keep him?'

'Don't rush me, Bunty.' It was so hard to do anything impulsive. Dogs were dirty, and a tie – everybody said so. On the other hand, they were also good companions. The puppy would be company when Charles was away. And they could always send him to dog-training classes, or restrict him to the kitchen.

Bunty's soggy features wrung themselves into an expression of rapture. 'Oh, please say yes. *Please.*'

Frances continued weighing pros and cons. They might even enjoy a dog. They could drive over to Acton and introduce him to Rilke. Ned would find a crazy name for him. Though why did Ned keep sneaking into things? He'd scoff at all her agonizing, take in half a dozen dogs. 'Well, all right, maybe . . .'

'Oh, *thank* you!' Bunty almost capsized her with the force of her hug. 'Magda will be over the moon! Here, hold the puppy and I'll go and get her in.'

The small furry body was trembling in her arms. Frances felt a strange sense of power. She could choose life or death for a dog, life or death for Magda.

Magda shuffled in, looking wary and embarrassed. The bottoms of her jeans were soaked and there was a three-cornered rent in her new corduroy jacket. She had trailed mud and water across the shining kitchen floor. There was something about the very sight of her which rankled. It always happened. So long as Magda wasn't there, she could revel in good resolutions and rapprochements. But as soon as Magda slouched on to the scene, shoulders hunched and hair defiant, her precious peace was shattered. She bundled the dog into Magda's arms and picked up the floor-cloth, stabbing at the footprints with unnecessary force. Magda watched her, jeering almost, kicking her muddy shoes against the table.

'Thanks for the puppy,' she growled.

Why couldn't she speak properly, and sit up straight, and cut her hair? 'Look, I haven't said you can have it, yet . . .' Frances squeezed the cloth into the bucket, as if she were wringing someone's neck. She knew she was being petty and unreasonable. But Magda never made it easy. The child almost flung her youth at her, flaunted her idleness, her foreignness, her dishevelled good looks. Everything about her screamed lies, infidelity, Piroska. She'd made enormous efforts, planned treats and expeditions, cosy little talks together, home-made fudge, visits to the Planetarium. But the minute she melted the butter, or set out in the car, the stars blacked out or the mixture burned. It was as if she and Magda were two chemicals which would not, could not fuse, but only consume each other or explode. She must have been crazy, refusing boarding school. Charles was right – it was the only possible solution.

'Bunty just told me you said yes. Well, didn't you?'

Magda's sullen whine went through her like a knife. She heard herself answering in the same harsh, grudging tones. 'There's your father to consider. We haven't asked Charles.' Your father, your father . . . Why was she always fathering and daughtering, when both words cut her into pieces?

Magda was gripping the puppy too tight, digging her nails into its skin. 'I don't care what he says. He can't say no, in any case. The puppy's mine. I rescued him. He'd have drowned without me. I've already got a name for him. So, fuck!'

Bunty's pale eyes almost disappeared in the worried folds of plasticine. 'Ssshh, Magda, don't be stupid. You'll only ruin things. Mrs Parry Jones was saying yes in any case.'

Frances had finished the floor and was slapping at the walls. They weren't even dirty. 'Oh no, I wasn't . . .'

Magda marched to the door, the dog clutched against her chest. 'Frances never says yes to anything. She's the one who always makes a fuss and then blames other people. If she didn't live here, I bet Charles would let me have a puppy. *And* lots of other things. He's my father, isn't he? And a father's more important than a stupid, rotten husband.'

Frances eased up to her feet and turned the gas out under the milk, which was almost boiling over. She kept her own voice down to simmering point. 'Well, I suggest you ask your father, then. He's in his study. And leave the puppy here, please.' She didn't add 'change your shoes', just watched the large, wet footprints writing their rude message on the floor; jumped when the study door slammed.

Five minutes later, the front door slammed as well. Bunty and the puppy cowered. 'Your husband said no,' Bunty whispered dully.

It wasn't a question and Frances didn't answer it. Bunty scooped up the creature from the corner where Magda had almost hurled him, and stood uncertainly at the door. 'I'll take him home, shall I? Mum won't mind. Then, if you change your mind . . .'

'I'm afraid we shan't,' said Frances, glancing at the child. Bunty was plain, like the puppy, dumpy and graceless, with the same pinkish eyes and short legs. 'I'm sorry,' she added, feeling her usual racking mixture of guilt, misery and failure. If only Bunty hadn't sprung it on her. Even Charles might have agreed to a dog, if she'd primed him first, inspected the kennels in the area, selected a decent specimen with a health certificate and a proper pedigree. And then drawn up a set of rules, limiting its freedom. 'Look,' she said desperately, 'don't just run away like that. Have a cup of tea before you go. Or I've got some cherry cake . . .'

'No, thank you, Mrs Parry Jones.' Bunty's voice was toneless. 'I ought to be with Magda.'

Frances drank the tea herself, slumped at the kitchen table. Since Magda arrived, she'd wasted endless time simply recovering from the arguments, upheavals. How could just one extra person cause so much aggravation? Her stomach felt curdled, as if she had mixed lemon juice with milk. There were so many layers of feeling, including wallowing self-pity, but also pity for Magda, pity for the trembling dog. But simple gestures of compassion could misfire. You took in a harmless puppy, and it grew into a snarling, thieving brute; you mothered a child and became a monster overnight. Magda was making her doubt herself in every smallest thing, undermining her values, wrecking her principles. She'd always assumed she could love a child. It was the next thing you did after setting up a home and writing fashion hand-outs. But love was proving screamingly impossible. Maybe it was simpler with your own child, but how could you tell? It had been easy in the past to condemn baby-batterers, or shudder when you read reports on cruelty to children. But if your baby was a Magda in miniature . . .

She abandoned her tea and walked upstairs. The lion was sitting on her bed, still grinning. 'Ned,' she whispered miserably. She'd christened it Ned – the first name she'd thought of, really. She cradled it in her arms like a baby. Toys were so much easier, didn't make puddles or noises, or wreck the house or deflower the garden, or grow up. Dogs did all those things, and so did babies. Yet she couldn't give up trying to have a baby. Her life was constructed now round a sacred fertility rite. She dared not halt the whole complicated process, the self-important visits to the gynaecologist, the special calendar, the sense of mission. She dared not fail. Magda had become almost part of the process, the precursor for her own child. She knew somehow that she would have her baby, when she had come safely through the storm and fire of Magda.

She held the lion against her shoulder and walked with it to Magda's room. Even with junk on the floor and punk on the walls, it still looked elegant. Too elegant. She arranged the lion in the centre of the bed, tail curled around its body. She threw out the dead flowers and replaced them with a fresh bunch from the garden – cheerful easy flowers: roses, daisies, marigolds. She brought up the tin of cherry cake and put it on the dressing-table, with a bowl of shiny apples. The room still looked wrong – all frills, all substitutes. The kid wanted a flesh and blood animal, a real, red-blooded dog, not a stuffed, synthetic toy and a vase of flowers which would die within the week.

She could have said yes to the puppy. Too easy to blame Charles, when he'd only underlined her own refusal. Fundamentally, it had been a choice between Magda's happiness and her own convenience. No, not just convenience – safety, order, discipline, all the things she needed for her own happiness, even her survival. It was frightening to realize her *joie de vivre* depended on a set of rules, a wire cage of restrictions. She had nothing to give Magda, nothing solid, nothing real. She couldn't even hug her. Every time she tried, some new barrier reared itself between them and turned her arms to wood.

She stood rigid in the centre of the room. One rose had already dropped its petals on the bedside table. Even the lion looked older. She paused by the bed to stroke its curly mane. 'Tell her I . . .'

She stopped. Pointless and ridiculous, talking to dumb animals.

10

That evening, Charles took her out to dinner, on her own. Magda had not returned. They studiously avoided the subject of pets; combining tolerable scampi and indifferent chocolate mousse with careful observations on the shadow cabinet's regional funding policy and the Richmond redevelopment scheme. Charles drained his port.

'Fancy a stroll by the river?'

'Well, yes, but haven't you got to work?'

'Not tonight. It's your evening. I wanted to spend it with you, darling. To – er – thank you . . .'

'What for?'

'For having Magda. You've done a lot for her. And I know it isn't easy.'

She didn't answer, seemed to have lost her usual easy habit of responding to Charles. Resentment had clogged it, like lumps in a cream sauce.

The evening was close, almost stifling. Small, swollen clouds were building up across the river, and a greenish light oozed its way between sky and water. A cloud of gnats buzzed above their heads. They walked in silence along the crumbling path, stepping gingerly around the puddles. In the early months of their marriage, they had walked the same path, but Charles had held her hand then, and stopped at every bench to kiss her, in the dark. It was light now, a blazing summer evening, and people were only dozing on the benches or reading newspapers which shrieked of strikes, inflation. They wandered on to where the river widened and the trees grew closer, trailing their branches in the water and staring at their own reflections. Charles stopped and took her hand, looked furtively around, to make sure no one was watching. 'I love you, Frances. You know that, don't you?'

She nodded.

'Don't let things be different.'

She shook her head, watched his neat, imperious eyebrows

draw down across his steel-blue eyes in a tense and wary frown. His brows were neither shaggy nor straggling, yet somehow they managed to dominate his face. Even when she was angry with him, she could still admire the way he was put together; each of his features carefully selected from Harrods and then set in place by a design consultant. Perhaps he was right – things needn't be different. Magda wouldn't stay with them for ever. They still had their own life, apart from Magda; perhaps even their own baby.

A couple strolled by, the young bearded man pushing a pram. Charles would never be a pram-pusher, but at least he could try to be a father. He'd done it once, for God's sake. But that was more than fifteen years ago, and with a Hungarian Earth Mother. Perhaps his sperm was tired now, worn out after years of jet-lag and tax conundrums. Or maybe she herself was too small, too cold, too old, and sperm only stirred themselves for hot Hungarian wombs.

But at least they could go on trying. It was absurd to swallow a fertility drug and then fail to be fertilized. How animal the whole thing sounded, except that animals got on with it, without all this fuss and bother. For them, it was becoming something of a chore. They hadn't even slept together since Magda had arrived. She hadn't wanted to, felt Charles was somehow polluted and defiled. Or maybe it was just a side effect of the Clomid. That would be ironical – to turn you off the sex you needed to conceive. She was taking her second month's dose now, and it made her feel nauseous, as if she were already pregnant.

Charles, too, had shown little inclination. Maybe it was guilt, or overwork. And yet he needed sex as a sort of safety valve, an indoor rugger match. She'd noticed herself how it sucked the aggression out of him and neutralized the electric shocks between them. Now it was all electricity. She must somehow switch it off and lure him back into the double bed.

She coaxed him over to a bench and put her arm around his shoulders. 'You're right, Charles, we can't let Magda ruin everything. There's still us.'

He removed the arm, so she took his hand instead. 'That's important,' she insisted. She could hear a magpie squawking at the top of a hawthorn bush, laughing at them almost. 'Let's go home and . . .' She didn't say it, just made a gesture with her hands against his body. It wasn't the vital middle of the month yet, but she must get him back into practice.

'What, now?' The magpie screeched with laughter.

'Yes, now.' She inched her fingers up his forearm, kept them stroking up and down.

Charles frowned. 'But supposing Magda's back? I know it sounds stupid, but I feel I can't perform if she's around.'

'She won't be,' whispered Frances.

She wasn't. But the front door had been left wide open, and a new set of muddy footprints serpented the hall. Charles strode up the stairs to the studio and knocked loudly on the door. 'Magda?'

No answer. Frances could hear her watch ticking almost apologetically in the silence, a tiny, golden sound.

Charles wrenched open the door. The bed was a heap of tangled blankets and dirty clothes. The exquisite Bawden watercolours had been taken down and flung on the floor, glass smashed and frames broken. The flowers were decapitated, lying in a pool of water on the stained and sodden desk. The lion was hanging upside down, its tail caught in the wardrobe door. And all over the new cornflower walls was written, in a bleeding crimson lipstick, 'I HATE YOU. I HATE YOU. I HATE YOU.'

Charles closed the door again, quietly and deliberately, as if trying not to wake a baby. Frances listened to her watch, tried to make her mind a blank. Charles took her arm and led her downstairs. He poured them both a brandy in the Victorian smoked glass goblets. Neither spoke. Charles took a sheet of headed paper from the bureau and uncapped his pen.

'I'm writing to the nuns at Westborough,' he said. 'Accepting their offer of a place. After that, we'll . . .' He leaned over, touched her face, ran a finger down across her breast.

'Go away,' she snapped, suddenly, irrationally. 'Go away. GO AWAY!'

11

Hate you, hate you, hate you, pounded the hammer in Magda's head. Three A.M. and still wide awake. Hated cats, hated puppies, hated Bunty's stupid snoring. Bunty was sprawled beside her on the bed, wheezing through enlarged adenoids. Two cats were curled together at the bottom of the eiderdown, the new white puppy snuffling in a laundry basket. Hate you, hate you, hate you, shrieked the blue flowered walls, back on Richmond Green. How would she ever get it off? Lipstick was indelible, like hate. Perhaps they'd forgive her, if she offered to pay, but she hadn't any money except Charles' allowance and that was meant for 'good' (boring) books and visits to the theatre. She hated the theatre. Frances had taken her to some stupid thing, where everyone spoke in poetry and you couldn't get ice creams. Frances had skin like the inside of a shell. She'd like to break the shell. Her own skin was coarser and there were blackheads round her nose. It would be nice to look like Frances. Frances didn't have dark hairs on her legs. She pulled up her jeans and peered at them. Disgusting. She hated hairs. That Miklos man had hairs all over him, even on his thumbs. She hated him, too. The way her mother called him '*szivecskem*' and used that stupid baby voice for him and kept ruffling his repulsive greasy hair. And then wasted all the money buying *beigli* for him, when they made do with plain bread and butter.

She turned over on her front. She was still fully dressed and the buckle of her belt dug into her stomach. She tore the belt off, flung it on the floor. She didn't believe all that crap about Grandma dying. 'We're only going to Hungary for the funeral.' Fancy talking about a funeral when someone wasn't even dead! Grandma wasn't old enough to die. She'd seen pictures of her, a small fuzzy lady who always looked out of focus and had a second set of china teeth for Sundays. People didn't go to Budapest for funerals. They went because some hairy Jew had a *lakás* there, two measly rooms in some rotten little alley. He was going to

132

nab her mother and shut her up in it, smarm his hairy hands all over her. His breath stank of pickled walnuts and he wore hideous shiny shirts. 'We'll send for you,' he'd said, in that flabby foreign voice. 'Later. We mustn't interrupt your English education.' It was a stinking lie. Of course he wouldn't send for her. And her education had been interrupted. She'd liked her old school. They had proper English sausages for dinner, not Hungarian *szalámi* which was crammed with bits of fat. And they'd just started judo and painting in oils.

Charles had taken her away, just like that, in the middle of her syllabus. He hadn't even asked. No one asked her anything – not the important things. 'Would you like your bacon fried or grilled, Magda?' 'How many of Shakespeare's plays have you read?' Oh yeah, they asked her junk like that all day long. But not whether she wanted to go to sodding Richmond Green instead of Hungary, or be ripped away from all her classmates, or share her mother with an odious little Yid. They hadn't even asked her whether she wanted fucking cornflowers on her walls. Lipstick-covered cornflowers. She wished she hadn't done it. Frances had searched through twenty sample books before she chose the flowers. Well, if the stupid bitch wanted to waste her time . . .

Frances wasn't stupid. She was fucking clever, spouted stuff out of encyclopaedias, and closed her eyes and went all trancey when she played the piano. Her own ma couldn't even play scales – or read French novels and German newspapers, and win at chess and golf and tennis and bridge, and all those other frightening Frances things. Charles was worse. He ruined mealtimes poking long boring words around his dinner plate, like those prissy wets on Radio 3 he took to the toilet with him. And if she didn't join in, he asked what was the matter, didn't she care about environmental thingummyjig, or something-something-something in the blah, blah, blah, blah . . .

It was easier with Frances on her own. Frances even smiled, sometimes, when Charles wasn't there, and they had fish and chips and ketchup in the kitchen, instead of sole Véronique off the poncy patterned plates. And Frances had given her a proper tape recorder, one that really worked, with fifteen blank cassettes and a leather storage box.

Fuck the lipstick! You couldn't ruin walls after fifteen blank cassettes. Perhaps bleach would shift it, or Vim, or nail varnish remover. At least she'd better try. But supposing all the flowers came off as well? If only she knew where Reggie lived, she could ask him for a piece of extra wallpaper to cover up the walls. But Reggie didn't like her. He'd tried to call her 'Missy' and she'd sworn at him.

Fuck, fuck, fuck – they hated her to use that word. The muscle on Charles' face twitched in and out when she said it and he looked like a goldfish. She knew what it meant. Grown-ups made such a fuss about it, but it was only what dogs did. Or what Miklos did with her mother all the time. Grown-ups all lied, anyway. Even her mother lied. 'We'll write to you every day, dear.' And she'd had two measly postcards. 'We'll send for you to come and join us.' Oh yeah, in a million years when she was dead and her mother had a dozen disgusting black hairy babies, all identical to Miklos.

Frances lied, too. 'You know I'm very fond of you, don't you, Magda?' Like hell she was! OK, Frances was decent to her sometimes, like when she was sick after the oysters. Frances cleaned it all up and sat with her for hours afterwards and put smelly stuff on her forehead. But she wouldn't be nice now – not after the lipstick. Frances would hate her now. She was sorry, in a way; wanted Frances to like her, call her 'Pootle' like Viv did with Rupert. Frances was special. You had to be someone, before she bothered with you.

Sometimes she made brandy snaps with real cream in the middle, then it was OK, or showed you her collection of old silver charms and told you where each separate one had come from, then you felt almost safe, but the very next minute she'd turn on you and do her nut about a speck of dust on the mantelpiece, or why hadn't you used a fork to eat your pudding.

She made such a fuss about her house. No one was allowed even to breathe in it. There were so many bloody things, you could hardly move. In their own flat, back in Streatham, they'd only had sensible stuff, beds and chairs and things, but Charles and Frances had freezers and dishwashers and microwave ovens and electronic tumble-driers and rôtisseries and charcoal grills. And they didn't have just one of everything, but two. Two cars, two pianos, two tellies, two stereos, two bathrooms, and three toilets, four radios, and fifteen bloody clocks. She'd counted the clocks. They all belonged to Charles – he collected them. Fifteen clocks, and he wouldn't agree to one piddling puppy.

Charles' study was so crammed with gear, it was like a shop. He had three pocket calculators and a mini computer, and a quartz digital watch with an alarm and a calendar, and a video tape recorder and a . . . The whole house was one sodding great machine, cold and shiny, and full of faceless factory inspectors, like that dump her mother worked in, where you had to wear a sterile uniform and even your hair was shoved into a net. Charles and Frances were Chief Inspectors, poking their noses into everything and pouncing on it – hands, nails, hair, underwear. 'We don't cut our toenails in the drawing-room, Magda.' 'Nice girls change their pants every day, Magda.' OK, so they'd given her a racing bike with five gears and cantilever brakes, but what was one lousy bike, when they had all that cash? You had to be so bloody careful all the time. They'd jump on you for nothing, or nag you into some fucking stupid chore like cleaning silver. Why buy grot that needed cleaning in the first place? Viv never did. And Viv didn't make you wash the bath out, or use a butter-knife, or turn puppies into dangerous monsters.

Charles had lied about the dog. Yeah, even he lied, her own saintly father who ponced about like God's elder brother. 'The puppy probably won't survive in any case,' he'd frowned. 'Not after a drowning.'

It hadn't bloody drowned. She'd saved it, hadn't she? He'd like to see it drown, that was obvious.

'Fuck you, Charles!' she'd shouted and he'd gone all white and tight and goldfishy again. Other kids didn't call their fathers Charles. She'd called him Dad once, and Frances had gone spare. Dad, dad, dad. Fuck, fuck, fuck. He wasn't a dad, anyway. Dads grew up with you and brought the coal in and mended things. He'd lock her up, if he found the lipstick. Or send her packing. She didn't want to go away. Well, back to her ma would be smashing, but that was impossible, and she'd rather stay in Richmond than be stuck in some hostel, or a prison. At least she had her bike and her tape recorder in Richmond, and Bunty was close by. She poked Bunty in the ribs and her breathing changed key. They couldn't send you to prison for writing on walls. 'Bunty?' she whispered.

'Mmmmmm . . .'

'Do you know what gets lipstick off?'

'Oh, cold cream or cleansing milk or something. Shut up. What's the time?'

'No, not off lips, off walls.'

'Magda, go to sleep, it's the middle of the night.'

'I can't go to sleep. I've put lipstick all over Frances' walls.'

'What?' Bunty grabbed at the blankets and pulled herself up. 'She'll kill you.'

'Yeah, I know.' Magda stared out of the window. There was only one curtain. The other one had been taken down three months ago for patching, and never been replaced. The moon was a mean little sliver, sneaking behind the trees. 'There's just a chance they haven't seen it yet. Your mum phoned Frances to tell her I was staying here, so they may not have bothered going to my room.'

Bunty yawned. 'Oh, you mean, it's only your room. I thought you meant the whole house.'

'Don't be stupid, Bunty. My room's bad enough, isn't it?'

'Yeah.'

'It's "yes", Bunty, not "yeah".' They both giggled, clutched each other.

'Mum's got a book downstairs. Sort of household hints and stuff. Mrs Parry Jones gave it to her last Christmas. It might tell you how to get lipstick off.'

'Bunty, quick, where is it?'

'Ssshh, don't wake the whole house. Can't we leave it till the morning?'

'No, we can't.'

They crept downstairs to the kitchen and Bunty dug out the book from the bottom of the cupboard, where it had been abandoned with half a dozen gumboots. She propped it open on her knee.

'Wait a mo – it's alphabetical. Lampshades, lentils, here we are – lipstick. "How to make your own lipstick. Melt 3 oz Peruvian basalm . . ."'

Magda grabbed the book from her. 'Let's look under "stains".

Beer, biro, bird droppings – ugh! OK, I've found it now. "To remove lipstick stains from fabric, dab with carbon tetra-something, then wash in soap and warm water."'

'You can't do that with walls. The paper'll come off.'

'Fuck! All right, let's look under "wallpaper". Hold on – here it is. "To remove greasy marks from wallpaper, rub stain with fresh white bread or with a soft India rubber." Christ! They must be joking.'

Bunty stretched out in a chair and shut her eyes. She was still yawning. 'Lipstick isn't greasy, anyway.'

''Course it is, fathead. It's made of shark's oil or something. Look, get me some bread.'

'Oh Magda, you can't start eating now. It's the middle of the night.'

'I'm not eating. I'm going back to Richmond.'

Bunty wrapped her nightdress round her knees and tucked her toes under. 'But you told me you'd never go back – told Mum the same as well.'

'I've got to remove the lipstick, Bunty, before they find it. I'm going now and I'm taking every cleaner I can find – bread, India rubber, soap . . . everything.'

'You can't go out in the pitch dark.'

'Why not? I've got lights on my bike, haven't I? It's only five minutes' ride, in any case.'

'But the house will be all locked up.'

'I've got keys.'

'But what about the bolts? And burglar alarms and things?'

'They don't bolt the little side door. It's only locked, and I've got a key to it. And the burglar alarm isn't on at night. I'll just creep in – they won't even hear me. My room's at the back.'

Bunty unwrapped her toes again and lumbered to her feet. 'All right. I'll get the bread.' She hacked a chunk from a large farmhouse loaf and wrapped it in a dish-cloth. Magda was collecting tins, jars and cartons of every household cleaner.

'I daren't use ours. Mrs Eady would notice – she measures everything. Half of these haven't been used for years. They've gone all hard and crumbly.'

Bunty found her a headscarf and a duffel coat from an anonymous collection in the cloakroom, then helped her wheel

137

her cycle round the front. The sky was already lightening, greyish round the edges now like a mouldy plum. The slice of moon had been cut so thin, it looked as if it would break.

''Bye,' Bunty whispered.

''Bye.'

Magda crouched in the shadow of the grandfather clock and listened. She could hear voices. Why were they still awake? Charles often worked late in his study, but he never spoke. She'd come down once or twice in the middle of the night and found him hunched over his papers, grey and frowning, like a gargoyle. He hadn't seen her, so she'd crept away again. But Frances was never with him. Frances went to bed at midnight and shut her bedroom door. Perhaps she didn't sleep. Perhaps grown-ups never slept. She was grown-up herself now, almost, so maybe she'd lie awake for ever, and nights and mornings would be all jumbled up together in a frightening grey fog.

She could hear Charles shouting. He never shouted. Even when he was cross, he spoke softly – it always scared her. He'd been clipping hedges with his Black and Decker whatsit last Sunday and she'd thought, that's how he sounds: an electric voice, a hedge-trimmer voice, smug and soft and humming on one even steady note. It wasn't humming now, it was roaring, as if his motor had over-revved and gone berserk. He was in his study, with the door open, and he was booming something at Frances who seemed to be upstairs.

She slunk along the passage and hid behind the oak settle. Frances' voice was muffled by the staircase and it was difficult to make it out. But she heard her name – Magda. Frances still pronounced it wrong. So they were discussing her, were they? She felt a prickle of importance. She almost didn't care if they were angry, so long as they went on talking. No one had ever held a conference about her in the middle of the night before. She'd even stopped Charles working. That meant she must be Somebody. Maybe they'd been up for hours, or hadn't even gone to bed at all. They'd turned her into an emergency. She liked the thought of that – being wicked enough to deserve an all-night sitting.

They were probably sorry, now, couldn't sleep for guilt. Perhaps they'd even change their minds about the puppy. Not that she'd accept it, not likely, after all that kerfuffle, but it would be nice for them to grovel. 'We're sorry, Magda, we were wrong . . .' She held her breath, as Frances' voice came nearer.

'I'm sorry, Charles, I just can't take any more. She'll have to go away.'

Charles had swooped to the door of his study. 'She *is* going away. I've told you, it's arranged. I've got the letter here. Term starts the eleventh of September. It's only a matter of a month or so. Just be patient, can't you?'

Magda jammed her face into the cold wood of the settle. She didn't want to hear. Nice to be made of oak, deaf and solid and unfeeling. She pressed her ear so hard against the carved frills of acanthus leaves that her own pain throbbed back at her. But Frances' voice was mingled with the pain, a smooth, slithery voice, squeezing through solid wood, snaking into everything. She was coming down the stairs now, slowly, one step at a time, the soft snake voice very quiet, very deadly.

'It's not only her . . .'

Her, her. She was an object now, a dumb household cleaner, a grotty tin of Vim.

'It's you, too. You're as bad. You're her father, aren't you? Well, we shouldn't really part you from your precious daughter, then. It wouldn't be natural, would it? You'd better go and join her. Yes, why don't you go away, the pair of you? Go on, go *away*.'

The voice wasn't hushed any more. It was rearing up on itself, surging down the staircase, swelling through the hall . . .

Magda fled. Back along the corridor, out through the small side door, slap into the grey almost-morning. The sky had paled into the colour of a dead fish, the moon dead now, decomposing. She rolled up her jeans. The steel frame of the bike bit cold against her bare legs. She pedalled wildly, Frances' voice jabbing round and round with the motion of the pedals, entangled with the chain. She tried to beat it off, but it was coiling down her throat, flailing through her hair, the two simple words striking at her, poisoning:

'Go away, go away, GO AWAY.'

12

He went away.

Mercantile International phoned him from Nassau at eight o'clock the following morning and requested him to catch the next plane. One of their directors had been accused of illegal speculation with company funds, for his own personal profit. Charles was required as an expert witness.

'Please don't go,' begged Frances, trying to rinse last night out of her mouth.

'Don't be silly, darling. You know perfectly well I have to go. It's a court case – a very nasty business by the sounds of it. God alone knows what Oppenheimer's going to say. It's one of his companies.'

'Oh, he's mixed up in it, is he? I might have guessed. Whenever there's trouble, it always seems to be our good friend Heinrich.'

'He *is* our good friend, Frances. The work he brings me pays for all our luxuries. It's not just trouble he's mixed up in, but all those little extras you insist on – your foreign cars, your couturier clothes, your . . .'

'All right, Charles, you've spent the last five years telling me how obliged we are to Oppenheimer. But all the same, you can't just disappear like that – not after what happened last night. I mean, we haven't even discussed it yet. I know I behaved badly, but . . .'

'You were tired, darling, that's all. Let's forget it, shall we? I'll only be gone a matter of days, a week at the outside.'

A week. If one night lasted a hundred years, a week might end somewhere in the twenty-seventh century. Normally, she didn't mind about his travelling. Charles dropped in at the Bahamas as other men took a spin to Bournemouth. She kept his suitcase permanently packed. But this time . . .

'But what about Magda? How on earth am I going to deal with her? It's much more awkward with you not being here.'

'She'd better stay at Viv's, then. I'll arrange it.' Another paltry item on his job list: clean car, trim hedge, dispose of daughter. Magda might be hysterical by now, or ill, or despairing.

'But I can't just ignore her for a week. And what am I meant to do about the walls? She shouldn't get away with vandalism like that. On the other hand, she must be in quite a state to . . .'

'I'll think about it on the plane, darling, and phone you. Now could you please do me a spot of breakfast.'

Frances cracked an egg into the frying pan. So Charles planned to deal with a delinquent daughter by long-distance phone call, with wires crackling and the pips going; fit her in among the formulae, no doubt.

'How's Magda?'

'Smashing up the house.'

'Fine, fine.'

Here he was, escaping again, using his work as a manhole to drop safely into and hide from all the hubbub on the pavement outside. All right, she'd shouted at him to get out of her way, told him to go, but that was only *in extremis*, and she hadn't meant a Bahamian business trip, lulled by labile secretaries and cushioned in a first-class cocoon of soothing schedules and self-importance, with a millionaire glittering on the sidelines.

Charles cut a neat square from his fried bread and matched it with a square of egg. He was already in the Bahamas, astounding the court-room, impressing the judge. His note-pad was propped against the coffee pot and he was smiling into it, jotting down inspired rejoinders. Last night had never existed as far as he was concerned. Her panic, her outburst, had dwindled to nothing in the face of a court case. A tenth of his income came from this Nassau company, and two-thirds of it from Oppenheimer. Heinrich was gold-dust, and she only a handful of loose change, in comparison.

'Got everything?' Ridiculous, of course he had. Charles had a check-list taped inside his head. He stood at the door, trying not to look too eager to be gone. He gave her his Bahamas kiss, longer and more ardent than the London peck, but slightly shorter than the full-scale Antipodean embrace.

'Try to relax, darling. Enjoy yourself. Play a bit of golf.'

'Yes.' She polished up her long-distance smile and clamped it on her face. How could he talk about relaxing when hate was crouching in the house.

'Take care.'

'Yes, and you.'

'I'll phone.'

'Yes.'

She closed the door. It was drizzling outside. Egg had congealed on the plates and the smell of bacon fat seeped into the hall.

'Shocking weather!' reported Mrs Eady, making a self-righteous hurricane with her plastic pack-a-mac.

'I'm afraid I can't be disturbed this morning. I've got a fashion job to finish.'

Mrs Eady pulled off a galosh and replaced it with a brown canvas beach shoe. 'Never did understand what good fashion did to nobody.'

Frances knew what she meant. Who cared whether skirts were longer, or bosoms back? But she had decided to get down to work. It wasn't an important job, only a paltry piece of advertising she had taken on as a favour to an old client, whose normal copywriter was coping with divorce and influenza, both at once. But at least it would return her to the iron rock of discipline and professionalism, at a time when things were crumbling like sand. She tried to sweep her problems off the desk. Magda must stay at Viv's, not keep creeping back into the in-tray, making ugly blots all over her clean page. She had locked the studio door, so that Mrs Eady wouldn't turn the lipstick into a National Disaster. Reggie had agreed to strip the wallpaper, and emulsion the walls in plain blue. That only left the hate . . .

She opened her folder with its collection of spring suits. It was summer outside, winter in her head, and spring in the advertising business. She read over the jaunty phrases she had written so glibly just a week ago. 'Trap your big-game hunter in these jungly camouflage colours', 'Ambitious little hat with a going-places feather', 'Bosoms blossom out'. Nonsense. Whipped-cream, rose-tinted, chocolate-coated nonsense. Reality was harsher. Reality was flowery walls blighted by red lipstick. Red for hate and danger, passion and Piroska. It was almost as if Piroska herself had written on the walls, etching her love for Charles into the very fabric of the house. Love and hate, both four-letter words, which socked you in the jaw and broke families apart.

Maybe it had broken Magda, too. How did it feel smashing precious pictures, and ripping the petals off roses? Only last week Magda had picked a bunch of McGredys Yellow for Viv, wrapping them in tissue paper from the laundry box and cradling them like glass. For Viv, though – not for her. She had only the hate.

She picked up her pen again and tried to write a headline for a wedding suit. 'Mother of the bride steals the show . . .' 'Bells are ringing for this . . .' 'I hate you.' She stared at the three black words polluting the pad. They had blotted out every word in the whole vocabulary of fashion. She couldn't work, had to talk to someone, to help to drown them out. But who? Magda had fled to Viv's, so she could hardly use Viv as an ally. And even if she did, Viv would be on Magda's side. Viv always took the 'crime is a broken home' line, and Magda would fit it to perfection. She and Charles would be the criminals, in Viv's eyes. Charles was phoning Viv, in any case. He'd promised to fit it in, between his duty-free brandy and passport control.

Her other friends were useless. How could she confide in them, when she'd fobbed them off so far, with convenient fictions. She couldn't turn a vague foreign cousin into an instant delinquent. They'd never understand, in any case. Someone else's pretty daughter sounded a delight, not a disaster – until you were actually in the ring with her, parrying every blow, or knocked senseless in a corner. Even if she told them, it would be all a charade. 'Little spot of bother with our guest . . . messed her room about a bit . . . yes, difficult age, isn't it?' The obligatory light touch and forced little laugh, feelings bandaged up, tourniquet on the tears.

There was no one she could turn to. Only stainless-steel acquaintances, neck-deep in their own problems, or their careers, or their children. Only empty formulae for standard situations.

She had been doodling on her pad, the blank page a tangle of flowers, feathers, numbers, squares, fighting and overlapping with each other. Only the numbers had arranged themselves neatly – into a group of three and then a group of four. A phone number. And she had no one to phone.

No one? She picked up the receiver and held it in her hand.

She shouldn't phone. She'd vowed never to use that number, even thrown the piece of paper in the dustbin. And yet the numbers had crawled into her head instead, and stayed there. And now they were shouting on her pad, growing bolder and more insistent, distracting her from working. Perhaps it would be more efficient to make the call, so that at least she could concentrate once she'd said goodbye. She dialled the first digit and stopped. Whatever could she say? Place an order for half a dozen cardboard sheep; tell him she'd found a fish-hook in her handbag; ask him for a crash course in astrology. Nonsense! As airy-fairy and unproductive nonsense as the polyfilla words on her pad. She must work at it harder. Wait a minute – she'd dropped an earring at the Poly dance? Pathetic. She'd set up her own mini-cab company and would he like details? Dangerous. She was desperate over Magda and needed his help. Right, honest, direct, and quite impossible. She put the receiver down again and replaced it with her pen. 'Spring fever sweeps to your feet – walk all over him with these man-eating mock-croc boots!'

He wouldn't be there, in any case. It was August, the long vacation, and any sensible teacher would be sunning himself on the Costa Brava, or earning extra money picking apples in Kent. August in Acton couldn't compare. August in Richmond wasn't too exciting, either. Charles was often too busy for a holiday, and even if he weren't, he refused to go away when everyone else did. So they took their sparse vacations in March or November and avoided raucous coach parties or queues at the airport. But even that would have to change, with Magda. Now it would be family holidays in the high season, with a teenager in tow.

'Would you like to see the Sistine Chapel, darling?'

'Nope.'

'Would you like to drown yourself in the River Danube, sweetheart?'

'Yeah.'

It was suddenly so easy – she had her pretext. Ned would know all about unaccompanied holidays for children, adventure trips and camping expeditions. He'd taught in that school, hadn't he? She could merely ring him up and ask for details.

'Oh hallo. Mr Bradley?'

'Yup.'

She grimaced – no wonder Magda never learned, when even teachers couldn't speak the Queen's English. 'It's Frances Parry Jones here. So sorry to bother you, but I wondered if . . .'

'Franny! Fantastic! Let's go down to Brighton.'

'Please, Ned, I . . .'

'Say it again. Your Neds absolutely ravish me! It's a magnificent day. Let's . . .'

'It's raining.'

'Ah, here it is, yes. But I've heard the weather forecast. They're already in bikinis in Brighton, collapsing from sunstroke from Dartmouth to Dover. If you want to dodge the clouds, my love, there's nothing for it – we'll have to head south.'

'Ned, do be sensible. I've got work to do and I only rang to . . .'

'How's Magda?' The doodles were submerging the spring suits – umbrellas, sunshades, starfish, waves.

'Fine.' Puppies, cornflowers, lipstick, hate. 'In fact I wanted to ask you about . . .'

'Ask me in person. You'll get much better answers. Meet you at Victoria Station as soon as you can get there. You bring the bikinis and I'll bring the jam butties.'

'Ned, if you can't be serious, I'd better phone you later.' She removed the telephone from the desk to a side table, and spread out her work sheets again. She stared at a picture of a pink suit with suede trimmings and frilled shirt. 'Frills and thrills, think pink, suede upgrades . . .' Why shouldn't she escape? Charles had. She couldn't work properly, in any case. The day stretched ahead like an endless piece of tangled string. The words had returned again. Every time she shut her eyes, she saw them bleeding down the walls – 'I hate you.' Terrifying words, fraught with fury and danger, hot with Magda's misery. Part of her wanted almost to beat the brat, for ruining her room and rejecting all her attempts at a relationship, and part of her felt guilty and petty and despicable for not being able to love even a puppy, let alone a child. She couldn't endure the battle raging inside her own head. She needed an ally or an arbitrator, someone to step inside the lines and win her peace with honour. And why shouldn't that somebody be Ned? The very fact that she hardly knew him was a distinct advantage. If she confided in any member of their

145

own sacred circle, it would compromise Charles and embarrass Magda. But Ned was outside that circle. He'd also had more experience. Working in that enormous comprehensive, he was bound to have had to deal with other Magdas. They needn't go to Brighton – that was quite unnecessary. But she could meet him in Richmond, or even at Victoria – somewhere safe and neutral – and merely ask his advice. Magda was clearly in need of some professional help, and Ned would know the procedures for teenage counselling or child guidance. Teachers always did.

She picked up the phone again. 'Look, Ned, I'm sorry I was sharp. I would like to talk to you, if it's no bother – just for half an hour or so. I've got a problem.'

Ned sounded so close, it was as if he had squeezed down the phone and catapulted into the room. 'Right, Brighton it is! We'll talk on the train and then collapse on the beach. I'll get the tickets, shall I? Meet you on Platform 16 about an hour from now.'

Frances frowned. 'I'd really rather not . . .'

Mrs Eady popped her head round the door. 'Will you be wanting coffee, same as usual?' She made the simplest question sound like her own funeral service. Even the hoover turned tragic when she used it, droning in mingled pain and protest. Frances gestured her away – she'd missed all that Ned was saying. She moved the phone to the other hand and started again.

'I'm sorry, Ned, but it seems a bit pointless for us to rush off to the sea. I mean, we haven't planned it, and I still don't even know you well . . .'

The phone almost rocketed out of her hand. 'Christ, Frances! You really are the most joyless, rule-ridden female I've ever met. Don't you allow yourself the slightest grain of pleasure, unless it's been weighed out and allotted to you on your ration book? Can't we just go to Brighton because it's *there*? I'm not planning to rape you or murder you, or wall you up in the Pavilion. You phoned me in the first place, for heaven's sake! It's a wonder you've got any friends at all, if you can't even catch a train without written permission from your husband or guardian. One day you'll be dead, my love, and you still won't have ventured a toe outside your impregnable fortress on Richmond Green. OK, I'm sorry, I've gone too far. Bugger Brighton! I'm sorry I even suggested it. I'll meet you in the Wimpy Bar in Richmond.'

146

A squall of rain spattered at the windows, nagging her like Ned. The room was always sombre, with its mahogany furniture and leather-bound books, but today it was even darker, grey clouds weighing down the morning. Now she'd offended all of them – Charles, Magda, Viv, Bunty – even Ned. He was right. She was a fossil and a curio, nailed down under glass with a label and a price tag.

Yet it did seem risky and ridiculous to jaunt off to the seaside with one man, when she was married to another. Just because Charles had behaved outrageously, was that any reason why she should change her own standards? Other women might plan sordid escapades, just to get their own back, but it wasn't easy to get even with a man like Charles. They had revenge and rebellion enough with Magda. On the other hand, Ned could be a genuine help with the child. She had only planned to see him, to help talk out the problems, and surely it was no more wicked to do it in Brighton over lunch, than in Richmond over coffee? If some solution resulted from their meeting, then it was Charles who would benefit.

'Ned?'

'Yes?'

'All right.'

'What do you mean "all right"?'

'I will come to Brighton. You're right – it's not the end of the world, either geographically or in any other sense.'

She almost heard the grin on the other end of the telephone. 'That's better. But are you sure, my love? I don't want to drag you kicking and screaming from your fastness . . .'

'Yes, I'm sure.' She wasn't. But, then, everything was confused and contradictory at the moment. Last night, she'd shouted and panicked and wished Charles a thousand miles away, but in the morning, when he'd gone that far and further, he seemed indispensable and precious. He and his daughter might be turning her from Minton china into barbed wire, but her life was still grafted on to his, like a frail scion on a strong branch, and without him she would droop and wither. It was humiliating to be so dependent on him, but she appeared to have no choice. He was her sap and root-stock, and no other man, no Ned, could be as strong. Her marriage was sacred, despite Magda.

147

There was still the Charles who was civilized, considerate, and cultivated – loyal and faithful even. After all, the Magda business was only a relic from the past. Was it fair to keep on blaming him for something which had happened sixteen years ago? It was simpler to snip Charles in two. Magda's Charles she could turf out and send away with no compunction, as she had done last night, but her own Charles she still needed as her rock and her lodestar. That left Magda – fatherless. The second Charles would somehow have to deal with her, not as a daddy, but as a distant relative and a strict disciplinarian – the only way the three of them could live together. And in the meantime, Magda must be sent to cool off. With a little help from Ned, they could choose somewhere bracing and remote, with friends her own age and a safe set of rules.

'We'll be able to have a serious talk in Brighton, won't we, Ned? I need your advice. That's why I rang.'

''Course. That's first priority. Didn't you know I'm Brighton's answer to Evelyn Home?'

He was. They got down to Magda almost as soon as the train heaved out of Victoria. It wasn't easy. Ned had met her with a huge scarlet beach-ball and a hug to match, a pile of peanut-butter sandwiches, a party pack of Mars bars and forty pigeons in tow whom he was teasing with the crusts.

'Ned, you're not *allowed* to feed the pigeons. There's a notice up.'

'I'm not feeding them, my darling, I'm preaching to them. It's my Francis of Assisi thing. Though I must admit they seem more interested in their grub than in their God. Christ – you look ravishing! Let's not go anywhere. I'll just put you on a pedestal and stare at you for ever and a day.'

People were already staring, especially when he bounced the beach-ball all the way down Platform 16. She tried to walk a step behind. The station was probably swarming with accountants, half of whom were Charles' bosom friends. She could imagine the phone call that evening.

'Hello, darling. How's Nassau?'

'Fine, fine. How was Brighton? *And what in God's name were you doing strolling arm-in-arm with an out-of-work lunatic in* shorts?'

148

The shorts had certainly been a stumbling block. They were cut-down jeans, sawn off so close to the crotch that his bare brown legs seemed to go on and on for ever. It was difficult to concentrate on Magda, with all that tangled golden hair creeping over the train seat and trying to involve itself with her severe brown dress. She brought out Magda almost immediately, as a shield and a defence. This was a problem-solving day, not a spree. Strangely, the lipsticked letters seemed almost to have shrunk. Ned had a way of rubbing things off with a little optimism and a lot of common sense. He turned rebellious teenagers into a temporary affliction, like a head cold, rather than a terminal illness. A wrecked bedroom, in his eyes, was a sneeze, not a death throe.

'Kids from the cosiest families do worse than that, Franny.'

'Yes, I know.' She didn't know. Teenager had just been a word until she'd met Magda – something she'd read about in the Sunday supplements, a species which roared around on motor bikes and stuck safety-pins up its nose, but always at a safe distance from her and Charles.

'But Magda's had a double shock. First no father, and then her mother running off . . .'

'One-parent families are here to stay, my love. Brent Edge was swarming with 'em. It's us who've got to change our attitudes. Lots of kids seem to thrive on Dad in jug, or Mum in Blackpool. We're just bloody hypocrites. If you're a famous film star, it's positively fashionable to have a baby without a father – the Vanessa Redgrave syndrome. I bet *she* even denies any bloke conceived hers in the first place! But try and get away with it when you're a humble office cleaner or a shop assistant, and all hell's let loose.'

'Look, Ned, that's not the point.' He was being far too pat. Perhaps he just wanted to dispose of Magda, so that he could get down to the Mars bars, or worse. People's motives were always so suspect. Hadn't she herself sandwiched Magda between her scruples and his shorts? But she must be fair to Ned. He was still up to his neck in Magda, only five miles out of Brighton. They hadn't even had a coffee in the buffet car.

'Her mother's not dead, Franny, only absent for a while. And meantime, you'll cope. You will, you know. Kids are tough. They adapt, and if they kick a bit in the process, just kick 'em back – gently. You're tough, too, Fran. My little blue steel whiplash.'

She was amazed that he could take it all so lightly, shrug off rebellion, joke about hate. She stared out of the window. Patchwork cows chewing contentedly while Concorde screeched over them, curdling their milk; stolid sheep munching all the way to the abattoir. Nature seemed as unconcerned as Ned. It was an ordinary sort of morning, half-awake, and drizzling with a lazy rain.

'Ned . . .'

'Yup?'

'I thought you promised sun.'

'Give it time, love. Have a while-u-wait Mars bar.'

She shook her head, closed her eyes. The black darkness behind them suddenly capsized into crimson, as if someone had unrolled a red carpet across her eyelids. The sun had come out, blazing with repentance, galloping after the rain. It jumped in at the window and sliced Ned in half, turning his hair from straw to champagne. The dust in the air between them exploded in a thousand colours. She felt his body leap in sympathy.

'Fantastic timing! I bet they pay the sun to do that on purpose – part of Brighton's tourist drive. You've gone all golden, Franny. Cheer up! Let's leave Magda in Richmond for a while. I refuse to let her spoil our day. It's just you and me and the sea.'

And half a million other bods, she thought, as they fought for a patch on the beach. Charles hated crowds, especially ones with transistor radios and progeny. But Ned knew everyone.

'See that lady there,' he whispered, 'the one with the double boobs.' Her purple-padded bikini top had shifted down, so that two purple cupolas abutted against her breasts, and all four mounds rose and fell in sleep. 'She's madly in love with her driving instructor – the one snoring beside her with the zebra-crossing on his swim trunks. They're staying in sin at the Metropole, but her husband thinks she's gone to a London clinic to get her boobs fixed. He's a conventional sort of chap who likes his ladies with the usual two. There he is now!'

He pointed to a small, swarthy man, waddling towards them with his trousers rolled up, and brandishing an ice cream cornet.

'There's going to be violence, I know it! Don't look, Fran. He's armed with a double-scoop strawberry.'

She didn't look. She was staring at Ned. He had just removed his blue cotton sweater and underneath was a dazzling white T-shirt printed with the words 'I'D SELL MY SOUL FOR FRANNY' in screaming scarlet capitals.

'Ned!'

'Do you like it? I got it done just before I met you. There's a place outside the station which prints them while you wait. I was going to put "Franny for Pope", but something told me you're an Anglican.'

'Oh, Ned.'

'Well, I suppose you must like it, if it's just earned me two Neds in a row. Give me a kiss, then.'

His face was moving towards hers. She dodged it and bestowed a safe peck on his shoulder. He deserved it. No one had ever plastered her name all over them before. He was like a walking advertisement for Franny. She had stopped being Franny fifteen years ago. Charles didn't approve of nicknames. But Ned had resurrected her. Sometimes she hardly knew who she was. Franny was almost dead, and Charles' Frances was too precious to be taken out of its case, and there didn't seem to be a central, essential Frances in between. She was one person with Charles and a different one with Ned, and another one still with Viv, and Laura and ... And yet none of them was authentic or spontaneous. But just looking at her name written on Ned's crazy chest made her feel better. Ned was like a rope trick. One flick of his wrist and the knotted, tangled piece of string she'd been all day pulled out into a simple scarlet ribbon. All right, she would be Franny – just for a day – one magic day, when the sun was shining and half of London had parked itself on Brighton beach and a marvellous mixed-up man thought fit to write her name all over his chest.

'Ned,' she said.

'Yup?'

'It's super.'

'So are you. Now close your eyes. It's sandwich time and I'm about to say grace in Latin.'

The peanut butter had melted into the bread and turned the

sandwiches into soggy cowpats. He'd sat on the swiss roll and flattened it. The Acton market pears were long past their first, firm youth. On Charles' rare trips to Brighton, he always ate at Wheeler's, or ordered lunch in his suite at the Grand. He avoided picnics unless they were socially unavoidable, as at Glyndebourne or Lord's. They had a picnic set, with proper china plates and small silver forks for the salmon and the strawberries. Ned was drinking out of the bottle and his table was two bare legs spread with a Mother's Pride wrapper.

Frances bit into a squelchy pear. The juice trickled down her wrist. Ned licked it off obligingly and kept his face, upside-down, below her chin. 'That's how you'd look to an Australian, I suppose. Smashing! Shall we swim after lunch?'

'I haven't brought my costume.'

'I have! I bought you a bikini for your birthday. It must be your birthday soon, if you're a Virgo. Christ, you really are a Virgo, aren't you? – so tidy and efficient. I've never seen a girl give hospital corners to dirty sandwich papers before. I bet your dustbins look like ornamental swans.'

Frances stared at the wrappers. She'd been giving them the Charles treatment quite unconsciously, smoothing them out and folding them into squares. She dropped them almost guiltily.

'Happy birthday!' said Ned, and passed her a package the size of a pocket hankie.

'But it's not my . . .'

'It's gotta be. Otherwise we can't swim. Try it on.'

It was nothing more than three Union Jacks – one to cover each of her vital territories, held together dangerously by skimpy scarlet ties.

'Ned, I couldn't possibly wear it! It's outrageous. Everyone will stare.'

'And so they should. You're a Michelin entry, "worth a detour". Come on, get undressed. I want to see the only walking flag in Brighton. I bought it at the same place as the T-shirt. It could have been worse. I almost got it printed with a message in morse code. Do you know, they tattoo people there. While you wait. I heard them – screaming! Shall we be done on the way back? "Why did the swiss roll?" plastered all over my belly!'

There wasn't much room on his belly. It was already thickly

152

tangled with honey-coloured hair, creeping down below his navel and disappearing into the top of his trunks. He had stripped off his shorts and his T-shirt and was standing naked except for six inches of striped poplin. Everyone else around them was more or less undressed, but somehow Ned looked nude. She couldn't understand it. The whole beach was jostling with bare bodies, but Ned's towered above them all like a naked bronze on a high pedestal. And yet he was small, made on a completely different scale from Charles, with narrower shoulders, tauter hips, a neat, tight bottom. Charles' swim trunks didn't cling like that, or plunge so disturbingly far below his stomach. Charles was a he-man, a bigger and better specimen than Ned, but Charles preferred to camouflage his form, hide it in a stern and unobtrusive uniform. Ned wore his body like an exhibit, even with his clothes on. 'Look at me!' it shouted, as he undid the bottom button on his shirt, or belted his trousers another inch tighter.

He was displaying it now, leaping around her, throwing up the sand. 'Hurry up, my love. We'll have the sea to ourselves if we get a move on. Half these bods will be tramping back to "Sea View" and "Mon Repos" for their braised-landladies-with-custard, any minute. The one o'clock curfew. Stewed prunes, pass the ketchup. Aren't you glad we've eaten?'

Frances nodded, felt ridiculously glad about everything – the sea pouncing on the pebbles; the sun squeezing between brown bellies and trying to find room for itself on the beach; even the gimcrack little plastic windmill, which Ned had bought her and stuck in the sand, where it shouted to the wind. A simple, stupid word, 'glad', not big enough for the clean, salty feeling that tugged at her hair and had washed all the lipstick from the walls. All right, he shouldn't be buying her bikinis and she shouldn't be profaning the national flag by wearing them, but she was Franny today and the rules were different if you changed your name.

He held a huge striped beach towel for her, and she tried to squirm out of her clothes.

'Oops! Dropped it. We should have gone to Cannes – they're topless there. Mind you, you look pretty stunning not topless. I've always yearned for a girl with red-white-and-blue breasts.'

She could feel him looking at her and the glance was like a red-hot finger, outlining her curves.

'Race you to the sea!' she said, to escape his scrutiny. They skimmed across the beach, stumbling over sandcastles and stubbing their toes on spoil-sport stones. She was a barefoot Contessa again, with a red rosette crowing on her chest. And this time no Magda to come between her and her crazy, barefoot Count. He collapsed into the sea on top of her.

'I won! Ouch, it's freezing. I've changed my mind – race you back again.'

She grabbed his hand and pushed him to his knees. 'Rotter!' he yelled. 'Now I've swallowed a starfish and I'll have a five-pointed stomach.'

They were sitting in the shallows like toddlers, with waves thumping over their knees and seaweed tangling between their toes.

'Shall I tell you something terrible?' Ned felt for her hand under the water and buried it in the sand. 'Promise me you won't rush back to Richmond, in sheer disgust.'

'What is it?' She felt a sudden twinge of fear, didn't want to rush back anywhere.

'I can't swim. It's shameful, isn't it?' He yelped with laughter. 'I've tried. Oh my God, I've tried. I got my best friend to push me in, once, and they scraped me off the bottom three weeks later. I even took fancy swimming lessons at the Municipal Baths in Penge with an All-England wrestler called Gladys. I sank her, all fourteen stone of her, and Penge Borough Council demanded compensation. The English don't like non-swimmers. I suppose they think it's unpatriotic, with all that water around us. They refused to serve me, once, when I tried to buy a pair of water wings . . .'

She was shocked, despite his banter. Charles could swim five thousand metres without stopping. He did it every summer, as his annual endurance test. Plunged straight in – no messing – and slogged backwards and forwards in straight lines, until the distance was up. On each occasion he tried to cut his time down. He didn't really like swimming, but it was a challenge and a discipline, a way of measuring his prowess and fitness, making sure he hadn't softened up.

Ned was walking on his knees and had reached neck-level, his head a smooth brown cup sticking up on a saucer of sea.

'You swim, love, don't let me stop you. You can pop across to Brittany and back, while I sit here and knit.'

She didn't want to swim. It was much more fun paddling and splashing and playing childish games. They jumped waves and collected treasures – half a crab, a cuttlefish, a barnacled beach shoe, even a message in a bottle. (Well, Ned swore it was a message.)

They returned to their six-inch square of beach and Ned wrapped the treasures in the dirty sandwich papers and spread the towel for Frances. She shut her eyes against the sun and the space between her eyelids filled with gold and scarlet sequins. The sun was like a velvet towel, mopping all the water from her body, and acting like an anaesthetic to dull the darts of guilt and doubt which still kept pricking.

'Happy?' Ned murmured. His mouth was unaccountably close to her cheek, but she felt too lazy to move. He was trickling tiny shells across her bare tummy, his fingers soft and languorous. She was lying in a gold and scarlet paradise, where there was no time, no rules, only indolent sensations she dared not analyse. Ned and the sun had gone into partnership and were taking her over. The shingle had turned into swansdown and the sky into goose-feathers and she was tucked up between the two of them, safe, snug and heavy.

When she woke up, there was something warm beside her, like a damp hot-water-bottle. It shifted a little and turned into Ned. His arms and legs were tangled up with hers and she was using his chest as a pillow. There was a strange roar in her ears – the noise of six thousand people trying to out-shout the sea. She opened her eyes to a kaleidoscope of colours. How could anyone drop off on Brighton beach, in the middle of a multi-coloured August, least of all Frances Parry Jones who often found it difficult to sleep in the padded darkness of her own hushed bedroom? But she'd gone out like a light. A transistor radio was blaring in her ear, and a posse of cockney kids was squabbling over Smarties, but she'd still fallen fast asleep in a damp bikini, on a bed of hard pebbles, and with a half-naked centaur by her side. She was astonished, almost proud. Charles would have punished her with ten black crosses, but she felt she deserved an accolade. Not gold stars – they were reserved for Proust and piano practice. Red letters,

155

perhaps, to match red-letter days and the scarlet message singing across Ned's shirt. 'I'd sell my soul for Franny.' Charles wouldn't. Charles didn't sell anything, unless he'd carefully calculated his net profit, after VAT, depreciation and capital gains tax.

She closed her eyes again and the red letters slipped behind her eyelids and arranged themselves into wicked, unprintable messages. She smiled. She was wasting time, deliberately lolling about doing nothing, and actually enjoying it. There she was, sandwiched between Ned and the sun, with no clock except the sea, and no plans except allowing one luxurious moment to fall, fat and somnolent, against the next. She dared not move, lest the idyll shatter into a thousand jagged pieces. So long as she stayed still, she was like the picture on the jigsaw-puzzle box, a perfect copy of how the puzzle should come out – no cracks, no missing pieces. But if she stirred a finger, if she listened to the little voices nagging in her head, the whole day might break apart, and all she would have left would be a boxful of rattling cardboard cut-outs.

Ned was lying half underneath her, her shadow turning him from gold to charcoal.

'Your eyelashes curl,' she murmured, tracing their barbed-wire fretwork on his cheek.

'Mmmm' – he fluttered them – 'they badly need a cut. I suspect that's the reason I can't swim. They're so thick, they drag me down.'

'Boaster.'

'Not!'

'Are!'

'Kiss me.'

'No.'

'Please.'

His mouth was so near, it was easier not to argue. His lips tasted salty. She could feel his body murmuring underneath her, his mouth opening and softening, his hands prowling along the hollow of her back. Her breasts were trying to reach him through the flimsy Union Jacks, pressing greedily against his chest. He was already growing out of his swim trunks. He was smaller than Charles, smaller everywhere. Her head reached higher up his body, so that when he kissed her, everything else seemed to fit together like another jigsaw puzzle. Little cardboard bumps fitting into slots and making a picture; unmatched lines and splodges joining up and forming a design; limbs slotting into limbs, heads into hollows. Neat, and very orderly. A million, billion gold stars. No – stars were Charles' notion, and she mustn't bring him into it. There was some new, raw excitement because this wasn't Charles. For fifteen years, she'd closed her mind and mouth to any other man.

'Men are all the same,' Laura had shrugged, dismissing a score of lovers, as if they were frozen peas. But they weren't the same. Ned even tasted different, stronger and sweatier, with a slight after-tang of brine. His body was different, easier to sprawl against, less of it to oppress and overwhelm her, the hair soft and strange against her stomach. He was licking the coils of her ear, his slow tongue meandering through a maze of pathways she'd never known were there. All the paths seemed to lead, dangerously, down between her legs. Her bikini bottom was shouting out rude words, egging him on. He shifted a thigh and let his damp swim trunks tease against hers. His tongue was busier further up. It had abandoned the ear for an armpit and was circling it in a tantalizing fugue. Charles had never included armpits in his timetable. She pushed the tongue away. She mustn't think of timetables, or include Charles as a threesome. The whole idyll would collapse.

She tried to close her mind against his name, to move out of her head again into the warm mix-and-match that was happening further down. Too late. All the pieces had already come apart. Charles had shaken up the puzzle and destroyed it. Even the sun had gone behind a cloud. She shivered. What in hell's name was she doing? Defiling a public beach, when she herself was private property; wasting time, playing games. Her bikini was damp in wrong, accusing places; there was sand in her hair; she was faithless, childish, cheap.

'No, Ned, no. Stop. Please.'

She was already on her feet, pulling on her dress over the damp, drooping flags. Yet she didn't want to ruin everything. She couldn't bear to climb back into the control tower of her head and wrestle with guilt and doubt again. Or litter the beach with apologies and explanations. Or wrap warm, simple things in Charles' fulminating phrases. Why couldn't Charles stay in Nassau? He had his own beach there, for heaven's sake.

Ned groped to a sitting position. 'What's wrong, love? Did I press the wrong button?' He grabbed the last, jammiest knob of swiss roll and crammed it in his mouth. She had expected hurt pride and reproaches, and there he was, cheerfully munching, as if a botched kiss were no more important than a broken shell. She loved him for it, for being so easy and greedy and relaxed, for not wrecking everything with complaints, recriminations. She was still Franny – his T-shirt said so. He had pulled it on again, and was doing a cartwheel on the sand.

'Let's go on the pier,' he said, as he landed wrong side up. 'I'll show you where I used to fish. I caught my first bass from Brighton pier – a six pounder. It took me twelve minutes to land it. I was half dead when I reeled it in, and d'you know what . . . ?'

'What?' She looked at his mouth in astonishment. How could it chew swiss roll and chatter on about bass, when it had just made her whole body turn cartwheels itself?

'I had an eight-ounce pout-whiting on one hook and a five-and-a-half pound chunk of driftwood on the other. I've never liked whiting since. I cook it for the cats. Tell you what, though, I'll win you a goldfish on the rifle range. I'm a crack shot with a rifle.'

He carried the goldfish back on the train in a jam jar. He had already christened it Edward. 'We'll give it gender confusion if it turns out to be a girl. But if I call it Franny, I'll spend my whole life trying to catch it. Or end up in the jam jar, sharing the same waterlily leaf.'

She didn't answer. She liked the crazy, dangerous things he said, but it was almost time to veto them. She was hanging on to the last dregs of Franny before all-change at Victoria. She didn't want to talk, just shut her eyes and lean against his shoulder. He still felt strange, after Charles. She was always looking up to Charles. Her head only reached his heart, so he made her feel frail and over-mastered. With Ned she felt equal. He was taller than her, but not king-sized, god-sized. Only a Puck, an Ariel, a lion-eyed leprechaun who

158

had cast a spell over her and turned her from Snow Queen to changeling.

Snow Queens didn't eat chips out of newspaper or scream in ghost trains or buy hats that said 'Kiss me slow'. Snow Queens would never deign to travel second-class to Brighton, in the first place. A town so tawdry, so blatant, a carbuncle on the coast, where tired insurance clerks took tarnished secretaries. Brighton was a joke, a nudge in the ribs, a dirty postcard. There were better parts, of course – the Lanes, the University, the Egon Ronay-recommended restaurants, the quieter streets of Hove. But Ned hadn't even glanced at them. Ned had chosen pier and promenade, candyfloss and jellied eels, paddle boats and palmists.

'I see romance with a fair young stranger,' whispered Madame Astra from her plastic silver ball. 'And twins.'

They'd laughed about the twins, but her heart had shifted into bottom gear. Twins meant charts and Clomid – subjects she had banned today. With Ned she felt at least two decades younger, too young and irresponsible to have children of her own. A whole day had passed and she hadn't even thought about fertility. There wasn't a baby in the whole of teeming Brighton. Strange, when every other Richmond resident was pregnant or a pram-pusher.

She sat on her bed back home and uncapped the Clomid. Day Seven. She tipped a smooth white tablet into the palm of her hand. How could something little bigger than an aspirin make her a mother? She wasn't even sure she wanted to be one. There were other, crazier things she wanted first – forbidden Franny things. The tablet was as heavy as a ball and chain, all the responsibilities of motherhood weighing like a burden. She'd passed Magda's room and stopped for a moment outside the locked door. Brighton slowly seeped away. It had been only a snapshot, a mirage. She was Frances now, back with the permanence of hate.

She slipped into her Harrods housecoat, and dropped her damp, dishevelled beach-clothes into the laundry basket. She showered the sand away and removed Ned's mouth with the electric toothbrush and the Listerine. Now, sterilized and plaque-free, she sat waiting for Charles' call.

It came, dead on ten, as promised. He was phoning from

the lawyers' chambers, where he was filling in the background to the case. It was still only teatime in Nassau, and he had several hours of gruelling paperwork in front of him. His voice was jaded, faint.

Yes, the flight had been fine; yes, Nassau was stifling; no, Oppenheimer was still in Buenos Aires. And how about her? Had she had a good day? Frances tried to remove the Brighton grin. Not bad, on the whole. Yes, of course she was missing him; no, she wouldn't forget to cancel his dental appointment; no, she hadn't played golf today.

'Where tomorrow?' Ned had asked, when he kissed her goodbye in a doorway off Victoria. 'Kempton Park, Kew Gardens, tea with the Queen at Windsor?'

'Windsor,' she said. 'Tea with you.'

'You're on!' He doubled the kiss. 'Hot buttered Franny on toast.'

'Try to get out a bit,' murmured Charles, between the pips. 'It'll do you good.'

'Yes,' said Frances, straightening the L to R directory, so that it lay at a perfect right-angle to the desk.

'Yup,' repeated Franny, doodling a six-pound goldfish on the cover, in wild red biro.

'Love you.'

'Love you, too.' She was talking to the goldfish.

160

13

They took it in turns to choose. On Ned days, they went by train to street markets and to stock-car racing, with shandy and fish-paste sandwiches in a plastic bag, and on Franny days, they drove to Windsor or Henley and picnicked on chicken breasts and Chardonnay. By the end of the week, Franny was buying shop-made Cornish pasties and Ned had tried his hand at making pâté. It was a sort of holiday. Magda stayed at Viv's, and Frances told lies about doing freelance work in London for a week. And yet Magda was the reason for it all.

Every time they met, they started with Magda. It was the first part of the ritual, which excused and justified the rest. With Magda away, Frances could hardly remember why the child had seemed so unendurable. She'd cleared away her things, which had strayed all over the house; her comic books littering the drawing-room, half-eaten bars of chocolate stuffed in the sideboard drawers. She sent her clothes to the cleaners, first removing stones and chewing-gum from torn and grubby pockets. It seemed wrong, in a way, to be rifling through the girl's possessions. And yet it was only because she longed to know her better, find some vital clue to this reserved and secret creature. The child was like her father, both of them closed and secretive. Magda had arrived with almost nothing, no photographs or books, or treasures, nothing personal, revealing. The things she owned now were mostly gifts from Charles: the leather-bound stamp album, the set of encyclopaedias, the French course on cassette. There was nothing else, except a letter in a cheap blue envelope. She recognized the writing – it was Viv's. Why in heaven's name was Viv in correspondence with the kid, when she had her in her house half the time? It was shameful to read other people's letters, something not even Frannys did, let alone Frances Parry Jones. The letter looked like Viv herself, sprawling, untidy and badly put together. She unfolded it uneasily.

'Darling Wombat'. A double shock, a darling first, and then a nickname. She herself never called Magda darling, and even her Magdas sounded wary and steel-tipped. But Wombat was a pet name, a cosy and affectionate one. Whatever was a wombat? She'd heard the word before, in connection with a zoo. She looked it up in Magda's encyclopaedia, the pages so immaculate she doubted if the girl had ever opened it.

'*An Australian marsupial mammal of the family Phascolomyidae.*' No wonder Magda didn't like encyclopaedias – they made everything sound fossilized. '*Thick, clumsy body, coarse hair, rough to the touch, small mean eyes, naked ugly muzzle.*' But that was nothing like Magda; Magda was beautiful. How could she stay with a woman who insulted her by calling her a wombat? She read on. '*A solitary nocturnal animal, reserved and retiring.*' That was more like it. '*The wombat wreaks so much damage on cultivated pastures, it has been widely destroyed and persecuted.*' A brute beleaguered pest, tamed and loved by Viv, kept as a pet in one home, when it had been snared and wounded in another. Not an insult, but a declaration of love.

She tried not to read the rest of the letter. It was too intimate, too painful. 'Little one,' Viv called her. 'You know I care about you.' How dare she care! And Magda wasn't little – she was a great hulking colt of a creature. 'Remember what I told you . . .' What had Viv told her, and why were they having secrets from her? How did Viv communicate, when she had failed? Love for Viv was something everyday and plentiful, dollops of it larded over everything like cheap strawberry jam. Love in the Parry Jones establishment was rarer; rationed; measured out like caviare, in tiny, precious portions.

Frances dropped the letter miserably back on to the desk. She'd tried, for God's sake, even read books on parenting and puberty. She'd coached Magda in history and offered to cook her favourite food. But Magda didn't have a favourite; didn't want her fancy dishes, or anything to do with her. The studio was empty now. The cornflowers had disappeared with the lipstick, under a wash of bland new paint. Magda had turned herself into Viv's daughter and gone off to be a wombat.

She always seemed more like a cuckoo, a rapacious, gate-crasher bird, taking over someone else's nest. Almost absent-mindedly, she replaced the W volume of the encyclopaedia and took out the C to D, leafing through the prim, print-crowded pages from Crusades to Cubism. She stopped at *Cuculus*.

'*A shy, brown, undistinguished, often furtive bird.*' Yes, that was all more or less correct. '*A summer visitor to these islands*' – right again – '*it departs for warmer climes in early September.*' (Would to God it did!) '*Famed for its habit of brood parasitism, the mother cuckoo selects its victim, then destroys or devours one of the host bird's eggs, to make room for its own.*'

Frances stared at the drawing of the cruel, predatory female stalking towards an unprotected nest. Wasn't it symbolic, some-how? The very word 'victim' was strangely apt. She had always felt duped and oppressed by Piroska. By infiltrating an alien chick into the nest, she had somehow destroyed her own capacity to be a mother in her turn.

No, that was quite unfair. She was taking her Clomid, wasn't she, preparing herself to conceive this very month, only days from ovulation. It was absurd to draw analogies between a cuculid parasite following its instinct, and a human child deprived of her natural rights. She tried not to see the drawing of a doting and devoted robin perched on the baby cuckoo's back, feeding it a grub. '*The fledgeling cuckoo soon grows larger than its foster mother.*' Well, that was true, at least. Magda towered above her, made her look puny and insignificant. '*It rarely receives attention from its real parents.*' How could it, when one of them was whoring in Hungary, and the other truant in Nassau? All the more reason for it to have the full devotion of its foster mother. But Frances was no tireless robin or self-sacrificing pipit. And there was no precedent in bird life for a fledgeling to fly away to another nest.

'I've failed, Ned,' Frances muttered, when they were climbing Box Hill with ice cream cornets and a home-made kite. 'Magda doesn't even want to live with us. I can't get close to her at all. Do you realize, I've never so much as kissed her goodnight. And yet she lets Viv give her bear hugs. How does Viv do it, Ned, when I can't even touch her?'

Ned swapped cornets. His was three-quarters finished and hers was melting. 'Viv's not married to Charles,' he said. 'Viv's not beautiful and talented. Viv's got Bunty.'

He didn't add 'Viv doesn't live in a showcase, or polish up her

163

own swingeing version of the ten commandments. She's a mother and you're a monster.' He didn't even insinuate that she hadn't kissed him goodnight, either. He could have hinted that she was the one who was scared of touching. She loved him because he didn't. In all the five days they'd been out and about together, he never nagged or criticized, or made everything complicated and accusing. Even when she shied away from him – his mouth, his dangerous body – he only grinned and teased her, and called her a gazelle or a unicorn. She let him hold her hand because he did it so matter-of-factly, and she allowed their bodies to touch and overlap a little, when they lay down to capture a view or digest their sandwiches. It seemed churlish to make a fuss about simple, easy things. She had to repay him with something, when he gave her so much time and understanding, listened unendingly to her fears about Magda. She knew he wanted more, impossibly more, but she tried to close her mind to it.

Brighton had been a dangerous precedent. She had been knocked off guard by sun and sleep, and then her own body had betrayed her. She almost marvelled at it. It seemed like someone else's flesh and blood, doing things spontaneous and sensual, without a nagging chaperon. But once was enough. Her body belonged to Charles and was trying to have his baby. It had no right to jaunt off on its own and help itself to barren pleasures.

Sometimes she longed to tell Ned everything. But how could she trot out Mr Rathbone, when Ned was playing hopscotch at the zoo, or launch into the topic of infertility when they were sitting in a teashop with butter dripping down their chins? They had constructed a Peter-Pan-and-Wendy world where grown-up subjects didn't stand a chance. It suited her, in fact; a never-never land, where the nevers weren't real and chilling as they were with Charles.

'We'll never have a baby,' she felt like shouting at him on the phone, when he rang so punctiliously from Nassau. It was already day eleven, so they should have been making love by now. It was so damned difficult explaining, long-distance, that her egg was bursting to be fertilized, primed and prepared by Clomid, waiting to turn them into pedigree parents, if only he weren't five thousand miles away. There were just three more days to go, three crucial, desperate days, before the whole thing was too late, the egg dead and dissipated. He *must* be back, he must be.

'I will be, darling, trust me.' Charles sounded solemn, like a bishop. 'I know how critical it is. I can't wait to get out of here, in any case. The air-conditioning's broken down and the court room's like an oven. Look, I should know more tomorrow. With any luck, the whole thing will be over when I ring you then. Miss you, darling.'

Oh yes, she missed him, too. She missed the circles round the dots, the rutting hallmarks on her blank, barren charts; she missed him as her partner and accomplice with the Clomid. And yet in some ways, she didn't want him back. Things were simpler and sunnier without him. Ned had turned a damp July into a sparkling August. It was bad enough, coming home each evening to a dark frowning house, after the bright patchwork days with a man who used the world as his playground, rather than his bank vault. She never asked him in. The house was Charles' territory. There were barricades around it, which even Frannys weren't allowed to enter.

It was Frances who sat there every evening, alone and dutiful, washing off Ned's hands, gargling away the picnics, filling in her charts. If it weren't for the charts, she might almost have welcomed a court case which left her free to walk barefoot in pine-woods or learn to beach a dinghy in a force seven easterly.

On day thirteen, she refused to see Ned – made up some excuse about a headache. She was so tense, she *did* ache – not only her head, but all of her. Charles had been due home the evening before. He was already two days late. There were only twenty-four more hours to fertilize that precious egg, which had become frighteningly important. The days with Ned had been only squandered time, a parenthesis between the real, serious business of life and parenthood. Ned was a bachelor, a layabout, a law unto himself. She was married, joined, a womb, a receptacle, a woman who must prove her womanhood, however high the cost. She belonged to Charles, she bore his name, his hallmark, and she must also bear his baby, before it was too late.

'N-no, Charles,' she had stammered. Her voice was ship-wrecked. 'I simply can't believe it. Y-you must come home.'

There were cracklings on the line, strange whistlings and buzzings. She wanted to scream. It was so grotesquely difficult to communicate.

'Charles, you don't understand. This drug has side effects. It may even be dangerous. What's the point in my taking it, when you're never here at ovulation time? We'll *never* have a baby.' Never-never land. The real one, the grey hopeless empty one, where the nevers stretched five thousand miles. Charles sounded a lifetime away, his whipped-cream voice curdled by all the interference on the line.

'I'm distraught about it, darling. Of course I realize what it means to you. I'd simply no idea the case would drag on as long as this. But now they've traced the missing funds to a Cayman Trust, so I've got to check all the transactions in between.'

'But why can't someone else do it? What about Bill Turner? He's got all the facts.'

'Darling, you're talking nonsense. Turner's just a lackey. I'm a key witness. I've been subpoena'd now. They simply won't release me. If it were anything else, I'd leave immediately, you know I would. But I can't defy a judge.'

She cried. It was a waste of money, crying long-distance. The phone turned her tears into a jarring dissonance. Charles hated tears, in any case. She tried to choke them back.

'Look, Charles, how about tomorrow? If you could make it by tomorrow, we might still be OK – just about.' It was so confusing with the time being different in their two parts of the world. She had to keep subtracting five hours. Charles' tomorrow might not even be her own.

'Impossible! Oppenheimer's flying in and I must be there when he arrives. He's king, Frances, and the courtiers don't run off when royalty arrives.'

King! She almost spat. Heinrich Oppenheimer was just a self-made millionaire with a first-class tailor. All right, she knew he was the power behind her camel coats and Citroëns, but she'd gladly renounce all that, to have a baby. With a child in your womb, who cared if you had only cheap rags on your back, or a Ford Fiesta in the garage?

'Listen, Charles, I've got a plan. It could still work out. You meet Heinrich first thing in the morning, have your briefing with him – explain the whole situation at home, if it helps – then catch the next plane back. We could just about make it then, by the skin of our teeth. I'll meet you at the airport, if you like. We could even book a room at the Heathrow Hotel, so we don't waste precious time driving back to Richmond.'

'Frances, my darling, you sound absolutely obsessed. It's simply out of the question. Oppenheimer's plane doesn't get in till lunchtime, and that's already evening, your end. In any case, he's relying on me to see this whole thing through to its conclusion. I'm not a free agent. The court's sitting and I must be there – at least three more days.'

Three more days! The egg would be long since shrivelled, her half of the baby flushed away like a tampon. Anger thrust between the crackling wires. 'What if I were dead, Charles? I suppose they'd leave me stinking and unburied, before they let you out.'

'You're *not* dead, darling. Do be reasonable. We've still got next month. Look, I promise you faithfully I won't go away next month. If it's anywhere remotely near ovulation time, I shan't even risk an overnight stay. That's a solemn undertaking. Now, come on, Frances, try and understand. I miss you. I love you.'

She didn't say 'love you too', she didn't even feel it. Only a bleak, gnawing pain, and horrible confusion. She couldn't really blame Charles – his job had always been like that. And for fifteen years, she'd enjoyed the fruits of it. Emeralds round her throat and Paris in her wardrobe, steak in the freezer, claret in the cellar, charge accounts at Fortnum's and Harrods, Lillywhites and Simpson's, her string of credit cards, her new McGregor golf clubs – all were Charles' bounty.

But there were other sorts of bounty – kites and cuttle-fish, peanut-butter sandwiches, puddles and paddle-boats. You could always opt for spam and shandy instead of salmon and champagne, and who needed diamond chokers to dam a river or reel in a trout? But that was only a week's new thinking, play-acting. Five short days of pretending to be a gypsy, dressing as a tramp. It was easy to lunch on bangers and mash in a transport caff, when she could top up in the evening with *caneton à l'orange*.

Or grub in the fields for fungi, when she had Fortnum and Mason truffles swanking in her larder. Hypocritical to swan around with Peter Pan and spend Tinkerbell days grabbing at rainbows, when she'd been made, saved, and subsidized by Charles and Oppenheimer.

She stayed in all day and tried to turn herself wholly into Frances. But Frances was empty, barren. She locked the door and took the phone off the hook. She didn't want Laura snooping round, crowing, 'So when did your hairdresser expire, darling?' or 'No wonder Charles stays away, sweet, if you will wear jeans from the Oxfam shop.' Or Viv to ring and explain that all Magda needed was love. Or Ned rocketing down the phone with a witch's potion for her headache and two free tickets for a pop festival. 'I'll bring the peace and the pot, and you bring the Snoopy blanket.'

She didn't want anything except a baby, a circle round her dot. She wasn't barren, there was a baby there – she knew it – waiting, only lacking a Charles to kick it into life. The week with Ned had primed and softened her; all that sun and sea, fresh air, wild flowers, new feelings, had worked like some lush fertility rite, blown out the gloom and tension from her womb, and made it fruitful.

Slowly, she walked upstairs to the top of the house, where she kept her filing system. Drawersful of past PR campaigns, promoting furs and fashion houses, bridal gowns and beachwear; details of all their Richmond furnishings – colour swatches and fabric samples; photographs – Charles as a young man, looking just the same but less assured about it, herself at seventeen, dumpier, and grinning in a way she hardly recognized. The bottom drawer was her baby file, full of articles and cuttings she'd been collecting since she gave up her career: the best form of childbirth, the advantages of breast-feeding, lists of equipment, nanny agencies. She took out the folder and sorted through it. The pictures of babies hardly moved her – they all looked much the same, chubby and torpid. It was the mess and mystery of childbirth itself that appalled and fascinated her. Something so natural and yet so strange and undignified, like sex. It both sanctified and sullied every woman who went through with it. Her mind felt prepared now, and her body ready – breasts fuller than usual on account of the Clomid, and a sick, expectant feeling in her stomach.

She went downstairs again, prowled through all the rooms. She couldn't eat. Books and music were impossible. Crazy schemes darted through her head. She'd rush to the airport and take the next plane to Nassau. But even then, it would be too late. The flight took at least eight hours, and by the time she'd waited for a plane and hung around for Charles at his hotel . . . She could hardly drag him screaming from the court room. 'Beg leave, m'Lud, for your honourable witness to fertilize an egg.'

Strange, how remote he felt. Not just on the other side of the Atlantic, but wafer-thin and dwindling on another planet. It was Ned who filled the room, sneaking up between the floorboards or grinning from the frames of the self-important pictures of Charles' ancestors. Ned felt real and solid – the only thing that was. She should never have put him off. Perhaps she ought to phone him and just say something casual and conversational – her headache was better, the rain had stopped.

She picked up the phone and began to dial . . . put it down again. It wasn't Ned she needed, it was Charles. And anyway, she'd always refused to see Ned in the evenings. She was Frances in the evenings, not Franny, and Frances was composed and self-sufficient. If she couldn't control herself enough to read or work, then at least she'd settle down and do a little cooking. They had an important dinner party later in the month and she could prepare a rum and orange soufflé in advance, and put it in the freezer. She stood at the kitchen table and set herself to grate the peel from seven oranges, a long and fiddly task. A man was talking on the radio in a plump, brandied voice about Balanchine's collaboration with Stravinsky. She tried to concentrate. She squeezed the orange juice and mixed it with a generous sloosh of rum. The long-case clock struck ten, echoed by the high bray of the chiming Delander, and, at the same instant, the spring door of the Victorian cuckoo-clock burst open and his absurdly smug cuckoo-ooo coughed across the hall. Ten cuckoos, ten chimes, ten peals, ten booms, ten . . .

All the clocks were so bloody obedient; none of them late or slow or out-of-time. How could they be, when they were Charles' property? She flung the pile of carefully grated orange peel into the sink, gulped down the tumblerful of rum and orange juice, and rummaged for the car keys. Sod the soufflé! Damn the rules! She needed air and space and action.

It was a soft summer night. The scent of stocks lassooed her as she walked across the garden to the garage. The grass looked grey and smoky. Tendrils of clematis reached out to touch her face as she edged along the wall. She was gulping air like rum.

The car knew where to go. It turned out of Richmond and along the Kew Road, over the bridge, past the old Brentford market. She hardly noticed the route. She was only out for a drive, a change of scene. She had no plans. If the car wanted to take itself to Acton, well, why not? It was as good a place as any. She cruised along the Vale, turned right, then right again.

The house looked taller and shabbier than she'd remembered it. There were no stocks in the front garden, only dandelions. A grey cat whisked round the side of the house and disappeared. She leaned against the cold stone steps. She'd drive off again in a moment. She was only getting a breath of air. Ned would be out, in any case. Or entertaining a girl, a young kid from Southmead Polytechnic with hair like Magda's. Why shouldn't he? He was young and unattached and bound to have a yes-girl. Frannys spent the whole time saying no.

It wouldn't hurt to knock. If they'd gone to bed, they simply needn't answer. And, if they hadn't, she could always say she was just passing and could she borrow a . . .

'I was . . . er . . . just passing . . .'

His legs were bare under the dirty towelling dressing-gown, his hair rumpled and on end. She'd obviously disturbed him with a girl. He'd be furious, embarrassed. She tried to back away.

'I'm sorry, Ned, I should have phoned. I . . .'

'Franny.' His voice was soft like fudge, an off-guard, sleepy voice without its usual banter.

Suddenly, her chin was grazing against his dressing-gown and she was drowning in rough brown towelling.

'I wondered . . . if I could borrow a . . .'

'Borrow anything, my darling.'

He pushed her down again. Her head was underwater. She clung to him. He was a buoy, a lifeboat. He was rescuing her, dragging her from the waves and setting her down in the cool green shores of his bedroom.

She was quite safe. It was only a continuation of the week. She'd lain beside him almost every day, on picnics and in parks, and nothing had happened. She hadn't let it happen. So it made no difference, really, that they were lying on his bed now, and his dressing-gown had slipped apart, and he was taking off her clothes. She was chilled – that was all – and she needed his hot nakedness to stop her catching cold.

She tried to keep talking, then she needn't think. It was just an ordinary evening, and they were relaxing together, putting their feet up.

'I was out for a drive, and . . .'

'Mmmmmm . . .' He was kissing the inside of her elbow and down along her forearm.

'So I thought I'd just drop by and say hello . . .'

His mouth was wet and open and had moved against hers. She dodged it.

'You taste of rum, darling. Delicious.'

She tried to fix her attention on the ceiling. 'I . . . hope I didn't wake you up.'

'Hush, my love, don't talk.'

It was so much worse in silence. All the guilts rushed in to fill the empty spaces where the words had been. Yet, it couldn't be entirely wrong. Rathbone had suggested it himself – well almost. Worse still to do it with the milkman and produce a bald, gingery infant, in a strawberry yoghurt carton. At least Ned was literate.

She mustn't enjoy it, that was the key. So long as she regarded it merely as a duty in the larger cause of procreation, a cold, sterile procedure like dilatation or laparotomy, then it couldn't be wicked. She must dispense with the kissing and the cuddling, cut out everything which smacked of pleasure. Ned was still nuzzling her neck. She rolled over on top of him, shut her eyes, put out her hand and groped down.

It felt different from Charles', smaller and more pliable. She tried to slot it in, still not daring to look down. It keeled over and slipped out. She tried again, closing her legs and squeezing. She wanted it to fill and overwhelm her, like Charles' did, to

171

grind her into pieces, so that she couldn't think of Charles, or anything, to whiplash her out of her head, into harbour. But the small soft thing was oozing out again, shrinking away from her. She mustn't let it go. Whatever happened, they must continue with this medical procedure. It was crucial day fourteen.

Ned crawled out from underneath her and stroked a hand along her breasts. 'I'm sorry, love, don't rush me. Let me kiss you first.'

She hadn't time for kissing. There was an egg more or less bursting to be fertilized, and every demon in hell ready to pounce if she wavered for a moment. Why were men so damned perverse, Charles dallying in Nassau, and Ned dawdling in Acton, still slowing down the pace.

'Hey, Franny . . .'

'What?' She wished he wouldn't talk, or use her name. She didn't want to remember who she was. Even Frannys wouldn't go this far. Safer to be just a body on Mr Rathbone's couch. She closed her eyes again, tried to steer and coax him in.

'Look, darling, just relax. You seem so tense, on edge, and it's affecting me, as well. There's no rush. Let's just cuddle.'

No rush! How could she relax when she was terrified he'd go completely limp, and her one chance of conceiving would peter out in cosy (barren) cuddles. They were already losing contact. She tensed her muscles and moved her body against him, the way Charles had taught her, circling her thighs and gripping. She could feel Ned stiffen a little, but he was still only a mollusc, compared with the mast that Charles was, and hardly moving at all. They were stranded, becalmed, but they must go on – it would be crazy to stop now. She needed Ned, his kiss of life, life not for her, but for her baby. She rocked backwards and forwards against him, slower, then quicker, using Charles' own tuition to betray him. Ned suddenly gasped and shouted underneath her. There was a shudder, a tin-pot explosion, and, as he slithered out, she felt sperm trickling down between her thighs.

She rolled over, bent her knees up right against her chest. She had to harvest every drop of sperm. Ned was kissing her and kissing her. She turned her face away.

'I'm sorry, love. I was lousy, but you took me by surprise. I like a bit of preparation first. Anyway, you've been saying no so long, I've begun to see you as a sort of Virgin Mary, and screwing Blessed Virgins puts me off. Give me half an hour and I'll recover.'

She felt rigid with embarrassment. Now she had his sperm safe inside her, the whole thing seemed shameful. How ever could she have got into his bed, a squalid hole with crumpled sheets that had never seen an iron, threadbare blankets, half a cheese roll mouldering on the bedside table, an outboard engine in pieces on the floor, the smell of naked, sweaty male? He was lying half on top of her, his nose jammed against hers. He didn't even seem mortified, just sleepy. She longed to creep away, but Mr Rathbone's instructions precluded it. She had to lie there a full thirty minutes on her back, and by that time, he'd be stiff again. Or fast asleep. He already had his eyes closed and was murmuring silly, sleepy things into her hair. His body felt damp and sticky against her own cool, dry one. She fought a strong temptation to push him off, alarmed by her own anger. She should be grateful, not vindictive. He had saved her, hadn't he, kindled the Clomid, serviced her egg. But she wanted Charles' baby, not a yellow-eyed pygmy who'd be born with an instant grin and a dandelion between its teeth. And, if it had to be Ned's, why couldn't it have been a beautiful encounter, an immaculate conception? Hot-house flowers blooming in a five-star bedroom, romantic music sobbing through a languorous night, not that sordid, five-minute shipwreck which had beached them on a wasteland.

Yet it was she who had made it sordid, by insisting on sperm instead of sensations. She had outlawed all ecstasy by setting up some pleasure-guilt ratio – if the one diminished, so would the other. But it hadn't proved the case. There was a different, harsher ratio – the more torpid it was, the more reprehensible. She couldn't even excuse herself on the grounds that she had been swept away by passion, or overruled by Ned's tempestuous feelings.

She was still surprised at Ned. After Brighton, she had expected something wilder, more akin to the last occasion she'd made love – well, hardly love, that time, the way Charles had forced her head against the floor and then rammed Magda into it. She had loathed his brutishness, yet there was something about it which now attracted her. Ned's passive, flaccid, rudderless performance had made her realize that Charles' thrust and vigour were not simply to be taken for granted as the norm.

Ned was leaning over her, his hair dripping in her eyes. 'I want you, Franny. I've wanted you ever since I found you in my front garden. Hold me, love. I want to have you properly.'

She couldn't say no. It was his bed, his sperm. She'd woken him up and she could hardly tell him to go back to sleep and forget it ever happened. Yet she didn't want him near her, especially not that part of him coiling damp and soft against her thigh. She'd never thought much about size before. She'd taken Charles as her gauge and her yardstick, and assumed most men more or less matched up. But now she found they didn't, it disturbed her.

Ned grew an inch or two as she used her hands to fondle him. She had to repay him for the sperm. She only hoped he'd come on top of her – Rathbone had made it clear she mustn't move. The egg had the best chance of being fertilized if she lay on her back with her legs drawn up. She drew them up still further, pretending she was excited by his mouth. The mouth moved lower down, rough chin scratching between her breasts, across her belly, and still on down. Suddenly, it had reached her thighs, his reckless tongue dipping and squeezing between them. She closed herself against him. That was not allowed. But, by drawing up her legs, she'd more or less encouraged him. He'd taken it as an open invitation, not just a practical procedure for retaining his sperm. Well, at least she needn't move, just stay on her back and pretend it wasn't happening.

His face had almost disappeared between her legs, his fair hair shading off into her darker, coarser thatch, his nose squashed sideways against her thighs. She mustn't look, or he'd think she was enjoying it. She *was* enjoying it. He was doing exquisite things with his teeth. His tongue felt barbed and dangerous. He was turning her inside out, adding pain to ecstasy, as he teased and nipped with his teeth and grazed his unshaven chin back and forth across her thighs. Part of her held back still, worrying and analysing in the prison of her head – she shouldn't be enjoying it; he'd expect her to do it back; supposing he licked away all his own semen and lessened the chance of conception. No, the sperm were already in her, rushing for the egg like lemmings, all four hundred million of them. She could almost feel them plunging and shoving deeper into her womb, an exhilarating feeling, somehow connected with what Ned was doing deep between her legs. His chameleon tongue changed shape and speed and texture from minute to minute. He was licking secret, shameful places which had nothing to do with sex, cul-de-sacs which had been closed and private all her life. She spread her legs wider. Everything was opening for him, the sensations taking her over. She could feel her own mouth imitating his, her tongue searching for him, restless.

'Ned,' she shouted. 'Ned!' Her voice came from somewhere deeper than her mouth.

He let his head move slowly up her belly. His face looked damp and crumpled, and his lips tasted strange when they fumbled against her own. No good recoiling – that was her own taste and smell – one she tried to drown with soap and douches. His tireless mouth was repeating what it had done further down. He had slipped his little finger between her lips, as well as his deft tongue, and there were incredible, tangled sensations she could only submit to. She had moved out of her head and into her mouth. She was no longer Frances, not even Franny, but just an object and an orifice. It was a shattering relief. All her life, sex had been monitored through her consciousness and conscience, obeying rules, observing boundaries, but now it had rebelled. She was suddenly a body – mouth, bowels, belly, arse – messy, sweaty, open.

He had still not entered her. She thrust her thighs up and out towards him, almost forced him in. He still felt small, as if he had been swallowed up inside her. She tried to move in time to him, but he was too slow, too feeble. She longed for him to slam into her, on and on, until her mind shrivelled with disuse. He was moving now, though only very tentatively. She slowed herself down to suit him, and suddenly, he yelled 'Christ!' and then lay still.

She was so wet already, she hardly knew he'd come. Her own body was still revving and thrusting underneath him, but there was nothing to fill or answer it. She tried to force him back, scooping up the small slippery thing between her hands and struggling to revive it.

He was spent, exhausted, his whole weight flat against her. 'You're wonderful, Franny, glorious! Put your arms around me, hold me.'

She didn't want to hold him. She wanted to screw him. That wasn't a Frances word. It had crept out of her new uncaged body and was crying out for a finale. She felt overwhelmed with contradictory feelings – white heat of frustration mixed with fury, amazement at the new, greedy whore she had become, but also a shame, a reticence, a slow return to the clogged, accusing strictures of her head.

There were black crosses everywhere, a hundred for adultery, a thousand for enjoying it, two thousand for wanting more. She felt guilt and terror towards Charles, anger and gratitude to Ned, delight and horror at herself. A civil war was raging in this small, poky bedroom, and one of the chief combatants was sleeping through the gunfire, slumped across her chest. She tried to shift from underneath him, but he clung on like a baby.

Baby! She'd forgotten all about babies for at least twenty minutes. God almighty! She was pregnant – she must be. Everything was primed. It was exactly day fourteen, the Clomid had made her super-fertile, all her tests were perfect anyway, Ned was young and virile, and above all, he was a different man with different sperm. If she was allergic to Charles' semen, as Rathbone had hinted, then this new, gutsy brand would mean instant conception. Now she had caught up with Piroska, and was Charles' equal in betrayal. A Ned for a Magda. She shivered. She didn't want to be his equal. One of Charles' attractions was that you could never catch up, not even in betrayal.

Charles would know the child wasn't his. It would be born with fair curly hair creeping down its navel, loll in its cot and never learn its alphabet. She could almost feel the foetus growing inside her, a soft-shelled, feckless thing, flinging its toys about, untidying her perfect houseproud womb. Cells adding to cells in the relentless drive towards creation; Ned's slipshod chromosomes forcing hers apart, and fusing with them. It was an alien growth, a cancer, slow-growing and inexorable, totally indifferent as to whether she welcomed it, or cursed it.

Even the act of conceiving it had totally confused her. Ned's thrusting had been almost perfunctory. Charles could do it at full throttle for at least twelve minutes. He probably even timed it on his quartz digital alarm. And yet, all that time, she had never felt the wild, inside-out sensations which Ned's mouth had exploded into her. Charles never moved his mouth any lower than her breasts. She tried now to imagine him, fusing Ned's tongue on to Charles' body and opening her legs, ashamed of her excitement. Not only had Ned impregnated her, he had turned her into some greedy, voracious slut, kindled strange new parts of her anatomy with wild new desires. And then he'd gone to sleep on top of them, leaving them still shouting out for more. He was crushing her limbs and lying on her hair, his mouth half open, one arm pinioning her chest.

She stared up at the ceiling. The bedside light was still switched on and she could see the paint stained and flaking on the dirty walls, and the overhead bulb bare, without a shade. She longed to be in her own bedroom, with its old-rose ceiling and the fragile elegance of the Bohemian tear-drop chandelier. The bed was too small for both of them. The mattress dipped and bulged, and there was only one small pillow. She'd never get to sleep. Another man's body was crushed on top of hers, another man's baby sprouting in her womb.

At least it was warm. There was something very comforting about lying against another naked body. She rarely did it. Charles always got up and took a shower after sex, and then returned to the chilly order of his own bed. There were a lot of things she rarely did. Her legs were still open. She trailed her hand down between them and left it there. She dared not move too much in case she woke Ned, but she turned her fingers into Ned's mouth and Charles' mast combined. The bed trembled in shock.

Rilke slunk through the open door and sprang on top of her. His soft fur brushed against her thighs and added to the tangle of sensations between them. She lay with Ned's weight against her breasts, and Rilke's warmth purring through her, further down. She was exhausted, even sore, so many guilts and pleasures breeding in her body, she doubted if she'd ever sleep again. But she might as well relax. The situation was so bizarre, all she could do was lie back and accept it for the moment. It would be light by five o'clock. She'd wake Ned then, and make her getaway. Meantime, she'd try to lull her frantic mind – work out logarithms, recite the whole of *Paradise Lost*, anything to dull the screaming ache of what she'd done. Charles had given her Milton, all twelve volumes, vellum-bound, for her twentieth birthday.

'Of man's first disobedience and the fall . . .'

It was noon when she woke. The sun was stampeding through the open curtains and the day smelled of toast. There were five hefty slices of it, glistening with butter, with Ned attached to them, trying to balance the marmalade on the teapot and kiss her, all at once.

'Your *petit déjeuner, madame*. Devilled kidneys on a silver salver, smoked Orkneys haddock in a chafing dish . . . and Tesco's tuppence-off teabags. Sleep well?'

'Mmmm . . .' She couldn't have slept. She had eleven and three-quarter more books of *Paradise Lost* to work through, and at least eight hours of guilt.

'Hungry?'

'Yes.' She couldn't be hungry. She was a wicked, unfaithful, pregnant, feckless bitch. An insomniac who'd lost her appetite.

He fed her with three-quarters of the toast and three mugs of tea, and tickled crumbs across her naked tummy. Rilke sat on her left foot and Werther licked butter from the empty plate. Ned spread the *Daily Mail* across the bed and thumbed through it for the horoscopes.

'Right, here we are – Virgo. "Stay in bed all day today and don't venture out. Intimate encounters with a fair, mysterious stranger can only prove fruitful."'

Frances tried to laugh. Fruitful – that terrifying, marvellous word. 'You're making it up, Ned. It probably says "Business interests prosper", or something boring like that.'

'No, it doesn't. It says "Stay in bed with lovely Ned." Which is halfway to a poem. Come on, love, move over. I don't see why Rilke can lie on top of you, if I can't.'

'Look, Ned, I ought to get back . . .'

'Whatever for?'

'Well, Charles . . .'

'He's away.'

'Yes, but . . .'

'How long will he be gone?'

178

'I don't know.'

'Roughly.'

'Three or four days, maybe.'

'OK, I'll settle for that. Three or four days in bed with Ned, and if the *Daily Mail* allows it, we'll get up on Friday. No, don't start objecting. I want to kiss you and it tickles if you talk. Shove up a bit, love, I'm falling out of bed.'

'Ned, I . . .'

'Hush, love. You taste of lemon marmalade, and I want some more of it. Look, we'll do it six times today, seven tomorrow, ten on Thursday, and go to Confession on Friday. Right? Right!'

14

Friday. Charles shut his eyes against the sugar-coated smile of the air hostess. He wished to God they'd leave a man alone. He didn't need all those airborne little simpers and the swish of skirts and petticoats interrupting his work, and no, he didn't want a cocktail, and yes, he did have a headache, but if only they'd remove themselves, he might feel slightly better.

He finished his report on the prosecution, making it sound less messy than it was. His own private report, locked inside his head, was a lot more damaging. He'd been reprimanded by the judge, in open court. Thank God Oppenheimer wasn't present at the time. But afterwards, King Heinrich had made it almost worse by being so magnanimous. That cold, well-mannered smile, that unctuous bottle of chilled Dom Pérignon, so cruelly inappropriate. It was humiliating, shameful.

He heard Mr Justice Lambton's damp-flannel voice echoing round the plane. 'Uncooperative, evasive in his evidence, muddled in his presentation.' He was never muddled – evasive maybe, but always clear, efficient. The whole damned business seemed to have fouled up right from the beginning. The crazy heat, the bungled advocacy, and worst of all, Frances' hysterical phone calls. She had never behaved like that before, filling his head so full of her obsessions, that he himself had lain awake in the frigid, air-conditioned Nassau nights, counting day thirteen, day fourteen, too late. The worst part was the small trickle of relief when it *was* too late, knowing that he couldn't be blamed, that a chance hitch in a court case had kept a child unconceived.

He couldn't risk a second round of fatherhood. The tie between parent and child was so close, so extraordinary, that if it failed, it took a gash out of your life. Magda had already chipped away at his defences. Even as a foetus, she had wormed her way between him and Piroska, and maimed the relationship. When she was born, he'd felt real pride, excitement, but only at a distance. And now that he had moved his daughter close to him, into the soul and strongbox of his house, she was threatening its very fabric, driving a wedge between him and Frances. And yet, Magda was so much part of him, that his anger was directed chiefly at himself, his own failure to love or control her.

He was failing Frances, too. Her phone calls only underlined it. He had tried to blot them out and fantasize about her, as a wife without a womb, the way she had been before Rathbone poked his prying speculum into their bedroom. She still excited him, her small, fastidious body, with its cool, tight, unadulterated innocence. He had missed her, genuinely. It was damned lonely jetting round the world, one aseptic hotel room a carbon copy of the rest, except the furniture was differently arranged. He often wondered why they couldn't enforce a standard layout for all executive suites – bed here, cupboard there. At least a man wouldn't have endlessly to adapt; wake up with his feet facing north in Tokyo, when they'd been south in Singapore; look out of a window that had turned into a wall; reach for a light-switch which wasn't there – reach for a woman who wasn't there – only the cold rump of a bolster rejecting his advances. Sheraton and Intercontinental probably planned it on purpose, to underline the fact that you were an everlasting exile in hotels. As soon as you'd signed with your American Express card, the sheets were stripped, the room deodorized, all traces of you aerosoled away, and the bed resterilized for another transient to toss and turn in.

Endless chit-chat with cardboard people, interchangeable faces and switch-on smiles. Self-important uniforms disguising empty robots – stewardesses, waiters, court officials, switchboard operators. And when, at last, your own wife came on the line, still no comfort or communion, only sobbing and reproaches. Laura had been as bad. Even she had phoned him, her water-bed drawl cooing snide remarks about his coming back with another little Magda, a Bahamian baby this time, via the chambermaid. Christ! All the female staff could have been flat-chested paraplegics with psoriasis, for all he cared. He'd been grappling with fraud and high finance, not chambermaids; Nemesis, not Eros. And yet, both the women in his life had belly-ached on about babies, as if nothing ever happened in the world above groin level. He shifted his own groin in the padded, ergonomic seat and

181

watched the dazzle of the blue Atlantic fade and dwindle into grey cloud. The plane seemed to fill with females, all demanding, all disappointed in him. Laura pacing up and down empty hotel bedrooms, Magda begging him for dogs and cats and ponies, Frances scrounging non-existent sperm. He wished to God he could return to an empty house, without a daughter or a mistress, without even a wife. He'd missed them when they were safely half a world away, but now the distance had shrunk to half an hour, he didn't want them back. At least, not yet. Just a few female-less days to recover from the court case and catch up with his other clients. Perhaps he'd go directly from the airport to the office. He could shut himself away there, tell his secretary he wanted no interruptions, not even any phone calls. He closed his eyes for touch-down, the roar of the jets as the engines reversed, the synthetic stewardess still oozing saccharin, the jostle and jar of customs.

'Charlie!'

Christ, no, not Laura. He'd forbidden her to come. Yes, he knew she always met him from the airport, but things would have to change. The whole advantage of a mistress was that she only turned up when you ordered her.

'Look, Laura, I told you . . .'

'I know, Charlie darling, but I've got a little piece of news for you that simply couldn't wait. It's really rather priceless.'

He put his suitcase down again, tried to blink away his headache, shut out all the noises – the endless drone of evidence and counter-evidence in the tense and stifling court room; the buzz of flies round the stinking hotel dustbins; Frances' tears crackling down the phone; and now Laura, shrill and gloating.

'Well, you'll have to be quick. I'm on my way to the office, and I've got a hell of a lot to catch up with.'

Laura picked up the suitcase herself, and headed for the buffet. 'Oh, it won't take a second, darling. It's just a little something about your precious Frances. I thought it might amuse you.'

Charles didn't go to the office – headed home instead. The house was untidy. There were dead flowers in the drawing-room, dirty cups and saucers in the kitchen, and his wife was wearing a crumpled skirt which looked as if she'd slept in it. He didn't kiss her. She was fussing with the tea things.

'Like a cup of tea, darling?'

'No thanks.'

'Coffee?'

'No.'

'What's wrong, Charles?'

'Nothing.'

'I'm sorry about your court case.'

'Yes.'

'Was it a good trip otherwise?'

'No.'

'Didn't you manage to fit in any sightseeing?'

'There wasn't time. Did you?'

'I beg your pardon?'

'Fit in any sightseeing?'

'Sightseeing? Why should I do sightseeing?'

'No reason.'

She was wearing a pendant round her neck, some gimcrack thing he'd never seen before. The collar of her blouse was grubby. In all the fifteen years he'd lived with her, she'd never been anything but immaculate.

'Well, what did you do?'

'Nothing much.'

'No trips out?'

'Not really.'

What was that supposed to mean? He stared at her small face. Her eyes were so audaciously blue, he felt almost angry with them. They should have paled or faded. He tried again.

'It must have been lonely for you, Frances, stuck in the house all day.'

'Not too bad. I've got my friends, and golf . . .'

'Oh, you played golf, did you?'

'Well, no, but . . .'

'Friends, then. Who did you see?'

She had her hair done in a different way – a foolish wispy fringe, which made her look much younger.

'Well, Evelyn. And . . . um . . . Jane. Oh – and Laura came round for a gin.'

'Really? How was she?'

'Fine. She wanted to know when you'd be back, said Clive had some business crisis and needed your advice. I promised her you'd phone.'

'Right. Who else?'

'What do you mean "who else"?'

Repeating his questions – a bad sign. She was stalling, playing for time. And did she normally leave her stockings off? It was a stifling day, but . . .

'Who else did you see?'

'Charles, this is like the Spanish Inquisition. What's the matter with you?'

'Nothing. You always complain that I don't take enough interest in your life, and when I do, you call it an inquisition. I'm merely concerned to know what you've been doing.'

'I told you, nothing much. A little cooking for the freezer, a bit of gardening, some freelance work for Fab Furs. And I finished the book on the pre-Raphaelites.'

'You finished that before I left.'

'Oh, did I? Look, why don't we have some tea?'

'I've told you, twice, I don't want tea.'

'You needn't be so touchy, Charles. In fact, considering the circumstances, I think you've got a cheek. The least you could do was say you're sorry, rather than keep badgering me.'

'Sorry? I wasn't under the impression that *I* was the one who had anything to be sorry for.'

'And what about the Clomid and missing ovulation? I suppose that doesn't count.'

Charles swooped on the radio, switched off *Woman's Hour*. 'I'm sure you found compensations.' He wrenched the dials, scorching through every station from AFN to Luxemburg. Brief, mindless syllables congealed in one squeal of sound. 'Stupid of me never to have guessed. I leave you alone at least a dozen times a year, trusting you implicitly, assuming you're the innocent you always play at being, the virtuous child-bride.'

'Charles, I don't know what you're . . .'

Flutes and violins swooped into the kitchen and almost swamped her voice. He had picked up a J.C. Bach recital on a German transmission.

'And anyway, I'm not a child. It's you that's always tried to keep me one – a hundred-year-old child, dead before she's even tasted life.'

Charles adjusted the sound a fraction. He hated melodrama. If Frances adopted that theatrical tone, he'd never keep his own cool. He listened for a moment to the steady beat of the harpsichord continuo, tried to keep his voice in touch with it, harmonious and even.

'Well I hope you enjoyed your taste of it, on this occasion.'

'Charles, what are you . . . ?'

'Oh, I know you said you hadn't done any sightseeing. I believe you. I'm sure you had more important things to do in Windsor.'

'Windsor?'

Still repeating him. She had dropped a teaspoon, and he could hear her fear reflected in the way it clattered to the floor.

'You'd hardly drive all that way, merely to visit the Castle, or walk in the Great Park . . .'

'What are you implying, Charles?'

'I'm not implying anything, simply reporting facts.'

'I don't know what you're talking about.'

There was fear everywhere, even in his own throat. He tried to clear it, speak less gruffly. 'A colleague of mine saw you leaving the Galsworthy Hotel in Windsor six days ago, hand in hand with a . . . er . . . young man. That was not, in fact, the term used to describe him, but I won't insult you.' He watched her closely, pretending not to. She didn't flush, or blanch, just fiddled with her pendant, twisting the chain round and round between her fingers, round and round . . . The suave, almost obsequious voice of the cellos was chasing its own echo through an ingenious web of sound. Round and round . . .

'Well?'

'Well, what?'

'Was my colleague correct?' He heard Laura's words again, bleeding from her wide, scarlet mouth, as it toyed with coffee in the airport lounge. Afterwards, she had blotted her lips with a paper napkin, leaving a perfect outline. A second traitor mouth mocking him on the soft white tissue. Scarlet and white, guilt and innocence. Frances hadn't answered.

185

'I'm asking you, Frances, was my information wrong?'

'Yes.' Her face was like a death-mask. Even her fingers were motionless now, the knuckles white and rigid as they gripped the edge of the table.

'I see. So you didn't go to the Galsworthy Hotel in Windsor? My colleague was lying.' The music had changed now from *andante* to *allegretto* and there were florid swirls and capers from the flutes, cavorting above the strict measure of the harpsichord.

'Look, Charles, who was this colleague? At least you could tell me his name. He's probably just a trouble-maker, some neurotic who got passed over in promotion. Frankly, I don't think much of a man who spends his free time sneaking round hotels, spying on innocent people.'

'Don't change the subject, Frances. All I want is a straight answer to a simple question. Did you, or did you not, go to Windsor with a young man?'

'Yes. I mean, no. You're making it sound all wrong, Charles. It wasn't what you think. I simply . . . All right, I *did* go to Windsor, I admit it, but we only had tea there.'

'We?'

'Well, me and just a . . . friend.'

'A male friend?'

'Just an odd acquaintance. It's not important.' A horn brayed derisively, isolated for a second above the unison of the strings.

'Do you normally hold hands with odd acquaintances? Or let them take you to hotels? And anyway, you said a little earlier you'd hardly been out, so what in God's name were you doing in Windsor?' He was the inquisitor now, the witness for the prosecution. The court case had moved from Nassau to his own cosy, split-pine kitchen.

'It was only tea, I told you. We were there less than half an hour, I've still got the bill. I'll show you, if you're so suspicious.'

'So, you were paying, were you? Not only do you allow strange men to take you to hotels, but the final irony is using my money to do it.'

'For Christ's sake, Charles, it was only a pot of tea and buttered toast. I'll pay you back, if you're that grudging.'

The word hit him like a punch in the gut, dislodging all the expensive gifts he had showered on her over the years – real kimonos from Tokyo; silks and snakeskins from Singapore; gold and scent and ivory; damask, diamonds, fur; and, even now, in his suitcase, the graceful necklet of moonstones and amethysts which had cost almost more than his entire fee for the trip. All right, even if some of it was guilt-money, hush-money, he had never, ever, grudged her anything. It was money earned by his own fatigue and endurance, swotting in planes and trains, working through colds and 'flus and holidays, so that she should never go without. If she remarked, sometimes, that she'd rather have his company, that was self-delusion. Frances had come, now, to take her cream-filled, chocolate-coated life for granted, conveniently forgetting that it was he who financed it. She complained because he worked so hard, and yet his punishing hours were the price her queenly life demanded.

Yet, there she was, scrabbling in her handbag, paying him for tea and buttered toast, hurling all her loose change on the table, pennies and ha'pennies scratching the delicate tulip-wood inlay. Delicate herself, her small hands white against the dirty coins. He couldn't bear the thought of anyone else mauling and devaluing her, trespassing on his property. She suddenly seemed precious, irreplaceable.

'Frances . . .'

Two flutes were bantering with each other, shrill, high-spirited. He took her in his arms. Her head fitted exactly into the hollow of his collar-bone. He hoped to Christ it had only been tea. Why in God's name couldn't she have denied the whole sordid story, showed utter incredulity, as he'd expected? Then he could have dismissed it as mere she-bitch jealousy on Laura's part, the lying tittle-tattle of a woman scorned. She could still deny it. There was still a chance of some simple, harmless explanation. He released her almost roughly. The first Sinfonia had ended and the German announcer's harsh guttural voice was introducing the second.

'Frances, listen to me, it was nothing, was it? Just a cup of tea with a friend. That's what you said. Can you swear that?' A friend. He didn't like the word. He knew all his wife's friends, and there wasn't one who wore Snoopy T-shirts and tartan laces in his sneakers. And why had she lied to him in the first place, told him she'd done nothing, been nowhere?

'Oh, Charles . . .'

She wasn't answering the question. Evasive. Mr Justice Lambton would have reprimanded her: refusing to face the evidence, confusing the plaintiff.

'Yes or no, Frances?'

'Yes.' The strings burst out again in a sudden, radiant flurry of arpeggios.

'You mean, there *was* more to it.' He was confusing her himself now, deliberately. Lies always surfaced in confusion.

'No, Charles. I mean yes, it was only tea.'

'OK, I'm sorry. Look, forgive me, Frances. I'm exhausted. It's probably jet-lag.' He tried to isolate the intricate line of the cello from the rapturous strings supporting it. He was home now, returned to her from an alien continent and a different time-scale, yet the space between them seemed even greater than when he'd been away. 'Only tea' solved nothing. Why should Frances be in Windsor at all, and least of all hand-in-hand with a layabout in dirty jeans and a bracelet? Amazing what an eye for detail Laura had. He had to admire her, really. The exact time, the precise location, the detailed dimensions of a silver identity bracelet, the colours of the Snoopy. A private detective could hardly have done better. Which made him suspect her, somehow. Laura had been gunning for Frances ever since Magda's arrival, when Charles had chosen wife and daughter over mistress. What better way to win him back, than cast aspersions on his wife's fidelity? The whole thing could be an elaborate trap. His own intuition was perhaps a safer guide. You could almost smell it if a woman were unfaithful and he could only catch the scent from Laura. Frances still had that cool, chaste virgin shell around her, something which both excited and provoked him. He wanted, suddenly, to tear her clothes off, to pound into her and repossess her, to establish without any shadow of a doubt that she was his exclusive property.

'Frances, I . . . I've missed you. Let's go to bed.' The music pleaded for him, violins cajoling, woodwind whispering.

'No.'

She never said no, not directly, anyway. That was almost proof. She didn't want him any more, because some filthy Charlie Brown, half his age, had been screwing her in Windsor, after or before the buttered toast.

'Look, Frances, it's important. We've been parted for a fortnight.'

She almost shook him off. 'Oh, it's important, is it, suddenly. And why wasn't it important a week ago? I begged you then, didn't I? Went on my knees for you to come home and make love to me. But it's only when *you* want it, it starts to be important. You can refuse and refuse, and then, the very second you step inside the door, I'm expected to roll over on my back with my legs open. Well, this time I shan't.'

Where, in Christ's name, had she learned such language? His bone-china wife had never spoken to him like that in fifteen years. He was wrong – she wasn't Minton any more, but rough, coarse earthenware which set his teeth on edge. There was something subtly different about her. He couldn't quite locate it, but she looked shop-soiled and unkempt. Her hair needed washing and she wasn't wearing any of his jewellery, only that bargain-basement pendant, which he was tempted to rip off. He tried to lower his voice into second gear, but it kept revving up again, slipping out of his control. He never shouted, least of all with J.C. Bach in progress. Yet here he was, an ugly, alien instrument, out of tune, wrecking and confounding the intricate order of a flawless Sinfonia. Yet he dared not turn it off, feared the empty space behind the orchestra, filled only with his own strident voice.

'It's never me you've wanted, Frances, only your blasted baby. You don't even *like* sex. For years it was a matrimonial endurance test, and now it's just a reproductive process. I'm not your husband, or your lover, I'm just your prize bull.'

'There's nothing very prize about you, is there? They'd have slaughtered you for beef by now, judging by your record.'

'Frances, how dare you ...' It couldn't be happening – these farmyard insults, this harsh discordant conversation. It must only be a recording. His life was measured and melodious. Even Johann Christian was jeering at him now, the smug, self-satisfied violas trifling with some fatuous phrase, soft-centred, out of harmony with the raucous dissonance of Frances' voice.

'I do dare. I've been thinking about things while you were away – all sorts of things. And I've begun to realize ...'

189

'Where's Magda?' he asked suddenly, didn't want to know what Frances had been thinking.

'She'll be back this afternoon. Viv's bringing her in time for tea.'

'You should never have left her at Viv's all week.' If Magda had been in the house, Frances would have had to act the mother, not the whore. 'I can't understand you, Frances. You object when I suggest a perfectly reasonable boarding school, yet have no compunction in getting rid of Magda on every possible occasion. I don't really know why I bother to consult you. She's my daughter, so it's I who should . . .'

Frances' voice was suddenly soft, conciliatory. She had picked up the silver teaspoon from the floor and was cradling it in her hands. 'How do you know she is your daughter?'

'I beg your pardon?' Charles stopped in his pacing of the kitchen, face to face with a skinny black knight, a framed brass-rubbing from the old church at Stoke d'Abernon.

'Well, how do you? There's no evidence, is there? She's ruined everything between us, and yet you can't even prove that she's your child in the first place. You've probably never had a child. Why should you have had one by Piroska, if you can't have one with me? She probably slept with scores of men and told them all they were Magda's father. Magda doesn't look like you. She's dark and foreign and . . . Her father was probably some swarthy, illiterate Hungarian. She isn't even fond of you. If she was really your flesh and blood, wouldn't there be some sign of it, some bond between you?'

Charles groped towards the door. Christ, holy Christ, not that! The tiny crack of doubt he'd been filling in and patching up for fifteen years, now wrenched apart by Frances; all his careful, rational arguments shattered into pieces, nothing but a shrieking hole he'd never fill again. Her voice was like a drill boring into his defences, cracking his foundations, mocking him with the sniggering bassoon.

She was still drilling him away. 'How does any man know if it's his child? Babies aren't born with a label round their necks, saying "X is my father". A woman can sleep with half a dozen men . . .'

Charles shut his eyes. He could see only blackness, an abyss with half of Windsor filling it. 'Can she, Frances?'

'All right, even if I had slept with someone else, whose fault would it be? You're never here, don't care a jot about trying to have a baby. Perhaps other men do care – other men who aren't so busy and unavailable and selfish . . .' The music was dark now, limping into *largo*, wounded, mutilated.

'So, you *do* admit it then – you did go to bed with that unkempt ignoramus at Windsor?'

'He's not an ignoramus. He's got a degree and a diploma and he's teaching himself Icelandic, and writing a play and . . .' She was stabbing at the strawberry jam, ramming the teaspoon against the dainty, cut-glass dish, slopping jam on to the table-cloth. 'Oh, I suppose that makes it better, does it? So long as he's educated and "our sort of person", he can screw the living daylights out of me. But if he's a loafer or a layabout, or blue-collar material or E-stream comprehensive, or any of those other condescending terms you throw around, then it's a sin and a crime and a . . . Well, what about *you*, Charles, how many A-levels did your Hungarian whore have? Did you make her sit an intelligence test before you fucked her? Check up on her grades . . .?'

Charles gripped the table. Whore, fuck, screw the living daylights . . . Words Frances didn't even know, words squeezing between the music and wrenching it out of key. Something appalling and unbelievable had happened to his wife. She'd been turned from gold into base metal.

'So you did go to that hotel at Windsor?'

'No, it wasn't bloody Windsor. Though I suppose you'd have preferred it – a royal town with a castle and a safe Conservative majority, and all the shops "by gracious appointment to her Majesty", and a four-star hotel with a top AA rating and a Michelin star. If you really want to know, Charles, it was a crumbling house in a squalid part of Acton, the sort of place they write "Pakis go home" on the lavatory walls . . .'

She was crying into the fruit dish, her tears shining on the glossy yellow skins of the Golden Delicious. 'I didn't want to, Charles. I wanted *you*. But you weren't there. You're never there. You drove me to it. I only went because . . .'

He put his hands over his ears, couldn't bear to hear. He tried to blot out everything, the coarse, disgusting details, the gloating jubilation of the flutes.

'It wasn't even much good. Well, not the first time. After that it . . .'

The first time. The phrase dropped like a stone into the echoing black hole the room had become. How many bloody times could that filthy lecher do it in a week? A hundred, a thousand? Even the radio was stunned. The German voice had disappeared, swallowed up in a frenzied surge of applause, five hundred hands clapping, a roar of adulation from the disembodied Munich audience. He picked up the knife from the table and ran his fingers along the blade. Fury was spilling out of everything, running down the walls. He watched Frances' mouth making stupid, senseless sounds.

'I must tell you, Charles, I must. You've got to listen, you've got to know what's happening.'

He turned his back, tried to stuff his fury in a drawer, tidy away jealousy and shock. But Frances was standing next to him, pulling at his sleeve, making him turn round.

'Look at me, Charles. Listen. I did go to bed with him, but not only that . . .'

Applause was still thundering through the room. Charles sat down slowly, stiffly, as if he were an invalid. 'Yes?' he said, seeing nothing save the pendant flashing on her neck. He shut his eyes, but it was still there, swaggering in front of him, like her preening, shameless voice.

'I'm pregnant by him, Charles, I'm going to have his baby.'

15

The convent smelt of brown paper, a stale, boring smell, as if nobody had unwrapped it for a hundred years. The nuns had no hair and no bodies, only cut-out faces and flat, black robes which glided on castors. They never rushed. Nor ate, drank, slept, unbent or smiled. In the chapel, they chanted foreign languages and worshipped some naked oddball trussed on a cross. Their breath smelt of fusty flower-water which had never been changed.

Mother Cornelia had cold pebble eyes set in a crazy paving face. She was sitting in the ante-chapel, her black back ramrod-straight. 'Well, my child,' she said, 'you are called after a great sinner who became a great saint.'

'Oh, yeah?' Magda kicked a lisle-stockinged foot against the prie-dieu.

'Your religious education has been most unfortunately neglected. No, it's not your fault, we won't apportion blame. All we're going to do is put it right. That's why your father brought you here, before term started. To give us a chance to catch up with your catechism, before the other girls return. We don't want your classmates calling you a heathen, do we?'

'Don't we?' Magda was jabbing at a loose splinter of wood sticking up on the prie-dieu.

'Please try to concentrate, child, otherwise we're not going to get through the Proofs Of The Existence Of God. God doesn't expect you to take Him on trust. We can prove He exists, just as the sun exists, or you exist, or . . .'

Magda had broken the splinter off and was poking it under her thumbnail. 'But supposing I *don't* exist?'

The mouth pursed itself into a smaller, harder pebble. 'Magda, don't be insolent.'

'I'm not. I've often thought about it. I mean, perhaps nobody exists. Perhaps we're all a sort of joke, or a shadow, or . . .'

'That's blasphemous, Magda, to deny God's creation. God made you in His own image.'

'But what's an image? Something that's nothing in a mirror and all the wrong way round. Anyway, Charles doesn't believe in God.'

'Who's Charles?'

'My father, of course. You met him, didn't you? He brought me down here.'

'Oh, I see.' The stone face set a few degrees harder. 'Well, we'll have to pray for him, won't we?'

'Charles doesn't need praying for. He's got everything – cars and videos and stuff. He's even bought a computer chess game with more than a million moves, stored in a sort of brain.'

'Magda, we're talking about God.'

Magda sucked at her thumb, which was bleeding from the splinter. 'I'm not.'

There was a faint dab at the door. Nuns never knocked, did everything low-key; fluttered like moths, closed doors with velvet hands. A second, younger nun had entered and the two black shapes were whispering together, joined at the top like a double-bodied monster.

Mother Cornelia stood up. 'Well, Magda, isn't that a strange coincidence? Your father's come to see you. We were just praying for him, weren't we? I'm afraid you'll have to tell him that we don't allow such frequent visits. He only brought you here three days ago. We have special weekends for visiting – just two a term. I'll let you see him this time, but not in future.'

Magda rammed the splinter further down her bleeding thumb. 'I don't want to see him.'

'Of course you do. All our girls love to see their parents.'

She watched as a drop of blood seeped slowly into the dark wood of the prie-dieu. 'He's not my parents. I haven't got any parents.'

'Magda!' The toad-coloured eyes darted in her direction. 'That's quite enough. Right, we'll receive your father in the parlour.'

Swish-swish went the black robe in front of her. You always had to walk behind nuns. They were the brides of Christ or something stupid. Well, no one else would marry them, the way most of them looked. Mother Cornelia had a wart on her chin, raised up on a sort of stalk, and Mother Gregory had traces of a beard.

They had reached the parlour now. Parents were always dumped in there – a cold, unfriendly room which swallowed everybody up. All the furniture stood stiffly to attention, as if Reverend Mother herself was forbidding it to slouch. There were grotty wax grapes in the fruit bowl, and pictures of Popes smirking round the walls. The Popes all looked the same, in purple dresses and fancy hats, with small piggy eyes and fingers raised in a sort of fuck-off gesture. They weren't exactly women, but they weren't men, either.

Charles was the only man there. She could see his shiny black shoes and three inches of frowning grey pin-stripe. Her gaze stopped at his ankles. The nuns had taught her to keep her eyes cast down. ('Only hussies look men in the face, Magda.') It was safer with Charles, anyway. If you started with his feet, it gave you time to prepare yourself, before you met the ice-floes of his eyes. She wasn't simply frightened of him, but proud of him as well. He was taller and richer and loads more important than most people's fathers. He'd flown on Concorde fifty-three times and had lunch with the Oma of Begin, and had written a book which had been translated into Japanese so that the pages read backwards. She liked being seen with him, longed to shout, 'Look at him, he's my father!' when he marched into shops in his posh camel coat and barked, 'Haven't you anything better?' to the quivering salesgirls, or ordered her French wine in restaurants and made the waiters pour hers first.

On the other hand, you couldn't touch him. His suits were made of steel, and inside his body he didn't have lungs and intestines and squashy, messy things like other people, but rows and rows of little drawers with labels on them – a sort of filing cabinet where his stomach should have been. He never hugged her and said 'Wotcha Lollipop!' or bought her sherbet suckers like Bunty's Uncle Bob did.

Her eyes had reached his fat gold watch-chain, paused at the middle button of his jacket.

'Say hello to your father, Magda.'

'Hi.' It was not the sort of thing you said to fat gold watch-chains, but whatever you said, it was bound to be wrong. Charles was always on about split infinitives or erroneous prepositions and all that crap. Except this time, he wasn't even listening. He had turned his asbestos smile on to Mother Cornelia.

'I wondered, Sister, if I could be alone with Magda for a while?'

You were meant to call them Mother, not Sister. Charles got it wrong on purpose. She was glad. She'd had enough of mothers – three in three months, and two of those had pissed off. First her own ma – oh yeah, she still wrote postcards – big deal, but the writing got larger on every one, and now it was only two lines and they were lies. 'Miss you, *kedvesem*. Wish you were here with us.' Well, if she bloody wished that, why not invite her over and be done with it? It was only that rotten Miklos who kept her out. She didn't *want* to go, thanks, with him around.

Then, precious Frances had flitted off as well, the very day Viv had returned her to the Parry Jones ponce-house. Charles had come back from Nassau, and looked all brown and cross and sort of simmering.

'Frances isn't well,' he'd said. 'She's gone to convalesce.'

Bilge! Frances couldn't bear the sight of her, that's why she'd walked out. Who cared, anyway? She'd won, hadn't she, driven Frances from her own house? Now she could queen it in Frances' chair at breakfast, and mess about with Charles' video recorder, once he'd gone to work. And, in the evenings, she had him completely to herself. It was nice, the first few days. He took her to a restaurant where the steaks were as big as doormats and gave her a fiver without even asking. But a lot of the time, he was out, and even when he wasn't, he locked himself in his study and hogged the phone. Most of the phone calls were to poor darling Frances. She'd listened outside the door and heard him saying, 'All right, Frances, if that's how you feel, there's nothing more to be said' – but he went on saying things. Once he'd said 'goodbye' seven times – she'd counted – and still not put the phone down. When he came out, his face was all locked up, and he went straight to the stereo and played some horrible wailing organ music. And they'd sat there all evening, choking in it, like church.

Then he'd packed her case and driven her to this other dump of a church, and rat-face Cornelia had pressed a pale, damp hand into hers and said, 'No, I'm not Miss, I'm Mother,' which was crap, because she was far too old and ugly to be anybody's ma, and Mother was a stupid name, anyway. Charles had stood with her at one end of the starched white dormitory, which was empty except for twenty staring beds and a picture of a bloke with golden ringlets and his heart on the outside. And he'd asked her a whole load of detailed questions about her mother and 'What was it like when you were little, Magda?' Well, he should know, shouldn't he, and how the hell could you remember stuff like that, when you'd just been marched off to some Jesus-freak prison, and were wearing a blue serge frock that rubbed the skin off your neck?

Christ! He was going to start it all again – the muscle in his face was twitching. The nun had disappeared, and he was leaning forward in that phoney, trust-me-darling way.

'Look, Magda, now you're living with us . . .'

'I'm not living with you.'

'Of course you are. This is just school. You'll be back in the holidays.'

'It *is* the holidays. Nobody else is here yet. It's like a bloody morgue.'

Charles shifted his chair, so that a new pig-eyed Pope glared at her over his shoulder. 'It would be worse at home, darling. Frances is still away, and I'm working very late most evenings, so you'd be all alone.'

She hated his darlings. They plopped out of his mouth half dead, like wet, struggling fishes. Of course she wouldn't be alone in Richmond. She had Viv and Bunty, didn't she, and all the animals, just a bike-ride away? They wanted to get rid of her, that was pretty clear. 'What have you come for?' she asked her father warily.

He was probably going to move her somewhere else. She hadn't budged from Streatham in all her fifteen years, but now it was all-change. First Richmond, then Westborough, and bloody borstal next.

'I've just come to see you, darling, to make sure you've settled in.' Another darling, another fucking lie. He'd never just come to see her, must be after something. Grown-ups always were.

197

He was sitting on the edge of his chair, his legs stretched out in front of him, dead legs, made of granite. 'Look, Magda, all I want is to get to know you better. I missed out on your childhood. That was sad. There were reasons, of course, but that doesn't mean we can't catch up now. I'd like you to trust me, tell me about yourself when you were small, fill me in on things.'

Trust him. He must be joking. You couldn't trust people who lied. 'What sort of things?' she asked.

'Anything. Your friends, your mother, people who visited the house. You and Piroska lived alone, didn't you?'

'Yeah.' Funny the way he called her ma Piroska. It sounded sort of weird.

'What can you remember when you were really tiny?'

'Nothing.' Christ, who the hell did he think she was – bloody Einstein or something, to remember things in her cradle?

'Your mother was working, wasn't she? Did she ever bring friends home?' He made his eyes all soulful like a basset hound. 'Try, Magda.'

Why should she bloody try? He'd been there himself, hadn't he? Not when she'd been old enough to have a memory, but years before, he'd visited. A tall man who didn't have a lap. She'd drawn him, sometimes, in her colouring book and never had to use her coloured crayons – he was always grey. Except the once she'd seen him lying on top of her mother in the narrow wooden bed. He'd been pale then, pale all over, except for his eyes. They'd gone almost black, when they saw her standing there. He'd never come again.

Perhaps she'd been mistaken and it wasn't him at all. Could such a stiff grey man be so soft and pink and pillowy underneath, or even take his clothes off? People looked so stupid when undressed, and Charles was never stupid.

'Did you and your mother have any – er – special friends?'

She remembered the way his legs had stuck out beyond the bed, almost level with her face, when she'd crept in through the door, and caught sight of him, feet first, crushing her mother. Miklos probably lay on her mother like that, but without the legs. He was so squat and dumpy, he hardly had legs.

'Yeah, there was one.'

'What, when you were a baby?'

'Yeah.' Miklos had only shown his ugly mug last January, but Charles wouldn't know that.

'He slept on my mother, right on top of her, smothered her.'

'Magda!'

'Well, he did. He put his hands all over her, and then he . . .' Disgusting. *She'd* never do it. Some of the girls at Streatham did, and then bragged about it in the lavatories, and giggled and went pink. But she'd refuse to take her clothes off in front of anyone.

'He was horrible. A Jew. A foreigner. He hadn't any legs.'

'No legs? Magda, please.'

She looked down at Charles' feet again. Black, smug, shiny feet. Could they ever have been naked, only inches from her face? Charles had moved his chair towards her. She suddenly wanted to hug him, like her mother had, crush into him and under him, strip off all the hard grey skin and find him pink and soft and loving underneath.

'This – er – foreign chap. Did your mother ever say how long she'd known him?'

'Oh, years and years.' If she couldn't hug him, at least she'd lie for him. These were the things he wanted her to say, she was quite aware of that. He was moving nearer to her now, and for the first time in her life, she had his total concentration.

'Before she knew me?'

'Oh, long before.' Perhaps he'd touch her now. She was answering correctly, she could tell. He was so close, she could smell the sharp spicy fragrance on his chin. She wanted that smell on top of her, overwhelming her. He took her hand, held it very tight.

'Look, Magda, I want to . . .'

'Time to go, Mr Parry Jones.' Mother Gregory billowed through the door, and Charles leapt up as if he had been doing something wrong.

'No!' Magda threw herself in front of him. 'There's something I've got to ask you.' The name had reminded her. 'I want to use your name – Parry Jones, I mean. Kornyai is such a stupid name. They teased me at the other school, and they'll fall about at this one.'

Charles had stopped, but he wasn't looking at her. He was staring at a picture of the Blessed Mother Foundress blessing a leper. Magda tried to squeeze between them.

199

'If you don't want me to have all of it, I'll just take half. The Parry bit, or even just the Jones. It's safer being Jones.'

Charles had turned to steel again. 'Look, Magda, names aren't important. They're just a legal fiction.'

She was speaking to his back. 'Well, if they're not important, why do you mind?'

'I don't mind.' He was lying to please her, as she had done for him.

'So I can, then?'

He straightened the picture, so that Mother Foundress's nose lay exactly parallel with the frieze beneath the whitewashed parlour ceiling. 'Well, not just at the moment, Magda. It'll only cause confusion.'

'Who with?'

'With whom.'

'Pardon?'

'Well, Frances doesn't . . .' Charles began.

'What's it got to do with Frances? She's got your name already, hasn't she?'

He was staring at the leper in the same desperate fashion as the leper was staring at the Foundress. 'Look, Frances isn't very strong at the moment . . .'

Bunk! Frances was the strongest woman in the world. She had Charles, didn't she? – his name, his house, all his books and desks and beds and cash and . . . She was bound to be back home again, now she had her precious husband to herself, devouring him, building herself up on him, swallowing his body like the nuns did at Communion.

Two more nuns were hovering in the background, fawning on her father, trying to lure him into church – well-fed nuns, stuffed to the ears with God. 'Time for Benediction, Magda, and perhaps your father would like to come along?'

He didn't. Magda knelt alone behind the nuns, and watched his car zip along the drive, the two five-pound notes he had given her tucked down the bodice of her dress. So that's what a name was worth. He'd bought her off, awarded her a tenner for giving up his name. He couldn't be her father if she didn't have his name.

She picked up the small silver cross on the end of her rosary

200

and held it like a pencil. 'Magda Rozsi Parry Jones' she etched across the pages of her prayer book. She could hardly read the name. The cross was blunt and hadn't made much impression on the paper. She whispered it instead: Magda Parry Jones. It sounded wrong – poncy and affected. She took the cross and scratched it to and fro across the faint marks of the letters. It ripped through the frail paper, leaving a hole.

She tried again. Magda Rozsi Kornyai. That sounded strange as well. It always had. Other kids didn't have stupid foreign names no one could pronounce. OK, she wouldn't have a name. You didn't need one – didn't really need a mother, come to that. Or a father. Or a dog. The less you had, the less they could take away.

The priest turned round with a blaze of gold-encrusted vestments. 'The Lord be with you,' he intoned. There was always God. The nuns said if you had Him, you had everything. Lucky nuns!

Magda grinned. She inserted the cross in the hole where her name had been, and twisted it backwards and forwards until it had torn through almost fifty pages of the prayer book. She joined her hands, as if she were praying, pressing them hard against her breasts, until she could hear the faint rustle of the bank notes tucked inside her dress. At least no one could take away the cash.

16

'I'm pregnant,' Frances whispered to the lion. She had brought him out into the garden with her, to use as a pillow. You had almost a duty to be comfortable, when you were carrying another life.

'I'm going to have a baby,' she repeated, in case he hadn't understood. She gazed around her. The whole lush garden was gloriously pregnant. Each pansy was a mauve and yellow uterus, every foxglove flower a purple cervix. The poppies had run to seed and their swelling pods were rounded, bursting ovaries. The golden rod curved over like fallopian tubes. Even the geranium leaves were foetus-shaped. Everything was budding and burgeoning into life, bees pollinating, small green apples plumping into full-term heaviness.

She stretched out on the bare brown patch Ned called the Earl of Rothmere's croquet lawn. Ned himself was out all day, at a weekend summer school on Icelandic Sagas. But better to be alone and becalmed in Acton, than buffeted by storms at Richmond. She had told Ned that Charles was abroad again, and had packed a suitcase full of bits and pieces, including the lion and extra vitamins. Ned's garden was a jungle and his house a disaster area, but it didn't matter any more. Nothing mattered except her swaggering uterus. She was a woman now, at last – sanctified and special. It was like receiving the Stigmata – pain and radiance combined. She had outlawed the pain for the moment, so that she could savour the full holy bliss of motherhood. Of course there were problems, so many and so complex, her mind trembled to confront them, but Ned was teaching her to leave problems, as he left the washing-up. Neither really mattered. She'd have the baby his way, not agonizing over guilt and paternity, but revelling in something she had wanted all her life. She wouldn't stifle it with lists and schedules, or expensive, unnecessary equipment, nor martyr herself with terrors and regrets. There wasn't even any rush. She had nine languorous months to change and blossom in.

She turned over on her back and stared up at the swollen white clouds. Even the sky was pregnant, labouring to give birth to an overdue sun. Rilke stalked across the grass and sprang on to her stomach.

'Not there,' she grinned. 'That's reserved!'

It was almost shameful how jubilant she felt, mooning about like some Mills and Boon heroine, in tune with all creation. She wasn't a career girl any more, but the highest sort of lowest woman, all womb and sentiment. Even her fantasies were disgracefully unoriginal – Ned pacing up and down the hospital corridor, minutes before the hushed Leboyer birth, with its soft lights and mystic music, the first cry, the first champagne. Well, perhaps not champagne, not on Ned's salary, but that was a detail. She might have twins, triplets even, her photo splashed across the *Daily Mirror*. No, she didn't want publicity, not with Charles' mother and the narrow-minded Golf Club crowd.

Best not to fill in the fantasies. There were too many complexities if she fleshed them out – awkward unromantic details like inlaws, illegitimacy, divorce, division of property, puerperal fever, complications of birth. She'd just *be*, for a change, live in the moment, as Ned encouraged. It was an almost revolutionary idea. With Charles, there had never been a present; only a strong-box of a future, a vaulted old age. She and Charles were always looking forward, waiting, expecting – when their annuities matured, when inflation eased, when a rival retired, or a senior partner died. Even the baby had been a future prospect – when the house was finished, or the mortgage paid off, when they'd established their careers . . . But now she had leap-frogged Charles' system and launched the baby as a here-and-now reality. Ned would say, 'Don't ruin it with fears for the future or regrets about the past, just savour the moment of it.' She closed her eyes, felt the sun sink into them, Rilke hot and heavy against her leg. She tried to remember her mantra, some strange gobbledigook which sounded like an opera singer's exercise. Ned had been teaching her to meditate. She hushed the cynical, mocking voice that scoffed at him – Charles' voice, which saw the life-force as a pound sign – and sought to sandwich herself between all creation, to become one with the sun, the cat, the grass, the summer afternoon.

'I'm pregnant,' she murmured. 'Now, here, in this garden, at this moment.' A DC 10 screamed over. She ignored it. She could feel the baby growing inside her, imperceptibly, like grass.

'Frances, for Christ's sake, get up. It's raining.'

Frances opened one eyelid a crack, and shut it hastily. A large, dark cloud was looming in front of her – Charles in his iron-grey suit, with a black umbrella over him. Cold, accusing drops of rain were stinging her bare legs, sneaking down her neck. Charles had brought rain on purpose. His influence reached even as far as the Meteorological Office.

'You've no right to be here, Charles.'

'We've got to talk.'

'We keep talking and it never gets us anywhere. I've told you not to come.'

'It's hardly your role to tell me what to do. If you don't want me here, then please return to Richmond. It's high time you came back and faced your responsibilities.'

'I am facing them. That's why I'm here.'

Silence. Charles had suddenly collapsed, like his own umbrella. He was squatting on the grass, thin, stiff, closed in on himself, the rain spitting on his suit. She picked a lupin from the border and stuck it in his jacket.

'Charles . . .'

'What?'

'Let's not fight. Our anger affects the universe.'

'Christ, Frances, you're impossible! Every time I try to reason with you, you churn out some pathetic mumbo-jumbo. The flower-child thing is twenty years out of date.' He snatched the lupin from his buttonhole and held it awkwardly. He was like a suitor, on his knees to her, flower in one hand, rolled umbrella in the other. 'I came to take you out to dinner.'

'You came to reason with me.'

'Can't we do both? I booked a table at Croft's.'

Croft's was fossilized Charles – his ancient and illustrious Club. He rarely took her there. It was reserved for top clients, a male sanctuary, private and inviolable.

'Let's eat here. I'll do you scrambled eggs.'

'I had scrambled eggs for lunch, scrambled eggs for breakfast, and scrambled bloody eggs for last night's so-called dinner. I haven't had a proper meal since you left.'

'Poor darling! There's not much here, either. Ned seems to live on tins. I could probably rustle you up some baked beans or . . .'

'I never want to hear that man's name again, and as for setting foot inside his house . . .'

'Well, let's eat outside then. A picnic in the garden.'

'In the pouring rain? I'm soaked already. It's bad enough having to chase after you over the whole of W3, without catching pneumonia on top of it.'

She laughed. It was easy to laugh when you were pregnant. 'Do you know, Charles, you're really rather comic.'

He shot up his umbrella, as if he were firing a rifle, and disappeared beneath it, stomping round the side of the house. He suddenly looked small – old, defeated, bowed.

'Charles!' she called. He stopped.

'I'll come.'

He didn't turn round. She ran after him and squeezed beside him under the umbrella. She was laughing again. 'So long as I can have the biggest steak they've got. I must admit I'm sick of beans, myself.'

His blue streak of a Bristol looked as if it had lost its way in Mayfair and landed up at Acton by mistake. She eased herself into the soft suede upholstery, draping her damp skirt in front of her.

'Aren't you going to change?'

'No need. If you put the heater on, I'll be dry in two ticks.'

'Yes, but I thought perhaps . . . another dress?'

'What for?'

Damn it, didn't she know what for? You didn't go to Croft's in some shapeless sack more suited to a Hackney stall-holder than a director's wife. She looked pregnant already, her neat, girlish figure swamped under cheap pink seersucker. But he dared not argue. The days and nights without her had put their cold hands around his throat and slowly squeezed, until he was left choking and retching with outrage, shock and murderous jealousy. He had forbidden such feelings ever to come near him in his life before, but they had sneaked up on him and grabbed him unawares, held him down, while he shouted out for a wife who wasn't there. It was humiliating, horrible – and worst of all, uncontrollable.

He stopped outside the Club and glanced across at her. She had her hands cradled on her lap, tuned in only to her own womb. He was shut out from all that growth and mystery, as he had been with Piroska. Fumblingly he leaned over and tried a tentative embrace. The girlish shape was still there, underneath. If anything, she was even slimmer. He felt her stomach, flat and innocent, sloping down to the slender thighs.

'Listen, Frances, are you absolutely sure you're pregnant?'

'Of course I'm not sure . . .'

He heard the windscreen wipers almost startle with relief.

'Not your sort of sure. Pregnancy tests and signed statements from three Harley Street laboratories and a nationwide broadcast from the Queen's gynaecologist. I just *feel* pregnant. It's a gut thing, intuitive. Oh, I know you'll scoff. You always insist on data and statistics, but I've started looking at life differently. It's feelings that count, not your universal Rule of Reason.'

'God almighty, Frances, this is the most critical problem we've ever had to face in our entire married life, and you're resorting to gibberish. You don't get pregnant merely by feelings.'

'No, that's not what happened.'

He winced. 'All right, let's have dinner and discuss it then. Perhaps you'll be more rational over a decent claret.'

He whispered to the head waiter to change their table, seat them in the darkest corner, where they could hide away. He'd never been seen there with a woman in no make-up and bare legs. He tried to lose himself in the menu, but the veal was sauced with some sod's semen, and Clomid had curdled the vichyssoise. There were no prices on the wine list, no vintages, only 'day thirty-two' printed over everything. He glanced around furtively, to make sure no one was listening. The place was half empty – it was early yet.

'Look, let's get down to hard facts, Frances. According to my reckoning, it's day thirty-two.'

She almost hugged him for getting it so right. It *was* day thirty-two, but she always felt she was the only one in the world who knew or cared. Day thirty-two meant four days late, and that was the most precious, incredible, terrifying thing she could possibly imagine. She was never, ever late. Her period started on day twenty-eight exactly, and had done since the age of thirteen and a half. And always in the morning. She could almost set her watch by it. But this month – nothing. She'd inspected herself at least a hundred times, checking and re-checking. No stained pants, no drop of blood, no pre-period pain. On day twenty-nine, she had ordered extra milk. On day thirty, she panicked and took six hot baths and three double gins. Still nothing. On day thirty-one, she hovered between hope and horror, spent the morning in Mothercare, comparing prams and prices, and the afternoon in tears. On day thirty-two – today – she had accepted the inevitable. She was pregnant, indisputably, so she'd damned well enjoy it.

She had almost succeeded, until Charles turned up – and all the horrors with him. So long as he kept away, she could concentrate on having Ned's baby Ned's way. But Charles brought complications – not only guilts and fears, but a reminder of all the things she missed and needed: steak, standards, security and strength. She looked across at his stern, sculpted features, his pained, prosecuting eyes. He was toying with the brown bread and butter which had come with his salmon mousse. His Club was almost part of him – the fine china and Georgian silver; the jealously-guarded membership, with instant recognition of a member, and suspicion of any stranger, even a guest; the low-key, reverential service; the impeccable address. He'd been coming here for years. The food was good, but not that good – he came for something else – old-fashioned standards, attention to detail, the solid continuity of tradition.

She loved him for his standards, for his own fastidious good manners. He was nibbling on a finicky morsel of crust. Ned would have stuffed the bread whole into his mouth and then kissed her through it; dolloped tinned spaghetti rings on to chipped and dirty plates, or eaten straight from the saucepan.

'Four days overdue hardly constitutes a pregnancy,' Charles was saying. Even the way he spoke was careful and melodious. Ned dragged words through hedges.

'No.'

It wasn't just a question of days. Admittedly they had been the longest and most frightening of her life, but she'd known she was pregnant almost the moment she conceived. It was something precious and primal you felt deep inside. You didn't count it on calendars or prove it with tests. It was a subtle sacred blossoming, which took you over and transformed you. There was nothing you could do to counter it, oppose it. You were only the receptacle, the instrument.

Her wine had arrived, decanted into a Georgian claret jug, and mixed liberally with homage. Charles was drinking a *Mersault-Charmes* '71. He waved away a posse of grovelling waiters.

'We need something more definite to go on. What about your charts? Isn't your temperature meant to stay up if you're pregnant? Is it up?' He was still talking in a whisper, as if they were planning crime or *lèse-majesté*.

'Well, sort of.'

'Sort of? Frances, you simply must be more precise.'

How could she tell him that she hadn't done the charts? Staying with Ned made it more or less impossible. What excuse was there for fussing with a thermometer, when you were clearly in the pink of health? She'd tried to pretend, one morning, that she was sickening for 'flu and had to check her temperature, but Ned had rushed around with steaming hot Ribena, and by the time she'd swallowed that, it was up in any case.

Rathbone insisted that you took your temperature before eating, drinking, talking, moving, but he hadn't calculated on having a Ned around. As soon as she woke, Ned was there, feeding her Ambrosia rice pudding out of the tin, or asking her opinion on Icelandic verb endings, or balancing his teacup on her navel. How could she lie still and silent for a full five minutes with a thermometer stuck in her mouth, when Ned was laying siege to all her other orifices?

'You're so extremely vague, Frances. It seems ridiculous to disrupt our whole existence, when we haven't got a shred of proof.'

'We don't need proof. I simply know I'm pregnant. My whole body feels quite different.'

'How could it, Frances, after only four days?'

'It does, that's all. Anyway, if you want statistics, there are plenty as far as Clomid's concerned. Very encouraging ones, I might add. In one study of women taking it, twenty-four per cent of them conceived, and they weren't even ovulating before they started on it. And in another group . . .'

Charles pushed his plate away. He didn't want a second helping of statistics. Even without them, he felt a stab of certainty, like a bone stuck in his throat. Sixteen years ago, he'd had the same conversation with Piroska. He had scoffed then – used almost the same words: 'It's merely stress, that's all. Wait another week or two. Of course you can't be pregnant.'

She had been. And so was Frances. It was obvious she had changed. Some new, careless lethargy clung around her body like a second skin. It wasn't just the shabby dress, but something very basic. He had seen it with Piroska. The only difference was, Piroska had been expendable and Frances wasn't. He leant across and took her hand, checking first that nobody was watching.

'Come back, Frances. Please. I miss you. I've wronged you over Magda – I admit it, and I'm sorry. But you've wronged me, too, and far more irresponsibly. But I still want you back – I know that. I've never told you this before, but I need you. Very deeply.'

She almost choked on a fragment of French bread. Charles never needed anyone. He was totally self-sufficient, moulded people, enlightened them, but *needed* them – impossible! She saw herself reflected in the pale wastes of his eyes, could hardly believe that he was pleading with her, begging.

'Frances, let's start again, darling. I love you. I want you.'

He had never told her he loved her in a public place before. And this was Croft's. Nothing was fake at Croft's, or insubstantial. Croft's meant genuine authenticity, true sterling value.

She forced down the scrap of bread. 'But do you want the baby?'

A waiter glided over and stared reproachfully at Charles' untouched mousse. 'Was something wrong, sir?'

'No, no, absolutely not. Everything first-rate as always.'

'Thank you, sir. I do hope you'll do justice to the sole, sir. They were sent up from Newhaven just this morning.'

Newhaven. That's where Ned had caught a conger eel. They'd gone there after Brighton, a lifetime ago, squatted on a breakwater and skimmed pebbles through the waves. Ned would teach the baby to fish, build it sandcastles, make it laugh. The crested silver soup-spoon suddenly felt too heavy in her hand. She put it down. 'Do you want me back with the baby?' she repeated.

That would be the perfect compromise – Ned's baby in Charles' house. If she tried, she could almost turn it into Charles' child. There were things a kid needed – a heritage, a legacy. You had to pass on values and traditions. This Club, for instance, symbol of all Charles represented, and all she'd come to prize herself. She couldn't deny those standards to her child.

Two waiters were already hovering, bearing the sole like the Blessed Sacrament. 'Shall I fillet it for you, sir?'

'Please.'

He hadn't answered her. He was fussing over his fishbone while her baby's fate hung in the balance. A third waiter swamped them both with vegetables – *épinards au beurre* and *chou-fleur Mornay* smothering an unborn child.

'Mustard, madam? The English or the Dijon?' Three waiters, four.

'Thanks, just a spot of English.'

'Certainly, madam. Tartare sauce for you, sir?' Four waiters, five. And now the head waiter salaaming in front of them, kneading his hands like pastry, an expression of pained subservience ironed and starched into his features.

'Everything all right, sir?'

'Excellent, thank you, Lewis.'

'Madam?'

'Yes, fine.' Everything just fine, except the baby. Soup fine, spinach fine, only the infant cooling on her plate, abandoned like a piece of gristle.

At last the tide of waiters ebbed away, leaving nothing on the beach except a small, forgotten foetus.

'Well, Charles?'

He picked up his wine glass and sipped. *Mersault* fine. Vintage fine. She could see his lips, full and generous, distorted in the glass. The restaurant had stopped breathing. His voice was so soft, she had to lip-read. His lips were pale, edged with a tiny wash of golden wine.

'No, Frances,' they were saying. 'I can't accept the baby. It

210

wouldn't work. I know I'd feel . . . look, leave it at that. It's simply quite impossible.'

He was sipping again, only to hide his face. Suddenly he drained the glass and rammed it back on the table. 'Look, you must come back. Then we can scrub the whole summer out, and start again. We'll make a deal. I'll send Magda back to Hungary and you . . . get yourself – er – fixed about the baby.'

Frances had ordered entrecôte. Slowly she cut into it and watched it bleed over the pale cauliflower, the waxy white potatoes. 'Fixed, Charles?'

'You know what I mean, sweetheart. It's simple nowadays. You can see the finest chap in London. We'll book you in at the best private clinic, with convalescence afterwards. I'll take you away. We'll go to the Seychelles, Corfu – anywhere. I'll make it up to you.'

Knifing into babies, cutting them out as easily as filleting a fish, the baby she'd waited fifteen years to bear. Buying the best murderer in London, paying for an execution, flowers for the grave, hothouse grapes for the funeral. Celebrating afterwards in a five-star hotel, washing the baby's blood away with *Moët et Chandon*.

A deal, he called it. The perfect word for the perfect business-man. I'll sacrifice my child, if you destroy yours. How many times would Magda have to be uprooted to pay the debts that were never hers? First to Richmond, then to Westborough, and now dragged half-way across Europe, back to Budapest, to balance the death of a baby who wouldn't even be her half-brother.

'We can't do that, Charles, it's criminal. Magda's suffered enough, and my child hasn't even got its limbs, yet. Let's have them both. Can't that be a different sort of deal – a better one? Let's get Magda home from boarding school and try again. I know I can be loving to her this time, if only you'll let me keep my own baby. Let's not even talk about mine and yours. Can't they both be ours, Charles? Our children.'

Charles' fish lay like a white shroud on the cold white plate, his face above it the same dead unnatural white. He shut his eyes. 'Magda's not my child.'

'What?' Frances' voice began as a whisper and finished as a

211

shout. Two waiters rushed. She waited, silent, for a moment, while Charles oiled them away. 'Of course she is. You're raving . . .'

Charles swallowed his first mouthful of fish, then laid his knife and fork down. 'No, Frances, you told me so yourself, only a few short days ago.'

'I didn't mean it, Charles. How could you think I meant it? I was just trying to get my own back. Of course she's yours. She's got the same proud, stubborn shell as you, to start with. And the same love and loyalty underneath. She's even got your mouth.'

'You didn't say that on Friday.'

'Well, no, but . . .'

'You didn't even mean it on Friday. You told me quite distinctly she was nothing like me in the least, that there wasn't even a bond between us, no love, no tie, no likeness.'

'Look, Charles, I only . . .'

'There *was* a bond, Frances, but you destroyed it. You took away the only thing I felt a sort of reverence for – the blood link with a child. It's sacred, somehow. I can't explain it, but it was there, all right. I admit I wasn't marvellous with the kid. I never even knew what she was thinking, or what the hell I ought to talk to her about. But the relationship was real, precious, until you ruined it. Whatever the truth is now – genes, or likenesses, or chromosomes – as far as I'm concerned she's not mine any more. You've killed her as my daughter.'

Frances shut her eyes. So she was a murderer, was she? But why, in hell's name had he never said those things before, let her see that a child was precious to him, instead of just a nuisance, an expense? How ironical it was. Here they were, almost united in the way they saw the holy bond of parenthood, and yet she'd only realized it too late, when she'd forged that bond with someone else. She felt terrible regret, but also anger.

'You've already had your kid for fifteen years. Mine's not even born. And, anyway, Magda's still alive, wonderfully alive. You can't just deny her as your daughter, because of some rubbish I let slip in a row. You must want to kill her, to react like that. Leave her alone – we've ruined her life enough. And leave *me* alone. *And* my baby. I intend to have this baby. I've let you mould my life for almost sixteen years, but now I'm going to smash the mould

212

and go my own way. This child's the first thing I've ever had without your rubber stamp.'

She hardly knew what she was saying. It was saying itself, pouring through the dam they'd built so carefully to keep out any flood. If only he'd stop her, interrupt, or make some bland remark about late Victorian watercolours, or the refloating of the pound. But all she could read in his eyes was murderer.

'Look, I didn't kill your daughter. And, if I did, you helped to kill her, too. We both killed her; our home killed her, our rules, our stupid, rigid, narrow barrenness. But that doesn't mean we have to kill another child. Why can't we change, Charles? We can still bring Magda back, resurrect her. We can resurrect ourselves, if only we'd stop being so terrified.'

'I'm sorry, Frances, I don't know what you're talking about, except that it sounds very uncontrolled. I don't want your lover's breakneck ideas served up with my sole.'

'How dare you, Charles! Don't you ever give me credit for thinking for myself? Just because I've stopped spouting the Gospel according to St Charles, does it mean . . .'

Nobody had ever walked out of Croft's Club in the middle of a sentence, least of all in the middle of a *Pichon-Longueville-Baron* 1967. Charles tried to staunch the flow of waiters. 'I'm sorry, my wife's not feeling well . . .'

'Perhaps she shouldn't have had the steak, sir, if she's unwell. How about a little steamed plaice, sir? Or we could do an omelette. We don't usually serve omelettes in the evening, sir, but in your case . . .'

Charles flung a wad of bank notes on the table, to pay for a dozen omelettes, and strode swiftly after Frances, through the hushed, mahogany-panelled hallway, past the obsequious shufflings of the doorman. She was already half-way down the drive, her damask napkin still clutched in her hand, trailing on the tarmac.

'Frances, wait!'

She didn't. He sprinted to catch up, stood in front of her, took both her hands in his. 'I'm sorry, darling. Look, don't let's act impulsively. Come back with me for coffee, and we'll try to sort things out.'

'No.'

'I want to talk to you.'

'You've talked.'

'Not really. There are lots of things I haven't even touched on. I love you.'

'You said that.'

'I do love you, Frances. I need you. Please come back.'

'You said that, too.'

'It's not just me. There are some things I can't manage on my own.'

'Like scrambled eggs?'

'No, Frances, more important things. I want to ask you a favour.'

'I know your favours. Just kill a child – that's all you want, isn't it? Rip it out, flush it down the loo, and then we'll all be nice and cosy again.'

She shrugged him off and streaked ahead. There were stones underfoot now, small obstreperous pebbles which ambushed her sandals and tripped her up.

'Frances, you'll break your neck!'

He grabbed her almost roughly and led her off the path, across the grass. A wooden bench basked in a puddle of moonlight, beneath a sagging cedar. Croft's cedars were as venerable as their port. It was no longer raining, but cold, lurking drops pounced suddenly from branch to bench, alarming the silence.

'At least come back for Saturday,' he pleaded.

'Why Saturday?'

'It's our wedding anniversary.'

'Oh I know that. I'd hardly forget, after sixteen years. But you don't expect us to celebrate it, do you?'

'Well, no, but Oppenheimer's coming.'

'Oh, our little friend again! How nice for you.' Easy to be sarcastic, but Oppenheimer's name was somehow a terrible reminder. He it was who had kept them apart at crucial ovulation time. If Charles hadn't been sent to save his company, the baby in her womb might well have been legitimate. She still wasn't sure whether she wanted Charles' baby, rather than Ned's, but at least it would have been simpler and more sacred. No rows and recrimination, then, no guilt and embarrassment, no threat of abortion, nor risk of poverty. Quarrels and conflict were bad for

214

any child. All the baby-books advised you to nurture a foetus in an atmosphere of radiant composure, not race about a shrubbery in the pitch dark, spoiling for a fight.

'Listen, Frances, I've invited him to stay. I didn't have much choice. He's off to South America to develop a stretch of jungle. It's quite a tricky business, so he's all keyed up about it. His plane arrives from Jersey in the late afternoon, and he's got a one-night stay in London before the morning flight. I asked him back with us. I couldn't not. He'll need a briefing with me, in any case.'

'So you plan to spend your sixteenth wedding anniversary closeted with a Lord of the Jungle. Well, at least you won't need me around.'

'Of course I'll need you, Frances. I want you there as my wife, to entertain him.'

'So that's what needing me means, does it? I thought for one crazy moment you might actually need me for myself, not just to be a smarming hostess, daintying your jungle politics with my veal *cordon bleu* and my Constance Spry flower arrangements . . . That's all I've ever been to you, isn't it? The perfect Mrs Charles Parry Jones, cementing your investment deals, advertising your happy, faithful marriage, your solidity, your credit-worthiness . . .'

'It has been happy, Frances, most of it. Just because . . .'

'Well, it isn't now. And it won't be on Saturday. I shan't be there.' She realized, suddenly, she had turned the tables on him. When she'd begged him to return from Nassau, he'd put Oppenheimer before her baby. Now she was doing the opposite, revelling in her power. All her married life she'd sat on the sidelines, while Charles and his kingpin clients diced for the world. Now she'd upset the board and hidden the counters.

'You can tell dear Heinrich Tarzan that your doting consort won't be around on Saturday. She'll be in Acton – knitting baby clothes for another man's child.'

'Don't be ridiculous, Frances, you must be there. I can't let Oppenheimer down. Not again. He asked after you especially. I even told him about our anniversary. He said he'd be honoured to help us celebrate. He'll have made all his arrangements by now, bought us a present and . . .'

'I see. So I'm to come back home, merely because some

215

stinking-rich parvenu has lashed out a fiver on a silver-plated egg cup, and I'm expected to rush back to offer humble thanks.'

He shuddered at the new, sarcastic language she had brought with her from Acton, like a souvenir. 'No, Frances. I need you there because Oppenheimer happens to be a very respected client, and I have a special obligation to him.'

'Oh yes, it's his millions you're obliged to, isn't it?'

'Don't be a hypocrite! I've told you already, Frances, it's money like his which provides your whole rich life style. You can't have one and damn the other.'

She was silent. Even at Ned's, she had her ritzy car to run about in, and a string of credit cards to splurge on anything that took her eye. One of her niggles against Ned was that he didn't come complete with a freezer and a tumble-drier, a nanny and a country cottage. She only realized how much she needed all those things when she was faced with losing them. Money wasn't simply meaningless possessions; money meant Charles and Croft's Club. Money meant Oppenheimer.

There *was* an obligation. They'd stayed in Jersey less than a year ago and Oppenheimer had flung open the flood-gates to them both, offering them his house, his yacht, his second Rolls, his influence and contacts on the island. He was a Croesus, not a Tarzan. And it was she who had wallowed in it all, sunning herself in his gold, which Charles had to quarry in the dark frowning pit-shaft of the boardroom.

Couldn't she cook them one anniversary dinner, in return? But it wasn't just a dinner. Cooking it would mean turning back into Mrs Charles Parry Jones. And Mrs Parry Jones was barren, her pit-shaft empty and worked-out.

'Look, Charles, couldn't you book him into a really nice hotel? I know it's not the same, but . . .'

'How can I, Frances? What reason could I give? I've offered him personal hospitality and I can't go back on it. He was decent enough about the court case. I can hardly mess him about a second time. Even if I said you were ill, he'd come rushing round with flowers. Anyway, all the hotels are full by now, especially at a weekend. It's still the height of the tourist season. You don't just dump a man like Oppenheimer on the town, when you've promised him your home. He'd take it as a slight.'

She stared up at the dark grid of branches barring the face of the moon. Wasn't it a slight to her, as well, that he was more worried about saving face with Oppenheimer than saving their marriage? But it wasn't that simple. She couldn't sling women's lib slogans in his face and still grab on to all the goodies he provided. The trouble was she wanted everything – security as well as freedom, ambrosia in Acton, on top of entrecôte at Croft's. But life didn't work like that. If you settled for a charge account at Harrods, then you couldn't indulge in midnight feasts and Mars bars with a feckless fisherman. She tried to strip everything away, claret and Kashans on one side, kites and candyfloss on the other, and see if anything was left genuinely indispensable. It wasn't easy. There were stumbling blocks like love and loyalty, morality, habit and tradition, and a crazy, contradictory impulse which leapfrogged over all of them with a Harvey Smith gesture. Only one small thing remained totally unyielding – that vital second heartbeat in her womb.

She turned to face Charles on the bench. Everything about him was unassailably familiar, his shape, his voice, the faint, stern whiff of power and after-shave combined. If her baby was so precious, then only he could be its guardian, a man who held the whole world together merely by frowning at it.

'Charles,' she whispered. Perhaps there would still be anniversaries – silver, ruby, gold ... 'I will come back, not just for Saturday, but for always, so long as I can come home with the baby.'

A lone drop of rain plopped on to his forehead and trailed slowly down his face. 'So we're back to that, are we? Back to blackmail.'

'It's not blackmail, Charles. The baby's part of me already. We're indistinguishable. I can't offer you anything unless you accept my child as part of the deal.'

Deal, thought Charles bitterly. So she was using his words now. It didn't make it any easier. It wasn't just a matter of accepting a baby he didn't want, but conniving at cuckoldry, deception, the mocking laughter of a man who had pre-empted his own wife's womb. Another sixteen years of grappling with a child who wasn't his. Yet, what was the alternative? Loss, emptiness, scrambled eggs, hotels.

He looked up at the sky. Even the nearest pinprick star was a million million miles away. How could one five-foot-nothing wife, one tinpot infidelity, matter so hugely when he was only a speck, a whispered syllable in the five-act cosmic drama? The sky seemed to shrug. A splatter of raindrops spat rudely in his face.

He got up from the bench and turned away. Frances was only a shadow now, a dark smudge muddying the moonlight.

'Look, forget Oppenheimer,' he said roughly. 'I'll manage on my own. Get in the car and I'll drive you back to Acton.'

17

Laura appraised her slim white hand in the silver-framed mirror of the Guildford jewellers. It was wearing five rings.

'This one,' she said, discarding the rest and handing Charles a narrow platinum band, studded all the way round with diamonds.

Charles whisked out his American Express card, then replaced it in his wallet. This time, he'd better pay by personal cheque. He didn't want Laura's snide remarks about expense-account jewellery. She was no fool. Even the ring she'd chosen was by far the most expensive. It fitted best, she said, but she knew as well as he did that size could be adjusted.

That was the last of the shopping, thank God. He'd trotted after her into boutiques and beauty parlours, emporiums and fashion houses. His credit cards were wilting with the strain. Laura herself was blooming. She festooned him with the heaviest of the packages, tucked her free arm through his, and squeezed it.

'Do you realize, Charlie, this is the first time you've ever granted me an entire day with you. The most I've ever been allowed before was four and a half hours, and that was only because your plane was delayed.'

Charles frowned. He preferred not to be reminded that he was missing a briefing with the President of Amalgamated Automobiles, and had left the licensing of a new off-shore bank to an incompetent colleague. It was madness to take a weekday off, and double madness to waste it in a one-horse town in the backwoods. He'd presented Laura with the gift of a whole day and let her plan it, almost sure she'd settle for their usual hotel – a light lunch, an afternoon of love, followed by the crucial conversation which was the whole object of the exercise. He'd hardly expected her to plump for this provincial shopping spree, followed by a matinée of *Love's Labour's Lost* at the Yvonne Arnaud Theatre. A matinée, for God's sake! He hadn't been to one since the school expedition to *Lady Windermere's Fan*, and that was unendurable – three hours of coach parties rustling chocolate papers.

'I suppose I must thank Frances for this unexpected favour,' Laura was carolling, as they laboured down the High Street. Every time she took a step, her bulky paper carriers banged against his thighs. 'So, she's not come back?'

'No.'

'You're sorry, aren't you?'

Charles didn't answer. He had no wish to broadcast his private affairs to the whole of West Surrey. He had hoped for a quiet stroll and a serious discussion in the secluded castle gardens, but every time he tried to steer Laura castlewards, she commandeered a lingerie department, or stormed a cheese counter, disgorging little snippets of his confidential life to grocers and salesgirls; mixing adultery with marabou and pregnancies with *Pont-l'Evêque*. He steered her off the main road, down the narrow, winding path which led past the church to river and theatre. Here, they could talk more freely.

'I was wondering, actually,' Charles cleared his throat, 'if you might – er – have a word with Frances for me.'

Laura unlatched her arm. 'Do your own dirty work!'

Charles plunged after her, across the road. 'Look, Laura, there are some things only a woman can say to a woman.'

'Balls! You sound like some soft-shelled Agony Aunt on the worst sort of women's mag. Why in God's name should I be the one to persuade Frances to return to you? It's preposterous! Using your mistress as an unpaid marriage guidance counsellor.'

Hardly unpaid, thought Charles, shifting two of the more substantial packages to his other arm. If they didn't talk now, Shakespeare would monopolize the whole afternoon, followed by at least an hour of Laura as theatre critic, and any chance of sorting out his future, with or without her, would vanish in a mixture of Clive Barnes and G. Wilson Knight. He glanced nervously around, but only the gravestones were listening. 'No one's talking about Frances coming back. All I'm suggesting, Laura, is that you try to persuade her not to have the baby – in her own interests. If she goes ahead with this pregnancy, she'll ruin her life.'

'And yours!' sniped Laura.

Charles strode towards the dead end of the river, a stagnant cesspool which coiled up almost to the theatre entrance, littered with chocolate wrappers and empty cans. The Yvonne Arnaud had once been an idyllic spot, not this tinny monster of a building, drowning in duckweed.

Laura was right. Of course his life would be ruined by Frances' pregnancy. A runaway wife and an illegitimate kid hardly helped to boost a man's career. Clients expected a tax and finance consultant to be a solid, conventional citizen, a family man with no messes in his life. And for fifteen years, he'd obliged them. Or he and Frances had. Frances had never let him down before. She'd always been serenely in the background, an unobtrusive presence, serving and supporting him, making the right remarks to the right people, choosing careful clothes and correct opinions, never late or shrill, rude or stupid, rebellious or unreliable. There was truth in the accusations she'd hurled at him at Croft's. Yet, until this incident, he'd never even thought about her side of things; just taken her for granted as another creditable aspect of himself – his good taste, his impeccable education, his congenial, British-Standards-tested wife. But, now, she had ripped the whole façade to shreds and left him in a cloud of shame and scandal. Gossip and tittle-tattle would creep up on his life like poison ivy and stifle his good name, lose him all respect, deny him new commissions. Yet it was only now he missed her, admired her even, in some perverse fashion, for standing up to him. He was furious with himself for not having valued her more highly, for perhaps even causing her to leave. And he was furious with her for risking and ruining everything he'd spent a lifetime carefully constructing.

Laura came up behind him, wrinkling her nose at the stench from the water. 'Don't sulk, sweet, it spoils your profile. Look, I can't talk to Frances, anyway. No one can. She's obsessed. She's always had this thing about babies. She'll never mention it directly – that's not her style. But she'll force the conversation round to motherhood in general. Can career women be totally fulfilled? Is it selfish to be sterilized? You know the sort of thing. I think she sees me as an authority on professional childlessness. Laura Doesn't Want One – is that monstrous, miraculous, or merely public-spirited? She never could decide. That's why she's pregnant now, I imagine – in order to find out. You can't stop her, Charlie. This baby's more than just a set of random genes. It's an intellectual exercise for Frances, a holy grail, a ritual, a philosophical experiment.'

Charles stared at a rusty pram, half submerged in the water, and coated in slime. 'Perhaps she isn't pregnant. I mean we're all assuming it, but there's no real proof or . . .'

'Oh, come off it, Charlie! She's got all the symptoms, hasn't she? And considering she's taking a fertility drug . . . A friend of mine was put on Clomid and conceived the very first month. Triplets, actually.'

Charles shut his eyes. Christ! Magda multiplied by three. They were bound to be all girls – six women in his life, all manipulating him, mopping up his strength. But could he trust what Laura said? Wasn't it in her interests to keep Frances pregnant, so the field was free for her? She had often hinted that their relationship should be more permanently established. Her husband was a farce and a nonentity – no risk there. But he wasn't sure he wanted Laura on the front page of his life. He'd considered it, of course – in his position, one had to consider everything. Laura had advantages, maybe more than Frances, and her gelded womb was not the least of them. But she wasn't Frances, and somehow that mattered fundamentally. He had tried to set the whole thing down on paper – pros and cons, strengths and weaknesses, but there were no conclusions; just an aching hole where Frances should have been.

Laura was nudging him in the back with her bag of French cheeses. 'Come on, darling, let's go in. I'm dying for a drink.'

The bar was closed, and a queue from the coffee lounge snailed out almost to the foyer. They joined a battalion of blue rinses and pink plastic hearing-aids.

'It's Senior Citizens' Day,' Laura whispered. 'They get in for 40p for these Thursday matinées, plus a free issue of Rowntrees fruit gums to keep their dentures busy.'

Charles ran his tongue round his own strong even teeth. His poker-faced business suit looked out of place amidst that gaggle of Crimplene cardigans and cut-price perms. There was hardly another man around. Only women survived old age – that was obvious. They killed off their men like black widow spiders – a night of love, followed by extinction for the male,

222

while the female swelled and gloated in cannibalistic pregnancy.

The queue was hardly moving. There were not enough staff, and the counter had been incorrectly sited. Give him a week, and he'd re-plan the entire theatre, streamline the catering, sack incompetent bunglers, and ship the whole huddle of geriatrics back to their bingo. Instead, he was dragging his feet behind some octogenarian crone who was whimpering for Horlicks, and wouldn't accept a no, or a lemon tea.

He removed Laura, himself, and his over-priced ham sandwich to the far corner of the lounge. Even here he was cramped. The chairs were too small, the tables ridiculously low, and he was still assaulted by bunioned feet and bossy handbags. It was a woman's world, like the real one. Yet, all the more reason why he had to have a woman in his life. He had no intention of landing up as a freak, or odd man out, a pathetic divorcé, living on his own, patronized and pitied. It was undignified, inconvenient, and strictly incompatible with his business obligations, especially those to Oppenheimer. You couldn't invite a millionaire to dinner, and then present him with baked beans on toast. And, since Frances had refused to rescue him from the tin-opener, then Laura must oblige. She was a dab cook and a dazzling hostess, and with any luck, she might have the weekend free. He glanced across at her. She was stealing the ham from his sandwich, leaving him the crusts, stencilling scarlet lip-prints on his clean white handkerchief. Once he was sure of her, there would have to be changes – a more unassuming brand of lipstick, for a start, and an embargo on his linen.

'I was wondering, darling, whether you might be available this Saturday?'

Laura lit a cigarette. 'Another matinée? You *are* brave! We haven't survived this one yet.'

'No, not theatre, dinner.'

'Lovely, darling! Except I'm already dining. Clive got in first, I'm afraid. He's booked a table at the Mirabelle.'

Charles coughed through her smoke. What the devil was she doing, dining with her own husband? If it hadn't been the Mirabelle, he might have persuaded her to cancel it. But Laura was particularly partial to their *contrefilet de boeuf Richelieu*. So as far as Oppenheimer was concerned, he was still to be a laughing stock, a deserted husband, a clumsy, bungling cook.

'Why not ask Frances? She should be eating for two, in any case. I shan't object. Just be sure you don't choose the Mirabelle. Foursomes are so boring.'

Charles banged down his coffee cup. The warning bell was sounding and a disembodied voice urging them to take their seats. Laura squeezed his hand.

'You could always accept the baby as your own,' she whispered. 'Had you thought of that?'

Charles stormed up the stairs behind her. Of course he'd thought of it, and every other damn solution – resident nannies, early boarding school. If he wanted Frances, that was the price he'd have to pay for her. She herself had Magda to contend with.

No, Magda was a teenager, not a babe-in-arms. He'd never inflicted her infancy on Frances. No broken nights or piles of dirty nappies. Magda was just a visitor, and almost grown up. But Frances had a smelly, screeching urchin squatting in her body, kidnapping her life, her looks, her love, for at least another twenty years. Easy for Frances to talk about having both their children, as she'd done at Croft's, but in actual cool objective fact, she'd proved herself incapable of coping even with one. She was idealizing Magda because she was a hundred miles away. If the kid came home again, the rows would resume, and Frances' milk-and-water fantasies about their united family would dribble away in nagging and recrimination. The same with the baby – blissful when it was only a whisper of cells in her womb, but nine months on, there would be blood and puke and shit to contend with. Of course the tie with a child was precious and unique – he'd told her that himself. But it was the concept, the ideal of parenthood, rather than the endlessly bleating and excreting reality.

He glanced up at the stage. Somehow they had reached their seats, squashed between rows of dotards, sucking toffees and adjusting spectacles. How in God's name could he concentrate on one of Shakespeare's lighter comedies, when his mind was primed for a five-act tragedy, a battlefield, a blasted heath? His problems had even spilled on to the boards. When the curtain rose, Clive was up there, tripping about in purple knee-breeches and a fair moustache. The programme called him the King of Navarre, but only Clive would preen and pontificate like that. He and his Elizabethan gentlemen had vowed to abjure the company of women, and devote themselves to learning. He envied them. Women were not only a snare and a distraction, but a source of everlasting complication and deceit. No man could even know whether the child a woman bore him was genuinely his. All the guilt and obligation he'd felt towards Magda might properly belong to that legless, lecherous Jew the kid had mentioned.

The irony was, he'd tried to get rid of Magda, even when he believed she was his own. He'd branded Frances a murderer, yet it was he who had bribed both women to destroy their babies in the womb. Both had refused. When Piroska handed him that blue-eyed, puckered creature, wrapped in a blanket ('She's got your mouth, exactly,' clucked the midwife), he'd felt horror and shame that this was the life he had wanted to snuff out. He tried to forget the incident, but somehow it had fuelled his guilt during the whole of Magda's childhood, and had finally persuaded him to take her in this summer, when Piroska returned to Hungary. But if she weren't his child in the first place, then the whole affair was doubly ironical, hopelessly confused.

> *Why, all delights are vain, but that most vain,*
> *Which, with pain purchased, doth inherit pain.*

He jumped. The actor had swept downstage, almost to the footlights, and seemed to be speaking to him alone, his sardonic blue eye fixed on Charles' own. He had all but forgotten he was at a play. The Kingdom of Navarre kept turning into Richmond Green or Streatham Maternity Hospital. The three French ladies he had been promised in his programme had all changed their names since it was printed. No longer Maria, Katharine and Rosaline, but Laura, Frances, Magda. Rosaline was almost Magda's double, the same dark, rebellious hair and secret swelling breasts.

Christ! If only he could exorcise his daughter – feel either simple love for her, or straight resentment at being made a fool

225

of. But to desire the kid, for God's sake, he hardly dared admit it to himself. He had even taken to fantasizing about her, imagining her sprawled naked on her bed, or wearing only a wet, transparent T-shirt. Somehow, her body was always fused with Laura's, to form some tantalizing female paradox – the virgin seductress, the voluptuous innocent. It was shameful, decadent, and almost proof he couldn't be her father. Could any natural father stoop so low, mix his own daughter's body with his mistress's, and then enjoy them both? He glanced sideways at Laura, sitting rapt beside him, the pale foothills of her breasts teasing him in the darkened auditorium. She always wore her blouses unbuttoned to the cleavage. Magda chose harsh, mannish shirts and fastened them to the throat. It was only he who swapped her round with Laura, unbuttoning, revealing . . .

He leaned forward and fondled Laura's knee. He must make her real, disentangle her from Magda. Or banish both of them and try to concentrate. Laura would quiz him on the play, even quote from it. How could he confess he'd hardly heard a word? Hanging on to all that painted verbiage was like a drowning man pausing in his struggles to admire a sunset. Endless strings of empty words, gin-fizz emotions frothing out of cardboard hearts. Up on the stage, the king and his three young lords were already reduced by Love to dribbling fools, their vows forgotten, creeping through the undergrowth, composing sonnets. Junes and moons and panting bosoms of the deep . . .

Twaddle! Or was it? He himself had never composed a love-letter in his life. Was that a virtue, or a failing? He didn't even know. Business was such a burden at the moment, it was all he could do to write his monthly financial reviews, let alone a sonnet. Even now, he should be closeted with the President of Amalgamated Automobiles, not this besotted King of Navarre. Perhaps his energies were failing. Once, he'd had time to mug up all the plays of Shakespeare, prided himself on knowing every last scraping and scruple of the footnotes, even the textual variations between Folio and Quarto. Now he felt only boredom and distaste, watching those clowns mortgage their studies and seclusion for a farthingale.

It was all too close to home, for heaven's sake. Hadn't he been duped himself, in the name of love? Crawling after one woman at Croft's, playing truant for another, saddled with children who weren't his. Even Laura guessed. He had tried to discuss Magda with her on the drive down to Guildford, but every time she said 'your daughter', he could hear the sarcasm glittering in her voice. Was every feckless father caught like this? You couldn't win. If Magda really were his child, then he was an incestuous swine to take her to his bed in fantasy, and if she weren't, then he'd not only been cuckolded, but squandered fifteen years of payments for her, in guilt and hard cash. The bills were getting steeper all the time. The nuns had sent the first account in advance, with extra charges for riding, tennis coaching, catechism classes. It hurt to have to pay for religious indoctrination. Though it wasn't the money he minded – he'd pay for anything, so long as he was sure the child was his. But how, in Christ's name, could any man be sure? If even Frances slept around, what hope was there that Piroska had been faithful?

Well, he wouldn't be fooled much longer. He'd contact Piroska and insist she took her daughter back. It was not impossible. She'd already written and hinted that there were thorns in her Hungarian bed of roses. Miklos' so-called wealth had materialized as three chickens and a goat, and the grandma was clinging grimly on to her life and property. Piroska needed cash. All he had to do was to make his cheque conditional. Bribery cost less than boarding school.

Maybe he'd even phone this evening, demand immediate action. He was weary of all the fuss and dawdle of foreign postal systems, the endless problems with a kid who had wrecked his marriage and shattered his self-esteem. He'd already lost Frances on account of her, and would lose Laura next, if he didn't get things moving. Magda must be transferred to Hungary – and fast. It was the only possible solution.

True, there were still all the problems they'd started with – schools, foreign languages, housing, Miklos. But Magda would cope. She'd have to. She was so damned miserable already, a move could only benefit her. He'd barter a generous cash allowance for her immediate summons to Budapest. A telegram, perhaps? Yes, why not? A telegram from Piroska sent direct to the school. Piroska was hopeless at letter-writing, and Miklos might even talk her out of it while she sat chewing on her pen.

But a telegram was instant and dramatic. He could more or less compose it for her himself.

'Found new flat and fine school. Stop. Longing to have you join us. Stop. Come immediately.' Not that he wanted to deceive the child. Perhaps he could find the flat and school himself, write to the Embassy, pull a few strings. Impossible – a Communist country, and Miklos breathing down his neck . . .

'Miklos moved out permanently. Miss you darling. Plenty of room with Grandma for the two of us.'

No, he couldn't lie to the kid. Christ! It was complicated. He couldn't even concentrate, with those cretinous lovelords leaping about the stage, ranting on about Fevers In The Blood and Love Learned In A Woman's Eye. He'd rather compose a thousand sonnets than wrestle with the guilt and deception of a dozen pre-paid words. Whatever he did, someone would be hurt.

He'd always prided himself on coping calmly in a crisis. This gibbering indecision was completely out of character. It was women again, wrecking his system, undermining his strengths. Was there really any need for frenzied haste and subterfuge? After all, the kid was safe at school. Couldn't she stay there, and let the nuns put up with her, while he sorted out his other problems? He could wait till the Christmas holidays and take her to Budapest himself, in mid-December.

Frances would be four months pregnant by December – an obscene little bulge for everyone to jeer at. God Almighty! Every woman should be sterilized at birth. Laura was right, as she was so often. Of course it was safer never to risk a child. Perhaps he should settle for Laura and be done with it. No possibility of babies, then. A neat, uncomplicated, adult life, drawn up like a contract. Laura was a skilled businesswoman and would appreciate a fair deal, spelt out in all the small print. They could even live abroad, to avoid the scandal; retreat to a tax haven with a decent climate, and combine financial advantages with a quiet life. He didn't want marriage, not yet. He needed time, and one last appeal to Frances. But meanwhile, Laura must be primed and feted, kept in hand as a reserve currency.

If those damn-fool lords could woo and win a woman, then so could he. Shakespeare had lavished twenty thousand words on nothing else. There was Berowne, the cynic, even he converted now, pouring out his love to a cardboard tree. He tried to concentrate. If he couldn't write his own lines, the least he could do was listen to someone else's. It was all part of the wooing. He leant back in his seat and closed his eyes.

There was only one interval. A visiting troupe of lutenists were playing Elizabethan songs in the corner of the still closed and shuttered bar. Laura stopped to listen.

'I suppose they're trying to compensate for a shoddy production,' she whispered. 'Total miscasting all round. Don't you agree, Charles?'

He muttered something he half recalled from the *Sunday Times* review and tried to lure her past the countertenor, who was bewailing the pains of Love, in yellow velvet doublet and laddered hose.

'I mean, fancy casting the King as a middle-aged bookworm, in spectacles. What's the point of his renouncing love, if he's past it anyway? Ice cream, darling?'

'No thanks. Fresh air.' He must entice her out into the garden, safely removed from all refreshments and distractions. She was still gabbling on about unsubtle lighting and anachronistic costumes. He chose the most secluded seat and enthroned her on it. They could hear the strains of the lute music echoing from the upstairs window. It should have been an idyll – river rippling in front of them, feet wreathed in flowers, ears lapped in love songs. But somehow, it was only another cardboard set, another bad production. The sky was pock-marked with clouds, the river sluggish and sludge-brown, brash French marigolds shrieking at shocking-pink petunias. He turned his back on the monstrous modern building glaring at them from across the river, and tried to blot out everything but Laura's pale white hand.

'Laura, darling, why don't you wear your new ring?'

He removed the silver band from its plush-lined box and held it out to her. Berowne would have gone down on one knee, but this was stockbroker Surrey, not rutting Navarre.

She wasn't listening, anyway. 'What do you think of the Rosaline?' she asked, swatting at a wasp. 'A little too coy for my taste. But then, when you've seen Dorothy Tutin in the role, no one else quite measures up.'

'No, I suppose not.' He slipped the ring on the safe, largest finger of Laura's non-marriage hand. The left hand, the dangerous hand, was already weighted down with Clive's booty.

'The set's not bad. Though I had my doubts about all those dead leaves. I suppose they're meant to symbolize the transience of love.'

Charles held on to the finger, pressed the tiny scratchy diamonds with his thumb. How could she keep jawing about symbolism, when he was more or less proposing to her? 'Look, Laura, I want to make it up to you, not just with theatres and presents, but with time. You're right – I have neglected you. But I intend to change.'

Laura had plucked a blade of grass and was tickling his face with it. Her laugh was like a scalpel cutting through his skull.

'Good God, Charlie, so love's labour *isn't* lost! I do believe wily old Shakespeare's made a convert of you. You sound worse than those love-lorn lords!'

'Laura, I'm serious. You matter to me, darling, and I want to prove it. I know I've taken you for granted, but things will be different now. Look, why don't we try and go away together. How about a weekend in Paris? Sometime in October, when the crowds have gone?' If he promised her Paris, she might even swap the Mirabelle for Oppenheimer, this all important Saturday.

The wasp was wooing Laura from the other side. She sprang up, to dislodge it from her hair. 'I'm afraid it's a little late, my love.'

He stared at her scarlet back. She was wearing all red, too harsh for the faded afternoon. 'What do you mean?'

'It's a very tedious journey from Johannesburg to Paris, darling.'

'Johannesburg?'

'Yes, my sweet. I didn't really intend to tell you, in the middle of a matinée, but your sudden protestations of devotion have rather forced my hand.'

Charles made an angry swipe at the wasp. 'What the hell are you talking about?'

'Relax, darling. They only sting you if you needle them. We're emigrating to South Africa.'

'Emigrating?'

'Yes, next month. Houghton Drive, just north of town. Five bedrooms and a swimming pool.'

'We, who's we? What in God's name are you saying?'

'Well, me and Clive, of course. Who else?'

'But I thought . . . Look, Laura, this is absolutely nonsensical! You always told me you had no future with Clive.'

'Poor love! I have been disloyal to him, haven't I? You've always encouraged me, but that's only natural, I suppose. Clive's very easy to insult – he's also very easy to get along with. I never realized that before. Funnily enough, it was you who made me see it. Clive loves me, Charles. He needs me. You don't need anyone. You use them. I don't exist for you as a person; nor does Frances, or Magda, or that poor, godforsaken brat Frances plans to bring into this wicked world. They're just inconveniences to you, cyphers to be slotted into your electronic calculator and assessed for their investment potential, or their scrap value.' She was still stroking the grass across his chin, cruel steel against soft flesh.

'When Magda loused you up, you handed me my cards. You didn't need me any more. Or, even if you did, I might prove dangerous. You never wondered how I might feel about it. In fact, you drove me back to Clive. It's probably better, that way. You stay with your precious daughter, and I'll stay with my old man.'

Daughter! That tone-deaf, blue-jeaned urchin who had lost him everything – his wife, his pride, his sex, his self-respect – and now Laura. Turned him into a cuckold and a laughing stock. He could see her now, picking her nose on his gilded Grecian couch, disposing of her chewing-gum on the underbelly of his Sheraton writing-table, dissecting meatballs with her fingers, dribbling gravy down her breasts, rinsing out her stained and bloody panties in his own private bathroom. This was the brat who had driven away his mistress, his voluptuous, witty, stylish, two-faced turncoat of a superwoman, who had the cheek, the insensitivity, to betray him with her own husband.

Well, she'd have to go, his 'daughter'. He'd had more than he could take. His so-called flesh and blood would be sent packing to her mother as soon as he could conceivably arrange it. He'd phone Piroska the moment he got home and more or less command her to send that telegram. Why should he fret any longer over threatened O-levels and damaged lives, lie awake agonizing over near-miss abortions, when the kid was almost certainly somebody else's? Magda could no more share his chromosomes than Clive could share a bed with dazzling Laura. It was time that Jewish dwarf took on the burden. If he'd fathered the brat, well, let him worry about her. Only he'd better do it back in Budapest. Because that's where Magda was going, as fast as a telegram could take her.

When he opened his eyes, the kid had already gone, packed off on an aeroplane, deported on a train. There was only Laura standing over him, tickling his neck with her cruel grass rapier. He almost slapped it off.

'I simply don't understand you, Laura. This doesn't make any sense at all. You always made out your . . . your husband was some sort of spastic mooncalf!'

'Come, my sweet, you're exaggerating. I admit he's not as bright as you are, but that's probably an advantage. And – no – his seduction technique isn't quite as slick and assured, but he's loyal and loving and a lot of other boring, dependable, old-fashioned things.'

Charles snatched the grass from her hand and crushed it into pulp. 'Seduction? What d'you mean? You always told me Clive was impotent.'

'Did I, darling? Or was that what you wanted to believe? Even now, you're not listening. The only word you heard was "seduction". You're still comparing penises with Clive. Perhaps that's what all affairs are based on – a sort of eternal cock fight, the lover gaining inches on the spouse. Well, I've finished with affairs. I'm off to Jo'burg to queen it on my floodlit patio, with my half dozen coloured maids. I might even go in for a family myself – adopt a little Bantu baby. I have to fill those five large bedrooms somehow.'

'You're joking . . .' He couldn't take it in – Clive screwing her, Clive zipping off to Jo'burg, Clive winning. Laura winning. Slipping in her insults, slapping him down.

'About the adoption, yes. You know how I feel about kids. Clive and I don't want any. Nor do you and Frances – if only you could see it. That's another reason I've finished with you, Charles. I rather despise a man who doesn't know what he wants, or where

232

the hell he's going. Clive's always been clear about the basics. He wanted me – and not much else. No kids, no other woman on the side, no driving ambition. You want everything, Charles, and you'll land up with nothing.'

The phrases slashed like knives. There was a tight ball, spring-coiled in his skull, a black sun scorching through his body, blistering his life, black humiliation mixed with fury.

Laura had sat down again, and was staring at her sparkling middle finger. 'Funny, really,' she taunted, in her Judas-kiss voice. 'This is what they call an eternity ring. Perhaps you didn't realize?'

He was silent, fighting a strong urge to tear the ring off, rip her strutting husband from her arms, blitz the prissy, preening house in Houghton Drive.

She was picking daisies now, white petals on her scarlet lap, pretending she was presiding at a simple country picnic, rather than a massacre. 'How long is eternity for you, Charles?'

He didn't answer. Two-faced hypocrite! She'd gulped down all the presents, grown fat and glossy on his jewels, allowed him to slip a ring on her finger, the very moment she was leaving him. He had given up a precious working day, simply so she could restock her wardrobe for Johannesburg; actually paid for the lingerie she was to seduce her husband in! And there she was, sitting demurely making a daisy chain, slitting the stems with her cruel crimson talons, in the same way she'd ripped his life apart, and smiling as she handed him the rejects.

It was all the more intolerable, because there was some truth in what she said. If only she'd accused him of stinginess or stupidity, he could have shrugged it off, but Laura had stabbed him in his most defenceless places. He could feel his anger ticking like a time-bomb. He must defuse it before it exploded in her face, blew up the whole of Guildford. Never before had he allowed himself to get so close to danger, to lose his self-control, throw away his shield and his defences. He shut his eyes, tried to concentrate only on the rhythm of his breathing, to count the notes in the rapture of a thrush's song.

Laura's voice had crept inside the song, and was wrenching it out of key. She was leaning over him, fastening the completed daisy chain around his neck. 'Let's not quarrel,' she murmured,

233

letting both hands tease and linger. 'I still fancy you, you know – even in a twenty-minute interval, surrounded by Guildford's geriatrics, and despite everything I've said. Crazy, isn't it?'

He felt a twinge of answering desire, clogged with only half-extinguished fury. Laura's thighs were spread apart on the seat, the flimsy fabric of her skirt straining over them. She wasn't just a bitchy tongue – there was a body attached to it, and it was the body he'd desired in the beginning. He'd first seen her sitting in the Golf Club, flirting with a bar stool, her long legs looped around the rungs, taunting him in black stockings. Today, the stockings were a paler shade of oyster. He placed his hand on her thigh, felt it warm and silky through her skirt. His head was a spinning roulette wheel. He hardly knew which colour would come up – the scarlet of desire, or the furious black of resentment and revenge. Even now, there was still some tantalizing overlay of Magda. He could feel the child underneath his hands, the long, sloping insolence of her legs, the swelling breasts pushing out her shirt, the neat, tight, dangerous, virgin bottom. Chewing-gum and nose-pickings hardly mattered any more – his hands were further down.

He sprang up from the seat, as if it had caught fire. Magda must go, if only for her own protection. If truth could be told in a telegram, it wasn't Miklos who'd be cited, but his own vile, unpardonable obsession:

'Magda, leave at once! Your brute of a father desires you.'

Except he wasn't her father. He couldn't be. Fathers didn't feel such lust and murderous violence towards their daughters; want to fondle them and rape them, then bash their bloody brains in. He shuddered, felt like some foul debris chucked into a wastebin. Back in his office, he could still parade with rod and sword, still receive homage as monarch and Führer, but closed in the filthy dungeon of his mind, he was only chaff and scum. He was so exhausted, he felt as if he'd lived and laboured through all the centuries from Shakespeare's to his own, yet this was a day off, a spree, a jaunt, a relaxation.

The interval was almost over. The lutenists had worked through Dowland, Byrd and Campian, and were now playing songs from the finale of the play itself.

234

> *When daisies pied and violets blue*
> *And lady-smocks all silver-white*
> *And cuckoo-buds of yellow hue*
> *Do paint the meadows with delight . . .*

That's all it was, paint. Even this theatre garden was plasticine and pigment. The tenor was flat in the upper register, the baritone had acne. He shaded his eyes from the pitiless purple-pink of the petunias, longed to lie down on the ground, and rot back into dust; or, at least, have Frances' frail, familiar form beside him, her small, soft hands curled around his misery.

Balls! His wife had gone. Her small, soft hands were curled only around her womb, or some other swine's filthy private parts. He kicked at a clump of daisies, decapitated their simple, smiling heads. He mustn't give in to this spinelessness, this wallowing self-pity. Frances was best forgotten. At least Laura was still sitting there beside him. He must woo her, recapture her, stand up to Clive, refuse to let him win. If some sexless nincompoop with thinning hair and a handicap in double figures could bribe her with five bedrooms and a swimming pool, then he must offer more.

'Look, Laura, I know things have been difficult, but just give me time. It can still work out between us . . .'

'Can it?' Laura broke the noose around his neck by plucking the largest daisy from the chain. 'Let's find out.'

She tore off one white petal and tossed it in the air. 'He loves me,' she chanted.

The countertenor's strange, metallic voice was shrilling from the balcony:

> *The cuckoo then on every tree*
> *Mocks married men, for thus sings he,*
> *'cuckoo'.*

Laura wasn't listening. All her attention was concentrated on the tiny white flower-head.

'He loves me not.' A second petal fluttered to the ground.

'Loves me.

'Loves me not.

235

'Loves me . . .'

Charles was mesmerized by her soft, mocking voice. How could there be so many petals on a common daisy? White flags of surrender littering the grass. The warning bell was sounding from the theatre, above the chorus of the song:

> *Cuckoo, cuckoo! O word of fear,*
> *Unpleasing to a married ear!*

He shivered. A spiteful wind was blowing off the river and the sun was all glare and no heart. He had no desire to return to Navarre – it was a vain and empty kingdom, and a cold one.

'Loves me not,
'Loves me . . .'

Stupid game! Laura's voice was like an incantation. There was one last petal on the mutilated daisy – only one. Slowly, teasingly, she pulled it off, handing him the scalped stalk.

'Loves me *not*,' she whispered. He could smell the pollen on her fingers, and her Benson and Hedges breath.

The final bell was pealing across the garden, mixed with the still insistent chorus:

> *'Cuckoo, cuckoo! O word of fear . . .'*

Charles turned away, head down. He couldn't endure that last act of the play, with its savage peasant songs, its jeering cuckoos. Laura took his arm, steered him back towards the theatre.

'Come along, darling, we don't want to miss it, do we? I doubt if there'll be much Shakespeare in Johannesburg!'

18

Frances was shelling peas. She dropped the last empty pod in the
waste bin, and laid out thirty-five green peas in a horizontal line –
a chart, a menstrual cycle, made of peas. She counted them again.
She was right – thirty-five. Day thirty-five. One week overdue.
A hundred thousand years overdue. How did giraffes endure
it, with fifteen-month-long pregnancies, or elephants, with six
hundred days to count? The way she felt, the baby should be
born by now, and yet it was still only a pinhead, smaller than
the smallest unripe pea. And still fatherless. How could Ned be
the father of something he didn't even know existed? She had
tried to tell him, practised openings to spring on him when the
moment was propitious. It somehow never was.

'Ned, how would you like to teach a son to fish?'

'Ned, guess what I found behind the gooseberry bush this
morning?'

He'd laugh, grab her round the waist and say, 'I'm your baby,
give me a breast to suck.' Or, 'Let's call it John Dory, after the
fish.' He wouldn't take her seriously. He never did. That was one
of the problems. It was fine to live his larky, lazy way, when there
were only the two of them, but a child changed everything. She
didn't want her precious baby shoved in an orange box with a
cat on top of it, or its Farex used for bait. And how would she
ever dry its nappies, when the airing cupboard was purple and
fermenting with home-made sloe gin? It wasn't easy to turn a
man like Ned into an instant pre-packed father. He complained
when she defrosted the fridge – claimed it disturbed the lugworm
– and refused to discuss wallpapering the bedroom. So long as
she was in his bed, he argued, why should he care what was on
the walls? Sometimes she submitted, and they lay indolent and
sweaty all day long. It was as if she had wallpapered over all the
doors and windows and they couldn't get out. Ned was the world
and there wasn't any other – no wars, no weather forecasts, no
share reports nor parliamentary crises. It seemed strange to her,

later, that a cabinet minister had died, or Israel had threatened Egypt, and she hadn't known or cared. She almost liked not caring. Strange how quickly you could sink into grubby apathy, the soft, delicious centre of your own abandoned world, switching off the universe, turning worktime into bedtime, playing at being full-time layabouts. It wasn't, after all, so difficult to renounce deodorant and dental floss, or eat chocolate cake for breakfast, or share your pillow with a self-opinionated cat. At least it wasn't hard until the nights. So long as Ned was over her, or under her, stopping her thinking with his childish, cheerful banter, telling her she was Salome and Venus and Bugs Bunny and the Blessed Virgin, then she didn't agonize. But when his breathing deepened, and he rolled away from her, to sleep, absurdly, on his stomach, then the small, niggly voices, stifled all day long, began to shout and hammer in her head. Why did he always feel so small inside her? Why did he come too quickly? Why did he pee with the bathroom door wide open and talk above the plash? Why was he idle and untidy, feckless, fatuous? Why wasn't he more like Charles? No, not like Charles. Then, he wouldn't push his face between her thighs and linger there over a four-course lunch, or use Werther's tail to do crazy, tickly things across her breasts, or sauté mashed bananas with marshmallows and feed her from the frying pan. Charles didn't perform Icelandic war-dances stark naked in the kitchen, or stick daisies in her pubic hair, or draw golden-syrup kisses on her porridge. Why couldn't she be Franny and settle for Ned and the syrup? Or, give him up and be a thoroughgoing Frances?

It was so confusing being half of two different people, warring with each other and wanting half of two different men. Sometimes she hated all the halves – theirs and hers, the whole complicated mix-up. It was like that game she'd played as a child – 'Heads, Bodies, Legs', each painted figure cut into three. You had to try to fit them back together, but you got some strange permutations on the way – a layabout's mouth with a paragon's penis on the end of it, a dirty fishing hat straddling a pair of Gucci shoes.

That's what her baby would be like – a hybrid. Now that Charles had refused to have anything to do with it, it remained a cross-breed, a monster, swelling in the nights, until it was a giraffe and an elephant inside her, accusing her of adultery, recklessness, betrayal. But if only Ned accepted it, it would shrink and mellow. It might still be a mongrel, but a happy, harmless one, with a name-tag and a home. Why was it so impossible to tell him? In old romantic movies, the woman didn't even have to spell it out. She merely reclined on the sofa, a beatific smile playing over her stomach, a fragment of white knitting fluttering in her hands. The man entered, their eyes met – sobbing violins, throbbing chords, et cetera, and he *knew*. Ned wouldn't. She'd tried the sofa and the knitting, and all he'd said was, 'Shove up, love, you're hogging all the cushions. And if you're knitting me a sweater, does it have to be white angora?'

She eased up from the kitchen bench. One last forgotten pea-pod was lurking at the bottom of the basket. She slit it with her thumb. Inside, just two tiny peas, identical and perfect. Twins. She'd have to tell him. You couldn't inflict twins on a man with a one-bedroomed flat and an out-of-work airing cupboard. She would break the news tonight, over a celebration dinner. Ned had gone down to Dover to try out a new Penn casting reel. She'd welcome him back with *boeuf Bordelaise* in the oven and a baby in her womb. No, not *boeuf Bordelaise*. She'd renounced her fancy Oppenheimer style of cooking, in favour of a new Ned simplicity. No more salmon soufflés or juliennes of ham, but pasta and tinned pilchards, which saved time and fuss and money. The Gospel according to Ned – though she wouldn't take it too far. The Simple Life needn't mean squalor and slumming, or baked beans from the can. Their new ménage must be a compromise, with the baby as the symbol of it. It had already united her and Ned, and they must follow up the process. She wouldn't ask too much. They needn't even move. She could merely renovate the flat and tame the garden. Ned's pad, with Franny's stamp on it. The same with dinner. They mustn't toast the baby in spam and chips, or lobster thermidor, but something in between. Simple soup and unpretentious chicken casserole. She threw on her mac and went to buy a Tesco's frozen chicken, no free-range Fortnum's darling, but a base-born cut-price broiler.

Burnt chicken was baser still, she thought, as she turned the oven lower, and scraped charred onions off the bottom of the casserole. Ten o'clock and Ned hadn't even phoned. He was always late.

In nine months' time, he'd probably miss the birth. 'Sorry, love, couldn't make it. Had a mermaid on the line!'

She smiled. He drove her crazy with his tomfoolery, his unpunctuality, but somehow he always managed to atone for it, when he kissed her entire body from right temple to left toe, or turned boring, basic things like shins or vertebrae into new erotic zones. He couldn't perform like Charles, but he bounced into bed with such exuberance that all her warning lights switched off and she swooped straight into overdrive. Sex with Charles was technically impeccable, but silent and controlled. He never took risks, or ventured out of lane. And there was no engine noise. Charles never purred or roared or hooted, as Ned did, never let her see his pleasure, let alone hear it. He must always be the stiff, munificent benefactor, the driver at the wheel; she the grateful passenger. It was quite a new experience to have Ned beg her to stroke his feet or squeeze his balls, and then yell, 'Christ, you're bloody marvellous, woman!' when she did it right. There was joy and power in giving.

Charles refused to be distracted from the road. Sex took his total concentration for the carefully calculated period he allotted it, and then it was back to verticality and work. But Ned stretched it out in all directions, made whole days horizontal as well as nights, interrupted kisses with date-and-banana sandwiches, told her fishing stories in the middle of a come. There was no structure, no timetable, just sex sprinkled over everything, like sugar.

So, how could she accuse him, when he accorded Dover beach the same lingering, day-long treatment? At least, when he did arrive, he'd probably be triumphant. Easy to slip a tiny baby in, when he was wreathed in ten-pound turbot. She only hoped he'd got a decent catch. Whatever happened, she mustn't be impatient. That would ruin everything. She could always use the waiting-time to rehearse her lines. She decided to keep them simple, like the meal.

'Ned, darling, I'm going to have your baby.'

She slipped gracefully into a broken chair, and tried it out aloud. 'Ned, darling, I'm going to . . .'

'Grub up!' shouted a familiar voice. 'Full bag! Fish supper! Frying tonight!'

Ned barged through the door, festooned with four dead dabs

and a still-expiring dogfish, and kissed her through the lot. The reek of Dover breakwater swamped the smell of chicken. 'Sling a lump of butter in the pan, love – I'm going to cook you Neptune's feast!'

She dodged a scaly tail. 'Let's save them for breakfast, darling. I've already made a chicken casserole.'

'Christ, Fran, I didn't flog all the way to Dover for plastic battery hen. Fish must be cooked the day it's caught. Fresh fried dabs are a knockout! Here, chuck over the butter and it can be melting while I clean the little blighters.'

'But the chicken's ready, Ned. It's been ready hours, in fact. I was expecting you at eight.' It had been something of a trauma cooking anything at Ned's, when there were tin-tacks in the spice jar instead of peppercorns, and half of last year's Christmas dinner still clinging to the oven.

'Never expect an angler.' He peeled off his anorak and flung it on the table, disturbing her flower arrangement. 'OK, love, we'll have the chicken afterwards. Fish course first, then poultry.' He was dripping fishy water over the newly polished floor, bunging up the sink with scales and fins.

'But I've made a soup to start with.' A Ned soup: leek and potato broth, earthy and unsophisticated.

'Better still. Soup, fish, poultry, pud. What's for pud?'

'Gooseberry crumble.'

He hugged her. He was still in his waterproofs and he felt slimy like the bottom of a pond. She pulled away.

'You don't cook dab with their heads on, do you?'

'Why not? More protein. Hey, where's the salt? What on earth have you done in here? I can't find a thing. The fridge is so bare, it looks like a toupee ad. Franny, you've springcleaned, you rotter! I smelt it as soon as I came in, or rather, I didn't smell it. You've ruined the bouquet. It took me years to build up that *je-ne-sais-quoi* fragrance of cobwebs and vintage bottled cat, and now you've gone and doused it all with Cleen-o-Pine.'

He was genuinely annoyed. She could hear it underneath the banter. He mustn't be annoyed – not on the night she was going to invest him with his fatherhood. She tried to distract him, take an interest in his catch.

241

'What's that one?' she asked, pointing to an evil-looking creature with a squashed back and a long whip-like tail.

'Thornback ray. The little bleeder almost dragged me in. Watch out! Those thorns are poisonous.'

All his fish looked poisonous. The charred aroma of her home-spun country sauce was outdone by the scorching smell of dab. Ned had left them to burn, while he scrabbled on his hands and knees, replacing the pile of ancient paperbacks on the bottom shelf of the larder. 'Look, Fran, if I want to keep my Enid Blytons next to the Branston pickle, that's my affair, right? Don't interfere, or try to take me over. You complain that's what your husband does to you. Well, I don't need any Charleses in my life. I'm happy as I am. I don't want Harpic sprinkled down my gut or my soul scrubbed out with Sqeezy.'

He rushed back to the frying pan, scraped the blackened fish off the bottom, then doused them with cold water from the sink. He stood over her, the dripping, sizzling pan still in one hand, her left nipple in the other.

'I want *you*, Franny – your crazy mixed-up cunt which isn't sure whether it's the Virgin Mary or the Whore of Babylon; your neon-tetra eyes. But I don't want your Minit-Mop or your Brillo pads, or your prissy little War-on-Dust Campaign. Kiss me.'

She did. Anything to stop him talking – she knew what would come next. 'I don't want your prissy little private-prescription, germ-free, Harley Street baby . . .'

She continued the kiss as long as the smell allowed. She seemed to be nose-to-nose with the entire dead-and-living contents of the English Channel.

'Shall I run you a bath?'

'Christ, no! I'm knackered. Grub first, scrub later.'

He plonked the frying pan in the centre of the table, grabbed a fork and skewered a dab on the end of it. It was black on the outside and still seeping water from the sink. 'Here, take a bite of this.'

'Ned, I've laid the table in the other room.' She had found some semi-decent china in the cellar and scrubbed off years of grime, improvised a clean white tablecloth out of a sheet. There were roses in a soup-bowl, paper napkins twisted into swans.

242

Things must be simple, but there was no need to pig it. She mustn't forget the compromise, the baby.

'I'm too whacked to move. Anyway, they're nicer eaten straight from the pan. Try a bit, it's bliss.'

He tore off a morsel with his fingers and popped it in her mouth. 'Know something? When a dab's born, it's got an eye on either side of its head, but when it grows bigger, the eyes sort of move, and it ends up with two eyes together, on the same side. Crazy, isn't it?'

Utterly crazy. The whole romantic evening had been shattered at a blow. Here was Ned, sprawling in his socks, smelling like Billingsgate, and spearing waterlogged flatfish from a frying pan. She'd planned low lights, hushed, tender conversation leading slowly but inexorably to the subject of paternity, not a clapped-out beachcomber explaining, with his mouth full, the ocular peculiarities of dab.

'Ned?'

'What?'

'I've got something to tell you, darling, something important.'

'Hold on a sec, I want some HP sauce – it'll cover up the burnt bits. Where the hell have you hidden it? Christ, Franny, you've moved everything out of its proper place.'

'Ned, I'm talking to you.'

'Look, Fran, I'm not often angry, you know that. I'm an easy-going sort of chap, but I don't like my house messed about. You're welcome to share it, live in it, use anything you like in it, but not dismantle it and put it back your way. That's what my wife tried to do and that's why I left her.'

Frances passed him the sauce bottle from its new home in the spice cupboard. She laid down her fork. 'Your *what*, Ned?'

'Look, forget it. I'm probably over-reacting. Let's have the chicken now. It smells a treat.'

'You said your *wife*.'

'Yeah. Shall I get the plates?'

'You never told me you had a wife.'

'Well, I haven't got one now. I told you, I left her. Want the last dab?'

'You're divorced?'

'No.'

'Still married?'

'Well, legally, I suppose, but . . .'

'You never told me.'

'No.'

'I mean, I asked you about your life and past and . . . We went over things like that . . .'

'Things like what? You're making it sound like a sort of contract between us.'

'Well, wasn't it?'

'Hell, Franny, one of the main reasons I was attracted to you was the fact that you made it so damned clear you *weren't* available. You told me about your husband the very first instant I set eyes upon you, and you haven't stopped embroidering on him, since. I've almost fallen in love with Charles myself, his brilliance and his business skills, his Ted Lapidus after-shave, his deodorant-impregnated socks. I knew I could never compete with a paragon like that. And, frankly, I don't really want to try.'

'What do you mean, Ned?' She tried to sound cool and uninvolved, as if they were discussing sea conditions in the Channel.

'We're friends, Franny, lovers, good pals, but that's all. I don't want a wife or a housekeeper. I've had both and it didn't work.'

'But why didn't you tell me, Ned?' The baby in her womb was drowning, flailing.

'Why should I? I didn't want to launch into that messy, miserable business and dig the whole thing up again. It's over – finished and done with. I should never have married in the first place. I'm a loner. You knew that, Franny. I never promised you anything or told you that I loved you. It's safer that way. Neither of us has lost our heart or head. I always assumed you were Charles' property – that was half the attraction. You were tied, tagged, accounted for, ringed like a homing pigeon. I don't like girls when they're single, or available. Oh, no doubt there's some devious psychological explanation. My mother didn't breast-feed me or my father wore a wig, but who cares? That's how I am, and I'm happy with it. Look, we're meant to be having dinner, aren't we? Where's this four-course feast you promised me?'

She got up automatically, surprised her legs still worked.

244

Someone had chopped them into pieces, floured them, and flung them in a casserole. She couldn't even think. Her mind was a soup, mushy and diluted. Somehow, she'd never put Ned in any context, or let him have a life story. He was simply there, ready and waiting, to fit any of her fantasies – lover, confidant, playmate, Peter Pan. Father of her baby. It was partly his fault. He'd always played along with her, never answering any questions, treating life as a game. But she'd lost the game. She was pregnant by a man who didn't even want to be a husband, let alone a father; who wanted to be free, untrammelled, single.

She tried to fix her attention on the blue and white squiggles on the cheap Woolworth plates. If she counted them like sheep, perhaps she wouldn't lose control. But even the squiggles were dazed and trembling, submerging under scalding chicken sauce.

'D . . . did you have children, Ned?'

If she lost the squiggles, at least she could still count peas. She knew there were more than thirty-five. One hundred and thirty-five. One thousand and thirty-five. Nine whole months of peas, stretching away to a fully-formed, deformed, unwanted baby. She continued spooning peas on to Ned's plate, until they were overflowing in a relentless green volcano.

'Hey, steady on! I know I said I was hungry, but . . .'

'Did you, Ned?'

'Did I what?'

'Have children?'

'Nope.'

'Did you ever want them?' She removed a sprig of mint from the potatoes, added a sprinkling of salt, a twist from the pepper mill.

'Can we stop this conversation? I find it tedious. I don't want to talk about my wife, or my mother, or my Serbo-Croat fairy godmother. I'm quite happy to tell you the difference between a bull-huss and a tope, or discuss the spawning habits of salmon. Mother Nature's very odd, you know. Salmon live in the sea, but break their bloody necks fighting back to the fresh water they were born in, in order to spawn themselves. Whereas silver eel live in fresh water all their lives, and then go bananas swimming three thousand miles back to the Sargasso Sea to lay their eggs. What a cock-up! All that unnecessary travelling. Now, if a broody eel could swap with a pregnant salmon . . .'

Pregnant, broody – why did he have to use such cruel words? He was explaining, now, which fish spawned their young alive, and which laid eggs. She let him talk, through alternate mouthfuls of dab and chicken. Her face made roughly the right sort of responses, but she wasn't listening. She was trying desperately to reassess the situation. She couldn't live with Ned – that was clear – she couldn't launch a baby on him, couldn't even blame him. She'd lied to him, not only over the Pill, but in other, fundamental things. Even after Croft's Club, she hadn't said, 'I've left my husband because he won't accept your baby.' She'd told him some fable about coming to stay, while Charles baled out a bank in Singapore. Just a few days; Charles wouldn't know. She'd even played the poor abandoned wife. She was lonely on her own, with her husband always abroad.

Ned had pressed her, 'Are you sure it's safe? Charles won't be suspicious?' And she'd lulled him with false assurances. She hadn't allowed Ned a life and a history of his own. Because he stressed the present, she'd abolished his past and kidnapped his future, taken him over and used him for her own purposes. Yet, all the time, she'd been using Charles as well. Even this Tesco's chicken had been bought with Charles' money, and all Ned's deficiencies patched and supplemented, courtesy of Charles. She had never really accepted that her precious infant would go to Acton Primary, or that she'd have the baby in a crowded, noisy ward on the NHS. If Ned had been her basic cake, then Charles was always the icing on the top. But neither man would go along with her. Why should they? She'd chosen a game they didn't want to play, and bent the rules to suit her.

She'd deceived herself, as well as them. Made up her own myth of Ned and swallowed it whole, assigning him the role of willing father, and expecting him to rewrite his entire life script, to fit her own needs. Or tried to believe that Charles would accept a child which wasn't his, when she'd failed to do the same, with Magda. There was something really repellent about having to face the truth about herself, seeing Frances Parry Jones as an insensitive manipulator, instead of a misused martyr.

Ned was making patterns of peas, laying them out in the

shape of a name, her name – Franny – with three broccoli kisses underneath.

'Cheer up, love. You haven't eaten a thing. Here – just eat the "F". F for my fabulous, fascinating, fantastic *femme fatale*.'

He picked up two tiny peas which formed the crossbar of the F, and trickled them between her lips. The twins. She almost choked.

'You're still my favourite, Fran. Don't be upset by what I said. Just let things be. Don't tidy cupboards or dig up wives. Remember the moment, comrade.'

She remembered it – the baby swelling, out on the summer grass. She still had the baby, but now it was doubly and permanently fatherless. Should she tell him, none the less? There was just a chance he might feel differently, when faced with a *fait accompli*. Even though she'd just admitted she was a manipulator, blind to other people's needs, she still craved the baby like a drug. Her mind could analyse and censure, point out just how selfishly and stupidly she'd acted, but her body didn't care. It was still murmuring 'I'm pregnant, pregnant, pregnant', lush and blossoming, back in the September afternoon.

Ned had abandoned the peas and was larding custard on to hot gooseberry crumble. 'Let's eat our pudding in bed.'

'No.' She struggled to her feet. The sick black night heaved against the dark uncurtained windows.

'Please, Fran. I'll have a bath, I promise. You won't smell a trace of plaice. That's a poem! D'you know, I'm the only living poet who . . .'

'Ned, I've got to go.'

'Go? Where? Why?'

It was suddenly so cold. Perhaps there had never been a summer afternoon. 'Oh, I don't know . . .' Where, indeed? Where could a pregnant woman go? There was always Viv – she would understand. But relations with Viv had been strained since Magda had been sent away to boarding school. Viv had swept round to see them, begged that the child should live with her, instead. And all Charles had done was repeat, 'Magda will be better with the nuns.' He hadn't even looked up from correcting the typescript of his latest new tax report. Viv had lost her cool, shouted at them both and rushed away. Frances had tried to mend the rift with a bread-and-butter letter, and a bunch of flowers. And then ignored her. It was the same with all her friends. She'd been so absorbed in herself and her predicament, she'd neglected and avoided them. She sometimes wondered if they really *were* her friends. She and Charles were always so busy, they treated friends like holidays – something you bothered with, if and when you could spare the time. Ned had taught her what true friendship was. He might be a loner, but he knew about caring and affection. Just-good-friends was everything with Ned. And she'd abused it. She couldn't walk away without repaying him, without some tangible farewell, one last crazy romp in his crumpled, fishy bed.

She lay in it, naked, waiting while he ran his bath. She remembered all the times they'd clowned together in the bathroom, when he'd scrubbed her back and soaped between her toes, drawn patterns on her breasts with shaving soap, conducted with the loofah while he thundered out Salvation Army hymns. He was singing now, out of tune, murdering the time. Charles would wince. But why was she still destroying Ned with Charles? She was no longer in the luxurious position of having two contradictory but complementary men, one to atone for the other. There was no man now – she was alone, with only a half-formed baby in a sparsely furnished womb.

'Shove over, love. I'm clean except for my middle upper back. Since you wouldn't come and scrub it, I can't guarantee it's free from barnacles.'

He was so puerile sometimes, so stupid, it would be almost a relief to be alone. His constant bantering was beginning to annoy her, so that she almost longed for Charles' high seriousness. Then, when she was back with Charles, she taunted him for being humourless. She wanted both of them, and neither. She moved over, almost to the wall.

He had brought his pudding with him, congealing gooseberry crumble in a dish which said 'PUSSY'. He daubed a blob of custard across the dark thatch of her pubic hair, then straddled her to lick it off. She felt his rough, familiar tongue spooning into her, licking her lips, going back for second helpings. Her mind shut off and she was only a sweetmeat now, a flesh-pot – milk and honey, gooseberries and cream. There was still the moment, even if it

248

was the last crowning moment she would ever have with him. No one could take it from her. She knew now what it was like to feel and respond through every cell and pore. And, somehow, the baby was part of it. If she hadn't wanted a child, she would never have known another man, never moved out of her haven, into the highway. She would have the baby on her own, and at least bequeath to it, from its absent and unwitting father, the importance of the moment. There was nothing else – only Ned devouring her as she shouted underneath him, only the flinging, furious now, slamming and soaring until it took over her whole body, her whole life.

She sank back, down, under, as Ned emerged, his face damp, his hair tangled.

'You taste different, darling, strange.' He dipped his fingers between her thighs, brought them out, dark and shining. 'Look, Fran!'

She didn't look. She had closed her eyes, still savouring the feelings, letting her body slowly spiral down.

He kissed her softly on the pubic hair. His lips were wet and scarlet. 'You're bleeding, darling. Your period must have started. Why didn't you tell me you were due?'

19

Frances had stuffed a double wad of Kleenex up her pants. She could feel the blood seeping through it, trickling on to the driving seat. She drove fast, watching the needle soar up to seventy and stay there. She was going home. Home was where her husband was, where she had her periods. Twenty years of periods. She had never, ever missed one, not even now. There was no traffic on the roads. It was too late (or too early) for fellow motorists. She was a migrating bird, flying back where she belonged, where nature and her instincts dictated, following her biology. Or was she merely running away from Acton? Where in hell could she go but home, at three o'clock in the morning? She could hardly wander the streets all night. Anyway, she needed Tampax.

She hadn't planned beyond the Tampax. There was too much else exploding in her mind. She'd already stayed far too long at Ned's. She should have left as soon as she'd realized her period had started, instead of lingering like that, and blurting out the whole stupid story. She shuddered as she played the scene again – Ned sprawling naked on the lino, with a cat on either side of him, and she upside down on the pillows, sobbing with . . .

No, she mustn't think of it. All she wanted was to mop up the wreckage of the night, return to base, start again. Perhaps she wouldn't stay at home, just camp in the house till morning, steal in, lie low, and be gone again by dawn. She needn't even go upstairs, just stretch out on the sofa like an uninvited guest. She blinkered herself, so that she could think of nothing but the sofa, a velvet-covered Mecca, with soft cushions and supporting arms. She didn't put the car away, nor dab at the dark stain on the driving seat. The house was hushed and dark, as she crept towards the front door and was engulfed by the familiar smell of wax polish and high principles. Her shadow groped along the hall, shifting and trembling towards velvet-sofa sleep. Suddenly, another, taller shadow intercepted it.

'Frances!' murmured Charles.

She froze. She had never even considered that her husband might be still awake. His voice was home, salvation. Their two shadows fused.

Her face was jammed against his shoulder. She didn't know if she should tell him, or even how. She couldn't just announce, 'My period's begun.' Yet she never used the more colloquial terms like 'the curse' or 'coming on'. Charles liked even menstruation to be grammatical, precise. Though this time, she knew he wouldn't care. The fact itself spelled Mafeking for him, victory, reprieve.

'Charles,' she stuttered. Her voice was muffled by his dressing-gown. 'I'm . . . er . . . not pregnant after all.'

He was too well-mannered to gloat, or jubilate. He just held her, tighter, so that she could feel his heart hammering into hers, his motor and machinery still powering her frail life.

'Happy anniversary!' he whispered. And, suddenly, he was undoing her zip, dragging her dress down over her hips, pushing her to the floor. She had left Ned's bed barely half an hour ago, still sticky with his sperm and her blood, and now Charles was repeating the performance, with no preliminaries, without even washing. He never made love to her when she was menstruating, found it far too messy and distasteful. Even if she wanted it herself, she never asked. It would stain the sheets, embarrass both of them. Ned's sheets were already stained and so was Ned. He hadn't been embarrassed in the slightest. And here was Charles, equally uninhibited, even more impetuous.

He hadn't spread a towel on the precious Persian rug. There was an urgency about him, a pleading, grabbing violence. It was a relief to feel him back in her again, large and inexhaustible. Ned had always been too small, too playful, a Peter Pan, U-certificate. But Charles was double X – slamming into her with wild, tearing strokes, crushing her body with his own, clawing her back with the pressure of his nails. And he was no longer silent, but making sounds she had never heard before, battle-cries of triumph and relief. She realized, suddenly, even while her body worshipped him, that he was competing with Ned, re-establishing his sexual rights, his ownership. He did not come at once – just went on stampeding her with pleasure, proving his superiority, his staying power, offering her everything he had and was.

Afterwards, they lay together on the rug, sprawled on top

251

of panting Persian dragons, their feet jammed against Charles' mother's priceless cellaret, Frances bleeding into him, shattered and sleepless. Charles fell fast asleep. She could hardly believe it, a man who found even hotel beds uncomfortable and who wore pinstriped pyjamas buttoned to the neck, reclining on the floor, clothed only in his own sweat. He was using sleep as a drug, a palisade, to block out all the facts he couldn't face, including his own messy, bloody, bellowing, unprecedented sexual act.

Morning was a long time coming. It crept up on them sullenly, with rain. Charles' eyes groped open, and for one brief, unacknowledged second, she saw terror and embarrassment flick over them, like secret pictures on a broken screen. Then he quickly slipped away from her, and she heard him run the taps, full blast, upstairs; soaping her away in a penitential cleansing rite, washing off her body, her blood, in an anniversary bath.

She stumbled to her feet and retrieved the stained wad of Kleenex, stuffing it back between her legs. She had still not fetched her Tampax, nor even glimpsed the sofa. So, what had she returned for? To be fucked by Charles? She slumped back down again. True, it had been wonderful, burst through all the rules and leapt new barriers, but Charles had already locked away the night like a dangerous aphrodisiac, to be swallowed only in life-and-death emergencies, and with the key in his safe keeping.

The drawing-room looked alien, like somebody else's house. It seemed to have swelled and stiffened in her absence, all its contents rigid and exalted, lowering down at her, as if she were a scratch upon their stern perfection. She stared around the room – everything so permanent and solid – furniture which had survived the centuries and increased its value at the same time. Stiff-spined chairs glared back at her, brass-footed bureaux pursed their lips, gaunt-eyed ancestors shrugged and turned away. There was no sign of welcome, or even recognition, no joy in her return. The house was always tidy, but at least when she was there, she added little touches to soften it or brighten it, ephemeral, insubstantial things which perished in a day – a bowl of cherries, a vase of fragrant pinks . . . But flowers and fruit had all been swept away. Now there was only highly-polished emptiness.

The doorbell cut across the vacuum. She started. Ned? No,

Ned never wished to set eyes on her again, not after the things he'd said last night. Postman, gasman, Harrods delivery van? She jumped up guiltily. You couldn't deal with Harrods, sprawled on the floor wearing nothing but a nappy. She pulled on an old raincoat hanging in the passage and sidled towards the door, trying to stop the Kleenex slipping. Mrs Eady was standing on the step, gawping in disbelief at her employer's bare feet and tangled hair.

'Oh, so you're back,' she said accusingly. 'Good holiday?'

'Yes ... thank you,' murmured Frances. 'You don't usually come on Saturdays, do you, Mrs Eady?'

'Not unless I'm asked,' snapped Mrs Eady. 'And not even then, unless I'm a fool. Which I must be.'

She was laden with shopping. Frances glimpsed steaks, nectarines, double cream – a Charles-and-Frances shopping list. There were also new potatoes, parsley, peas. God, not peas! She turned away.

'Brenda's coming later,' Mrs Eady announced, plonking her hat on the kitchen table and surrounding it with lemons.

'I beg your pardon?' Had Charles shacked up with another girl already, summoned Mrs Eady to lay on a lover's feast?

'My daughter – the one that cooks. And don't say you won't be needing her, now you're back. How am I supposed to tell her that, when she lives in Epping and isn't on the phone?'

'I'm sorry, Mrs Eady. I don't quite understand. I've only just returned.'

'You been out like that?' asked Mrs Eady, her pale eye fixed on Frances' unbuttoned raincoat which revealed a lot more than bare feet.

'Well, no, but ...'

'Oh, I suppose your husband hasn't told you yet. Well, he's expecting company tonight and asked me to help him out. My daughter cooks, you see. Fancy stuff. She's got exams an' all. Dinner for three, he said.'

'Three?' Had Charles invited Ned, arranged some terrible confrontation with him – dinner before their duel? Ridiculous. Couldn't she think of anything but Ned?

'The foreign gentleman's bringing his wife with him. She

phoned yesterday – I took the call myself. Couldn't hear a thing. Dreadful phones they got in Jersey.'

'Oh, I see.' Jersey. Oppenheimer. The anniversary dinner with Mr and Mrs Millions. The man she had blamed for the illegitimate child she wasn't even carrying. No baby, no Ned, no future. But steak and double cream, courtesy of Brenda. Polite cocktail-party conversation, when their whole world was changed, their entire marriage hanging in the balance, calling out for re-negotiation. Charles divided into four, and she left with only a superficial quarter of him, a polished façade, when she needed him whole, real, and undistracted.

Mrs Eady had donned her overall and was already gouging eyes out of potatoes. Frances murmured her excuses and limped upstairs, slowed down by her bottleneck of Kleenex. Charles had locked the bathroom door. She knocked, but got no answer. He hated being disturbed halfway through his toilet, before he was public and immaculate.

'Charles . . .'

'Can't it wait?'

'No.'

He was listening to 'Record Review' on Radio Three, rival recordings of Bach's *St John Passion*. Reluctantly, he turned down the soprano. 'What, darling?'

'Charles, you've got to cancel the Oppenheimers.'

Silence.

'Charles, did you hear?'

'Yes, darling.'

So he was flinging in a few darlings, was he, to celebrate their anniversary.

'Well, will you do it, or shall I?'

The taps were running now again, at top C, outsinging the soprano.

'Just a minute, darling. I don't like discussing things through bathroom doors.'

Oh, a touch of humour now, to spice the darlings. Any tactics, so long as they prevented that crucial conversation, stopped them sitting down and facing each other alone across the table, with no guests and no disguises, not even any music.

She was still waiting for him when he emerged, all traces

of the Persian rug purged away. She followed him into his dressing-room, switched off *St John*.

'Listen, Charles, we've got to be alone today. Our whole marriage is at stake, our future. We can't just carry on as if nothing's happened.'

Charles frowned at her reflection in the mirror. 'Of course not, darling. The Oppenheimers will be gone first thing tomorrow. We'll discuss it then – all day, if you like.'

'No, Charles, now. This is real life, not a shareholders' meeting. We can't just postpone things, like "business carried over". We've got to discuss it while it's actually happening. I've come back. That means something, doesn't it? If we don't talk now, I may not be here to talk to.'

Charles dropped his comb. She could see that he was nervous. 'It'll be easier tomorrow, Frances, on our own. We can't really talk with Mrs Eady here.'

'Well, get rid of her, then. We don't need her now the Oppenheimers aren't coming.'

'They are coming, Frances.'

'No.'

'Look, darling, we've been over all this already. I told you at Croft's why I couldn't put them off, and now it's even more impossible, the very day they're travelling. Do be reasonable.'

'It was entirely different then. I thought I was pregnant. Now I know I'm not.'

'I should have thought that made it easier.'

'Oh, really? And what do you know about . . .?'

'Look, Frances, I'm sorry about the pregnancy.'

'Of course you're not sorry.'

'What I mean is, I'm sorry you're sorry.'

'And who says *I am* sorry? Have you even bothered to . . .'

'Frances, you're upset. Of course you are. I do understand. It's rotten luck we can't be on our own today. But, it is only a day. It's hardly fair to let your period disrupt everybody else's plans. The Eadys, the Oppenheimers – they've all got lives as well, you know. You can't just bulldoze everyone because it happens to be day one instead of day thirty-six.'

She winced. He was right. She was trampling over everyone again, being selfish, boorish, totally unreasonable. Ned had

255

yelled at her last night, and now it was Charles' turn. Somehow, she couldn't stop herself, or didn't even want to. Some foiled, frustrated part of her wanted to shout and storm. It was almost desperation. She was like one of those roly-poly Russian dolls, which could only rock and wobble from side to side, since they had no legs or feet. If she couldn't stand on her own, at least she must keep bouncing back, bumping into everyone. Better than lying down and giving in, letting Brenda and the nectarines take over. She jumped up from the window-seat, and stood face to shoulder with Charles in front of the mirror.

'Day one, is it? That's wonderful. Fancy you remembering! We really ought to celebrate. A Day One Party. Death of a Baby Party. Of course we'll have Oppenheimer. He'd love it. He loves celebrations – you told me so yourself. All this would never have happened without him, anyway. I'll ring him up this minute and ask him to come early, stay the whole week, if he wants, bring his wife, his sisters, his secretaries, his race-horse trainers – anyone he likes . . .'

She glimpsed two faces grimacing in the mirror; distant, contorted faces, nothing to do with her and Charles.

'Frances, you're hysterical. You'd better go and lie down. This baby thing has obviously upset you.'

'Oh, no, it hasn't. I'm thrilled about it! I told you, I want to have a party, a proper one. Not just two guests, two hundred. I refuse to spend my anniversary lying down.'

'Frances, please. How can we have a party at this late stage? We haven't even planned it. I've only bought steak for three.'

'Who needs steak? Or grouse, or nectarines, or all those other fancy foods your fancy friends were weaned on? Let them eat bread and cheese for a change. It'll do them good! We'll have a bread and cheese party in our dressing-gowns. Wouldn't that be fun, Charles?' The smaller face was jeering in the mirror. It couldn't be hers – she didn't mock and snarl like that, or wear dirty, faded raincoats beneath lank, unwashed hair. She turned her back on the reflection and strode towards the bedroom. 'You shift the furniture – we'll need a hell of a lot of room. I'm going to phone every friend we've got!'

She pounced on the prim grey phone by Charles' bed. 'Viv? Hello, darling. It's our wedding anniversary. Yes, a hundred happy years together. We thought we'd have a party. Can you come? No, tonight . . .'

The tall, contorted man in the mirror had followed her, and was trying to drag the receiver from her hand. She hung on grimly. 'Sorry, Viv. A bit of interference on the line. No, don't bring anything – we're going to keep it simple. Just yourself. Oh, and a few records for dancing. Charles has only got Bach fugues, and we want to let our hair down. Right? See you later, then.'

Frances slammed the phone down, then picked it up immediately, began to dial again. She was squatting on the floor, the blood-stained mac trailing out behind her. 'Laura? Frances here . . .'

Charles reached across and cut her off.

'What's the matter, darling? Surely you want Clive and Laura to come to our little party?'

'Frances, I absolutely forbid you to phone Laura. You don't know what you're doing. You're not well.'

'I'm perfectly well. Never felt better in my life. And Laura would love the Oppenheimers. You know how she worships money.'

'Frances, you are not to phone her. She's . . . got a bug.'

'A bug? Poor Laura! *She*'s ill, *I*'m ill – there must be an epidemic. All the more reason to phone her, so we can swap symptoms.'

'Frances, listen, Laura's not available. She's going to the Mirabelle.'

'The Mirabelle, with a bug? That's not very kind of her. She'll give it to all the waiters. How do you know, anyway? You haven't seen her, have you? Oh, hello, Laura. It's Frances. You shouldn't spread your germs about, you know. What? No, Charles told me you were unwell. Have you been in touch with him? Oh, I see, you thought *he* was sickening. No, he's not, we're both fine. In fact, we're planning a party. Tonight. Yes, it is rather sudden. Yes, a little celebration – how did you guess? Just a minute, Laura. I can't hear. Charles keeps interrupting. (Be quiet, Charles! Yes, I know they've booked a table at the Mirabelle, but Laura's going to cancel it. She says our party sounds too intriguing to miss. Isn't that nice?) Laura? Hello? Are you still there? Listen – Charles is thrilled you're coming. We both are. No, don't dress up, any old thing will do. See you at eight o'clock, then.'

*　　*　　*

257

Eleven o'clock. Blasting trumpets and wailing synthesizers terrorizing the quaking porcelain; guttering candles weeping scarlet wax; hot, half-naked bodies, playing blind man's buff with the furniture; wine in slow, red rivers, bleeding down a stricken sideboard; peanuts pulverized into priceless Persian rugs.

Charles stood at the door of the drawing-room and watched the party engulf his house. A celebration, that's what it was called – girls whose names he hardly knew, wounding his parquet with their cruel stiletto heels; neighbours he hated, guzzling his *grand cru* wines; blue-jeaned Mafia stubbing out their fag-ends on his gasping Sheraton. Frances had scraped the barrel for her guests. At such short notice, she hadn't had much choice. Their overweight, under-dressed butcher was entangled on the sofa with Brenda Eady's pink angora breasts. And Mrs Oppenheimer, standing, nervous and neglected, by the window, nibbling on a twiglet, awaiting, no doubt, the caviare and canapés, hot crab vol-au-vents, lobster mousseline – all traditional fare at Parry Jones parties. Frances had kicked tradition in the teeth, sent Charles out to Sainsbury's for simple bread and cheese, hacked it into chunks, and flung it on the kitchen table with a jar of Branston pickle. Nobody had touched it. Even the steaks and nectarines were still in their cellophane coffins in the fridge. He had tried to compensate with his best malt whisky and the choicest offerings from the Wine Society, but all it had done was embolden their autistic solicitor to blow up Mr Men balloons and burst them with a lighted cigarette, and remove the last of Brenda Eady's inhibitions, along with her fish-net stockings.

Mrs Eady hadn't noticed, yet. She was deep in emergency first-aid with floor-cloth and bucket. 'I said I'd look after three,' she grumbled, 'not a houseful. And why say steak, when he means peanuts? It's like a monkey-house in here!'

Charles turned his back on her dustpanful of nuts. He was busy enough himself, for Christ's sake, trying to act as host, barman, bouncer and furniture restorer, not to mention nursemaid to his wife. Frances had subsided for the moment, thank God, sprawled in a chair with her legs wide apart, grinning grotesquely at her empty glass. He shuddered as he glanced at her. She was wearing her unwashed hair and some strange athletic garment in purple towelling. He had asked Viv to keep an eye on her, but Viv was deep in the benefits of breast-feeding with their breastless next-door neighbour. He tried to catch her eye.

'Well, I did get an abscess with my third, but that was only because he *bit*. What's the matter, Charles?'

'Er . . . nothing.'

How could he yell to Viv across a mob of lurching John Travoltas, would she please muzzle his wife with Valium, or lock her in the lavatory before someone refilled her glass? He couldn't even reach her. It was impossible to cross that palpitating dance floor, which had once been called a drawing-room. Forty-three revellers loose and whooping in his house, friends of the friends of the friends Frances had telephoned that morning. 'Yes, of course bring your sister along – ask anyone you like – the more the merrier!'

His face ached with the polite pain of introducing people, yet he was the one who needed an introduction. Everyone else smiling, swilling, junketing – but he a stranger and a gate-crasher at his own party, stiff, cold, sober and alone. There was no one he could count on. Laura had arrived early, on purpose, and found him still minus his shirt and quarrelling with Frances over the merits of disposable paper plates versus the Royal Doulton. Viv had arrived late and smashed a Ch'ien Lung vase. Even his own acquaintances had turned into fools and drunkards. Their local estate agent was on his knees to Amanda Crawford, sporting a burnt-cork moustache and a funny hat, and the asinine Clive was labouring to prove that he knew the difference between the Manhattan Hustle and the hand-jive.

He joined the group by the piano and forced his face into the ruins of a smile. Perhaps he could initiate a little serious conversation about the new production of *Idomeneo*, with Janet Baker as a ravishing Idamante, and Colin Davis in the pit.

'And then he said he'd have to take the ovaries as well. He told Dave he'd never seen fibroids like it. Veritable grapefruits. I haemorrhaged for weeks.'

Christ! What hope was there for Mozart, when every bloody female was up to her neck in gynaecologists? It must be Frances' influence. Wherever she was, the conversation turned to wombs. He'd already escaped from a double prolapse and a hysterectomy.

Laura wasn't much better. Her line was storks and gooseberry bushes. He could see her now, out of the corner of his eye, flagging him down with a bottle of gin. She was resplendent in a Zandra Rhodes creation, set off with all Clive's diamonds. His own eternity ring was still on her middle finger, looking puny and insubstantial in comparison with her husband's mocking sparklers. He could hardly bear to look at her, now that he'd lost her, and if he did, Magda was still entangled with her, both of them mocking and denouncing him, ex-mistress and ex-daughter in a double exposure. Black letters were punching into his head, branding the cold white paper of his mind. The telegram! It would be on its way, by now, scalding over Europe, crash-landing at Westborough. His hands were damp with sweat. Perhaps he shouldn't have phoned Piroska at all. How would he ever know if . . .?

No, he mustn't think about it. Those perjured, pre-paid words must be erased from his mind for ever, the whole business of the telegram consigned to a section of his life marked 'File Closed'. He was sweating more profusely now, shameful droplets beading on his forehead, as fat and rank as Laura's diamonds. She'd edged so close, he could smell the faint, intimate odour of her hair.

'Darling, do tell me what we're celebrating. I was wondering, actually, whether to bring a little gift along. Blue bootees, for example?'

Charles turned his back and stormed into the kitchen. He'd chill more wine, replenish the ice – anything – to keep away from her. He sneaked a look behind him, to make sure she wasn't following. But Laura had already turned her charms on the most important guest.

'I adore these simple little spur-of-the-moment soirées, don't you, Mr Oppenheimer?'

Oppenheimer murmured something indecipherable through a mouthful of potato crisps. He was gallantly pretending that Golden Wonder's Onion Flavour were the perfect partner for a *Latricières-Chambertin* 1973.

'This is a very noble wine. I can highly recommend it. May I get you some?'

'No thanks, I always stick to gin. Besides, it's all gone.'

Laura had watched the last bottle disappear into Brenda Eady's holdall, aided by the butcher's sleight-of-hand. The *Chambertin* was the pride of Charles' cellar – he had been cosseting it for Christmas, two whole crates of it.

'Well,' said Oppenheimer, caught between Laura's gin bottle and the last broken fragments of the crisps. 'Shall we go and say hello to our hostess? I've hardly seen her.'

'I think she's keeping what they call a low profile,' sniped Laura, gesturing to Frances, who had slipped from her chair and was sprawled ignobly on a pile of cushions.

'Hi!' giggled Frances, watching Oppenheimer's calf-skin shoes glide purposefully towards her. She reached out a playful hand and grabbed his ankle. 'Great party, isn't it?'

'How are you, Mrs Parry Jones? I haven't had a chance to say hello to you.'

'Call me Fran.' She kidnapped the other ankle. Five foot ten above her, Oppenheimer tried to keep his balance.

'It was most gracious of you to offer us hospitality. You have a very beautiful home, if I may say so.'

Frances burped. 'Think so? I've just run away from it. Only came back today. That's why we're celebrating. Return of the prodigal.'

She released the ankles and pulled him down towards her on the cushions. 'You don't believe me, do you? I ran away to have a baby. It was your fault, really. Except I'm not having it. We're celebrating that, as well. The death of a foetus. Did you ever have a baby – your wife, I mean?'

'Er, no. We . . .'

'It's safer, isn't it? Babies are such messy things. Disgusting. They ruin everything. Heinrich . . . may I call you Heinrich?' She squeezed closer to him, fingered his Victorian cravat-pin. 'Would you be an angel and fill me up? Charles is such a spoil-sport, he says I've had enough. But it's my party, isn't it?'

'Yes, of course. What are you drinking?'

'Anything.'

Frances was suddenly alone again. She could hear the party roaring all around her, out of key. She stuck out her tongue at a smug bronze figurine posturing on a low table. 'Hap-py ann-i-vers-ary,' she whimpered to it. 'Hap-py, hap-py, hap-py, hap-py, hap-py . . .'

She wasn't sure how happy she was. The room was thick and coated, and there seemed to be two of everything, and her glass wouldn't stay where she put it, and her head had turned into a stereo and was playing dreadful roaring music, and underneath the roar there were little niggly voices imploring her to pull herself together.

'You're behaving outrageously,' they whined.

'Yes, outrageously!' she agreed. And giggled.

'Making a fool of Charles.' Charles? He was the tall one, with the terrifying grey smile. They must have got it wrong – you couldn't make a fool of Charles.

The voices were still nagging. 'Messing up your clothes, swaying on your feet . . .'

She grinned. Not on her feet – she couldn't be – she was swaying on the floor. Just one more tiny drink, and then she'd stop. She'd only downed a glass or two, to drown the pain of her period. It was the heaviest one she'd ever had, with cramps.

Heinrich had returned with two glasses. She struggled up to grab one.

'Oops – sorry!' Why on earth did the floor have to shift like that, when it was her turn to move?

'It's quite all right.' How could it be all right, when that greedy red stain was gobbling up his pale oyster suit?

'But I've soaked your trousers.'

'Please don't mention it.' No, mustn't mention anything – Charles had told her that. Not trousers, nor babies, nor Neds, or beds, or wombs, or periods, or Charles, or . . .

She stroked a sweaty finger down his arm. 'What do you think of Charles?'

'I beg your pardon?' Heinrich was mopping his knees with a white silk handkerchief. She wished to God he'd stay still, instead of bobbing around like that. It hurt her head.

'Charles. Charlie boy. My other half. Do you like him?'

'Your husband is a very brilliant man.'

'But do you like him, Heinrich?'

'Well, yes, of course, I . . .'

'You don't like him, do you? I don't blame you, actually. I don't like him much myself.'

'Mrs Parry Jones, I simply . . .'

'Call me Fran. I'm drunk, aren't I? I'm a rotter. Don't like my own husband. I use him. I use people all the time. Charles says so. Charles says I use *you*. Do you think I use you, Heinrich?'

'No, of course not, Mrs Par . . .'

'Oh, listen! They're playing our tune. Someone's put on the Anniversary Waltz. Shall we dance?'

'I'm sorry, Mrs Parry – Fran . . . I'm afraid I don't dance.'

'Oh, you don't dance. The richest man in the world and he doesn't dance. What a shame!'

Oppenheimer had taken two steps backwards. That was stupid. You were meant to move towards people when you danced with them. Frances crawled after him on her hands and knees. 'I don't believe you, Heinrich. You just don't want to dance. But I want to dance with you. Charles says we've got to dance. I've got to entertain you. That's why I'm here. You're his most important client and . . . Oh, please don't go away.'

She pulled herself up, using his leg as a lever, and then laid her head against his shoulder. Except his shoulder wasn't there. Only a sort of awkward gap between them, which made it impossible to waltz, let alone stand up. And suddenly, the rhythm had changed and she had swapped partners. They must be doing a Paul Jones, because Heinrich had disappeared and the tall, terrifying one had grabbed her, with the smile. The smile was cutting her to pieces and the sharp, splintered voice had crashed into the music and was spinning at the wrong speed on the dizzy turntable inside her head. 'Go away, Charles, I'm teaching Heinrich to dance.'

And now there was Viv, vast and rustling in puke-green taffeta, wanting to waltz with her as well. They were tugging her in two – the stiff, steely one, yanking at her right side, and the soft, flabby one lungeing at her left. It felt strange, as if one leg were shorter than the other.

'No, Viv, I don't want to dance with you, I want to dance with Heinrich. Let me go, Viv, I don't want to go upstairs . . .'

When Charles came down again, Laura was draped across the banisters. 'Frances unwell, darling? A touch of morning sickness, I suppose. Or is it that bug you said *I* had?'

He stared past her sequins at the wreckage of his house. The Sex Pistols had kidnapped his outraged stereo; retching ashtrays were sicking up their contents on the pale wild-silk upholstery;

a fourteen-stone bruiser was standing on the sideboard, looping multi-coloured streamers from the antique chandelier.

'Off the sofa, everyone – we need more room. Shove that table back. Wow, mind the wine!'

Charles groaned and turned away. He could see Oppenheimer, like some silent portrait of a cursed and hunted ancestor, cowering in the shelter of a tallboy, pale and wary, glancing at his watch.

How, in God's name, could he turf out forty-three barbarians, some of whom he didn't even know; how ensure his most respected client a decent night's sleep, before a crucial flight to Bogota? It wasn't even midnight. The party might rollick on for hours, yet. Drinking on empty stomachs had made everybody reckless; last trains or morning church or baby-sitters, all conveniently forgotten. There were not even any clocks. Frances had removed them from the whole of the downstairs area. It was another of her crazy, new-wave whims, some Rousseau-esque rubbish she had picked up at Acton, along with her cave-man hairstyle and tomboy clothes. Clocks killed spontaneity and natural body rhythms – or so guru Frances claimed. Those she couldn't hide, she had castrated, by insisting he remove their pendulums. Even his long-case clock was neutered now. God Almighty! A month or two ago, he would never have allowed her to dictate to him like this, mess around with expensive fragile mechanisms, in the name of some mumbo-jumbo mysticism. It was proof that he was weakening. Yet now she wasn't pregnant, he felt he had to humour her, indulge her, even in absurdities. He couldn't bear to lose her, not a second time.

Besides, it unnerved him, somehow, to know that she had never liked his clocks. Why hadn't she told him so before? In all the sixteen years they'd been chiming and pealing in what he saw as gloriously conformist harmony, she had been gritting her teeth, clenching her fists, longing for silence, or discord, or some millennial myth of sun-dial randomness. And he hadn't even known.

So, tonight, he had conspired with her in silencing his clocks, as if a single evening could compensate for all those jangling, booming years. Frightening, really, to see how easily their hands and pendulums surrendered, as if he himself had been muzzled or unstrung.

It hadn't paid. He'd given way to irrationality, and now his rule and territory were overrun, his drawing-room under siege. It was time to take a stand. His clocks must be his allies in the return to order. If he replaced or re-hung them all, their so-called guests might take a hint and go. It was nineteen minutes to midnight. Fifteen clocks, striking twelve times each, could hardly be ignored. Once he'd boomed and chimed them off the premises, he'd be left only with the Oppenheimers, and they were more amenable. He'd bundle Mrs off to bed with a mug of charm and Ovaltine, and woo Heinrich with his strongest five-star cognac, and a man-to-man apology (wife unwell, women's troubles, hormones playing up). Then, with any luck, bed and oblivion until the morning plane.

He fetched a screwdriver from the kitchen drawer, concealed it in his pocket. Mrs Eady was scraping squashed piccalilli from the hall rug.

'I'm sorry, Mr Parry Jones, but if you call this a quiet little dinner for three, then I'm the Duke of Kent.'

He'd start with the cuckoo clock, since it was nearest him, in the hall. Frances had been unable to remove it, so she had gagged and stifled it, instead. It was one of his favourites, a collector's piece with its carved acanthus leaves and early fusee movement. The cuckoo itself was hand-painted, with two-tone grey wings and a speckled breast, every detail perfect. He hated it to be out of action, time stopped arbitrarily at six o'clock. He turned it round and removed the backplate. Mercifully, he was almost alone. The hall was too dark and chilly for most of the guests.

The little spring door burst open and the cuckoo bowed its head and flapped its wings, as if in jubilation at its reprieve.

'Cuckoo-oo!' it whooped, prematurely.

'Not yet,' mouthed Charles, inserting the screwdriver into a delicate brass pawl. It was only eleven forty-six, for Christ's sake, and he didn't want anyone alerted until his grand finale at midnight.

'Cuckoo-oo, cuckoo-oo, cuckoo-oo,' cheered the unabashed yellow beak, dipping up and down, up and down, wooden wings flapping. Charles slammed his hand over its mouth, as he had done with Frances in the bedroom, when she kept struggling up and asking him to dance. The wretched bird was equally perverse. Its beak jabbed up and down against his palm, the cuckoo-oos spilling through it and tumbling out across the hall, rallying all the guests. 'Cuckoo-oo, cuckoo-oo, cuckoo-oo, cuckoo-oo . . .'

'Oh, how lovely!' cried Amanda Crawford. 'A cuckoo clock!'

'A drunken cuckoo clock,' corrected Laura. 'Don't they say pets take after their owners?' she added, *sotto voce*.

Charles was using his hanky as a gag, while he tried desperately to release the jammed mechanism. But he couldn't halt the cuckoo-oos, only made them hoarser.

'For God's sake, stop,' he muttered.

The cuckoo ignored him. So did all the guests, who were thronging into the hall, as if to attend a cabaret, egging the cuckoo on with cheers and catcalls.

'Pretty Polly, pretty Polly!'

'It's gone cuckoo – ha ha!'

'At the third stroke, it will be . . .'

The cuckoo was merciless. It had even woken Frances, who had staggered to the top of the stairs and was gazing down at the heaving, seething circus in the hall below. Laura had started cuckooing herself, and now all the mob was joining in, shouting out in unison, 'Cuckoo-oo, cuckoo-oo, cuckoo-oo . . .'

Yellow beak and speckled chest flashed up and down, up and down, as if conducting a massed chorus. How could such a tiny thing resound like that? Forty-three human throats were now outshouting it, but Charles could hear the bird above them all. However hard he struggled, he couldn't silence it – his screwdriver was impotent. He was suffocating in hot, sweaty bodies; elbows jammed into his side, flailing hands grabbing at the clock. The whole panting, braying herd had hemmed him in. He could smell their cheap scent, their whisky breaths, their reeking underarms. Their throats were open scarlet traps, devouring him and jeering; 'cuckoo, cuckoo' mocking in his ears, Laura as their ring-leader.

He grabbed the bird by the neck and wrenched it out. There was a sudden snapping sound as the metal rod broke off, and the bird came away in his hand, mute and mangled, wings rigid now, beak silent. The broken mechanism whirred on for a moment, and then ran down into a final, gasping wheeze. As if in sympathy, the whole house held its breath. Every guest stood motionless. Even Frances had stopped whimpering on the landing. The silence was oppressive, ten foot thick. Suddenly, she lurched forward and fell halfway down the stairs. Charles made a move towards her; the tiny wooden corpse still clutched tight in his hand.

'Murderer,' she shouted. 'Bloody murderer!'

20

Frances tried to open her eyes. Someone had glued them together, taken her legs away and left only a pair of bobbing yo-yos. She reached out for her watch, which wasn't there. She didn't need to look at it, knew already it was late. Winter had come that morning, and old age. She eased painfully out of bed, stumbled to the curtains and opened them a crack. There would be only bare brown earth and fallen leaves. She blinked against the glare. The sun was sizzling on to shrieking purple dahlias, the lawn blazed with emeralds, and whooping red carpets had been flung across the hot geraniums. How could the sun be so insensitive, tossing tinsel and bunting across half the world and roistering on with the party, when . . .? Party. She shuddered at the word, hardly dared remember it. Horror and remorse were clogging up her works like a broken clock.

Her period was still taking its revenge. Dried blood was streaked across the sheets, and someone was dragging barbed wire right through her stomach. There was an angry bruise on her knee and another on her forehead. The entire contents of the compost heap had been emptied into her mouth. She felt sick and hollow and ravenous at once.

She limped and crawled downstairs. The hall smelt stale and smoky. There was blood on the floor, or was it only wine? Broken glass sparkled in spears of sunlight, squashed lumps of cheese patterned the dark sofa, bloated shipwrecked olives floated in puddles of whisky. The cuckoo clock still had its back off, all its private parts exposed. The spring door was turned to the wall, so she couldn't see the broken rod, the empty, gaping house.

'Charles,' she faltered. 'Charles . . .'

Viv appeared from the kitchen, with an overall atop her taffeta. 'Oh hello, love. How are you feeling?'

'Where's Charles?'

'He left with the Oppenheimers about two hours ago. They

had to catch their plane. I stayed to lend a hand. Here, let me make you some tea. You look really rough.'

Frances walked slowly across the drawing-room and stopped in front of the bronze figurine. That was the exact spot she had sprawled last night, drunk and out of control. She was almost surprised the cushions looked so normal. Shouldn't they be stained – everything she'd touched in that disgusting swinish state be shrivelled and polluted? Some shrill, insistent voice was screaming in her head, accusing her, accusing.

'Come and sit down, love. I've made some nice strong tea.'

'Viv, last night . . . I hardly dare remember.'

'Don't! You'd had a horrid shock and were just reacting to it. Charles told me all about it. I hope you don't mind, but he was in such a dreadful state. I stayed behind to help him and it all sort of came out.'

'What did?'

'Oh, you know, your . . . pregnancy. Look, why didn't you tell me, darling? I could have been some help.'

'I wasn't pregnant, Viv.' Frances spat out each word slowly, as if words were too much trouble for her mouth.

'Yes, I know that. Charles explained. But, all the same, perhaps I could have . . . Look, I'm sorry, Frances, I really am.'

'Why be sorry?'

'What d'you mean?'

'Well, I'm not. I'm glad I'm not pregnant. I'm over the moon about it.'

'Frances, don't be silly, darling. You don't have to pretend with me.'

'I'm not pretending. It happens to be true. D'you know what I did when I realized my period had started?'

'What?' Viv sugared her tea for the second time.

'I laughed! I simply rocked with laughter. I couldn't stop.'

'That was just shock, another form of crying.'

'No, Viv, it wasn't. It was real, good, old-fashioned laughter. You don't understand. I was absolutely delirious with relief.'

'Relief?' Viv looked shocked herself. 'But I thought you said you wanted . . .'

'Yes.' She nodded. 'But I didn't. That's the whole point – I was wrong. I've been wrong all my life. Everybody tells you, if you're female, you've got to want a baby. So you do. It wasn't until I saw that blood between my legs, I realized how much I *didn't* want one.' She stopped. Why did talking hurt so much? Every syllable banged against her head and made it judder. And yet she had to talk. Words were piling up inside her, fighting with each other, trying to escape and explain themselves to all the world, herself included. 'I know it sounds crazy, Viv, after all those months of poring over charts and baby books; all the times I've wept because my period has come. But, this time, when it came, it was almost a deliverance. If anyone had told me that, I'd have laughed them out of court. I was absolutely convinced I wanted to be pregnant. And I did, Viv, it was true. But that's all I wanted. Just the *achievement* of pregnancy – the status, the specialness. But pregnancy without a final term, without a baby at the end of it.'

Viv kept trying to interrupt. This was her special subject which she'd studied five times over. 'Expectant mothers often feel like that, Frances, especially with the first one. It's difficult to visualize the baby, that's all. If you'd really been pregnant, and gone ahead and had it, you'd have been overwhelmed with joy when it was born. All your doubts and fears would have simply vanished.'

Frances slung a cushion from sofa to floor. 'I'm sorry, Viv, I simply don't believe it. That may be true for you, but not for me. Oh, maybe there's something wrong with me – I'm the first to admit it. But my period was actually like a victory sign, a great reprieve, a peal of bells. I felt as if I'd been brought back from the dead.'

Viv swallowed her tea too fast and spluttered through it. 'But that was only because of the circumstances. Don't you see? Of course you'd be relieved, when the baby wasn't . . .' She broke off in embarrassment. 'But supposing it was Charles' baby . . .'

'I don't want anybody's baby. I was just obsessed with my own mysterious womb.' Frances pushed her cup away. One small cup of tea was useless against the gritty thirst raging through the room. The entire Niagara Falls couldn't wash that rank taste from her mouth. All her words seemed coated with it. 'Do you realize, Viv, I totally believed that I was pregnant, didn't have the slightest doubt. Yet there was no real proof at all. It was far too early, anyway. But I managed to talk myself into all the signs and symptoms. I'd almost had my labour pains by day thirty-five! I can hardly believe how ridiculous I must have sounded.'

'It's hardly ridiculous to want a baby, Frances. Most women do.'

'That's exactly it. Most women do, so all women must. And, if you don't, you're a freak, and a monster and a . . . Yes, Viv, I admit I feel ashamed. It's so much easier to be normal and maternal and want the things which other women want. It's almost wicked and unnatural to realize you've no desire to procreate, that the thing you've set your heart on for the past few years suddenly means less than nothing. What do I do now, for heaven's sake? Return to the fashion world and write hollow puffs about thigh-length boots and bat-wing sleeves? Or take refuge in Good Works? Or buy a goldfish?' The words were pouring out, struggling past her throbbing, grudging head, blasting through the sewer of her mouth. It was as if she had been wound up to some frantic fever pitch, and all the wine she had gulped down at the party had turned into spurts of clumsy, drunken rhetoric. 'My whole existence feels as if it's been wrenched inside out. I hardly dare examine it too closely, in case I find out something even worse about myself. God! I realize now why women daren't be different. It's just too terrifying.'

Viv took her hand and squeezed it. 'You're just upset, that's all. Don't you see, you've had such an awful shock about the baby, you're trying to drown it in a tide of words. It's just a form of rationalizing. You wanted that child so desperately, now you've got to persuade yourself you didn't – just to make it bearable.'

Frances snatched the hand away. 'I'm sorry, but that's rubbish! You're as bad as Charles. You both refuse to allow me any opinions of my own. You're rationalizing things as much as I am. You're so horrified that any woman might prefer not to be pregnant, you've got to twist it round.'

She groped to her feet and started clearing up. Her body seemed to be blundering a pace or two behind her, as if she were dragging it along on a broken string.

Viv tried to sit her down again. 'I don't want to sound smug, but you can't really know about having babies, until you've actually got one in your arms.'

Frances swung round to face her, almost fell. 'And what

271

d'you do then, I'd like to ask, if you find you still don't want it?'

'But you will, Frances. You told me yourself you'd been longing for a child. That's a true, natural, undistorted instinct. It's stupid to disown it, just because you've been disappointed once. You go on trying, love – with Charles, I mean – and I'm sure you'll have one soon. Then you'll realize that all this intellectualizing is nothing but sour grapes.'

'Oh, shit, Viv! Look, I'm sorry, but you haven't heard a word I've said. I keep trying to tell you, what I actually wanted all the time had nothing to do with babies. It was only a sort of pride. Trying to prove myself, that's all; do what was expected of me, not let anyone down, least of all myself.' Frances leaned her head against the cold glass of the bookcase. Her tongue had been taken away and swapped with somebody else's. The new one didn't fit, just sat there, hot and swollen in her mouth, choking all her words. Yet, she had to go on talking, had to tell the world what she believed.

'Look, Viv, what's the very first word we all learn? Mama! We don't even know what it means, before we're lisping it. We *have* to be mothers. That's what we're made for. Society tells us, and so does our biology. Even all the great religions put in a plug for motherhood. It's like the Annunciation, in a way. You just fold your hands on your cosy little prie-dieu – and lo! – God fills your womb and your life, and everyone bows down to you as a Sacred Receptacle.'

She stopped. Nobody was listening, not the world, not Viv. All she was doing was mouthing soggy, reconstituted words which she had picked out of other people's mouths like scraps of food. She wasn't even sure if she believed them herself, and they were hardly flattering to Viv, who had filled her life with five Annunciations. Perhaps it *was* sour grapes. So much easier to cloud the air with slogans, than face up honestly to your own conflicting feelings. She slung an empty bottle in the wastebin. Why was she always so confused? Other women seemed to know what they wanted, whether it was half a dozen pregnancies, or a seat on the Board. All she was certain of was a labyrinth of question marks. 'Forgive me, Viv. I don't know why I'm ranting on like this. I sound like a fanatic women's libber, yet really, I'm so muddled. It's not just this baby thing, it's the whole of my life. It's all in such a mess, I just don't know what to do.'

'What d'you mean, do?'

'Well, Charles . . . last night and everything. I mean, how on earth . . .'

'He'll forgive you, Frances. Oh, I admit he was horrified, but I talked him out of it. I told him what a shock it must have been for you.'

Frances rammed an ashtray back on to the sideboard. 'Forgive me? I don't want him to forgive me. It's me that should . . . OUCH!' She clutched her hands across her stomach. 'This blasted period! I've never had one like it. It's so painful, I can hardly . . .'

'You shouldn't be clearing up, then. I'll get you a hot water bottle, shall I? There's plenty of hot water in the kettle.' She stopped suddenly, with her hand on the door knob. 'Hey, Frances . . .'

'What?'

'I've just thought of something.'

'Well, what?'

'Perhaps it isn't just a period. I mean, couldn't it be an early miscarriage? Did you think of that?'

Frances laughed, unconvincingly. 'No, Viv.'

'Well, it could be. You might be pregnant, after all. You might even save it.'

'No, Viv.'

'Don't keep saying "No, Viv." You can't be sure.'

'Oh yes, I can.'

'Don't be silly, Frances, there's no real way of telling – not at this early stage. It would seem like an ordinary period, only heavier.'

'And that's exactly what it is: an ordinary period, only heavier.'

'Honestly, Frances, you're so determined not to be pregnant, you're simply overreacting. You must be. I mean, when you can't even admit . . .'

'Look, you don't know what you're talking about. I haven't told you everything.'

'You haven't told me anything.' Viv flounced through the door, towards the kitchen.

Frances stared out of the window at the cruel, green brashness of the lawn. It still seemed incredible that it should be morning, summer, bright. It was dark in her head, like her last dark night at Acton. She had stayed there till the early hours, listening to a Ned she'd never glimpsed before. She'd vowed never to mention it to anyone. She closed her eyes a moment against the insolent dazzle of the sun. Her body wanted to creep into darkness, close down on itself, hibernate for a hundred torpid years . . .

Something warm and clammy nudged her in the belly. Viv had lumbered in again and slipped a plump pink hot water bottle into her arms. It was cradled in a soft white towel like a baby in its shawl. Frances held it close. Her phantom baby. She remembered the absurdly premature things she'd done for it, gulping extra vitamins, buying a guard for Ned's electric fire, even a Dr Spock.

'Look, Viv, I really don't know how to tell you. It's so – well, humiliating.'

'Oh come on, love. I shan't mind. You know me.'

Frances trailed back to the sofa and slumped down against the cushions. 'Well, you see . . . I . . . I couldn't have been pregnant, anyway.' She yanked the towel almost roughly from the hot water bottle, leaving it naked and exposed.

'Frances, you're driving me mad with these dramatic pauses. What d'you mean, you couldn't have been pregnant?'

Frances was twisting the towel tighter and tighter around the rubber neck of the bottle, as if she were trying to strangle it. 'Well, Ned . . .'

'Who's Ned?'

'Oh, Viv, you know, the father.'

'Oh, I'm sorry, love, I didn't know his name. Charles didn't give him one.'

'No, he wouldn't. Well, he – Ned, I mean . . .'

'Yes?'

Frances flung towel and bottle away from her. They fell with a muffled gasp on to the carpet. 'He had a vasectomy two years ago.'

'*What?*'

Frances began to laugh. She sprawled back against the sofa and let her body fall into it, heavy and helpless with laughter. Tears were running down her cheeks, gusts of laughter grabbing her by the throat, shaking her whole body, colliding with her breath. 'Oh, Viv, it's so funny. It's so terribly funny . . .'

Viv tried to smile herself. 'Why on earth did he do that, Frances?'

'He . . . he . . .' Frances could hardly speak for laughter. It was a harsh, grinding pain between her ribs, rocking the sofa, tearing at her chest. 'I mean, there I was, mooning around being gloriously pregnant by a man who had . . . had . . . hadn't . . .' The guffaws cut her off again.

Viv plaited and unplaited the silk fringe on the cushion. She could hear the radio droning in the kitchen, almost drowned by Frances' splutterings. She waited. Frances wiped her eyes. She was still laughing, but weakly now, her body limp like a piece of crumpled paper.

'Well, you see, his . . . wife was terrified of having children. She'd had a botched abortion in her teens. Every time they made love, she got into a panic, imagining she was pregnant. She couldn't take the Pill – some medical reason – I'm not sure exactly what. So, in the end, Ned agreed to a vasectomy – much against his will. He wanted kids.'

How flat it sounded. The story of a life. Or half a life. Ned had made it comic, played it as a farce. The surgeon rambling on about the test score while he snipped Ned's balls with nail scissors, Ned borrowing his little sister's bikini bottoms to keep the dressing tight. The sequel wasn't quite so funny. Six months later, his wife was pregnant by another man.

She realized Ned was bitter. He had still kept up the banter, but she'd heard the resentment scowling underneath, curdling all his jokes. Ned survived by clowning. It was a life-escape, like Charles'. But, now she had discovered there was hurt and bitterness behind it, it wasn't so diverting any more. She needed Ned to be her court jester, a sparkling, surface person, whose job was only to amuse. Once she'd found the scars beneath pierrot's painted face, the whole carnival collapsed.

She had lain there, silent, on Ned's crumpled, sway-back bed, feeling like a stillborn child herself. First, the shock of her period, and the double shock of realizing she was glad about it. Next, the crazy laughter, which ended up with their making love again. Then while they were still bloody and entangled, she had somehow blurted out the whole, stupid story of her phantom pregnancy. Which Ned had countered with his Eunuch's Tale. She'd been so angry, so astounded, she'd simply stared at him. Why, in God's name, couldn't he have told her at the start of their relationship, saved her all that crowing jubilation, those wrenching conflicts, that absurd, agonizing build-up to Day Thirty-Five?

Ned had been angrier still. He didn't want a clucking, broody hen fussing into his nest and trying to take it over, some woman he had valued as unobtainable and independent, helping herself to his sperm, so that she could turn him into a father by stealth and subterfuge.

'How could you, Fran? You can't go around using men like that, creating life one-sidedly and irresponsibly.' He had sat cross-legged on the lino, raging at her, repeating her own most secret and shameful self-accusations, while midnight sulked into two A.M. and the whole happy myth of pastoral parenthood shattered into a thousand tiny fragments.

'I can hardly be accused of creating anything, now you tell me you've been . . . neutered.'

He winced. 'But you didn't know I had, Fran.'

'And whose fault was that? At least, you might have told me at the time.'

'I've told other women. And they never believe you, anyway. I'm beginning to think it's more or less impossible to have an honest relationship with any female at all. That's probably why I live with two male cats.'

The bantering again, disguising the hurt. All those jokes she'd laughed at were not just a bachelor's simple-minded clowning – there were treacherous currents swirling underneath. But, like Charles, he disguised them. She'd assumed she could read Ned like a book, but she'd never got further than the jolly, blue-skied picture grinning on the front.

The Ned inside was different. Almost as limited as Charles, in some respects. Because he'd been hurt, he wouldn't take life seriously again. She was right to have left the lion behind at Acton – a plaything for a little boy, a Peter Pan who refused to grow up, or build a new relationship, or believe in the future. Whereas Charles could live *only* in the future, barricading himself

276

from the terrifying impact of the present. She was caught between them, uncertain of the way out of the maze she'd made by circling round them both, knowing only that both were wrong.

She was surprised to look up and see Viv still sitting there, pouring a second round of tea. A hundred thousand hours had passed since the last bloody dregs of that aborted Friday evening, to this hung-over Sunday morning in her own pale and shaky drawing-room. Only Viv looked real, substantial, bright. 'I'm really sorry, darling,' she was saying. 'You've had a rotten time of it. Never mind – at least it's over now. You can pick up the pieces and pretend it never happened.'

'Viv, for heaven's sake . . .'

Oh, what was the use? Viv would never understand. She didn't really understand herself. It was easy to whoop with laughter because your period had started, but what did you do when the laughter died away? You still had all those empty years to fill. A child would take care of a score of them, at least. Twenty years less to fret and agonize in, twenty years less to wonder who you were. But, if you didn't want a child . . .? The women's libbers always claimed their freedom with some goal in mind; a career, a mission, some social or artistic purpose, even self-fulfilment. But Frances Parry Jones was just a selfish little rich girl who didn't even like her job, and had no real aim or ambition in her life. She had never panted to discover a lost tribe, or itched to write a symphony. She tried hard to care about underpaid garment workers in the Midlands, or the dwindling numbers of the blue whale, but she knew she'd never be marching in Hyde Park, or setting light to herself with petrol cans. All she could feel was a grey, echoing emptiness.

For the last few years, she'd had her goal, marching to the stirring music of her own menstrual cycle. An easy way of filling up the days, eyes fixed only on the month ahead, clear battle orders from Major General Rathbone, and support from every mother in the land. Now, she knew it was only the myth and mystique she'd wanted, the discipline, the ritual, something to swell the hollowness inside. The charts had been comforting, like Charles' notebooks and yearly planning guides – lists and tabulations to keep the terror out, to stifle any possibility of mystery or chaos. Without them, life was no longer tidily divided into twenty-eight-day pieces, but stretched out to a limitless horizon that was only a terrifying haze. Hundreds of women would envy her her freedom. She didn't even have to earn her living, or her luxuries. How could she admit she almost craved to be a low-paid garment worker? Nose to the grindstone at least stopped speculation, mopped up that eternity of days.

She picked up the dishcloth and made a half-hearted swipe at the table. Better to be a plodding skivvy than a paralysed philosopher. Or was it? Germaine Greer would disagree – not to mention Mrs Eady. It was all so complicated. If only she'd been born a hundred years ago, and could divide her time between bottling damsons and her drawing master, without being branded as a traitor to her sex.

Viv eased the dishcloth gently from her hand. 'I'll do that. You go and lie down.'

'No, I'm going to bottle damsons.'

'Damsons? Now? What for?'

'Oh, just a joke.' Frances didn't laugh. 'Viv, d'you ever feel . . . everything's so . . .?'

There was a sudden uproar in the passage. The front door slammed and feet pounded up the hall. Frances froze. Charles? No, he'd never run. Ned? Laura? Oppenheimer, come to get revenge?

'Viv, I'm not here. I can't face anyone.' She dashed to the door to hide, collided with a panting figure in odd shoes and a shabby coat flung over its pyjamas. Bunty. The child pushed Frances to one side, grabbed her mother by the arm.

'Quick, Mum!' she shouted. 'You must come home. It's Magda. She's run away from school.'

21

'Frances, you can't send her back. It's downright cruel. Even if the nuns would have her, which they probably won't . . .' Viv was baking in her steamy, crowded kitchen. She flung sliced apples into a pyrex dish, showered them with brown sugar.

Bunty was licking out the mixing bowl. 'They read all her letters,' she announced, through a fingerful of uncooked dough. 'She told me. That's why she didn't write. And they make you wear your PT shorts just below your knees.' She giggled. 'All the girls had to kneel in the assembly hall, and two nuns marched round inspecting them, and if their shorts didn't touch the floor they had to let them down, go and fetch their sewing things, and miss tea and recreation. Magda cut hers off, instead. They were so short, they were like a pair of knickers, and all jagged round the edges. The nuns were furious. She had to wear her Sunday frock on Monday as a punishment, and a black veil on her head, and kneel in the chapel for two whole hours.'

'What's a Sunday frock?' asked Philip, who was bashing nails into a block of wood. Frances and the table jumped every time another nail went in.

'Oh, it's all sort of prickly, with a white collar, and the name of your patron saint embroidered on the bodice.' Bunty removed Rupert from the golden syrup tin. 'Magda's saint is Mary Magdalen. That's twelve whole letters and she can't even embroider. It took her hours to do it, but then Mother Annunciata snipped the whole thing out again with a pair of scissors, and said it was an insult to any patron saint.'

'Weird,' muttered Philip, missing the nail and knocking in his thumb instead. Midge screeched in sympathy.

'Hush!' shouted Viv, above them all. 'Look, kids, Frances and I can hardly hear ourselves speak. Why don't you go out into the garden?'

Frances almost prayed they wouldn't. The last thing she felt like was a morning-after playgroup, but even that was better than

279

a heart-to-heart with Viv, on the subject of Magda's future. That future was all too entangled with her own. If Magda returned to Richmond, then she herself would have to stay and play mother. She didn't want to be a mother, not even to her own child. What was the point of proving that, if all she did was settle back again with someone else's offspring? Nothing would be changed, nothing learned or gained, if she and Magda both slunk back to Richmond, and the whole tragic farce restarted.

She hadn't even seen her yet. From the moment that Bunty had burst in with the news, Viv had taken over, giving orders, acting the part of Magda's nurse and mother, pushing her into a sick-bay on the sidelines. 'You stay here. I'll cope. You look far too rough to do anything but rest.'

She'd tried to remonstrate, but she knew Viv didn't want her. One part of her was secretly relieved. Easier to take the role of invalid and play nursemaid to herself. While Viv dashed back to Magda, rushing around with blankets and beef tea, she had stayed behind in the ruins of her drawing-room, breakfasting on Alka Seltzer and bandaging her wounded house.

Viv had found Magda barricaded in the garden shed, filthy, exhausted. The child had been up all night, trekking the hundred miles from Westborough, hitching lifts in lorries where she could. Viv had bathed and changed her like a baby, then put her to bed with two aspirin and warm milk. She was still asleep. Thank God, thought Frances, who had arrived at Viv's an hour ago, and been talking Magda, Magda, ever since. So much had happened in the last few frantic days, she could hardly cope with it, let alone this new crisis.

Charles had phoned from the airport, before she left for Viv's, so suave and courteous, she'd been thrown off guard. She had been expecting retribution, but all he said was 'Hello, darling, I'm afraid I'll be late for lunch. The Oppenheimers' plane has been delayed.' Surely the name of Oppenheimer should strike her down like Voodoo, but Charles pronounced it calmly, almost nonchalantly, as if last night had never been. He had rubbed out the party, and her assumed pregnancy, like a misspelt paragraph in an otherwise impeccable life report, and then filed it away and started on a clean page. She heard herself responding in the same careful, treacherous fashion.

'It's quite all right, darling, don't worry about lunch. We'll eat this evening, shall we, then you won't have to rush?'

Eat, when her stomach was a battleground; prepare his dinner, when she wasn't even sure whether she was married any more; finish up the party wines, when his daughter had just run away from school? She hadn't dared to tell him that. It didn't seem to fit with the quiet return to order and good sense he'd so carefully prepared. That was the stumbling block. Too much order, white-washing all the mess and questioning inside, blotting out drunken wives and rebellious daughters. Drunkenness was disgusting and rebellion terrifying, so safer to pretend they never happened. But some part of her kept shouting out that she had been drunk, would be drunk again, and not only drunk, but wild, unfaithful, and impulsive.

But if she could rebel, then why not Magda, too? If Magdas went wild, they were bundled off to boarding school, or worse. The trouble was, Magda did things too precipitately. It had taken her fifteen weary years to bend the rules, and here was Magda, stamping them to bits after only six short weeks. She felt a twinge of jealousy, wished she too could run away from things she didn't like, from having to play mother. Even now, she was being forced to shovel spinach into Rupert, sit down to a hectic, unhinged lunch, with five gabbling children and assorted dogs and cats, instead of nursing her headache in a darkened room. And all because of Magda. Midge was dumping chewed lumps of gristle on her plate, Philip had poured Pepsi in her wine. She pushed the glass away. She couldn't eat or drink, in any case. Her head was a rifle-range and her stomach a roller-coaster. The noise, the chaos, the constant battlefire of kids . . .

Bunty leapt up, suddenly, spraying her with gravy.

'Hey!' she yelled. 'Magda's awake. I can hear her on the stairs. She must be coming down.'

Frances jammed a cold potato in her mouth. She shut her eyes and slowly forced it down. When she opened them, Magda was standing in the doorway, tousled and embarrassed in a pair of striped pyjamas, one bare foot jabbing against the floor.

Frances dropped her fork. 'Magda,' she gasped. 'Your *hair*!'

Viv had warned her, prepared her, but how could anyone prepare you for such massacre? The long, luxurious tresses were cropped short like a jail-bird's, sticking up around her head, jagged and uneven. The hair had been hacked and mangled off, longer in some parts than in others, butchered at the back into a lopsided shingle. All Magda's beauty had been shorn away. Without her crowning glory, her face looked pinched and thinner, her body bulkier. Frances wanted to storm and weep for such barbarous destruction, to hug that mutilated head on its slouched, unsmiling body. She kicked her chair back, jumped up to her feet. Magda stiffened. Even now, she couldn't touch the child. She longed to take her in her arms and turn pity and horror into some loving, caring, flesh-and-blood gesture. But Magda was recoiling, backing away from her, locking up her face.

'Excuse me,' Frances muttered, blundering to the door. She couldn't bear to see those cold, accusing eyes. She escaped into the kitchen, mumbling something fatuous about a headache.

Yes, of course she had a headache, but what was that, compared to Magda's scalping? She'd been so concerned with her own paltry little pains, she'd hardly even listened when Viv had explained about the hair. It was the nuns, apparently, who'd first pressured Magda to have it cut. They told her it was injurious to her health to wear her hair so long. It was the health of her soul they were more concerned about. A well-developed girl with such a wild and sensual mane was a temptation to men, and thus a danger to herself and an attraction to the devil – though Magda had shown no interest yet in either men or Satan. She vowed she'd never marry, and refused to let the Brides of Christ lay a finger on her hair. When she swore at them for trying, they locked her in the dormitory. Two hours later, they brought her a glass of water and St Ignatius' Prayer for Obedience and Humility. She was crouched in a corner, staring at the wall, surrounded by dark, limp swathes. She had cut her hair herself – hacked it off with the nail scissors, exorcized her beauty and the devil, with the same self-destructive strokes.

And there was Frances, Lord Justice Frances Parry Jones, planning to treat her like a convict, to lock her up again, and refuse to take her in, for no more reason than to wallow in her own selfish freedom, spread her own wings. And even that was sheer hypocrisy. She'd made no plans to fly away. Ned was right. He'd called her a homing pigeon, ringed and tagged by

Charles. In whichever direction she was pointed, she speeded back to the safety of the nest. Just an hour or so ago, she had laid the table in the dining-room, ready for Charles' return, decanted the port, left the steaks to marinate in wine. Wasn't it safer to observe the rules? Magda had only lost her strength like Samson, by refusing to conform, and what had she herself gained by her petty little outrages? – a thick head, a wrecked house, and a bellyful of remorse. She couldn't even deceive herself that she'd been striking a blow for feminist freedom. She didn't want freedom – only goose-feather cushioning and jam in her sandwich. By betraying Charles and insulting Oppenheimer, she'd been biting the hands that fed her. It was all too easy to twist things into slogans. Ned would say she'd challenged Oppenheimer as a filthy-rich fascist grinding the faces of the poor. But that was far too pat. Heinrich was a self-made man, who had attended the Frankfurt equivalent of Brent Edge Comprehensive. He also happened to be a model employer and generous patron of the arts, his cheque book ever at the ready for any deserving cause or charity. She herself had basked in the warmth of his largesse. And, even if she left Charles, Oppenheimer's wealth would still follow her and coddle her – alimony, maintenance, a separate bijou residence, the best divorce lawyers money could buy.

But it wouldn't come to that – she wouldn't leave Charles. She knew it, just by looking at his daughter. Magda was a victim now, with no other home than theirs. She would take her to that home and start again. And if Charles was wary, she could always talk him round. He was far less perverse and prickly now he knew she wasn't pregnant, had overlooked her outrage at the party, shown himself ready to be merciful. Well, Magda must be included in that mercy. They must work at being a family again. It needn't be as disastrous as before. Things were different now – Ned had changed her, taught her more than simple slogans. She'd been only a diversion in his life, the froth on his small beer, but all the same, he had leavened and unstoppered her. She could still winkle out the gems from his dustbin and bring them back like souvenirs from Brighton. Ned would survive, with his clowning and his cats, and she would survive on his precious, threadbare legacy. She could always swell it out with Charles' more solid one.

'Frances? What are you doing out here? You haven't had your pudding!'

She jumped. Viv had burst into the kitchen, with Rupert burping in her arms and Midge trailing behind her, clutching at her skirts.

'What's wrong, love? Why did you rush off like that? Magda's quite upset. She thought you . . .'

Frances struggled to her feet. She'd been sitting at the table snapping spent matches into tiny fragments. The table was littered with black heads and broken limbs. 'Listen, Viv, I want to take her back with me, this evening. For dinner.' There were still three steaks, three nectarines – exactly right. One each, not for Charles and the Oppenheimers, but for Charles and his wife and daughter. It was fitting somehow, meant. 'Charles will be back any minute, and he'll want to see her.'

'Will he?' Viv griped. She had picked up the custard saucepan and was scraping out the dregs.

'He is her father, Viv.'

'Yes. Funny, I keep forgetting.'

So, even Viv could be sarcastic. Frances marched back to the dining-room and collected up her things. She wanted to escape. If she were going to be Magda's mother, then why wait for dinner to make a start on it?

'Look, if you don't mind, Frances, I'll just pop over this evening, to see how she is.'

'There's no need, Viv. You sound like some social worker checking up on baby batterers. I know I've been a bit . . . well . . . unreliable, but that's over, finished. I . . .'

'Look, all I want to hear is what you've decided – you know, school and things. We haven't discussed it yet.'

'Charles and I will discuss it, Viv. This evening.'

'Fine. And I'll pop round to hear the verdict. Any objections?'

When Viv knocked, after dark, they had only reached the nectarines. Charles had opened a bottle of sparkling wine to wash them down. Not champagne. They weren't exactly celebrating.

'Thanks,' said Viv, accepting a glass and subsiding on the sofa. 'Where's Magda?'

'Upstairs.'

'Doesn't she eat with you?'

Frances fiddled with her fruit knife. 'Well, yes, of course, but . . .' How could she admit that Magda had banged out and marched up to her room the minute she'd made her 'announcement'? That's all she had returned for, not fillet steak and a prime-cut, medium-rare family reunion.

'She's tired,' Charles shrugged, finishing off his nectarine and starting on the nuts.

'She slept all morning, didn't she?'

'Look, Viv, don't be scratchy. Charles only meant . . .'

Viv drained her glass in one gulp. 'OK, cut the cackle. All I want to know is what you've decided about her education. I mean, if it's all right with you, I'll take her down to Highfield first thing in the morning, and make an appointment to see the headmistress. Then, with any luck . . .'

Charles cracked a walnut so hard, the shell splintered and flew across the table. 'No, it's not all right with me.'

Frances stood up. 'Ssshh, Charles, let me explain. Look, Viv. Charles and I haven't decided anything – honestly, we haven't. It's Magda herself. She wants to . . .'

'You're not trying to tell me she wants to go back to that atrocious boarding school? I'm sorry, Frances, I simply don't believe it. And if you send her back, I'll . . .'

'We're not.'

'Well, where are you sending her?'

'Nowhere.' Frances was wringing out her napkin, as if it were soaking wet.

'What do you mean, nowhere? She's got to go to school.'

'Viv, for heaven's sake . . .' Charles exploded the silence with another walnut, then sat there, picking morsels from the wreckage of the shell. 'She's going to Budapest.'

'Budapest? How could she? The schools are completely different over there. She doesn't even speak the language properly. How will she ever . . .?'

'It's her own decision, Viv. She asked to go. She wants to.'

'Rubbish! Of course she doesn't want to. You want to get rid of her, more like it.'

Charles slammed the nut-crackers back on to the table. 'Viv, I think you may regret . . .'

'*Me* regret? And what about *your* regretting something? Treating your own daughter like an outcast, packing her off to outlandish places, just so you can lead your own selfish life . . .'

Viv was standing, trembling, with her hand on the door. Frances tried to edge her through it, away from Charles, and out into the hall.

'Viv, do be reasonable. Hungary's not outlandish. It's almost her own home, in a way, her second country.'

'Of course it isn't! She's never been there in her life. She was born in London and schooled in Streatham and she's English to her toenails – English by law and language and upbringing and every other damn way.'

'Yes, but what about her mother? Her mother's not English, she's Hungarian. And she happens to be in Hungary now. That's important, Viv. Of course Magda wants to join her – it's only natural. You said yourself a child belongs with its mother.'

'Not a mother who deserts her own flesh and blood and runs off with some . . . gigolo. How d'you know she even wants Magda back? Have you checked? She may have scooted off somewhere else by now – with a new boyfriend, I wouldn't be surprised. I suppose you'd let the poor kid trek half-way across Europe to find a scribbled note saying they've moved on.'

'Don't be silly, Viv. Piroska's not as irresponsible as that.' Ironical to be defending a woman she'd vilified to Viv only a month or so ago. 'Anyway, Charles seems to think everything's all right, and he ought to know. He's kept in touch with Piroska all along.' Frances had shut the door behind them. She couldn't bear to see her husband chomping walnuts like an angry animal. He hated walnuts.

Viv stormed down the passage, towards the front door. 'I'd hardly rate Charles as an authority on anybody's happiness. Anyway, what about all those objections he raised in the first place – Magda's education, and so on? He'll muck up all her O-levels, and how the hell's she going to get a job out there, when she's older and left school? I don't like the sound of it at all – having to share her mother with that . . . pick-up! They may even kiss and cuddle in front of her. That's the last thing Magda needs, when she's been starved of love herself. Look, let her come to me, Frances. I've said I'll have her all along. At least I can be sure she gets a stable home and plenty of affection.'

'It's no good, Viv. She wants to go. She . . .'

'And did you even try to talk her out of it, make her feel loved and wanted here? Didn't you stand up to Charles, or think about someone else but yourself, for a change? I'm sorry – I'd better go before I do say something I regret. I'll phone in the morning and hope to God you've changed your minds by then.' The front door slammed behind her. 'Give my love to Magda,' she shouted through it.

Frances mooched along the passage. She could feel the blood oozing between her legs; thirty-five days of mockery and delusion weeping into a Tampax. The dull, cramping pain was like a continual reminder, dragging her down, jeering at her. 'Give my love to Magda.' Yes, Viv had love for the child, for every child, enough to last them through a hundred lifetimes, enough to take in the whole, abandoned, battered, unloved world. Her own heart wouldn't even open to one neglected, wretched teenager. It was so crammed full of conflict and exhaustion, there wasn't room for love. Despite her new resolves to start again, to return to base and make a nest for the fledgeling, she had felt a whoop of incredulous delight when Magda had announced she was going to Budapest. Relief had poured across the dinner table like hot, sweet custard. She was bitterly ashamed of that relief.

Yet, Magda had decided for herself. No one could say they'd forced her hand, or turfed her out. They had offered her a refuge and a peace-treaty, and Magda had rejected both. Anyway, whatever Viv said, it was surely only natural for a child to seek its mother, return where it belonged. Why should they try to talk her out of it, when it was a solution which seemed to satisfy them all? Mother and daughter reconciled, she and Charles reprieved, a new start both for cuckoo and for host-bird.

Yet, supposing Viv were right? Could they really send Magda off to an unstable household or an empty flat; disrupt her education? Charles had been so vague about it all, leaving everything uncertain, undefined. Strange, for a man who normally checked every smallest detail of a change of plan, examined all the problems, and insisted on solutions. On this occasion, he'd

287

merely sat in silence, looking pained and secretive, and let a fifteen-year-old seditionary dictate to him.

She opened the dining-room door a crack, paused a moment, just outside. Charles was sitting at the table with his head in his hands, surrounded by empty walnut shells. She felt a stab of pity. The last few days had pounced on his neat and tidy life and torn it into shreds, presenting him, in turn, with a pseudo-pregnant wife, a drunken hostess, an illegitimate, non-existent baby, and a runaway teenager shorn of all her hair. His skin looked taut and greyish. Even his breath smelt slightly sour and tainted, unthinkable for Charles, who was always tingling-fresh with mint and vigour.

'Try not to worry, darling.' She took his hands, still felt stunned herself, as if she had been flung into a pestle and mortar and pounded into crumbs. But there were things to be done – Charles to be appeased, Magda's future to be safeguarded.

Charles had already snapped up straight again. 'I'm not worrying,' he said, picking up his glass. The frown cut so deep between his eyes, it looked as if it had been gouged out with a chisel.

'Look, Charles, I admit Viv's a bit outspoken, but she's right, you know. We shouldn't really have agreed that Magda could leave – not before we'd phoned her mother. I mean, perhaps she doesn't want the child. Isn't that why she came to us, in the first place? That, and her education?'

'It was an experiment, Frances, and frankly, it hasn't worked. Anyway, if she's run away from school and is refusing to go back, she's hardly going to achieve much in the way of education.'

'Yes, but how do we know that Piroska's got room enough, or money enough? I mean, Viv just said that . . .'

'Could we kindly leave Viv out of this? She's hardly in a position to know the facts. I've never kept Piroska short of anything. She's written to me, on and off, and, as far as I can see, everything's perfectly all right. You and Viv are simply over-reacting. Anyway, of course I plan to phone. It's top of my morning list. I'll go over the whole thing with Piroska in detail – schools, housing, money, job opportunities . . .'

'Why don't you ring her now, darling? I mean, if there is some problem, we don't want Magda lying there all night, planning a trip she might not even . . .'

'I've told you, Frances, I'll do it tomorrow. It's too late now, in any case. Hungary's an hour or two ahead of us, and they'll all have gone to bed. Which – quite frankly – is where I'd like to be myself.'

The skin beneath his eyes looked almost bruised. He had gashed himself shaving and a cruel red line cut into the pallor of his cheek. He was like some wounded bird, but a proud, dangerous species, which refused to let anyone approach it, or show it tenderness. She longed for some warmth between them, so that they could turn towards each other and shut out all the pain. Not sex, not even caresses, just a quiet, united front against the world. But Charles was already on his way towards the door, his back a cold grey gravestone.

'You go on up, then,' she murmured, 'and I'll clear the supper dishes.' Best to give in to him, leave him on his own. He'd be more amenable after a decent night's rest. They could phone Piroska, first thing in the morning. Maybe she'd even speak to her herself. Her husband's mistress no longer seemed so vile. Ned had somehow bridged the gulf between them.

Yet, all that Ned had taught her seemed to fade and shrivel when faced with Charles' frown. Even now, with pain in every part of her, she was still scouring out saucepans and sweeping up nutshells when she should have been asleep upstairs. Why couldn't she leave the bloody dishes? The kitchen was like a museum, as it was. Where were her new resolves, her determination to live more casually, to let both Ned and Magda creep inside the palisade, which she and Charles had built fifty foot high around them? She replaced the silver fruit knives in their rosewood box, rubbed at a scratch on the table, trickled disinfectant in the wastebin. Were habits stuck with you for ever, imprinted like genetic instructions on DNA? Or was it just something about this house? It was Charles' house, so perhaps it was a tyrant, like its owner. The only time she'd escaped from it, she'd managed to cock a snook at dust and dishes. But, back in its dark, forbidding clutches, duty nagged and flogged.

Forty minutes later, she crept into the bedroom. Charles was already asleep – or pretending to be. He feigned sleep as she feigned climaxes. She undressed as quietly as she could, had already had her bath. Only Neds and Frannys went to bed unwashed. There was hardly room for her in her single bed, which was crowded with a raucous mob of gate-crashers, all quarrelling among themselves and confusing her with contradictory advice.

'Be a tramp, be a gypsy!' grinned Ned, biting into a giant-sized Mars bar. 'Pawn the sodding fruit knives and buy a horse-drawn caravan.'

'Back with Charles?' mocked Franny. 'Cramped by his Ten Commandments, crushed by his Tablets of Stone? What happened to that Brighton sybarite, that Barefoot Contessa?'

'Love me,' Magda pleaded. 'Hug me, hold me. Let me know you want me.'

'I don't bloody want you,' snarled Miklos, in his brutal pidgin English. 'It's your ma I fancy, and there's not room for the two of us.'

'Selfish, sterile, sour-grapes intellectualizer!' Viv accused, popping another orphan under the blankets.

Frances struggled up. The voices slunk into the shadows, and were coffined in silence; silence so thick, she could feel it smothering her like a duvet, pressing down on her eyes, her mouth, her life. Even the bedroom furniture seemed to be holding its breath in an accusing, tight-lipped circle all around her, the whole house screwed up to breaking-point.

Could Charles be there, beside her, still breathing, still alive? She reached out her hand and touched the rough beard of the blanket, the curve of an elbow underneath.

'Charles?'

No answer. Only another swirl and shiver of silence. She couldn't wake him; it was sacrilege. With Ned, you could jump on his tummy in the middle of the night, or make him three A.M. milkshakes and share a coloured straw. Not any longer. That Ned was dead and buried, like her baby. There was only gelded Ned and supine Charles.

She was free, now. No baby to bind her, no life-plans to blinker her, not even any Ned to confuse her with his teasing. But was that really freedom, or just sterility and loss? Anyway, how could she be free, with Magda's future undecided, with that morning phone call hanging over her, still threatening and uncertain? One wrong word from Piroska, and the longed-for trip to Budapest might shatter and collapse. Freedom and duty were fighting a duel inside her head.

She pressed her hands against it, trying to banish both conflicting voices. Would people ever understand how one hopeless, hapless, almost grown-up schoolgirl could tear your mind apart like that, make such a difference to a home, a life? She could hardly explain it to herself. Except that with Magda in the house she felt flattened, threatened, trodden underfoot; crushed like a flower in a flower-press, all the sap and colour which Ned had allowed to blossom in her stamped out and dried up. But wasn't that Charles' doing? Didn't he, even more than Magda, have the power to trap her between the pages of a heavy, musty tome, and leave her gasping for light and air?

But Charles was impossible to fight. She couldn't turf *him* out, or send him packing to his mother. It was his house, his flower-press, and all those weighty tomes which bludgeoned her bore his name, his crest, his imprint. All she could do was try to work towards a truce with him, and to remove the biggest obstacles between them. Magda, herself, was one of those big obstacles, a danger to their truce. The kid couldn't help it, but there was something about her which would always lead to uproar and upheaval. Even now, she was causing rifts again, alienating Viv, splitting apart their precarious post-Oppenheimer peace.

Christ! How confused it all was. She threw back the blankets and swung her feet out of bed. The darkness was diluting a little, now that her eyes had grown more used to it. She could make out the hump of Charles' shoulder, the lowering bulk of the wardrobe, the pale gleam of the charts, beside her on the bedside table. She was still thinking in terms of charts. It was hard to break the habit of all those dots and dates and graphs. Tomorrow would be Day Four, almost time to start her last course of Clomid. Except she'd be chucking it down the lavatory, instead.

She groped in the shadows for the bottle, tipped one tiny smooth white tablet into her hand. White for innocence and safety, purity, fidelity. White for blank pages and clean sheets. White for breast-milk, baby-gowns, delivery rooms. Was she really sure she didn't want a baby? There was still time, still hope. She'd been so wrong about herself for fifteen years, perhaps she was wrong again, and the last few days had been merely shock and self-deception.

She flung the tablet on the floor. She couldn't endure her frenzied, circling thoughts, her endless speculation. She poured out the rest of the tablets, let them fall between her fingers. Only cold, unfeeling things were as white and pure as that – ice and alabaster, marble lilies on a grave, Charles' principles . . .

She lurched to her feet, swept the charts off the beside table, heard them sigh and rustle to the floor. Her body felt as if someone had wound it tighter, tighter, like a fire-hose on a reel. 'Let Magda go,' she prayed, the entire fire brigade clanking through her head, in the startled blaring silence.

She fell back into bed, turned over, away from charts and Clomid towards the second bed, and the dark shape called her husband. The long-case clock was booming through the hall, echoed by fourteen faint and muffled chimes. One A.M. All the clocks were back again, on duty, carving night and day into manageable pieces, reminding her that Time ruled in the universe, and Charles in Richmond Green. How could she have even thought to silence them? More foolish than Canute! If she chose to live in the bank-vault of her husband's bounty, then she must accept his rule, his clocks.

Half a lifetime later, fifteen throats struck two. Sleep was an impostor, like herself. She crept out to the bathroom, and sat on the cold white shoulder of the bath, peering at the moon. Was it Hungary's moon, as well? Was Piroska staring at it, even now, through the grandma's greasy curtains, weeping for a lost daughter, or praying to some moon-goddess that she would never be sent back?

Frances drifted to the window. Thin steel knives of moonlight cut across the floor-tiles, flickered on her feet. She realized, suddenly, and almost with astonishment, that there was no decision to be made. All her tossing, frantic agonizing had been completely purposeless. It was Piroska herself who must and would decide. If mother opened heart and home to daughter, then she, too, would be freed. But, if Piroska hesitated, if there were the slightest frown or obstacle in Budapest, then Magda must stay with them in Richmond Green. However much she longed for the child's departure, that was her basic duty, and she would follow it. No more reason to lie awake. It was simple now – Piroska held the final card. Softly, she closed the bathroom door, and climbed back into bed. The sheets stretched clammy arms around her neck.

'Let her be happy,' she whispered, to the darkness.

Charles flung out a hand and snorted in his sleep.

22

When she woke, the silence was still there, but pale now, like sour milk. She looked across at Charles. The blurred black shape he had been all night had changed into cold white sheets, sheets turned neatly back, pillows smooth and plumped.

She dragged herself out of bed and leaned over the banisters. 'Charles?' she called.

Why hadn't he woken her, to cook his eggs and bacon, before his early meeting in the City? She'd laid the table late last night, left the grapefruit ready in the fridge. She trailed downstairs, pulling on her housecoat. Her head was clearer now, her period pain reduced to a nagging ache. The kitchen was unscathed. Charles hadn't even made a cup of tea. She wondered, suddenly, if he'd bothered to eat or drink at all while she'd been at Ned's. It was almost beneath his dignity to boil a kettle, or poach an egg.

The kettle sat beside the telephone. In the interests of efficiency, Charles had fitted phone extensions in almost every room. The kitchen one was red, as a slight concession to frivolity. She picked up the receiver. Charles should be beside her now, making that vital phone call to Piroska – red-hot Piroska, who would pale to white and innocent, if only she would have her daughter back. Frances dialled the first digit of Charles' private office number, then banged the receiver down again. She'd ring from the study, where the phone was grey and businesslike. There was nothing frivolous about this call.

The ringing tone sounded querulous, impatient.

'Charles?'

'Mr Parry Jones is in a meeting.' The voice was pedigree barbed wire. 'Who's speaking, please? Oh, I'm sorry, Mrs Parry Jones, I didn't recognize you.' Barbed wire with icing sugar sprinkled on the top. 'I'll see if he can speak to you. Though it is a little tricky, I'm afraid. They're right in the middle of a breakfast session.'

'Tell him it's urgent, please.'

'Yes? Well? What is it?' Charles was on the line now – grudging and abrupt.

'Charles, what happened? Why didn't you wake me? I've only just got up. I couldn't understand it when I went downstairs and . . .'

'For God's sake, Frances, what do you want? My secretary told me it was urgent.'

'Well, it is urgent, Charles. We've got to ring Piroska. I must know what's happening, before Magda gets up. I'll phone her myself, if necessary. I'd rather do that, than have to let Magda down this evening, when she's . . .'

'I've already phoned.'

'Already? But when, Charles? It's only half-past eight.'

'So? I thought it would be safer from the office. No chance of Magda overhearing then, just in case there was a hitch.'

'And was there?' The study held its breath, the blotter sprouting doodlebugs beneath her trembling pen.

'No. Everything's fine.'

'You mean Piroska's glad about it? She wants Magda back?'

'Yes. Delighted.'

'Are you sure, Charles?'

'What d'you mean, am I sure? I've just spoken to her haven't I?'

'I'm sorry, it's just that you sound a bit – well – flat. Did you check on all the problems? I mean, are you certain they've got room for her?'

'Well, they are a little cramped, but they'll manage.' She could hear him tapping a pen against a desk and an electric typewriter stuttering in the background. 'There's an attic they can use, apparently.'

'An attic! We can't send Magda to an attic. She's not a suitcase, or a piece of lumber.'

'Don't be absurd!' The pen tapped faster. 'Magda won't be sleeping there. It simply means they've got a bit more room, if they find they need to expand. Anyway, sooner or later, they'll have the whole flat to themselves, which is quite a stroke of luck. Flats are scarce in Budapest. A lot of the bigger ones are still held by the State. Now, look here, Frances, you've dragged me out of a very important meeting . . .'

'Wait, darling, wait! This is urgent, too. I'm still a bit worried about all the formalities. You know, visas and permits – all that sort of thing. I mean, it's a Communist country, isn't it? They might not let Magda in, unless she. . . .'

'No problem. My secretary's looking into it right now. It's much easier apparently than it was ten years ago. It should only take a matter of days to get her in. They can complete the formalities once she's over there.'

'Days, Charles? But surely you don't want . . .?'

'I'm sorry, Frances, but I simply can't talk any longer. They're holding up the meeting for me, as it is. I've got two bank managers in there, and the President of American Continental.'

'Please, Charles. Just one more minute. I must get things clear, before I see Magda. Look, what about Miklos? Is he still there?'

'I'm not sure.'

'Not sure! But couldn't you have . . .?'

His 'goodbye' was like a steel bolt rammed home in her face. She sat at the desk, staring at the messy blotter. Well, she'd got what she wanted, hadn't she? Magda off her hands, room in the flat (just about), a delighted mother, even a secretary's capable help with the visa. So why did she feel so joyless?

It was probably just Charles' irritation rubbing off on her. He always sounded strained at work, hated interruptions. When he got home that evening, he'd fill in all the details. The main thing was that Piroska wanted Magda. She was free!

She plodded up the stairs to change her Tampax. It still seemed strange to have a period, when she'd planned on no more tampons for at least nine months. She stared at the fierce, dark blood trickling into the lavatory bowl. Why were physical things so messy and barbaric? Babies themselves were squalid, primitive – as *she* had been at Ned's, and at the party . . .

No, she mustn't think of that. If only she could stick a tampon in her brain, to plug it up, stop it analyzing. Better to keep busy. She marched back to the kitchen. The kettle had boiled and turned itself off. Even kettles were well-trained in the Parry Jones household. She'd take Magda tea in bed – not just tea, a full-scale breakfast. She wanted, suddenly, to spoil the kid, shower her with treats and affection, now that she was leaving.

The trouble was, Magda didn't eat breakfast, just grabbed a piece of toast, or stuffed a bar of chocolate in her pocket. She didn't like bacon, she wouldn't touch eggs. She was always finicky and critical at meals. All she ever wanted was trans-Atlantic junk-food – hamburgers and ice cream, pecan pie and Pepsi. You couldn't serve up triple-scoop Banana Boat for breakfast.

Perhaps she'd make real French brioches, or a plaited loaf with poppy seeds on top. But yeast needed time to rise, and it would be lunchtime before she got it in the oven. She thumbed through her cookery books. What did you give a runaway for breakfast, a refugee, a hostage?

Pancakes. That was it! Pancakes with maple syrup and thick whipped cream on top – a real American breakfast. She sieved the flour in a basin, cracked eggs, added milk, humming as she beat the mixture smooth. It was only now that relief and elation were beginning to surface, like the froth on the batter. She was ashamed of that elation, ought to stifle and disown it; yet to have the house to themselves again, to remove that sullen, slouching presence, stop the bumpy seesawing between guilt and resentment, pity and anger . . . It was the only way she could survive, the only hope of saving her relationship with Charles. They were equal now. Both had lost their children, both been unfaithful and unreasonable, and both preferred to rip out a messy, blemished page, and begin again on a clean one. She didn't even want to be his equal. Safer to be his child, his only child, loved and spoiled, with no rivals, no siblings; protected from the harsh world outside, from having to earn her own living, or struggle for her own identity.

She beat and beat the batter, till her arm ached, refused to use the painless electric mixer. She must put everything she had into those pancakes, even the strength of an elbow, the discomfort in a wrist. She tipped an inch of the frothing batter into the pan. The syrup was already heating with cinnamon and butter; the cream whipped stiff with sugar. For a few more days, there would still be another child, but not a rival. Now Magda was indisputably departing, she was no longer any threat – only a cropped and branded orphan, a displaced person, temporarily squatting in a foreign land. There wasn't any love, but there was pity, guilt, regret. And, so long as the kid was with them, there must be white flags and olive branches, penitence and peace.

She knocked at Magda's door with the loaded breakfast tray. 'Magda?'

'Go away! I'm busy.'

'But I've brought your breakfast up . . .'

'Don't want any breakfast.'

Frances put the tray down and opened the door a crack. All she could see was the spiky outline of Magda's butchered head. 'But it's pancakes, darling . . .' She took a step inside.

'Yuk!'

'I thought you'd like them. They eat them in America for breakfast.' Magda was kneeling on the floor, on a pile of jumbled clothes.

'So? This is Richmond, isn't it?'

'Yes, of course, but . . .'

All the dressing-table drawers were open and Magda was scooping out her underclothes and flinging them on the pile. 'I don't like pancakes.'

'You haven't tried them. They've got cream and maple syrup on, and . . .'

'Double yuk!'

She mustn't get annoyed. No point starting all those rows again. If Magda didn't want pancakes, well, let her go without. She banged the tray down on the dressing-table. The child hadn't even glanced at it, had ignored the mug of chocolate, the frosted glass of orange juice.

'Charles has rung your mother.'

'Oh?' The hands stopped scrabbling in the drawers, the head looked up. The girl was far too proud to say anything directly, but she must be hoping desperately that there had been no change of plan.

'It's all right, you can go. Piroska's longing to have you back.'

The hunched shoulders capsized with relief, the knuckles unclenched. So she and Magda were both relieved. Couldn't they build a bridge out of that one common feeling?

'Look, Magda, you don't have to rush off immediately, you know. Of course, I realize you're longing to see your mother, but . . . why not stay with us for a while, and let your hair grow?'

'No.'

'Wouldn't you rather Piroska saw you with your hair a little prettier? I could take you to Evansky's and ask Geoffrey to tidy it up a bit . . .'

'*No.*'

'All right. It's just that – well – I didn't want you to think you weren't welcome. I mean, Charles and I are happy to have you here, just as long as you want to stay.' All lies. She had nothing else to offer the kid but lies. 'You don't have to go at all, unless you're absolutely sure about it. You do understand that, don't you?'

Magda was sweeping all her possessions off the desk and dumping them in a plastic bag. 'I want to leave today.'

'Today, Magda? But that's impossible.'

'Tomorrow, then.'

Relief was swirling round the room, swelling up like yeast. Frances could almost see herself stripping off the sheets, ripping down the posters. Relief like that was wicked and unnatural. She had failed as a mother, even as a human. No wonder Viv was so contemptuous. Magda would be better off without her.

'It's not quite as easy as that, darling. You have to have a passport and a permit. Charles is looking into it, but it takes time. And then there's your ticket and all your stuff at school. Mother Perpetua phoned, you know – and Mother Gregory. Yesterday morning. They didn't sound too pleased.'

'Why not? They should be bloody glad to get rid of me.'

'No one's glad to be rid of you, Magda.' Shameful how glibly the lies tripped out, easy honeyed lies.

'Who cares, anyway? I still want to leave tomorrow.'

'Well, it won't be tomorrow, I'm afraid. That's simply not feasible. But I'll see what I can do to make it soon. Charles can sort out your visa, and I'll phone the airport first thing in the morning.'

Magda was scrabbling in her cupboards now, tossing out shabby slippers and broken shoes. Half of them were Bunty's. 'I'm not flying.'

'Not flying? Then how . . .'

'I'll go by train.'

'Train? No one goes by train to Budapest.'

'I do.' Magda tugged a shoe-lace with her teeth.

'But you can fly first class. It's really nice, first class. They give you special meals – super things like caviare and strawberries. And free champagne.'

She yearned to drown Magda in champagne, stuff her with celebration meals, swaddle her in smiling, soothing air hostesses. Anything to make it easier. Cardboard coffee and plastic sandwiches in a jolting railway carriage were more suited to an orphan or an exile, and would only swell the guilt.

Magda was scraping dried bubble-gum off a pair of dirty jeans. 'I don't like champagne.'

'But you'd be there in just two hours, darling.'

'Don't call me darling.'

'I'm sorry, I . . .'

'That's three darlings in the last three minutes, and not one at all before. I suppose I'm only "darling" because I'm leaving.'

'Magda, how could you think . . .'

'Oh, forget it.' Magda ripped a paperback in half, and hurled it in the bin. 'Look, I don't intend to fly, OK? I want to do things my way. Charles flies. I don't.'

Frances was silent. So that was it. Magda despised her father so much, she couldn't even bear to board an aeroplane, in case he'd been there first. She wanted to rip his life and genes to shreds, and build herself from nothing. Frances sank down on the blue frilled bedroom chair. Even a darling was a *casus belli*.

'All right, then, you'd better go by train. I suppose there are trains? You'll have to take the ferry, first. I'll get Charles to look up the connections and he can drive you down.'

'No.'

Christ! How many more 'no's would line the route, before that train roared into Budapest? Why did Magda make things so damned difficult? They could have seen her off at an airport with far more ease and ceremony – a decent meal at Heathrow's plushy Terrace restaurant, coffee and comfort in the first-class lounge.

'I don't want him to take me.'

'Well, you can't go on your own.'

'Why can't I?'

It was just like the early days. 'Don't want to.' 'Why can't I?'

Except Magda sounded tired and broken now – still defiant, but despairing. She was mouthing the same rebellious words, but all the stuffing had gone out of them. What difference could words make now, in any case? They had only a few short miles to drive before they tipped her over the edge of England. If only they could strew those miles with roses, make the going soft and painless, line the road with love and coloured streamers.

Magda had shoved her clothes and shoes aside, and had made a separate pile of treasures on the floor. She was stretched full-length beside them, almost lying on them, tatty, dilapidated cast-offs, the flotsam and jetsam of Viv's house: an airgun which had once belonged to Philip, one of Viv's trailing velvet skirts, a chocolate box without the chocolates. No sign of the things which she and Charles had given her – they were probably left at school – the sensible shoes and the five-language European dictionary, the pocket calculator, the brown leather gloves from Harrods. All she had saved were Bunty's faded T-shirts, Rupert's teething ring, a broken china dog.

Frances squatted down beside her, amidst the tarnished treasure-trove. One short tuft of hair stood up, absurdly, on the shingled head.

'Won't you let me help you sort your things? I'm good at packing.'

'No.'

'It'll be easier with two of us. Are you going to take your books?'

'No.'

'Just this one?' Frances picked up a small, dog-eared copy of *The Secret Garden*, which had been stowed inside the chocolate box. On the cover was a frail, blue-eyed angel child, with blond hair blazing down her back. She made Magda look tonsured in comparison, clomping, rough, unruly.

'It's Viv's copy, isn't it? I remember her reading it to Bunty. I loved it myself, when I was a child.'

'Leave it alone!' Magda made a grab at it. A small white envelope fluttered from its pages to the floor, and landed wrong side up. 'International Telegram' was printed in bold blue letters along the bottom edge, and above it, smaller but quite legible,

Saturday's date. Magda snatched it up, stuffed it in the pocket of her jeans, and turned her back.

There was a sticky, strangulated silence. Frances felt last night's dinner nudging her gently in the throat. A telegram was somehow always sinister, presaged death, disaster. Magda was picking at her nails, tearing down the little tags of skin around her cuticles, one finger sore and bleeding. Frances glanced at her. Why a telegram? And why, in God's name, had Magda kept it secret? It could only be her mother who had sent it – Magda knew no one else abroad. Charles must have heard about it when he phoned Piroska, just an hour ago. But why hadn't he mentioned it? Was it news too terrible to share? Miklos and Piroska were married and expecting twins . . . Hell! Even now she was still obsessed with twins. News like that wouldn't send Magda rushing off to Budapest. Her mother must have sent for her – that would explain everything – her escape from boarding school, her sudden insistence on leaving them. Perhaps the grandmother had died and Piroska now had money and a decent place to live. No, Charles would have heard that, on the phone. Maybe she was near death. Hadn't Charles said something about having the whole flat to themselves? That's what he must have meant. But surely Piroska wouldn't want her daughter involved in all the grief and disruption of a funeral. Wouldn't she have waited until the death was certain, the mourning period over?

It could be different news. Something strange and unexpected; a new, complicated chapter about to burst upon their lives. God forbid! Perhaps Charles hadn't really listened on the phone. With a breakfast session looming, he was bound to have been rushed, and could well have rung off before Piroska had a chance to get it out. Charles often cut phone calls short. And people.

But why hadn't Magda told them – any of them? Even Viv knew nothing about a telegram, nothing about Magda's plans to join her mother. Viv despised Piroska. Any woman who abandoned her own flesh and blood was anathema to Viv. That was reason enough for Magda to keep it secret from her – besides the fact that Magda knew Viv wanted her to stay – as a friend for Bunty and a new chick in her nest. Frances felt a sneaking sense of pleasure. Viv had been thwarted – no longer the trusted confidante, sharing secrets with Charles' daughter, excluding his own wife. This time, she, alone, was aware of the latest twist.

All the same, it was worrying. Didn't she have a duty to prise out the contents of that mysterious telegram? Magda was far too young to deal with death and dilemmas on her own. At least she should tell Charles. Perhaps Piroska was deceiving him, double-crossing all of them. But why?

She walked slowly to the door. She'd have to phone Charles at work again, and only hope she'd catch him in a coffee break. He'd be frostier still, a second time. She paused, with her hand on the door knob. She shouldn't really interrupt him in the middle of a meeting. American Continental was worth five hundred million dollars and had just got a grip on the Middle East. Its President owned two Greek islands and a chunk of Scotland, only bothered with London twice a year. You didn't disturb a man like that with anything less than the collapse of the dollar or failure of the Federal Reserve.

What could Charles do, anyway? Even if she waited until he was home with them that evening, there would only be uproar and defiance, another sleepless night. She tried not to hear the tiny traitor voice whispering inside her. 'Don't make an issue of it, don't tell Charles – he might change Magda's mind. Or force her to change it. Supposing she stays in England, after all? Then you'll have to share him again. Rows again, chaos again, endless complications.'

Didn't Magda have every right to be secretive? She'd been the same herself, as a child. She remembered the almost superstitious feeling that if you told an adult some treasured plan or project, the whole thing would burst, like a multi-coloured bubble pricked by a grown-up's lighted cigarette. Besides, Magda barely was a child. Sixteen next birthday – girls could be married and leave home by then. It would be absurd for them to shackle and restrain her.

If Magda had chosen to go to Budapest, then she must have reasons. Her mother had summoned her, was missing her, had every natural right to her. A telegram could be *good* news, didn't always mean a crisis. Charles accused her constantly of over-dramatizing, and here she was again, turning a greetings telegram into a death warrant. Charles had actually spoken to Piroska, would have sussed it out if anything were wrong. It could well be a happy ending for them all. She and Charles could settle back less culpably together, knowing that Magda was loved and wanted somewhere else, and not simply running off in desperation, as Viv had implied.

She walked back across the room, knelt down beside Magda's bowed and silent back. Why risk rows and explanations over a simple loving message from her mother? The important thing was to make the child feel loved at both ends of her journey. She shuffled round on her knees, until she was level with Magda's pale, shuttered face. 'Magda?' she whispered.

'Yeah?'

She could see the pile of pancakes, cold now and congealing. The whipped cream had capsized; a skin was forming on the mug of tepid chocolate. 'Would you do something for me?'

'What?'

'Let me take you to the ferry.'

'Why?'

'Just because I'd like to.'

Magda punched her fist through the bottom of the chocolate box. 'So you can see the back of me, make sure I've really gone.'

'Of course not, Magda. Nothing like that. It's just . . .' How could she explain, with all that hostility crackling round the room? Magda had already edged away, out of reach, out of touch.

'I'd rather say goodbye here. Get it over and done with.'

'No, Magda. Let's not get it over. Let's do it properly. I think that's very important.'

She tried to grapple with the silence. Strange to be pleading with a kid she was only too happy to push over the white cliffs of Dover. No, no, not that. She couldn't build her own reprieve on a child's destruction. Almost desperately, she groped for Magda's hand.

'Magda, please say yes. I do really want to take you. I can't explain, but . . .'

'Dunno what you're on about. What's it matter, anyway?'

Magda had shrugged her shoulders, tossed out the words like crumpled chocolate papers, but she hadn't let go the hand.

'You'll let me, then?'

'OK, yeah – I don't care.'

304

They stood, embarrassed, foolish, joined by their tense fingers. Neither dared be the first to pull away.

'Know something?' Magda was still staring at the ground.

'What?'

'I'm terrified of planes. Stupid, isn't it? I've never ever been in one.'

Magda terrified? Magda was tough, cast-iron, double-insulated, throwing down her mocking gauntlet to the world, challenging fathers, mothers, Reverend Mothers, God Himself. And scared of a tin-pot aeroplane.

Frances swallowed. So it was nothing to do with Charles. 'Know something else?' she asked the girl, still holding her hot hand, her fingers twisted, sweating.

'What?'

'I'm frightened of them, too. Absolutely petrified! Every time I go on one, I want to curl up and die. And I've never even admitted it before. You're the only one in the world who knows.'

Magda was looking at her now, incredulously. 'But that's crazy,' she objected. 'You're not frightened of anything. You can't be.'

Frances walked towards the window, now smirched and grey with rain, a glum, persistent rain, which seemed to be submerging half the world, from Richmond Green to Budapest. She traced a shaky 'F' on the blurred and steamy pane.

'Can't I?' she asked, watching her fingerprints mist up.

The 'F' was already half obliterated.

23

It was still raining when they drove into Dover. Frances nosed her way around the roundabout, on to the harbour road and the new ugly concrete viaduct, which led from the clifftops down towards the sea. Sea was the wrong word for that flat expanse of almost greasy water, lying dense and torpid beneath a pasty sky. There was no horizon – just grey wash blurring into greyer wave. Even the white cliffs were a delusion, not white at all, but dulled by wind and weather into a grubby shade of beige.

Frances swung left at sea-level and turned along the prom-enade, following the signs for the Western Docks and Marine Station. The windscreen wipers panted from side to side, masking the human silence in the car. They stopped outside a dingy mausoleum, flanked by weed-infested railway tracks and muddy rutted puddles. The rain tapped a mournful requiem on the bonnet of the car. There was nowhere to park.

'Think we ought to risk a yellow line?' asked Frances. She never had, not once in fifteen years of driving.

'Yeah, why not?' Magda hadn't seen the sea. She was staring at the photo in her passport, with its docked head, slouched shoulders. Frances had to coax her from the car.

They struggled up the grey stone steps of the station, weighed down by massive leather suitcases. Charles had insisted on leather. It was twice as heavy, but also twice as elegant. He had bought up half of Harrods for her, in relief, or reparation; sent her off with a whole new wardrobe, a full-scale library, a battery of gifts – things he would have chosen for himself: his favourite authors, favourite records, favourite (bitter) chocolates. Magda had arrived with one scruffy bag; she was leaving with a matching set of calf-hide cases, initialled in gold italic – M.R.K. When she'd seen them, all she'd muttered was, 'They're not my initials, anyway.' Most of her shabby treasures had been left behind: the football boots, the faded photo of Viv on her wedding day, the Brent Edge cords, *The Secret Garden*.

They paused, for a moment, at the end of the corridor, arms aching, fingers rubbed red from the stiff leather handles. The only thing Charles had overlooked was someone to carry his cornucopia. He hadn't been able to face the farewell himself, was too terrified of 'scenes'. Emotion might surface, or guilt, or something equally unthinkable. The formal excuse was a business trip to Douglas, one he assured her it was impossible to postpone. Strange, he had chosen the Isle of Man, turned his face in the opposite direction and run away from them, winged north and west when Magda was going south and east.

'Look at the sea!' said Frances. She had to say something – the silence was as heavy as the luggage. It was imperative to change this last crucial day from mute overcast to sunny bright.

Magda looked. The sea had reappeared through a gap in the wall, still grey, and almost solid like old glue. It seemed too tired for waves and tides. The girl shrugged and turned away. Too much sea. She blinkered herself along the corridor again, humping and dragging the cases down the iron stairway to the platform.

The station was almost deserted, looked abandoned like a branch line closed for lack of passengers. The boat trains had not yet arrived from Victoria, and without them, this quayside terminal had no real life or function. Rusty rails trailed away to ramshackle sheds. A cleaner swept rubbish from a waiting-room, leaning morosely on his brush.

'It's not exactly Piccadilly Circus.' Frances tried to keep talking. She was furious with the place, wanted to send Magda off in an atmosphere of hope and radiance, not this sullen no-man's land. She had planned a special farewell, with the sun smiling and the clouds lifting, as she poured out all the things she had never dared; wrapped the girl in affection, as her final gift and recompense.

So far, all she had managed was small talk. Magda had been silent the whole way down to Dover, despite every effort to distract her. They had struggled through traffic-sick miles of suburban sprawl, and out into a dismal countryside of grey farms and sodden fields, with Frances trying every subject in the book. She had moved from puppies to pop stars, from Kawasakis to karate, fallen back on fatuous topics like the weather and school food, even tackled the Top Twenty and the First Division; but the hunched figure beside her only bit its nails and fiddled with its passport. There was still time. They were far too early, anyway. The boat didn't leave for over an hour, and they were banned from the quay until noon, marooned on a dingy platform, side by side, with nobody else and no distractions.

She almost jumped when Magda broke the silence. 'It's like a cage,' she muttered.

Frances glanced around. Stark iron pillars frowned up to the ceiling, handcuffed into the horizontal girders of the roof, to form a prison of steel bars. The glass beyond let in almost no light. The day was overcast, in any case, and the panes themselves were stained and yellowing. There was a yellow tinge over everything – the jaundiced brick, the rusting iron, the bleary blemished glass.

Magda, too, looked sallow. Her skin was pale and waxen, like a sickly plant dumped in a dark cellar. Frances had tried to tidy up her hair, but there was little she could do until it grew again. She had trimmed it more or less even, then bought her a pretty headscarf to conceal it. The girl had left the scarf behind.

She was wearing new, stiff cords and a sensible raincoat. The clothes looked wrong on her, as if they had been bought for someone else, or hired out for the day. The prim brown gaberdine engulfed her, like a child swamped in its first school uniform. It had flattened her breasts and censored her curves, so that she was only a crop-haired kid again, too young to cross Europe on her own. Frances longed to put her in charge of the steward, or ask a kindly lady to keep an eye on her. But Magda didn't believe in kindly ladies, and had categorically refused to let anyone look after her. She was unaware of all the dangers – rape, murder, interference with a minor. Frances shivered.

'Chilly, isn't it? Shall we have a coffee, to warm us up?'

'Don't mind.'

The buffet was damp and fuggy at the same time. Rust-red lino clashed with pond-weed walls. They drank two *cappuccinos* each, spinning out hot froth in place of conversation. Magda put a coin in the juke-box. The barrier between them rose a notch or two higher, as the silence was assaulted by wild, whip-crack music. Frances was still struggling to remember her lines. She had to say something final and momentous, but all the words were trampled down by slamming drumbeats and snorting guitars, drowned in the orgiastic transports of the Clash.

She strode over to the book-stand and scanned the rack of paperbacks. She had to give Magda some treasure to take away with her, some wisdom to remember. But there were only cheap romances, trashy thrillers, comic-strips. She piled the counter high with them, added chocolate, popcorn, bubble-gum, a pocket torch, a key-ring with an M on it. Still only cardboard rubbish. She glanced at the stale fruit pies, the leaden sausage rolls. Even the girl behind the counter looked plastic and disposable.

'Haven't you got anything more . . .?' She stopped. You couldn't buy affection and farewells in station waiting-rooms. She tossed down a handful of bank notes, mooched back to their table. Magda was fiddling with a matchbox, didn't even bother to look up. Frances handed her the bag.

'Thanks,' she muttered tersely, and dumped it on the floor with the rest of her luggage.

The juke-box was silent now, the four empty cups like an electric fence between them. Frances had done nothing to dismantle it. All she had managed was to burden the kid still further.

'Shall we see if it's time to go yet?' Maybe it would be easier to talk outside.

Magda stood up and tripped over the bag, a fragile paper bag which broke and spilled its contents on to the floor. A plastic Snoopy rolled into a puddle of cold tea. Magda left it there. She simply couldn't carry any more. She struggled through the door with her half of the luggage, inching along the platform after Frances. The barricade was still closed. They stood outside the war memorial, drooping like the pigeons which shivered on the cold grey stone behind them. Magda had turned her back on Europe and was facing the other way, gazing along the station towards Richmond Green and Charles.

Suddenly, Frances saw Charles standing there, not in person, but in Magda. The resemblance between them struck her like a blow. She had never really noticed it before, or perhaps she had never dared to. She and Magda rarely met each other's eyes, always looked down, or looked away. Maybe it was the shorn head, revealing Charles' stubborn profile underneath, his uncompromising bone structure. She had always had his mouth, that sensuous, unlikely mouth, but now all the other similarities were almost shouting out. Even allowing for the difference in their colouring, this was still Charles' child; his imprint and his lineage stamped across her face like initials on a set of luggage. She had never really doubted it, and now there *was* no doubt. Magda was Charles' daughter, indisputably.

Frances stood motionless, like the stiff and sculpted figures on the war memorial behind her, weeping women mourning the departed. Here was Charles' offspring, torn from her school, her friends, her father; travelling on her own, without even the expiation she had so carefully prepared. There was still time. The station clock had turned to marble, its hands too cold to move.

'Look, Magda, I don't know how to say this, but I wanted to try to . . .' There was a sudden roar behind her, and the station racketed into life. Porters poured from nowhere, crowds surged from slamming doors, announcements blared and crackled over bellowing loudspeakers. The first boat-train had arrived. Frances and Magda were almost trampled down, shoved aside by burly men and boorish women, battered by cases and rucksacks. There was no chance of a porter – they had all been immediately snapped up. They were swept along like rubbish towards the barricade. It had now been lifted and the passengers were butting through it, like a herd of animals. Most of them were foreigners, returning from a summer in Britain; French, German, Japanese, all prattling in their alien tongues. This is farewell, thought Frances, the parting of the ways. Four or five policemen were controlling the gate, allowing only those with tickets and passports to proceed through customs and out on to the quay.

They couldn't part like this. It was far too drab, too sudden. She hadn't even said goodbye, and here was Magda being herded through a cattle pen, kenneled in the dungeons of a ship, without a glimpse of sky or sea. She had imagined wide horizons, leaping waves, not these prison bars, these sweaty, jostling aliens.

Frances almost threw herself on a uniformed official. 'Look, please let me through the barrier. I want to see my . . . daughter off. She's travelling on her own, and I promised to be there when the boat leaves. I know it's not allowed, but . . .'

'Sorry, lady, the quayside's strictly out of bounds. But if you

310

walk back along the station and out on to the jetty, you can see the boat depart from there. It's quite a tidy distance, though.'

Frances hesitated. She was holding up the crowds. A Frenchman swore at them in German. Magda wasn't German – she was British, the same nationality as her blue-eyed, light-haired father. Viv was right – she belonged here, and with him. Yet, she'd dealt so cavalierly with all Viv's fears, kidded herself that Magda was simply going home. It wasn't home. Magda would be a foreigner in Budapest, with a thick accent and strange English ways; teased and isolated as an alien in both her homelands. She'd allowed one rushed and suspect phone call, which Charles had made in private, to lull all her objections. Magda would undoubtedly be harmed. The school-leaving age in Hungary was as low as fourteen. Charles had talked about further studies at the State *Gymnasium*, followed by Budapest University, but supposing her mother pushed her into a dead-end job instead? Her whole future could be ruined, her life cut off before it had begun.

And what about that telegram? She'd almost glamorized it, in the end, assumed quite arbitrarily it meant an automatic reunion between mother and daughter, with Miklos safely out of sight, and everything cosy. But what proof did she have? As Viv had pointed out, if Piroska was cruel enough to abandon her child in the first place, was it really likely she'd be begging to have her back again? Magda might arrive to a frosty, grudging welcome, to illness, poverty, or worse.

Frances was standing like a dummy in the queue, people swearing as they bumped into her or tried to push past. She remembered suddenly the C to D encyclopaedia. '*The newly-fledged cuckoo leaves its foster mother and flies unaided to its winter quarters. It may cross two thousand miles of land and open sea, risking storm and starvation, completely unguided, and with no assistance from its natural parents.*' She glanced at the drab brown plumage of Magda's raincoat, the speckled jersey underneath. The child had found a porter and was watching him load her cases on a trolley. She was already half-turned towards the barricade, head down, hands plunged deep into her pockets.

''Bye, then,' she muttered, scuttling sidewards like a scared bird, following the porter, edging out of reach, towards the sea and Hungary and oblivion.

311

'No!' Frances shouted. 'Wait a minute.'

Magda stopped, defenceless now, no luggage to lurk behind, no cases to hide her. She looked smaller, almost shrunken, as if she had crawled back into herself, only another blob among the crowds. The porter was whistling impatiently, tapping his foot, annoyed by the delay. Frances moved her lips like someone dumb and screaming in a dream. She could feel the words straining to get out, struggling to form themselves into a credible farewell, but they were blocked and panicked aliens, gibbering in a foreign tongue, who didn't know the English for 'goodbye'.

She snatched the cases from the porter's trolley, heaved and banged them back on to the pavement.

'Don't go!' she cried to Magda. 'Please don't go – you mustn't. Come back to Richmond with us. You belong with us. We want you.'

Magda slowly unfurled. All her height and strength had been telescoped before. Now she was towering over Frances, a dark shadow blotting out the light.

'Piss off!' she screamed, tearing off the stiff brown coat and flinging it on the ground. 'This is the last time I'll ever bloody see you and you're still giving me a pack of lies. Can't you ever say what you mean? You don't want me. You never did. And Charles doesn't, either. He didn't even want me to be born, so why give me all that crap about coming back with you? I'd rather die than go back to that dump! I don't belong there. It's not my home. It's not anybody's home. I can't even breathe there.'

Frances could hardly find her voice, a voice of ashes, dust. 'Magda, I . . . I didn't mean . . .'

'No, of course you didn't! You never mean anything you say. You're a liar and a cheat and a . . .'

'Magda, be quiet, please. We're in a public place.'

'That's all you fucking care about – what other people think. Well, I don't give a shit about it!'

'How . . . *dare* you speak to me like that! I was only trying to help. I thought . . .'

'I don't want your rotten help – or anything to do with you. I never want to see you in my life again.'

A little knot of people was gathering to watch, whispering

and pointing. Suddenly, Frances didn't care, began to shout at Magda, screaming across their dumb and gawping faces.

'And I don't want to see you, either! You're right. I never did. I wouldn't have you now, if you went down on your knees to me.'

'Oh, you'd like that, wouldn't you? That's what you've wanted all along – some poncy, slavering little creep, telling you how wonderful you are, to take her in off the streets and share your crappy home, giving you a medal for it.'

'Anyone who lived with you would deserve a medal! You're the most, rude, ungrateful, boorish child I've ever had the . . .'

'I'm not a child.' She was stamping on the raincoat now, trampling it deliberately.

'You're right, you're not! You're a great overgrown monster of a . . .'

'And what do you think you are? A lazy slob who sits on your arse all day and never stops moaning about how busy you are, boring everyone with your stupid wingeing headaches and your little specks of dust. You don't do a bloody thing, except complain – can't even keep yourself. Charles pays for everything.'

'You leave Charles out of this, you impertinent little . . .'

'Why should I? He's my father, isn't he?'

'No, he's not.'

Magda stared at her a moment, then swung round and kicked the largest of the cases with the full force and fury of her tough-soled boot. It didn't even dent. She went on kicking, again, again, again. There was a gasp from the crowd, but the case remained unscathed; shiny and impervious. Magda pummelled at the leather with her fists, tore at the straps, battered the locks. All she achieved was bruised and smarting fingers.

She aimed one last savage kick at the case, then reeled back with a grimace. 'Fuck off, Frances!' she yelled, louder even than the blare of the loudspeakers.

The crowd drew in its breath.

'Fuck off yourself, you destructive little bitch!'

Silence. Dover had rotted and dissolved into the sea, leaving only a pile of rubble, a foul and lingering smell. This was the solemn sacred leave-taking, yet all they had bestowed on each other was four-letter words and fury. She would carry that fury to the grave with her, and Magda would lug her share to Budapest and taint half Europe with it. If only she had settled for a brief, anodyne farewell – a shuffle, a mutter, a quick embarrassed wave. Anything was better than those shameful words, that terrifying outburst, those stupid sniggering onlookers. She could feel her heart still pounding against her ribs, her whole shocked body fraying and unravelling. How, in God's name, could she have answered back like that, joined in a brawl like a fishwife, lied to an orphan kid about her father? It was too late now to make amends. There were only a few stragglers trickling from the boat-train, shuffling towards the customs hall. Once they were through, the barrier would be closed, she on one side of it, Magda on the other, forced apart by far more than a gate. A second porter was already reloading the luggage. She hardly dared look up. 'Magda, I . . .'

'You said fuck.'

'I know, I'm sorry. I'm so terribly sorry.'

'I can't believe it.'

'I don't know what came over me. I'm so bitterly ashamed, I've never . . .'

'It's *great!*'

'What are you talking about?'

'Your saying fuck. I like it.'

'Magda, you're . . .'

'It suits you. It's the best thing you've ever said. You really meant it, didn't you?'

'Of course not, Magda. How could you think I meant it? I was just . . .'

'Crap! You meant it. Fancy Frances saying fuck! Wait till I write and tell Bunty. She'll have hysterics.'

'Magda, how can you . . .?'

Magda was grinning. She couldn't be. Neither of them could ever smile again. They shouldn't even be speaking to each other. Everything was finished, smashed.

'Say it again.'

'What?'

'Fuck. Go on, just say fuck. I want to hear you.'

'You're crazy, you're . . .'

'There's not a law against it. You won't be struck down dead, or swallowed up, or something. Just say it once, to please me.'

'I can't, I . . .'

'Go on, it's easy.'

'But people are listening, Magda.'

'Who cares? I'll say it first. Fuck.'

'All right, then . . . f . . . fuck.'

Magda giggled. 'Great! I like it. Fuck!'

Frances grinned herself. It was so stupid, so miraculous. There they were, dwarfed on a cold stone station, and laughing, for God's sake – yes, both actually laughing, falling about, making a spectacle of themselves, almost hugging each other. Christ knows how it happened – she couldn't tell – but suddenly they *were* hugging each other, not the brief, formal gesture she'd planned as a farewell, but a real, messy, gutsy, unpremeditated hug. She was treading in a patch of pigeon-shit, Magda's chin was digging in her eye, but they could feel each other's bodies clinging on to each other, holding each other up.

She had changed from dark antique mahogany to something light, new-born – something which could leap and soar and fly. She and Magda were reconciled, but it wasn't only that, or simply that she'd cleared the air, at last, by saying what she meant. There was another still more crucial issue, more dangerous, more permanent, and Magda herself had put it into words. She could still hear those blazing syllables, echoing round the station. 'I'd rather die than go back to that dump. It isn't anybody's home. I don't belong there.'

Magda didn't – and nor did she. She hadn't any home, and there was nowhere to go back to. Like Magda, she was a displaced person with an odyssey in front of her. Neither of them had really planned it. They weren't noble martyrs or stalwart pioneers, just messy, mixed-up, bloody selfish people who liked their own way. She had changed her mind a hundred times, dithered, doubted, cheated. But suddenly, astonishingly, she had come to a decision. Everything was clear. Magda was travelling east to Budapest, and she was going westwards, to find her own new world. It wouldn't be easy – she'd curse, grumble, whine, despair, even change her mind again, fret over specks of dust, bore people with her stupid, wingeing headaches. But one thing was certain – it wouldn't be

315

Charles and Magda she'd be boring, any more. She didn't have a husband or a child – and she no longer wanted either.

Magda would survive. She was going where she wanted, returning to her mother. They couldn't stop her, anyway. The child was obstinate, like Charles. If they tried to keep her with them, she'd only run away. Even if they poured out love like seawater, they still couldn't make her happy. After all, she'd turned her back on Viv, as well as them. She was a wombat, not a lap-dog; a cuckoo, not a cage-bird; and tougher than any of them knew. Ned had told her that, a hundred years ago, in a red-letter place called Brighton. Let her off the leash, he'd urged, don't clip her wings; the kid knows what she wants. He was right. Magda had just screamed out to the whole of south-east England that she didn't belong in Richmond. And she herself had picked up the echoes, and realized that neither did she. She was slipping her own leash, smashing Rule and Order, escaping on the same day as Magda, but with no destination, no belongings. All she had were a few red letters in her pocket, and some crazy candyfloss belief that there would be other, better Brightons for them both.

'For God's sake, Miss, get a move on!' The porter had finally lost patience and was jabbing their backs with a corner of his trolley. 'If you don't look sharp, you'll miss the boat and be camped here for the night. They're closing the barricade!'

She stepped away. 'Goodbye, Magda.' It was easier to say now. '*K . . . kellemes uta . . . zást!*' She struggled with the unfamiliar syllables – the Hungarian for *bon voyage*. She had learned them specially for this last farewell; sitting, sleepless, half the night, poring over a Hungarian pocket phrase-book.

Magda grinned. 'That's not right. The s's are pronounced like "sshh" and the accent's on the first syllable.' The words sounded strange on Magda's tongue; outlandish, almost dangerous.

'*Kellemes utazást,*' she repeated. How could a language feel so alien?

'Not bad,' Magda grudged. '*Sok szerencsét!*'

'What's that?'

'Good luck.'

'Well, *sok sze . . . ren . . . csét*, then.' She stumbled on the 'sshh's'. 'It's not easy, is it?'

'No, it's not.' The grin had faded now, Magda tense again, and

316

shuttered. The raincoat was a brown puddle on the ground, an obstacle which barred her way. Frances picked it up.

Magda dodged away from it. ''Bye,' she muttered. She was looking eastwards now.

The porter had already crossed the barricade. Magda followed, haltingly. Frances was left behind, the wrong side of a barrier, still holding Magda's coat. She pressed her body against the cold unyielding metal of the gate.

'Goodbye!' she shouted. 'Take care, good luck . . .'

She watched the hunched grey back dwindling down the corridor marked 'British Passports'. '*Kellemes utazást!*' she called, tugging at the bars. She'd still got the accent wrong, but there was no one to correct her.

Magda had gone.

The barricade clanged shut. One bird had flown the cage. Now it was her turn. She tore back along the station, up the stairs and out on to the harbour wall. If she hurried, she'd see the boat depart, and she and Magda could wave each other off. She pounded along the jetty, out towards the open sea. It was still drizzling, but she didn't care, didn't even want the raincoat. It would only weigh her down. It was Magda's coat, bought with Charles' money, at Charles' favourite store. Expensive, serviceable, and made to last. Dreary and confining. She should post it on to Magda, or return it to the shop and credit it to Charles' account. Or at least offer it to Bunty, or give it to a jumble sale. Duty, conscience, common sense . . . They weighed heavy, too.

She bundled the raincoat into a ball and flung it over the wall, into the sea. The waves closed over it. A seagull swooped, thinking it was food, and screamed back, disappointed. She was so light now, so insubstantial, that the wind could blow her like a spore. She was no one, nothing; not Frances, not Franny, not Mrs Parry Jones, not Ned's mistress, nor Charles' wife; not even Mr Rathbone's patient any more. The sea stretched to vacuity, the sky faded into void. Magda herself was only a pinprick now; the huge black haunches of the boat reduced to a splodge on the horizon, a flurry of white gulls.

She went on running. Whatever happened, she mustn't look

back. It wouldn't be easy, but Magda had shown her how. All you had to do was renounce your treasures and keep going. And, with any luck, the rain might even stop.

'*Sok szerencsét!*' she panted, to herself.

She had got the accent right.